SAFE AT FIRST

THE BOYS OF BASEBALL #3
MAC DAVIES

by
J. Sterling

SAFE AT FIRST
Copyright © 2021 by J. Sterling
All Rights Reserved

Edited by:
Jovana Shirley
Unforeseen Editing
www.unforeseenediting.com

Cover Design by:
Michelle Preast
www.Michelle-Preast.com
facebook.com/IndieBookCovers

No part of this book may be reproduced or transmitted in any form or by any means, electronic or mechanical, including photocopying, recording, or by any information storage and retrieval system without the written permission of the author, except for the use of brief quotations in a book review.

This is a work of fiction. Names, characters, businesses, places, events, and incidents are either the products of the author's imagination or used in a fictitious manner. Any resemblance to actual persons, living or dead, or actual events is purely coincidental.

ISBN-13: 978-1-945042-53-9

Please visit the author's website
www.j-sterling.com
to find out where additional versions may be purchased.

OTHER BOOKS BY J. STERLING

Bitter Rivals—an enemies to lovers romance
Dear Heart, I Hate You
10 Years Later—A Second Chance Romance
In Dreams—a new adult college romance
Chance Encounters—a coming of age story

The Game Series:
The Perfect Game—Book One
The Game Changer—Book Two
The Sweetest Game—Book Three
The Other Game (Dean Carter)—Book Four

The Playboy Serial:
Avoiding the Playboy—Episode #1
Resisting the Playboy—Episode #2
Wanting the Playboy—Episode #3

The Celebrity Series:
Seeing Stars—Madison & Walker
Breaking Stars—Paige & Tatum
Losing Stars—Quinn & Ryson

The Fisher Brothers Series:
No Bad Days—a New Adult, Second Chance Romance
Guy Hater—an Emotional Love Story
Adios Pantalones—a Single Mom Romance
Happy Ending

THE BOYS OF BASEBALL
(THE NEXT GENERATION OF
FULLTON STATE BASEBALL PLAYERS):
The Ninth Inning—Cole Anders
Behind the Plate—Chance Carter
Safe at First—Mac Davies

ABOUT THE AUTHOR

Jenn Sterling is a Southern California native who loves writing stories from the heart. Every story she tells has pieces of her truth in it, as well as her life experience. She has her bachelor's degree in Radio/TV/Film and has worked in the entertainment industry the majority of her life.

Jenn loves hearing from her readers and can be found online at:

Blog & Website:
www.j-sterling.com

Twitter:
twitter.com/AuthorJSterling

Facebook:
facebook.com/AuthorJSterling

Private Facebook Reader Group:
facebook.com/groups/ThePerfectGameChangerGroup

Instagram:
instagram.com/AuthorJSterling

DEDICATION

Not every guy who plays on a team is a player.

This is for all the girl's who pushed past his defenses to find the diamond inside.

This is for all the guys who try so hard to be tough when all we want is your soft.

The right girl is worth opening up for.

The right guy is worth fighting for.

PROLOGUE

LAST JUNE
MLB DRAFT

Mac

IT WAS STUPID, and I was being an idiot. Here I was, back in my and Chance's shared hotel room, feeling sorry for myself. I was happy for my best friend and teammate. I'd always be happy for him because he deserved to get drafted, but I wanted it too. That was why I'd left the second he sat down with the reporters. I was afraid that he'd be able to see my jealousy. And I didn't want to ruin that moment for him.

When the rest of the days came and went and my name was never called in the Major League Draft, I couldn't help but feel that pang of disappointment in my guts. I wondered if that was how my other teammate Cole had felt when he didn't get drafted in his junior year. I thought about calling him and asking. I needed someone to talk to, but I didn't want to sound like a pussy. Plus, he'd eventually gotten drafted, and he was already in spring training for the season. The last thing Cole Anders wanted to hear was my whining.

I had one more year of baseball eligibility left. One more year to show the scouts that I was worth it. That I was good enough to play professional baseball for them and the team they worked for. But honestly, I wasn't sure that I was. I was good enough to play for one of the best college baseball teams in the country, but that didn't mean that I had what the scouts were looking for to go beyond that. So far, not a single one had approached me. There were no agents banging down my door, hoping to represent me when the time came. No emails, no phone calls, no messages through Coach Jackson. No nothing.

And as much as I hated to admit it, there was a pretty damn good possibility that I'd be going back home to Arizona after my senior year and taking a job with my dad's company. It had always been the backup plan. One I hoped I'd never need. One my dad assumed I always would. The thought alone made me want to get on a plane and disappear forever. Having my failure thrown in my face daily wasn't something I looked forward to. I really fucking wanted to prove my dad wrong, but so far, all I was doing was proving him right.

After our appearance at the College World Series, Chance and his girlfriend, Danika, had left for Florida. The Mets had sent him to their Class A Advanced team instead of regular Single A. I knew he wouldn't be there long either, so I hoped Danika liked packing up and moving because she'd be doing it often. They seemed really happy though. And that was when I realized that playing professional baseball wasn't the only thing I wanted in my life.

I wanted the one other thing that had kept eluding me—or maybe I'd pushed it away—a real girlfriend. I knew I came off as the team's biggest player, but it was all a front. A defense mechanism. As long as I called all the shots and kept the ladies playing by my rules, I couldn't get decimated, like I had during my freshman year. All that needed to change, and I had no idea how to do it. Especially when girls only wanted to hook up with me because I was a baseball player. What happened if I was no longer one? Who would want me then?

My phone vibrated, and I looked down, seeing a new private message waiting for me on one of the social media apps. I clicked on it, noticing that it was from Sunny, Danika's best friend. We'd started following each other a few months back, but I'd done my best to never comment or like any of her pictures even though they were fucking spectacular. That girl never seemed to have a down day. She was always smiling, looking happy, and quoting *glass half-full* type of shit in her captions. Sunny was a ray of fucking sunshine, just like her name, and I was drawn to all of it.

She was also one of the few girls at Fullton that I'd hooked up with who didn't chase me after the fact. Sunny accepted that I didn't want a relationship, and she never tried to talk me out of it or change my mind. Other girls didn't work that way. They were always pushing for more. Which always pushed me away. The problem was, I would have actually considered changing my ways for Sunny, but I knew that she deserved way better than someone as damaged as me. So, I kept her at arm's length, and she let me do it.

I clicked on the message and read it out loud, "*I'm sorry you didn't get drafted this year. I'm here if you want to talk.*"

She included her phone number, and in a moment of clear

weakness and vulnerability, I found myself dialing it. We talked for hours that night. Longer than I'd ever talked to any girl before in my life, including my ex. It was easy. Comfortable. And I felt like Sunny understood me when it seemed like no one else had ever even tried to.

She gave me stellar advice, listened quietly when I wouldn't stop talking, and reminded me that everything I felt was totally normal and justified. Sunny made me feel less crazy when I felt like I was completely unraveling. She calmed me in every way.

I wasn't sure what I would have done without her, but I was pretty positive I would have self-destructed and sabotaged it all if left to my own devices. She saved me that night.

So, what did I do after we hung up?

Never fucking called her again, of course. And I left her on Read anytime she messaged me after that, which stopped pretty quickly because, apparently, Sunny had self-control. I knew that I was doing the wrong thing when it came to her, but I couldn't seem to stop it. I hid behind a million excuses and reasons, convincing myself that she was better off without me. Which was most likely the God's honest truth.

What the hell did I have to offer a sweet, perfect girl like her?

Nothing.

And I damn well knew it.

SENIOR YEAR

Mac

MY DAD PULLED over to the curb in the departing flights section of the Phoenix airport. He wasn't even parking in the short-term lot and walking me inside to say good-bye. Nope. Just a quick drop off for his only son. Richard Davies—or Dick, as I mostly called him in my head and not to his face—would never waste his time coming inside an airport he wasn't leaving out of. Did I mention that we had driven in *my* car? My stunning two-door charcoal-gray 3 Series BMW that Dick Davies—aka DD for short—had bought me for my high school graduation. It'd had one of those big, fucking obnoxious red bows on it and everything. It would have been completely embarrassing if it wasn't so fucking cool.

I'd driven this car all of about three months total since the moment I got her because in true Dick Davies fashion, he'd bought that beautiful piece of machinery more for himself than he ever did for me. DD wanted other people to see how successful he was, how prominent, how *rich*. Everything DD did was for show. If things appeared perfect on the outside, no one would dare question what went on behind closed doors. And what went on behind the doors of our house was anything but perfection.

"It's my senior year. Just let me take my car to school," I'd begged my parents.

But they'd both said no. It was the one thing they seemed to agree on. The only thing really.

My mom firmly believed that me not having a car in California kept me safer somehow. Like car accidents couldn't happen if someone else was driving and I was in the passenger seat. I'd actually stopped myself from looking up statistics to prove her wrong, knowing that it would only backfire on me somehow. The last thing I wanted was to be stuck here for any longer than necessary. My mom would most likely read those stats and demand I never leave Arizona—or the house—again. Not that she could stop me. It was hard stopping your only kid when you were too drunk to walk in a straight line anymore.

She hadn't always been like that, and I wasn't sure when it'd even started in the first place, but she had seemed to be drunk more than she was sober lately. Clearly, my mom hated her life, and I couldn't even blame her for it. My dad really was a miserable, selfish prick. It fucking killed me, seeing her that way, but I knew that I couldn't be the one to save her.

At least, not yet. I had to save myself first.

"Are you still going to play this year?" my dad asked me from the driver's seat. Of my own damn car.

"What?" I looked at him like he'd grown twelve heads when it was just more proof that my old man didn't understand me at all.

"Baseball. Are you going to play? I mean, you didn't get

drafted, so what's the point?"

He's serious. He's absolutely fucking dead serious, asking me this question right now.

"I have a scholarship to play baseball. I have one more season. I'm the starting first baseman. It's not over yet. Of course I'm going to fucking play."

"Don't take that tone with me, Mackenzie. And watch your damn mouth when you speak to me," he chastised, using my full name.

I cringed. He was the only person who ever called me that. *Ever.* No one, not even my teammates at Fullton, knew my real first name. I couldn't wait to get the fuck out of Arizona and out of *my* car.

"I've been gone all summer, playing. Why would I stop now? I just don't understand the question," I tried to explain in a calm tone, but I knew I sounded anything but.

Dick Davies lived to piss me off.

My dad had never been an athlete, so trying to get him to relate to my state of mind when it came to baseball was futile at best. He had no idea what it felt like to have this kind of passion burning you alive from the inside out. For better or worse, baseball gave me purpose. And in the blink of an eye, it could all be gone.

DD shifted in his seat and pulled at his tie. It was something he did whenever he was frustrated. And I was clearly frustrating him. "You're just wasting time when you could be focusing on working for me and learning the ropes."

Here we go again.

"You should have been spending your summers in the

office, so you don't have to start in the mailroom and work your way up the ladder."

"I want to play baseball for as long as I can," I said instead of picking a fight with him.

There was no use in saying all the things I'd already said a thousand times before. Dick Davies refused to listen to me anyway. He didn't care what I wanted.

"Doesn't look like that will be for much longer." He looked me dead in the eyes without blinking. It was a challenge. He was baiting me. I'd tried to avoid the fight, but he wanted one.

My mom had stopped arguing with him years ago, and in return, DD had started picking battles with me instead. I'd accepted it at first because it meant that he would give my mom a break, but the dynamic had taken its toll. I thought DD liked it—the arguing. It made him feel powerful somehow. He used his words to wage war, to cut down his opponents and make them feel like nothing. He felt bigger that way.

Today, I refused to play. I knew he was just looking for an opportunity to remind me of all the ways in which his *career* was superior to my *hobby*. DD's main point was always about how much money I'd be making if I gave up baseball already and came to work for him. As if money made a person happy. We both knew that it didn't.

Money might buy you a bunch of nice and pretty shit, but that was the extent of its power. I should have thanked him for teaching me that lesson early on in life, but I didn't. There was no point. And he never deserved my thanks anyway.

"Baseball's been a fun hobby for you, but it's time to get

serious, Mackenzie."

Cringing again at the sound of my full name, I suggested, "Maybe if you came to a game and actually watched me play, you'd understand why I love it so much." I knew he'd never in a million years do it.

"You know I don't have time for that," he bit back, his tone a mixture of disgust and annoyance. "And even if I did, why would I watch you play something that's done nothing but stop you from being the man you're supposed to be?"

I held myself back from punching the fucking dashboard. I couldn't remember the last time my dad had gone to one of my baseball games. I knew he'd watched me play when I was a little kid, but at some point, that'd all changed. Maybe it was once I'd started obsessing over playing professionally.

Once, back in high school, I'd asked him if he was coming to the championship game, and he'd told me that watching me play gave me the wrong idea. DD said that it filled my head with false hope and gave me the impression that he supported nonsense, which he considered baseball to be. I thought he believed that if he never showed up, I'd stop wishing he was there. Or maybe he thought I'd stop wanting to play altogether without his support. Neither had proven to be true.

A loud whistle blew, scaring the shit out of me. I jumped and looked out the passenger window to see an airport cop waving us along. We'd been sitting at the curb for too long.

Thank God.

"I gotta go," I said before getting out of *my* car and heading toward the trunk, where my bags were waiting.

It would be so much easier to have my car with me in

California. I really hated asking people for rides. It was embarrassing. And now, I had to ask someone new to tote my non-driving ass around since Chance was gone.

The least he could have done was leave me his car, I thought for a moment before remembering that he had given me the master suite in the baseball house, so I couldn't really be too pissed.

The most coveted room in the house was about to be mine. Although I would have preferred getting drafted instead and not needing the room at all.

I walked toward the double glass doors when the sound of DD's voice stopped me. "Focus on your future, Mackenzie. It's time to start letting this pipe dream go. We made a deal," he reminded me before rolling up the window and driving off.

I stood there, bags in hand, heart on the fucking floor.

The deal.

My dad had forced me to agree that if I didn't get drafted, I'd come work for his tax prep company after I graduated. He even made me sign a contract. At eighteen years old, I wrote my name on the dotted line, too naive to know better. He'd used Fullton State as his bargaining chip. It was the only way he'd allow me to move to California and pay for what the scholarship didn't cover, which was some hefty out-of-state tuition costs. I'd like to think I'd have rebelled and gone to school there anyway without his help, but I wasn't sure that I would have. More than likely, I'd have opted to stay in Arizona and played baseball at some second-rate college instead. And I would have felt like I was drowning in all that hot air.

It burned like hell, knowing that my dad, of all people,

didn't believe in me or my ability. Every time he told me to give up on baseball, it felt like a fucking knife to the chest. I'd barely been able to breathe the first time I heard him say it. He knew how much I loved the sport. He saw how hard I worked, how much I planned for a future in it, and how dedicated I was to the game. But none of it mattered. He never believed in me, and that was the kind of shit that left you with scars you couldn't see.

Punching in the numbers at the kiosk, I waited for it to print my baggage claim stickers and wrapped them around the handles of my duffel bags before heading toward the counter to drop them off. The ticket lady was sort of hot, but even flirting with her didn't make me feel better, and I walked in the direction of the security line, my head all sorts of fucked up.

BOYS ARE SO FRUSTRATING

Sunny

I WAS SIMULTANEOUSLY looking forward and dreading heading back for my senior year at Fullton State. Danika, my best friend and ex-roommate, was in Florida with her boyfriend, Chance Carter, the baseball superstar, and I was all alone.

I hated being alone.

Anytime Danika had left to go visit her dad back home in New York when we lived together, I'd drive the whopping forty-five minutes away from campus and go home too. That was how much I hated being in our apartment by myself. Most people reveled in their solitary, but I just wasn't one of them. To put it bluntly, I was scared and uncomfortable. It wasn't like I had some giant guard dog to keep me safe from intruders or anything.

But over the summer, I'd decided that it was time to face my fears. I had to grow up and start adulting at some point, so I moved into a one-bedroom apartment in the same complex where Danika and I had lived for the past two years. A single bedroom, where I could do whatever I wanted.

Alone.

By myself.

With no one else around.

I wouldn't have even been in this situation in the first place if I hadn't switched majors. It put me a full year behind, so when Danika graduated last year, I still had one more to go before I got my degree. It was my own fault, but I wasn't too mad about it. I had no idea what I wanted to do with my life, and this bought me a little more time before I felt like a complete loser.

I envied that part of Mac, even more so after our phone call. He had so much passion and drive. I never talked about anything in my life the way he talked about baseball.

I pondered that for a minute before remembering that I really freaking hated the quiet, so I started wearing a hole in the carpet by walking back and forth, trying to calm myself down. Turning on music didn't help. Distracting myself with some stupid flying bird game on my phone wasn't enough either. For the most part, I was fine during the day, but it was the nights that seemed to wreak havoc on my imagination.

Maybe I should ask my parents for one of their dogs. Something to cuddle with whenever I thought the boogeyman was going to murder me in my sleep. Or worse, while I was still awake.

Without thinking, I found myself in the kitchen, pulling out the ingredients I needed to bake some chocolate chip cookies—with sea salt flakes sprinkled on top, of course. Concentrating on baking seemed to quiet my mind even though I could do it with my eyes closed. Mixing and measuring helped me forget to be scared. Or that I was alone in a ground-floor apartment that anyone could access if they really wanted to. I glanced up at the giant sliding glass door that led to a small patio for only a second before checking my mixer, making sure the butter and sugars were thoroughly combined.

The only other time I could remember forgetting to be terrified was the night I'd spent hours on the phone with Mac after the draft. He confessed so many things about the state of his heart when it came to baseball that the fact that I was desperately alone in my apartment had completely slipped my mind. I loved getting to know him that way, and I honestly thought we'd shared something special during that conversation, but then the little jerk went and ignored me for the rest of the summer. All of my texts and messages went unanswered. Eventually, I stopped sending them. I could only take feeling like an idiot so many times. He'd gotten what he needed that night, and then he'd moved on like I'd never existed.

I shouldn't have been surprised that Mac disappeared on me right after opening up. I had known exactly what kind of guy he was, and I'd gone and caught feelings for him anyway, against my own better judgment. Where all the other guys in the past had lied and spewed out promises and pretty words to get what they wanted, Mac had been open and honest right from the start.

There were no false pretenses with him. He gave you exactly what he told you he would. And then it was up to you to decide if you could handle it or not. When we'd first met, he'd let me know right off the bat that he wasn't looking for anything serious and that he wasn't boyfriend material. We'd made out all night, no strings attached, and I'd convinced myself that it had been refreshing to meet someone like him, someone who wasn't lying just so they could get in my pants.

I'd even told Danika once that I respected Mac's honesty. She'd laughed.

Laughed.

And then told me that I deserved more than a guy who wanted to *make out and walk away in the same breath.*

It was the truth. Of course I deserved more, but at the time, I pretended that it was enough. Then, he'd had to go and give me a peek at the real guy inside, and it'd wrecked me. I remembered hanging up the phone that night, shaking with the weight of his confessions, all of his words swirling inside my mind and tugging at my heart. I'd realized that I wanted to continue being the one Mac confided in, and I didn't want to lie to myself about it anymore.

I'd known better than to have more than a crush on him, but damn if every girl in the history of the world didn't want to be the one girl a guy altered his heart for. We all craved being the one who was different than all the rest. The one girl who changed it all. The one he broke all his rules for. And I wanted that girl to be me.

There was something between us, and I knew it. My head told me that was exactly why Mac had disappeared on me … because he knew it too. It was his defense mechanism, and I'd let him use it on me. I'd gone away quietly even though I didn't want to. Even though I wanted the exact opposite, but I had no idea how to go about getting it.

I'd eventually gotten so frustrated with being ignored by him that I talked to Danika about it, who in turn talked to Chance about it, but neither one of them was any help at all. Chance didn't even offer to call Mac and force him to fall in love with me or anything! No, he'd basically said that Mac was a lost cause and he couldn't figure him out either. Which I knew was a lie because boys never tried to figure out shit. That was what women were for.

Pulling the first batch of cookies out of the oven, I opened up a social media app on my phone. Someone had posted earlier that there was a welcome-back party at the baseball house tonight, and I still wasn't sure what to do. I was a walking contradiction of feelings and emotions, trying to navigate waters I was completely unfamiliar with.

Mac would obviously be there, but I didn't know if I could handle going there all by myself. The last thing I wanted to do was look like some desperate groupie, and I was afraid that if I went, that was exactly how it might come off.

I decided to text Danika.

SUNNY: BASEBALL PARTY TONIGHT. SHOULD I GO?

DANIKA: WHY WOULDN'T YOU?

SUNNY: UH, BECAUSE I'D HAVE TO GO ALONE. AND MAC'S IGNORED ME ALL SUMMER. WHAT IF HE IGNORES ME TONIGHT TOO?

DANIKA: ALL THIS COMING FROM THE GIRL WHO FORCED ME TO GO TO THE PARTY LAST YEAR. SAID SHE WAS GOING WITH OR WITHOUT ME. NOW, YOU'RE SCARED TO GO ALONE? WHO ARE YOU, AND WHAT HAVE YOU DONE WITH MY BEST FRIEND?

SUNNY: I'M NOT SURE I CAN HANDLE BEING REJECTED BY MAC IN PERSON. OVER THE PHONE IS ONE THING, BUT REAL LIFE ...

DANIKA: I GET IT. I'M NOT SURE I'D PUT MYSELF IN THAT SITUATION EITHER.

SUNNY: YOU'RE NO HELP.

DANIKA: YOU'RE WELCOME. :)

Ugh.

Danika's texts were less than helpful, but at least she'd made me feel a little better. Knowing that she wouldn't put herself in the position to be dissed in front of other people helped me feel less crazy about the whole thing.

My phone pinged again, and there was another message from Danika.

DANIKA: I MEAN, WHAT IF YOU SEE HIM HOOKING UP WITH SOME OTHER GIRL? THIS IS MAC WE'RE TALKING ABOUT.

My stomach dropped as I read her words. Mac didn't belong to me, and he wasn't mine, but that didn't mean I wanted to see his face attached to someone else's all night long. Watching him with another girl might be the exact opposite of what I could handle. Even though the rumor mill was filled with stories of Mac's numerous sexual conquests, I wasn't sure I believed a word of it. I'd never seen him slip off with any girls or disappear into his room with one during a party. He was always in the middle of a crowd, openly making out with whatever girl had agreed to his rules for the night. One time, that had been me. But that was last year. And last year felt like it'd happened eons ago.

SUNNY: YEAH. NOT SURE I'D BE ABLE TO KEEP MY FOOD DOWN.

It was in that moment that I realized I was terrified to face him. I genuinely liked Mac, and I wanted him to like me back. But I didn't want to put myself in an embarrassing situation or look like a fool in order to prove my feelings. I still had no idea what to do.

NOT READY FOR THIS

Mac

WHEN I LANDED in Orange County, I was still in no better mindset. If it was possible, I might have been in an even worse mood. I got into my ride-share, put my head back on the seat, and dropped a pair of sunglasses over my eyes, not wanting to make small talk with the driver. He got the hint, only asking me for our destination before getting on the crowded freeway.

If you had asked me last season, I might have admitted—most likely in a drunken state—that there was a decent chance that I'd get picked up by a Major League team. There were forty rounds in the draft, and about thirty-two guys went in each round. So, yeah, the possibility of me being one of about twelve hundred seemed achievable. Even if it happened in the last round, that shit still counted. And I would have taken it, by the way, skipping all the way to whatever farm team they sent me to with a smile and never looking back.

But it hadn't worked out for me.

And everyone knew it.

I'd be facing that reality in about T-minus twenty minutes

when I arrived at the baseball house. I thought that a tiny part of me never thought I'd make it here—to my senior year at Fullton State. At least, I'd always assumed it was small, but when the draft had come and gone and I wasn't one of the names called, it was clear that I had believed in something for myself far more than I'd had any right to. It'd felt more like the entirety of my being had hoped and pulled for a dream that was getting further and further out of reach. And now, the countdown was on, the pressure intensified. It was this year or nothing. Get drafted or hang up my cleats for good and go work for Dickhead Davies.

How the hell would I ever walk away from baseball and stay whole?

My disappointment had grown into bitterness over the summer even though I had been kicking ass on my summer ball team. I found myself pissed off that my friends were getting paid to play baseball, but I had to go back to our fucking university and take a bunch of classes for a future I didn't want. I hated the way that getting a degree was forced on our shoulders in order to do the one thing we loved. As if we didn't have enough pressure and stress as it was, being a Division 1 athlete.

The only saving grace was the fact that my courses came pretty easily for me. Where Chance had struggled last year to stay eligible, I never had to worry about that kind of thing. I passed my classes with ease. I just didn't want to fucking take them anymore. I was so sick and tired of school ... of pretending to give a shit about classes like business economics when I had zero interest in it.

I knew that I wasn't the only guy on the team who hadn't gotten drafted last year, so there were a few of us seniors in the same boat, all knowing that it was our last chance, praying we'd get the opportunity to make our dreams come true. But none of that made me feel any better. As much of a team sport as baseball was, it was still every man for himself. We didn't get the chance to go pro as a team; we got the chance separately, as individuals, and we were ranked as such.

As my ride pulled into the driveway of the baseball house, I wondered if everyone would see a giant neon sign that read *FAILURE*, flashing over my head when they looked at me. I wondered when I'd stop seeing it every time I saw my reflection in the mirror.

With a groan, I carried my shit across the threshold and opened the front door to boisterous yells and whoops that hit my ears the second I stepped inside. My name was being shouted from somewhere in the kitchen, and I looked around until I saw Dayton Mawlry, our star pitcher; Colin Anderson, our shortstop; and Matt Sanders, our new left fielder, who I'd heard all about over the summer, doing shots before starting to pour more.

I'd lived with Dayton and Colin last year, but Matt was a new addition to the house.

Shaking my head, I knew that a baseball party was imminent.

"We're pregaming!" Dayton yelled.

"I can see that," I said, hoping I sounded as genuinely uninterested as I felt. I was still in a shit mood, and partying sounded fucking awful.

"Party tonight," Colin said as he walked toward me, a brown-colored shot in his hand. "Gotta welcome the new guys! And break Matt in," he added with a laugh as he handed me the shot glass.

"Some things never change," I practically groaned but took the shot anyway. It burned as it passed down my throat and into my stomach. "What the hell was that?"

"Tequila!" the three of them shouted in unison.

Tequila was always a bad idea, especially if it was cheap. I frowned, and Colin's expression shifted.

"What's up?" he asked. "You don't seem excited."

"I'm not."

"You, Mac Davies, king of all women on this campus, are not happy about a party at our house for our senior fucking year?" Colin reached out, touching the back of his hand to my forehead. "You okay, man? Got a fever?"

I slapped his hand away, wanting it off me. "I'm just tired," I lied.

"Well, get untired, bro. Females will be here in an hour," Dayton shouted with a grin, seemingly pleased with himself. Or drunk already. Most likely, it was the latter.

I watched as Matt braced himself on the counter. "Hey. It's nice to meet you. But I need to slow down, or I'll be passed the fuck out in an hour."

That made me laugh even though I wasn't in the mood. "Nice to meet you too. Don't pass out. You'll regret it. Our parties are legendary," I said, deciding that maybe getting lost in some attention from the female variety was just what I needed to forget about how shitty my life was.

Sunny's image flashed in my mind before I forced it away with a shake of my head. She wouldn't show up alone tonight, would she? Chance had told me that Sunny was living by herself this year. And Danika had actually asked me to keep an eye out for her before telling me something about how she had an intense fear of being alone, but I never agreed to do it. At least, I didn't think I'd agreed to do it.

I wasn't sure I could even face Sunny, let alone watch out for the girl without wanting to spill all of my darkness into her light. She brought me comfort in a way that no one ever had before. Not even my own mother could get me to open up and tell her things the way I had with Sunny that night.

And I'd been such an asshole to her after. She should have hated me, but Chance had told me that she asked about me over the summer, so I knew that she didn't. I owed her a thousand apologies, but I wasn't sure I could give her even one of them.

Everything about me was fucking toxic. I came from a fucked up family that was only getting worse. I had no control over my own life, no baseball prospects in sight, and no scouts even interested in me, as far as I knew. The last thing I wanted to do was drag Sunny down to my level. She deserved to be in a place filled with goodness and hope, and I didn't live there.

How could I give her any part of me when I currently hated all of it myself?

Why the hell would she even want me?

She wouldn't.

And that was why I planned on staying inside my bedroom all night and not coming out for anything or anyone, no matter what. It would be easier that way.

PARTY OF ONE

Sunny

SINCE MY TEXTS with Danika, I'd been debating on whether or not I should go to the baseball party tonight, and I was still no closer to an answer. On one hand, I wanted to go because... Mac. But on the other hand, I was nervous because... well, Mac.

My phone rang, distracting me from my inner dialogue that was getting me nowhere.

"Hey, Mom. What's up?"

"Just checking in," she said, and I knew she wanted to make sure that I was okay before the semester started. "How are you doing?"

"I'm fine." I tried to reassure her, but she knew how nervous I'd been about living alone.

She'd called every day the first week I moved in, but her calls had grown a little more infrequent lately. It was a good thing. I needed to be able to survive on my own without my mommy checking up on me daily.

"Are you sure, honey? Your dad and I can come out and take you to lunch, or go grocery shopping, or take you to

Target if you still need anything for the apartment." Her voice was so soothing.

Something about my mom's tone always made me feel better, and I was just about to tell her that when I suddenly heard a lot of barking in the background.

"Did you bring home dogs again?" I asked in a sarcastic tone, already knowing the answer.

My dad owned a local vet clinic, and my mom ran the front desk there. It was the family business, but I wanted nothing to do with it. It wasn't that I hated animals or anything like that, but my heart couldn't handle being around sick pets or putting them down, even when I knew it was for the best. Thankfully, my older sister was all about it, so the Jamison Family Vet Clinic would be falling on her shoulders and not mine.

"We have a couple of rescues that are waiting for homes. It's fine," she said, and I pictured her waving me off like it was no big deal, but we both knew that there were far more than just a "couple" there.

My mom had started bringing home pets to foster when my sister and I moved out of the house, making my parents empty nesters.

"The house is too quiet without you girls. I need some chaos," she used to say before filling it with stray animals in need of their forever homes.

My dad only wanted her to be happy, so he never complained or said a word about it.

"A couple? It sounds like you have a hundred dogs, Mom!"

She laughed. "I wish." She sounded dreamy, like owning

a hundred dogs would be the greatest thing in the world. My mom was officially insane. "You could take one, you know?"

"I actually thought about that, but no. The last thing I need is to worry about a dog living in a one-bedroom apartment," I said because I had considered it. But the idea of a dog living here with no backyard or doggie door to go outside and potty stressed me out. I knew that I'd never be able to go to class and not worry the whole time about getting back fast enough.

"You're probably right. Well, if you change your mind, you know who to ask."

"I know, Mom. Tell Dad I said hi. I'll call you guys tomorrow. I have to go get ready."

"Ready for what?"

"I'm going to a party," I said without thinking.

"Ooh! By yourself, or have you made new friends?" she asked, making me feel like I was a schoolgirl.

"By myself. Don't worry. I know a bunch of the guys on the team, so I won't be alone for long," I said before realizing how scandalous that sounded.

"What team? What guys? Sunny—" She started to get that concerned timbre to her voice, and I cut her off.

"Mom, it's fine. I just meant that it's the baseball team. You know, the one Danika's boyfriend was on. I know all the guys. We're friends," I exaggerated, hoping she'd buy it and not worry once we hung up.

"Okay," she said, and more barking ensued. "Well, have fun. Shoot. Comet! Get off the kitchen table! Don't eat that!" she yelled before I heard the phone clatter. She must have dropped it. "Sunny, I have to go. Be careful!" she shouted, sounding somewhere far off in the distance, and then the call ended.

I laughed and rolled my eyes before realizing that talking to her had helped me make up my mind. I was definitely going to the party.

ONE OF THE downsides to living alone was that I had no one to get ready for parties with. There was no one to tell me that I looked cute, to compliment my outfit, or to make sure I wasn't making a complete fool of myself with my chosen attire. It was an adjustment I hadn't quite gotten used to yet, I realized as I picked out clothes. Danika had always given me her honest opinion whenever it came to this kind of thing, but now, I had to trust myself when I looked in the mirror, and I wasn't always the best person for the job. Sometimes, I wore things a little too inappropriate without realizing it.

I never tried to be racy with my clothes, but it could look that way to people who didn't really know me. I'd learned in college how quickly character assumptions could be made about a person simply based on what they wore. Excuse me for being short and having a tiny, little waist and super-toned abs that I tended to leave exposed in my belly shirts. Wearing a half-shirt didn't mean that I wanted to sleep with every guy I talked to, but try telling that to the girls who stared at me with venom in their eyes.

Another thing that sucked about being by myself was that I had no one to *go* to said parties with, just like I'd told my mom. That's right; Sunny Jamison would have to walk into the infamous baseball house, alone. I wasn't even sure if girls did that kind of thing or not. I'd never paid attention before because I always had Danika by my side, but now that I was alone, I felt exposed and vulnerable. It wasn't a comfortable way to feel, to be honest.

Why the hell hadn't I made any other friends besides her over the years? Oh yeah, because once I'd met her, there'd been no need for anyone else. Danika was the best roommate and friend I could have asked for, with her no-nonsense attitude and almost-all-black attire all the time. I'd never met anyone like her before in my life. We complemented each other perfectly, and I missed her.

With a single deep breath, I grabbed my car keys off the counter before I lost what little nerve I had left. Going to a party had to be better than sitting in this apartment with two-dozen cookies for another night with no one but my shadow and myself to eat them all. At this rate, I was going to have to start wearing oversize shirts if I didn't stop baking and eating my feelings.

My text exchange with Danika popped into my mind as I got into my car and started the engine.

Please don't be making out with some other girl. Please don't be making out with some other girl. The words became my mantra as I drove and eventually parked on the side of the house.

I almost put my car in reverse and pulled right back out,

but when another car parked directly behind me and blocked me in my spot, I took it as a sign. I had to go inside and face Mac. Or at least attempt to.

A loud knock on my car window caused me to jump in my seat, and I let out a squeal. I turned toward the glass and saw three guys walking away from me and stumbling toward the party. They must have hit my car on their way past it just to mess with me. One last look at my reflection in the rearview mirror, and I pushed open the door and stepped out.

The house was packed, which I'd expected, but it was loud and dark, which I hadn't expected. Usually, music played in the background, and the lights were on. But tonight, the music was blaring, making conversations damn near impossible, and there were only strobe lights flashing. I could barely see, let alone recognize anyone.

My focus was on finding Mac—or at least seeing his gorgeous face—so I started walking from room to room, my confidence shaky at best.

"Sunny?" a voice said, and I got excited for only a second before realizing that it wasn't the right guy's voice.

I turned around and gave the giant shortstop a hug. "Hey, Colin!"

"Hey, girl. How's Danikas?" he shouted over the music.

"She's great!"

"Tell hers I said hi's the next time you talk to her, yeahs?" he added extra *s*'s to the end of random words, but I still understood him.

"I will. Hey, Colin, have you seen Mac around?" I asked and watched his face transform into something that made me feel a little stupid. I'd asked about a specific player on the team, and that only meant one thing—I was interested.

Colin was grinning, his head moving as he smiled.

He looked around before leaning close to my ear. "You know, Suns, I haven't seen hims for some hours now that you mention it. He's probably in his rooms."

Dread filled me. Hadn't I just convinced myself that Mac didn't sleep around with random girls at parties? But he was currently not in the center of the room with his latest conquest, like I'd said he always was. I was such an idiot. A fool who'd convinced herself that he was one of the good ones because that was what I wanted him to be.

"You can goes back there, I'm sure. You know which rooms is his? Chance's old one. The big ones," Colin slurred, and I wanted to laugh, but I couldn't. I was too busy choking on what was left of my pride.

"That's okay. I'd rather not," I said, wanting nothing more than to leave the same way I'd come in.

"Want me to tell hims you were lookings for him?" Colin balanced himself on my shoulder, almost making me fall.

"No. It's okay. Please don't," I begged as I wrapped an arm around my stomach and wiggled out from under the weight of his drunk body.

"Bye, Suns. See you laters." Colin smiled as I maneuvered through the crowd, my eyes suddenly focused on the door that led to Mac's room.

A small light shone from underneath it, and I knew he was in there.

The door flew open, and a stunning girl walked out with a

satisfied smile on her face as she pulled down on the world's shortest skirt. Mac followed quickly behind her, his face contorted as his eyes looked around briefly before crashing into mine, stopping me dead in my tracks. He was tanner than the last time I had seen him, his muscles pulling the shirt taut around his arms. And his hair was a little longer, unrulier and sun-bleached at the ends. It all suited him. His expression softened for a millisecond before he composed himself again and continued walking. Right. Past. Me.

Like I didn't even exist.

Like I wasn't worth his time.

I shouldn't have come tonight. It was stupid, and I was a fool. Mac wasn't into me. We'd shared one phone call a few months ago, and I'd been acting like it was some life-changing moment when it clearly meant nothing to him.

I meant nothing to him.

And the sooner I got that through my head and my heart, the better off I'd be.

THE UNIVERSE HATES ME

Mac

THE PARTY RAGED outside of my bedroom, and even though people pounded on the door throughout the night, I never budged. I wasn't in the right frame of mind to socialize, and though I'd contemplated the distraction of some female attention, I realized that I didn't fucking want it.

I was tired of the same shit. If I opened this door and walked out of it, I'd repeat the patterns I'd started my freshman year. I was over playing the same old games. It was exhausting, being this fake version of me, and I had zero energy for it anymore.

Grabbing my pillow, I pulled it over my face and fell asleep, only to wake up to the sound of my ex-girlfriend's voice outside of my bedroom door. I wasn't sure if I was having a nightmare or if her being here was real. I thought she graduated last semester.

"Mac, I know you're in there. Open the door, or I'll have someone do it for me," she demanded.

I wouldn't put it past her to do exactly that. Hayley could most likely convince my own teammates to remove the entire door if she asked them to.

Begrudgingly, I stood up and slowly made my way over, half-annoyed, half-curious. I still had no idea why the hell she was even here in the first place. Throwing the door open, I saw Hayley standing there in the shortest fucking skirt known to man, her long, tanned supermodel legs on display for all to see as she shoved her way inside my room and closed the door behind her.

"What do you want? And what are you doing here? I thought you graduated." I shocked myself at how pissed I was feeling more than any other emotion. When it came to Hayley, I was never sure how I'd react. But the fact that she was in the baseball house right now when I'd thought she was long gone angered me beyond reason.

My one saving grace in having to come back to Fullton State for my senior year was that she wouldn't be here. It was going to be the first time I could walk to classes without looking over my shoulder, wondering if I'd run into her at a party or see her pointing and laughing in my direction with all her shitty friends following suit. I was her personal jester, and the joke was on me.

I'd always wanted to hate her. And there had even been nights in the beginning of our breakup when I prayed to a god I wasn't sure I believed in to help me get over her. I begged him to put anger in my heart because still wanting her back after everything that had happened felt incredibly pathetic, and I didn't want to be that guy. But I was. I'd wanted her back more than anything at the time.

And as I took in all five foot ten of her dark skin and jet-black hair, I knew exactly why I'd fallen so hard in the first place. Hayley was jaw-droppingly gorgeous. Way out of my league physically, even now, three years later. She'd given an eager freshman with confidence and daddy issues the right kind of attention at just the right time. And in return, I'd given her my heart and fallen head over heels into what I thought was going to be some sort of epic fairy-tale romance for the ages.

Instead, I'd fallen for the spawn of Satan who got off on humiliating me in front of my entire team and never once apologized for it.

"I'm two classes short," she started to say, and I'd almost forgotten that I'd asked her a question. "I have to take them this semester, or I never would have, and my dad would kill me if I didn't get my degree." She popped a piece of bubble gum that was in her mouth before seductively licking her lips and batting her eyelashes at me.

"Why are you at my party? Why are you in my room?" I tried my best to sound like a dick, but she was fluent in wielding her body for power, and she knew it. Too bad her satanic charms no longer worked on me.

"Heard you had a great summer in Washington," she practically purred.

She wasn't wrong. I'd had a stellar summer, but how did she know about it?

"What's your point?" I asked, realizing that she thought she could jump right back into my arms if I was stupid enough to let her.

"My point is that I bet those scouts are looking at you now.

You'll probably get drafted this year, and you know that's all I've ever wanted for you."

She took a step toward me, and I took one back, a sick laugh escaping from my throat.

"You don't give a shit about me," I growled.

Her jaw dropped open in mock shock. "How can you say that? After everything we've been through?"

This chick was seriously delusional.

"After everything we've been through? Don't you mean, after the hell *you* put me through? You crushed me," I admitted, and it felt good to say it out loud. Maybe because I wanted her to feel bad about what she'd done to me, and here I was, giving her the chance to admit she was an actual human with feelings.

"I crushed you? I crushed you?" she shouted. "You embarrassed me! In front of the whole school!" she kept yelling, and I realized that she wasn't sorry for any of it and she never would be.

Only a demon or a robot could look at our situation and not feel even an ounce of remorse. I decided that she had to be both.

"Get the fuck out of my room," I said, and she pretended to be shocked by my dismissal.

"But we could be great again, Mac. A true power couple," she added, and I wondered what part of the power she provided to this fictional coupledom because the last time I'd checked, she was looking for some coattails to ride.

"Get. The. Fuck. Out. Of. My. Room," I said, enunciating each word so there would be no misunderstanding.

"You can't be serious." She cocked her head and glared at me. "I know you haven't dated anyone since we broke up."

"Don't take that the wrong way, Satan. It has nothing to do with you and everything to do with me."

"Maybe you're not over me, and that's why you can't move on. You miss me. You still want me."

She closed the space between us, her acrylic nails running down my chest, and I wanted to give myself a blue fucking ribbon for resisting her. I'd never thought I'd be able to do that, but here I was, wishing she'd choke on her own tongue rather than ever putting it in my mouth again.

"Get off me." I moved out of her reach. "Didn't you hear me? I said, it has nothing to do with you. Now, go find some other athlete's life to ruin."

She huffed. "Well, I heard Dayton's getting drafted. Maybe I'll go see what he's up to," she goaded, assuming that I'd care because I was jealous when that was the furthest thing from the truth.

"Stay away from my teammates. Don't go near any of them, Hayley." I was angry. Not because I gave two shits about her, but because I cared about my teammates and I didn't want any of them going through what I had with her.

"You can't keep me away from an entire team, Mac. I mean, you can try"—she ran her hands down the sides of her body—"but you know it won't work."

"I can, and I will. Get out of my house. Now."

She pulled open the door she'd closed, walked out of my room, and straightened her skirt like I'd messed it up, giving anyone who might see her the absolute wrong idea. But I couldn't worry about that shit right now. In order to make sure Hayley actually left the party and didn't try to ruin any of my teammates' lives, I needed to follow her out.

I was hot on her heels when my heart almost exploded inside my chest. I saw Sunny standing there, watching me, her eyes big and round and filled with sadness. I'd forgotten how beautiful she was, how much just seeing her made me want to get lost in her.

Looking at Sunny hurt, and it took every ounce of willpower I had inside of me to walk straight past her when all I wanted to do was take her in my arms and kiss the hell out of her. But I couldn't. At least, not yet. I had to focus on getting Hayley off my property and out of my life for good. So, I kept chasing after the wrong girl, leaving the right one behind.

WHEN I HAD come back inside the house after forcing Hayley to leave with all of her demonic friends, Sunny was long gone. Believe me, I checked. I'd looked everywhere, and once I realized that she really had left, I had gone to bed. Alone.

I woke up the next morning without a hangover. That was what happened when you didn't drink like the rest of the guys. But I was starving, like I hadn't eaten in days.

Stretching my arms over my head, I wandered through the living room and into the kitchen, hoping like hell that someone had done some grocery shopping before I got in yesterday.

The house was a fucking disaster. A few people slept on the couches, and there was some guy I didn't recognize on the floor, cuddling with an inflatable doll. Empty plastic cups and bottles were everywhere. *Why was throwing things in a trash can so fucking hard for people to do?*

Shaking my head, I pulled open the refrigerator door and cursed silently. The damn thing was empty—unless you counted the lone pizza box that had nothing inside of it, except a single piece of crust.

Who the hell had left that in the fridge anyway? *Idiots.*

When I yanked it out, my eyes widened. Hiding behind the stupid box was a carton of eggs. I knew better than to get too excited though. With my luck, it would be empty too.

Reaching for it, I smiled at the weight. There were definitely eggs in there. Scanning the packaging, I made sure that the expiration date was still in the future and pumped my fist in the air when I read that it was. Just as I opened the carton to see six eggs inside, Colin walked into the kitchen, yawning.

"You found the eggs," he said, holding his head between his hands.

"Only because I moved the pizza box."

"I put that there, so no one would see the eggs," he started to explain before sitting down at the counter. "You know how stupid we get after drinking. We eat all the things. So, I hid them."

I laughed. "From yourself?"

"From all of us. Especially myself," he said. "But you'll make them, right? I need food, or I might yak."

"Yeah, yeah. I'll make them," I agreed before grabbing a

pan and some cooking spray and getting to work. "Take these." I tossed him some aspirin that I'd grabbed from the drawer.

Colin worked on the cap before finally getting it off and dumped two pills inside his hand, taking them without water or any liquid. "You know, Sunny was here last night. Did you see her?"

I stopped cracking the eggs into the pan and walked over to where he was sitting, spatula in hand. "I saw her for two seconds before she left. Did she say anything? Who was she here with?" I pointed the spatula at him with each question.

He put up his hands. "Not so loud, man. I don't know who she was with, but she asked where you were."

"She asked where I was? What did you say?" At this rate, I was never going to start cooking the eggs.

He shrugged. "I don't know. I think I said you were in your room. I don't really remember."

Damn.

That was why Sunny had been right there when my bedroom door opened and Hayley walked out of it. She definitely thought something was going on between us, and I couldn't blame her. I would have drawn the same conclusion if the roles had been reversed.

"What's up with the two of you anyway?"

"Nothing," I said a little too quickly, and we both knew it. Denial came out fast, especially when it was a lie.

"Doesn't seem like nothing," he pushed, but I walked away from him and turned on the stove instead, cracking all six eggs into the pan.

My stomach growled, and I pressed my palm against it.

"How long until the guys are up? I want to go to the field and get some swings in."

"Come on, Mac. It's, like, our only day off," Colin started to whine, and it irritated me.

Fall practice began tomorrow, and even though our team was bound by all sorts of NCAA rules and regulations, we skirted our way around them, rarely taking a day off until winter break.

"I'll go alone," I said as I continued scrambling. "Doesn't matter to me," I lied. It mattered but not enough to make me not go.

I missed Chance. He was always down for going the extra mile, and he never said no when it came to baseball.

"I'll go wake up the guys," Colin finally relented, and I knew that they were probably too hungover to be productive anyway.

Splitting the eggs onto two plates, I started eating before anyone else woke up and wanted me to share with them. Six eggs weren't nearly enough food for four guys.

Colin reappeared with a frown. "They're not getting up anytime soon. But I'll go to the field with you."

"Eat up then." I pushed the other plate of eggs in his direction before planning exactly what I wanted to work on today. Weights. Sprints. Hitting off the tee. Ground balls. Sunny.

Sunny?

What the hell was I going to do about this girl?

STUPID, PERFECT JERKFACE

Sunny

I'D LEFT THE party last night, beyond pissed off. I'd gone through a wide range of emotions on the drive home but kept coming back to anger.

And when I woke up this morning, I was still angry. It was the one thing that made me feel the best. Being mad meant that I wasn't sulking—or worse, crying. I didn't want to do either of those things.

Sitting up in bed, I tossed the covers off of my body and huffed. Screw Mac and his deliciously gorgeous face, stupid surfer hair, and hot baseball-playing body. Who needed any of it? Not. Me.

I had no idea what I'd truly expected from him, but I guessed I hadn't counted on him being able to walk past me like I was nothing. He didn't even acknowledge my existence. No. All he had done was give me a quick glance and then continued chasing after a girl who looked like she belonged more on the cover of a magazine than at a college baseball party. *How typical.*

He could have sent me a text message afterward,

apologizing for being such an asshat. I knew he still had my phone number. No one deleted people's numbers anymore. But he hadn't apologized or texted or done anything. It was June all over again.

Reaching for my cell, I pressed Danika's name without stopping to calculate the time difference, something I usually did by habit.

"Hey," she answered, sounding happy to hear from me.

"Hi," I responded, but my tone was less than happy.

"What's wrong?" she asked before adding quickly, "Oh no. The party. What happened? What did he do?"

"What did who do?" I heard Chance ask in the background, and Danika tried to cover up the phone, but I heard her say Mac's name.

I sucked in a long breath, determined not to cry. "He just..." I started. "It sounds so dumb when I say it out loud."

"You haven't said anything out loud yet," Danika chastised.

"Fine, it sounds stupid in my head before I say it out loud to you."

She groaned through the phone, "Spit it out, Sunny."

"He ignored me. I mean, first of all, he was in his room with some girl who was ridiculously pretty, and then he just walked right past me while he was chasing after her," I explained, and she was quiet.

"What did he do? Tell me," Chance whispered, and I rolled my eyes even though they couldn't see me.

"Just put me on speaker."

" 'K. We're both here."

"So, he ignored you? Maybe he didn't see you," Danika suggested, and Chance agreed.

"Mac can be dumb sometimes, you know." That was Chance.

"He saw me. He looked right at me and walked on by."

"He didn't even say hi?" Chance again.

"No. He barely even acted like he knew me. It was embarrassing. I felt like an idiot," I said, feeling vulnerable and dumb all over again. Being mad was so much better than this crap.

"I'll talk to him," Chance said, and Danika squealed.

I'd never heard my best friend squeal before.

"Did you just ... *squeal*?" I asked, making sure the sound of that word was as unbelievable coming out of my mouth as it had been from hers.

"Be quiet. Chance just said he'd call him. Did you hear that part?" she asked.

"I heard, but you don't have to do that," I said, and I meant it.

Maybe if this had been a few months ago, Chance might have been able to make a difference, but I wasn't sure there was any point now. Mac clearly didn't care.

"I'm not going to let my best friend be a dick to you, Sunny. I'll handle it. And I'll find out what's going on and put a stop to it."

Before I knew it, the phone clicked off speaker, and Danika was on the line alone. "Well, I guess he's handling it then," she said with a little odd-sounding laugh.

"Oh God. You're turned on right now, aren't you?"

"Wouldn't you be? Did you hear him? I need to go jump

his bones for all that macho, bossy shit."

"Go away. Call me later and let me know if Chance actually talks to him," I said, and she made another weird sound. At least one of us was getting the baseball player we wanted.

"I will. And you should think about coming to New York and working with me. 'K-thanks-bye," she said really fast before ending the call, knowing that if she stayed on the line, I'd argue with her about it.

Danika had mentioned a couple times since she'd started the new division in her dad's company that she was going to need help eventually and that I'd be perfect for it, but it always made me nervous whenever I tried to work through the logistics in my head. I knew absolutely nothing about real estate, and I'd never even been to New York before.

How could she even think that I'd be good at matching high-end clients with properties when I knew nothing about any of it? I had to admit that it sounded exciting, and Danika had never been happier, but I thought that had more to do with Chance than anything else. Don't tell her I said that.

AFTER SHOWERING AND washing my hair, I decided to run to the campus bookstore and pick up some things. It was hot out, and even though I was in cutoff shorts and a crop top, I still felt the beads of sweat starting to form. I reached for my long blonde hair and twisted it around my fist before tying it into a knot on top of my head.

Campus was pretty crowded for a Sunday with people milling around all over the place, staring down at their phones and almost walking into things. I couldn't remember a time when we didn't have cell phones, but my parents did, and they talked about it a lot. They made it sound so appealing and freeing, not having a phone attached to you twenty-four hours a day. But the idea of turning mine off for said *freedom* gave me this weird level of anxiety instead. It made me feel unsafe and uncomfortable to be so disconnected.

As I approached the two-story stucco building with a *Get Your Books Here* banner hanging from it, I noticed a *We're Hiring* flyer underneath some Plexiglas by the doors. They were looking for part-time help, and I briefly considered applying before hearing my parents' voices in my head once again.

"*You have the rest of your life to work. Don't start now.*"

They had both emphasized my not working while I was a full-time student, insisting that once I started, I'd never stop. It wasn't like I'd never had a job before. I'd worked over the summers, helping my parents in the vet clinic, which I was sure might not have counted to some people, but it did to me. I'd learned all kinds of skills just from working the front desk.

So, the idea of picking up a few hours had been crossing my mind lately. Nothing too serious, just something to fill my free time. I had far too much of it with Danika gone, and I figured that anything that stopped me from focusing on Mac had to be a good thing.

Pulling open one of the glass doors, I was hit with a wave

of air-conditioning before Mac's stupid, grinning face painted on the wall with the rest of the team from last year's College World Series greeted me. So much for not thinking about him or trying to escape his hazel-colored eyes. They'd even gotten the color right on a freaking mural.

Who was I kidding? I couldn't work here, not with Mac's eyes following my every move. Growling at his giant-sized painted face, I decided that it was all his fault the store was so crowded. The lines for the cashier were about twenty people long, and I had zero interest in waiting when all I'd wanted in the first place were some cute pens and stuff.

I spun around to leave and literally ran into a rock-hard chest. An apology was on the tip of my tongue when I realized that it was none other than Mac himself.

"Sunny," he said my name so sweet as he moved to reach for the pieces of hair that had fallen around my face but stopped himself.

His eyes roamed over the entire length of my body before stopping back on my bare midriff and my belly-button piercing. He liked what he saw, and it took everything in me to not say that out loud and call him out.

"It's not enough that you're on the freaking wall, but you have to be here in real life too?" I grumbled to myself, but Mac clearly thought I was talking to him.

"What? Oh," he said as he looked toward the wall, obviously forgetting that *he was painted on it*! "It's a little obnoxious, right?"

He actually looked embarrassed, and I figured that he probably was. For as much as Mac acted like he loved the attention, some part of me knew better.

"Are you asking or telling me?"

"I was asking, but damn, Sunny, you sound mad."

Is he serious right now?

I narrowed my eyes, hoping they might shoot lasers at him or something as equally destructive. "I am mad," I admitted before realizing that we weren't alone and his teammates were watching our interaction with rapt attention. "But it doesn't matter anyway, does it?"

"What doesn't?"

"How I feel."

He gave me a one-armed shrug, and I wanted to sock him in it. When had we turned into two people who couldn't even have a normal conversation with each other anymore? Instead of waiting for him to figure out what to say to me next or formulate the perfect response, I gave him mine instead.

"You're an asshole," I tossed over my shoulder before walking away from him, hoping like hell that he'd come running after me but knowing he never would.

Why did I keep hoping he'd want me when he kept showing me that he didn't?

Mac

DAMN IT.

Every time I saw Sunny, I screwed it all up. I turned into a tongue-tied idiot who couldn't speak, and instead of fixing things between us, I kept letting them get even more sideways. Everything I'd confessed to her during our talk last summer would rush back into my mind, and I'd just get *so ... fucking ... embarrassed.*

I found myself consumed with how she must see me now that she knew all those things that no one else did. I'd told her my innermost thoughts when it came to baseball and my future, shared my deepest fears, and practically cried into the damn phone. And if *I* was thinking about our conversation every single time I ran into her, I assumed that she must have been as well.

I was almost surprised she hadn't laughed in my face yet even though, deep down, I knew Sunny wasn't the type of girl to do that. She wasn't evil, like my ex. Even if I didn't know Sunny all that well, I knew at least that much. And it scared the hell out of me because I had no idea how to trust females anymore.

"What was that?" Matt asked as I watched Sunny leave through the glass doors, her long hair swaying from side to side with each step. It had been up when I first saw her, so she must have taken it down.

"Nothing." I tried to blow him off. I refused to get into it with him, the one guy who I knew the least of all. Plus, I didn't want him checking her out. She was barely wearing anything!

"You sounded like a dick," he boasted, acting proud.

"I know, and I didn't mean to be."

"You didn't? Girls like that anyway. You know, the

meaner we are, the more they want us," he said like he was some kind of professional on the matter.

"I'm not interested in a girl who wants to be treated like crap. And Sunny," I said, not meaning to tell Matt her name, "she's pissed because I was mean, and she doesn't like it."

"You should go after her, man." Dayton stepped toward me, his eyes still on her before she finally disappeared out of our line of vision.

I knew he was right. I should be chasing after her, telling her how sorry I was and promising I'd never be mean to her again. But I didn't. My stomach was tied up in knots. I was in unfamiliar territory here—wanting this girl but not knowing how to go about it. All of my fears kept me rooted firmly in place.

My phone buzzed in my pocket, and I pulled it out, praying it wasn't my dad. Chance's name flashed on the screen, and I swore my face must have looked like a schoolgirl with a crush.

"Gotta take this," I said with a grin as I sprinted outside for some privacy.

"My man. What's up? How's ball?" I said as I answered and searched for an empty place to talk, where no one would eavesdrop or accidentally overhear.

"Why are you making my life so difficult?" Chance asked, and I furrowed my brow in confusion.

"Come again?"

"My life. Why are you messing with it?" he said once more, and I had no idea what he was talking about.

"Uh ..." I stopped walking and stood still.

"Sunny, Mac. What are you doing?"

Pulling the phone away, I breathed heavily into the air before getting back on. "What did you hear?"

"I heard you were a jerk to her last night at some party." He sounded annoyed, and I knew that if he were here, he would be lecturing me in person.

If Chance already knew about last night, then Sunny must have been really upset when she left. She must have called Danika.

"I wasn't a jerk per se—" I started to explain when he cut me off.

"Why are you being mean to her? I know you like her. You've liked her since last year. So, what's up?"

I couldn't very well sit here and tell my best friend that I was having a hard time letting my guard down because I was scared, so I improvised. "I don't know. I just see her, and I turn stupid. I'm not sure why." *Lies. Lies. Lies.* I knew exactly why.

"You see her, and you turn cruel. That's not like you. Sunny doesn't deserve that, and we both know it. What's really going on? Talk to me, man. Is this because you didn't get drafted?" He asked the last question quieter than the rest, his voice cracking a little under the weight of it.

It was the one topic that most of us ballplayers avoided and never talked about after the fact. It was too sensitive a subject. Too touchy. Too painful.

Looking around, I noticed a few girls staring in my direction, so I started walking again, realizing that standing in one place was going to pose a problem. "Um ... I mean, yeah, that's part of it," I admitted reluctantly.

"Don't think I haven't noticed that you seem ..." He

paused. "How should I say this? Sadder, I guess."

"You think I seem sadder?" I asked, hoping I sounded crazy.

When did Chance think I was sad in the first place?

"Mac, I'm your best friend. I might be distracted with my own career right now, but I know when you aren't a hundred percent yourself. And you haven't been since last June."

"Why are you just saying something now then?" I asked, feeling a little disappointed that it never occurred to him to ask me if I was okay before today ... especially if he'd noticed. It had been months.

"I thought you'd snap out of it. I was letting you work through it on your own, but from the sound of it, you're not getting better. How can I help?"

A small huff mixed with a laugh escaped from deep in my throat. "Make sure someone picks me up this season, so I don't have to go work for my old man."

Chance blew out a loud breath. "Ah, fuuuck. I forgot all about Dick. How could I forget about your dad? No wonder you're so stressed out."

"Yeah," I said, agreeing with nothing in particular. "I'll figure it out. Not everyone gets drafted, right?"

"Don't talk like that," he snapped. "It's not over yet. Hell, it hasn't even started. Don't forget about Cole and every other guy who got picked up his senior year. It doesn't mean anything that you didn't get signed last year. You know that."

Cole Anders. I always circled back to him in my mind as well since he had been in the same situation as I currently was—worried that this dream would end when senior season did.

"I know," I said, hoping to placate Chance, but the nagging feeling in the back of my mind wouldn't go away. *What if I wasn't good enough?* A lot of guys weren't, and that wasn't me being a whiny little bitch; it was me being realistic. "And hey, I'll apologize to Sunny, okay?"

"Yeah, all right. But don't play with her feelings. Only apologize if you mean it. Let her in, Mac. I think she might be exactly what you need."

I heard Danika's voice in the background saying something I couldn't quite make out, and I realized how much I missed having them around.

"Trust me, I know. Why the hell do you think I keep trying to stay away from her?"

Sunny wasn't the kind of girl you dated and then let go of when the semester ended. She was the *bring her home to Mom* type. The kind of girl you fought to hold on to, not the one you let go. Sunny Jamison was the girl you married.

"I know exactly why," he said with a laugh. "You're a pussy."

"You are what you eat," I fired back without thinking, and I swore I could see him rolling his eyes from here.

"Mac," Chance said, his voice turning serious, "one last thing."

"Yeah?" I kicked at the dirt while I waited for him to say whatever was coming next.

"What happened freshman year was fucked up, but it wasn't your fault. And not all girls are like that. Hell, most girls aren't. Sunny would never do something like that to you."

"I know she wouldn't," I practically whispered, feeling a little caught off guard.

Even though Sunny was a good girl, what if I wasn't enough for her? What if she looked at me and only saw a guy worthy of being a fling? I wasn't sure I could handle the rejection. Believe me, I noticed the hypocrisy.

"You deserve to be happy. And you deserve a good girl. Even if you don't think you do."

"Jeez, Carter, you're the last person I ever expected to get all this lady advice from, Mr. I'm Never Falling in Love."

"Yeah, yeah. What can I say? I was an idiot. Danika's the best thing that's ever happened to me." He sounded so confident.

"Better than baseball?" I asked even though I was only teasing.

"A hundred times over."

I gasped. "Only a hundred?"

"If there were a choice, I'd pick Danika every time," he said without taking a breath. My best friend had fallen head over heels in love. "Hey, I gotta get to the field. Call me if you need anything, but fix it, Mac. FIX. IT," he repeated sternly, emphasizing the words as if I needed the additional reminder before Danika yelled from somewhere in the background, "Fix it, Maaac!"

I laughed. "Tell your girl I will. You know where to send the bill." I tried to joke about him being my therapist, but I was honestly grateful for the talk as we ended the call.

I knew what I needed to do, but I had no idea how to go about doing it.

YOU'VE GOT TO BE KIDDING ME

Sunny

DANIKA VIDEO-CALLED ME when I was in the hallway of my apartment, following behind a girl I'd never seen before with crazy green-and-black hair that I sort of loved. It was almost like Danika sensed that I was this close to making a new friend. Granted, I hadn't said two words to the girl yet, but I had just been about to introduce myself when my phone rang.

"What's up, cockblock?" I said with a laugh as I answered her video call, the girl with the fun hair turning around to eye me for only a second before she kept walking.

"Wait, what? Cockblock? Where are you?" She narrowed her eyes and moved her head as she tried to see around me.

Unlocking my front door, I stepped inside and locked it behind me. "Home. But there was a girl I wanted to meet, and you ruined it."

I tossed the food I'd just bought onto the counter and plopped down on the couch, holding the phone in front of my face.

"Oh, you were trying to replace me. Good thing I called."

She smiled, and it made me smile back. I really missed having her here.

"What are you wearing?" I asked, squinting at the bright blue T-shirt.

"It's a team shirt. Chance has a game, and I like to be supportive."

"Does it have his name on the back?"

"Of course it does. What kind of girlfriend do you think I am?" She moved around, so I could see the back of the shirt, but it didn't work. Everything turned into a blurry blue blob instead. "Anyway," she said as she walked around her place, "I just called to tell you that Chance talked to Mac today."

There was no way I could hide the surprise on my face. "Shut up. He did? What'd he say?"

Her face contorted a little, and her eyes pulled together. "Basically, he told Mac to pull his head out of his ass and talk to you."

I pondered this information for a minute.

"What's wrong? I thought you'd be happy," Danika asked, making a pouty face.

"I don't want Mac to talk to me because Chance told him to. I want him to WANT to talk to me."

She rolled her eyes all dramatically. "Oh my God, Sunny. He does want to talk to you. He said he turns stupid whenever he sees you—or something idiotic like that. Whatever happened to him freshman year really messed him up, I think. He has trust issues. And I overheard Chance saying something about his dad, but I don't know what it was exactly."

"That doesn't give him an excuse to be shitty to me," I

argued because it was true. As much slack as I was willing to cut Mac, I didn't want to be treated like crap in the process. I hadn't done anything to deserve it.

"No, it doesn't. I totally agree."

"I'll let you know if he reaches out," I said in a sarcastic tone because I wasn't going to hold my breath or anything.

Danika nodded her head before telling me she had to go and ended the call. Her face disappeared, and I sat there for a second, holding on to the phone before remembering that I had food waiting for me.

I spent the rest of the afternoon and evening cleaning my apartment and organizing my baking drawers. I liked all of my things to be in just the right place. And even though there was no one else around to mess it up, sometimes, I was the one who ruined my perfect order.

Everything I did only served as a slight distraction. I kept checking my phone like a crazy person, making sure it was turned on, the battery hadn't died, or that it wasn't on silent. But Mac never texted. Or called. Or emailed. Not that he had my email address, but still, he could have found it if he looked hard enough.

And I kicked myself every time I logged in to social media and checked his profile for updates. There weren't any. But that didn't make me any less anxious. At least when he was posting in his stories, I knew what he was doing and what he was up to. His silence only made my mind go into overdrive, making up all kinds of reasons as to why he wasn't posting in the first place. Most of them involving girls, like the one I'd seen walking out of his room that night.

Speaking of that girl, I thought to myself as my finger hovered over the list of people he was following on the app. It was a way smaller number than how many were following him, so I pressed it, looking for her face as I scrolled down the list.

Aside from a handful of girls, myself included, Mac was following mostly other baseball players and baseball-related profiles. The girl from the party wasn't one of them. I wanted to throw a freaking celebration for that tidbit of knowledge alone. I had no idea why that brought me any sense of relief, but for whatever reason, it did.

Feeling more than a little stalkerish, I clicked on each one of the other girls' profiles that he was following to see if they went to school here and to look at their pictures because … I was a female, and we were curious—aka competitive—but they were all private. It was probably for the best. The last thing I needed was to fall down the rabbit hole of Mac's social media and get myself all worked up, which would have definitely happened.

And that was exactly why I stopped myself from scrolling through his likes and comments on his regular feed too. I'd done that more than once over the summer, and it hadn't gone well for my emotional state. Seeing the number of comments the guy racked up with each picture, plus the kinds of things that girls posted, I only imagined what they said in his DMs.

Walking into my room, I tossed my phone on my bed and headed toward the shower before promising myself that I wouldn't log on any more tonight. School started tomorrow, and I needed the sleep, not the headache.

THE NEXT MORNING, the usual thrill of the first day of classes rolled through me as I stretched my arms over my head and smiled to no one. I couldn't help it; a new school year always made me a little excited. You never knew who you might meet or what might happen.

Practically hopping out of bed, I grabbed a pair of jean shorts and a plain white T-shirt. Simple but still cute. It was too hot to wear combat boots and socks, so I opted for a pair of sandals instead. Liking what I saw in the full-length mirror, I walked into the bathroom to put on some makeup but couldn't stop staring at my hair.

It was long and blonde and had been for all of my life. I'd never once colored my hair or done anything different with it. And while I loved it, it suddenly felt a little stale. Maybe it was the girl I had seen yesterday with the Billie Eilish hair that seemed to work so well on her that got me thinking. NOT that I wanted to color my hair black and green, but maybe I could pull something else off. *Lavender maybe? Silver? Icy blue?* I pulled at the strands, deciding I'd mess with them later. For today at least, I'd have the same old blonde hair that I'd had forever.

After finishing my makeup, I grabbed my bag and my keys before heading into the kitchen. I stuffed a bottle of water and a protein bar into my bag. I rarely woke up hungry, and to be honest, I had to force myself to eat breakfast most days—

hence, the protein bar. Phone in hand, I glanced at it one last time and started to hustle.

I liked being early to class. Not on time, definitely not late, but early. And since it was still morning, I knew that there were most likely no classes before mine started, so I could get in there, find a seat, and get comfortable. School was technically close enough that I could walk if I wanted to, but in this weather, I'd be sweating through my shirt by the time I got there. And even though parking could be a total pain in the ass, I decided to drive anyway.

It was a typical morning, the streets were crowded and I'd just accelerated to make it through a yellow light when I heard a loud thud. My car immediately started pulling to the right as horns honked, and I gripped the steering wheel like my life depended on it. Maybe it did. I was confused, and my car wasn't cooperating, pulling to the right as I tried to navigate it toward the left.

The sound got louder and more consistent, and my car felt like I was driving over a gravel road. I looked in my rearview mirror, signaled, and pulled over to the side of the road with my heart in my throat. Stepping out of my car, I noticed the flat tire.

Shit.

I'd never changed a flat tire before, but I was a smart and capable girl. I was sure I could figure it out. They didn't keep a spare in the trunk for no reason, right? I thought about calling my dad, but what could he realistically do? He'd probably tell me to call AAA, but I didn't have hours to sit here, waiting on the side of the road.

Checking the time on the dashboard, I realized that I was most likely not only going to be late for class, but I might also miss it completely. I couldn't miss my first day of school. Popping the trunk, I walked back there, making sure no one hit me while I did it. It crossed my mind that being on the side of the road with a flat tire wasn't the safest situation to be in. A driver could lose control of their car and hit mine—or me. It wasn't unheard of.

Staring at the spare tire and the equipment to change it sitting there, I tried to pull the tire out, but it wouldn't budge. While I was stared at it, frustrated, a car pulled up behind me, and I looked over, a little nervous at first. The passenger door flew open, and a guy in a baseball hat stepped out before the car even came to a complete stop.

Great.

Mac Davies was either here to rescue me or make it all worse.

THERE MIGHT BE A GOD

Mac

I THREW OPEN my bedroom door with a smile and heard my roommates already chatting it up in the kitchen. As I rounded the corner, I saw Matt standing at the stove, cooking.

He turned around, a giant, goofy grin on his face as his eyes met mine. "First day of class, man. I am pumped!"

I smiled back, sitting down at the counter between to Dayton and Colin. "Should be cool. It's whatever. What are you making?" I asked, curious if it was going to be edible or not.

"Eggs, toast, and sausage for everyone. Don't even think about leaving this house without food," he insisted, pointing his spatula in our direction, and I shot both Dayton and Colin an inquisitive look.

Colin shrugged. "It's a little weird that you're taking on the role of mom in the house since you love to party so much, but I like being fed, so thanks."

"Yeah, man. Thanks for cooking," I added as I noticed four glasses all filled with orange juice, sitting just out of reach.

Matt must have seen because he scooted them toward us

before hustling back to the stove like a gourmet chef.

If Matt hadn't let us know he could cook, we all would have attempted to switch off at some point, burning shit or making it poorly. We'd learned pretty quickly last year that none of us were any good in the kitchen if the meal was more complicated than spaghetti, ramen noodles, or protein shakes. Every athlete seemed proficient in making shakes to survive on if we had to. And pasta was a no-brainer. Except that one time when Cole hadn't cooked it long enough and we'd ended up eating crunchy noodles that almost broke our teeth.

"I'm fired up," Matt yelled as he divvied up the eggs and sausage evenly onto four separate plates before shoving them our way.

As we reached for the plates, we hit each other like we'd never eaten breakfast before.

"About?" I asked around a mouthful of food before realizing that it was hot as fuck.

"Class. Being here. I'm excited to be at this school and on the team. I've heard so many things," Matt explained as he buttered the toast and gave us each a slice.

"It's still school, bro. And you have to pass your classes, or you can't play," Dayton said, suddenly sounding like the parent. He was always so serious.

"I know that, Dad," Matt teased, clearly thinking the same thing I was.

"Just don't forget: no passing grades, no baseball." Dayton nodded before finishing off his glass of orange juice.

"I'm excited, not stupid," Matt fired back, getting agitated.

"So, who's taking me to school this morning?" I asked,

hoping to change the subject before Dayton started dishing out one of his famous lectures and pissing Matt off. One of the worst things was having two guys who ended up not getting along, living in the same house. "I have class in thirty," I said because if someone wasn't giving me a ride, I needed to leave now and start walking.

Dayton raised his hand. "I'm driving you. Actually, I'm driving all of us this morning," he added with a smile.

"You don't have a car?" Matt asked, and I realized that we actually knew very little about each other.

"My parents don't let me bring it out here," I explained.

He grimaced like that was the worst thing he'd ever heard. "So, it just sits at your house? I've never understood why parents do that," he said.

I agreed, "Right? Incredibly fucking annoying that I have to rely on everyone else to drive me around when I have a perfectly good car sitting at home, collecting dust."

"That sucks. If you ever need to borrow my car, just let me know, okay?" Matt said as he grabbed our plates and tossed them into the sink for one of us to clean later.

He was far more generous than I'd thought he'd be, but I appreciated it.

"Thanks."

Colin clapped a hand on my shoulder. "Let's go. I hate being even remotely late to class. It's embarrassing."

Grinning, I stood up. "Couldn't agree more. Let me get my stuff."

We all piled into Dayton's car, and on our way to campus, my skin buzzed with awareness.

Craning my neck as if that would help me see better, I told Dayton, "Pull over," but he wasn't slowing down. I smacked his shoulder hard, getting his attention over the sound of the radio. "I said, pull over!" I shouted, and he gave me a quick glance.

"Jesus. I'm pulling over. What the hell, man?" He looked around at the cars on the road before pulling off to the side.

Pointing at the lone car leaning to the right up ahead, I said, "It's Sunny."

"Oh shit. It is Sunny," Colin agreed from the back, practically sitting between the front seats. "We have to help her."

"I'd like to help her," Matt interjected with a smirk, "with my cock."

I whipped my head in his direction so fast that I thought it might spin off. "Don't talk like that. She's not for you."

Matt shrugged. "Who's she for then? 'Cause I've never seen her with anyone in this car. Looks like she might be for me."

Dayton slowly creeped toward Sunny's car, her tire flat, as I tried not to lose my cool on the new guy.

"Don't get out. I mean it. Everyone else can help but you. You stay in this fucking car," I demanded before opening the door and hopping out before Dayton even stopped.

I heard Matt say something in complaint, but Dayton and Colin both told him to do what he had been told. Jogging toward Sunny, I felt satisfied when I heard only two other doors slam shut from behind me. I glanced back to make sure Matt was doing as I'd asked. He was fidgeting around in the backseat, most likely cursing my name.

"Hey. Are you okay?" I said as soon as I reached her, wanting to pull her into my arms and hold her against me.

She looked fucking stunning but flustered. Her face was flushed, and I assumed the tire popping must have rattled her. The desire to take care of her overwhelmed me.

Her eyes skirted past me, like she didn't want to answer me until the rest of the guys caught up. I was probably the last person in the world she wanted to see in this moment, but Sunny needed a knight right now, and it was going to be me and not anyone else. That fact was not up for discussion.

"Hey, Sunny," Colin said, and her face practically lit up.

What the hell?

"I got a flat. I have no idea how to change it, and I really don't want to be late or miss class. Should I just call AAA? What do you think?"

I stepped toward her, and her eyes crashed into mine. "I'll fix it. Do you have a spare?"

"Yeah. It's a full-sized one in the back." She swallowed. "I couldn't even get it out. I tried."

I knew that must have pissed her off, not being able to get the tire out and handle this herself. But she was a tiny little thing. How did she think she could pull a giant spare out of her car without any help? The damn thing probably weighed more than she did.

"You ever changed a flat before?" I asked Dayton and Colin, who both shook their heads.

They'd be no use. I knew I could change it on my own, but having at least one other guy to help would make it go quicker.

Matt leaned out the now-open back window. "I have!"

Of course he had.

"Get out here and help then," I shouted, and he popped that door open so fast that I thought it might come off in his hand. He sprinted over to us and went to say something to Sunny, but I cut him off and turned him away from her, "Don't talk. Just work."

His mouth snapped shut as he glared at me, obviously wanting to fight back; instead, for whatever reason, he seemed to know better and listened.

"Dayton, do you want to get Sunny to school, so she isn't late?"

"Wait. What? You want me to just leave?" She looked at me, thoroughly confused, as she pulled her shirt away from her body and fanned her chest with the movements.

I touched her shoulder, and I swore she shivered even though it was already ninety degrees out. "Only so you aren't late. I'll handle your car."

"But where are you going to take it after you're done? To school somewhere or my apartment? How will I get the keys?"

She was rattled, and it was fucking adorable. Everything about this girl bordered on the sweetest damn thing I'd ever seen, even when she pretended to hate me.

"Let me do this for you."

"You don't have to," she argued.

"I want to. Sunny, go with Dayton. Where's your class at?"

She told me the building and class number, and I knew I'd figure out all the details later. Right now, I wanted to do this for her. Take care of her the way she'd taken care of me when

I needed someone. Apologize to her without actually saying the words. At least, not yet.

"Go."

"Are you sure?" She looked uncertain, her eyes all pulled together like it was a tough decision.

"I'm sure. I got this. I got you."

She fidgeted with her hair, brushing it back from her shoulders and tucking it behind her ears. "Okay. Well, thank you. I really appreciate it."

"Come on, sweetheart," Colin said, and I lunged toward him to tear out his vocal cords before he started laughing. "He's just jealous."

I couldn't hear Sunny's response, but the tone of her voice told me she didn't believe him for a second. That girl had no clue how twisted up I was inside because of her.

I waited until they drove away before I looked at Matt. "We can do this in twenty, right?"

"Pshh"—he waved me off—"more like ten."

Arrogant ass.

"So, what's up with the two of you? You have history or something?" he asked as he jacked the car up off the ground, and I started to work on loosening the bolts, sweat dripping down my head from where my hat was.

"Not history. A future."

"So, I can't shoot my shot with her then?" he asked with a shit-eating grin on his face, and I had no idea if he was busting my balls or if he was really asking.

"Not if you want to play this season," I threatened, but what was I going to do, break his arm? And why was I acting that way? This wasn't like me, all broody and intimidating.

He stood up as I pulled out the last remaining bolt and removed the janky tire. It was shredded. I laid it down on the ground next to me.

"I'm only joking. I'll stay away from her. But what about that chick you made leave the party the other night? I was pretty drunk, but I think she might have been the hottest girl I've ever seen, and you were throwing her out of the house." Matt was practically foaming at the mouth, just talking about Hayley.

I stood up and reached for the bad tire. "Get past her looks and remember that a fire-breathing devil lives inside that body. That's why it's so smoking hot."

"Come on," Matt complained as he rolled the good tire toward me and took the flat one. "Seriously? She can't be that bad."

"Stay away from her."

"Jeez. You can't forbid me from screwing all the girls on campus." He maneuvered the good tire on and held it in place while I started with the bolts. "Can you?" he genuinely asked.

"That one's for your own good. She will ruin your life. But Sunny's mine—whether she knows it yet or not. And if you mess with her, I'll ruin your life."

Matt saluted me, and I rolled my eyes.

"I thought you were supposed to be the fun one," he practically huffed, but he wasn't wrong.

I used to be the happy-go-lucky guy without a care in the world, who hooked up with new girls every weekend if I wanted to. At least, that was what I always pretended to be before this year started.

"Done." I spun the tire, and Matt double-checked it before lowering the jack.

We put everything in the back of Sunny's car, and I hopped in the front seat, not fitting inside.

I moved the seat back right as Matt got into the passenger side, and we took off. By some kind of stroke of luck, we weren't going to be late. I dropped Matt off on the other side of campus, where our classes were located and parked Sunny's car in the lot closest to her building. When I got out, I noticed a planter filled with fresh flowers for the semester. I picked a purple daisy and left it on her dashboard.

Strutting across the great lawn toward my class, I was feeling confident and good, which had been a rare feeling lately. Maybe seeing Sunny this morning and being able to help her gave me some sort of solace I hadn't realized I was craving. Fixing her car had been easy, but I knew it wasn't enough. At some point, I needed to actually talk to her and explain my side of things. I just wasn't ready to do that yet, and I had no fucking idea why not.

CAN'T BELIEVE I'M DOING THIS ... AGAIN

Sunny

MAC HAD FIGURED out a way to get my keys to me that day after he fixed my car. When I walked out of class, there was a young guy I'd never seen before, holding them in the air along with a note that I assumed was from Mac. It showed exactly where my car was parked with a little hand-drawn map and everything. When I went to my car later that afternoon, I saw the purple flower inside. It hadn't been there before, so I knew it was from him, but I had no idea what it meant.

I'd texted Mac, telling him thank you, and included a picture of the flower, which was still on my dashboard because I was never taking it out of my car—ever—and he responded a few hours later with a, *You're welcome*, but that was it.

There had been no other communication since, and it was driving me freaking batty. That was almost two weeks ago. TWO WEEKS, and I hadn't seen Mac in person one single time. I hadn't run into him on campus or spied him from a distance or anything.

He wasn't in the commissary, or in the commons, or the

library, or even at the field the one time I'd worked up enough nerve to pass by it. It was infuriating. When the last person on earth I'd wanted to see was Mac, I'd smacked right into his chest. But now that I was hoping to at least catch a glimpse of him, he was nowhere to be found. Our school was spread out, but it honestly wasn't *that* big. I should have been able to see him if I tried hard enough.

I was currently in my kitchen, whipping up a batch of my famous chocolate chip cookies. The act of baking was soothing me, which I appreciated, but knowing why I was making them in the first place was working against me, forcing me into a ball of nerves. There was a get-together tonight at the baseball house, and since I hadn't talked to Mac in what felt like forever, I thought I'd bake him cookies to thank him for what he'd done with the car. I knew how much he loved them and figured the rest of the guys would, too, if I brought some with me.

My cell phone beeped, and I glanced down at it before picking it up and moving it closer to my face. I didn't recognize the number even though it was local, and it wasn't saved in my phone. Pressing on the text button, I read the message.

UNKNOWN: DON'T FORGET ABOUT THE KICKBACK TONIGHT!

SUNNY: WHAT KICKBACK?

UNKNOWN: DON'T PLAY DUMB WITH ME. I KNOW YOU PUT IT IN YOUR CALENDAR. I WATCHED YOU, REMEMBER?

SUNNY: WHO IS THIS?

UNKNOWN: IT'S COLIN! DON'T TELL MAC I'M TEXTING YOU, OKAY?

I LIKE HAVING ALL MY LIMBS.

As I added his name to my Contacts list, I laughed, picturing Colin hiding somewhere in the dark and texting me without anyone seeing.

SUNNY: HOW'D YOU GET MY NUMBER?

COLIN: YOU HAVE IT ON YOUR PROFILE. IT'S ALL LINKED TOGETHER SOMEHOW. PHONE NUMBER AND EMAIL. SPEAKING OF, YOU SHOULD PROBABLY TAKE THAT DOWN. IT REALLY ISN'T SAFE.

I had it on my profile? Shit. How come I never noticed that before?

SUNNY: I DO? THANKS FOR THE HEADS-UP.

COLIN: THE PARTY. TONIGHT. YOU'RE COMING. RIGHT?

SUNNY: UGH. I'LL BE THERE.

COLIN: DON'T UGH ME, SUNNY. YOU NEED TO BE THERE. MAC IS DRIVING US ALL CRAZY.

That was interesting ...

SUNNY: WHAT DO YOU MEAN?

COLIN: I'VE SAID ENOUGH. BE THERE, OR I'LL COME KIDNAP YOU. OPERATION SUNNYMAC IS IN EFFECT.

SUNNY: DO I WANT TO KNOW?

COLIN: NO. SHIT. GOTTA GO. SHOW UP, SUNNY. OR ELSE. I MEA—

His text cut off at the end, and I wondered if he'd gotten caught. For whatever reason, I was nervous for him, like he could actually get in trouble somehow.

I'd pretended that I didn't remember about the kickback at the baseball house, but Colin had known I was lying. I'd put it in my calendar the morning they dropped me off at school. Mostly because they'd forced me to, Colin and Dayton both hovering over me until I typed it in and pressed Save.

They had talked the entire way to campus about it, telling me that it wasn't a normal party like they usually had, but something more casual and with way less people. They insisted I be there. Said it was *invite only* and I was invited. I never actually said yes or even agreed to go, but somehow, I had known I'd find myself in this position when the night finally came around.

WHEN I PULLED up in front of the house, once again, someone pulled up right on my bumper.

That's going to make leaving virtually impossible, I thought before realizing that I was already planning my escape.

There were way too many cars here to just be a little kickback, like the guys had promised. This was a normal full-blown party. There was nothing laid-back or casual about it. And there was no way that all these people had been invited.

I briefly considered leaving and going back to my apartment, alone, where I could possibly get murdered in peace, but

Colin's text messages lingered in the back of my mind. I had no idea what Operation SunnyMac was, but I had to admit that I liked the sound of it. Color me intrigued. Or a glutton for punishment. Either way, I was going in there to hopefully find out.

I walked through the courtyard and into the baseball house when I remembered that I'd forgotten the cookies I'd made earlier. They were sitting on the table by the front door, where I'd set them down and fumbled for my keys. But looking around at the sheer number of people here, I was happy I'd left them at home. I would have looked so stupid, walking into this house, carrying a tray of baked goods. I was self-conscious enough already.

Scanning the immediate area, I didn't see anyone I recognized. There was no Mac in sight. No Colin or Dayton either. And the guys who did look like baseball players, I'd never seen them before. Nothing made you feel more insecure than standing in a crowded room by yourself.

"Hi. I'm Matt. Welcome to my house." He waved an arm and almost lost his balance. The liquid in his red cup sloshed out and splashed onto his forearm, but he didn't seem to notice. "You're not leaving, are you? Wait, do I know you? I think I know you."

He dramatically squinted his eyes, and I recognized him as the fourth guy from the morning of my flat tire. The one who had been sitting in the backseat until Mac asked for his help.

"I'm Sunny." I gave him a forced smile, but my attention was elsewhere, and even in his drunken state, he sensed it.

"Sunny." He rolled my name around on his lips like he

should know who I was but couldn't place it. "Operation SunnyMac, right? I can help you find him," he offered, his eyes opening and closing slowly as I tried not to laugh at this whole SunnyMac thing. This guy was hammered. "Unless you'd rather hang out with me. Want to hang out with me, Sunny?"

"Not a chance in hell she wants to hang out with you." Mac's voice broke through the noise and pierced the air between us.

I wasn't sure how my legs didn't give out on the spot, but I managed to stay upright as I took him in. There was something about Mac that just did it for me. No matter what he wore, if his hat was on or not, the guy pressed all my buttons.

Matt snapped his fingers and pointed at me. "I know. I know. *Stay away from Sunny. She's off-limits.* Sorry. Don't kill me," he said toward Mac.

I marinated in every drunk word that he'd said. *I'm off-limits? Since when?*

"Hey," I said, offering Mac a small smile. I hadn't forgotten that he'd ghosted me during the summer and been kind of a dick so far this year.

"Hey, gorgeous," he said before leaning close and giving me a kiss on the cheek.

I hadn't expected either of those things—the compliment or the kiss—and I wondered how much he'd had to drink. *Was he as drunk as Matt?*

"Sorry again, Operation SunnyMac," Matt slurred his words as he stumbled away, and I pressed my lips together to stop from giggling.

"New recruit?" I asked, assuming Matt was a new freshman.

"Transfer," Mac corrected, and I nodded in surprise.

For whatever reason, I'd expected a transfer student to be a little less sloppy than a first-time freshman.

"Any idea what he's talking about? The operation thing?" I tried to question, but Mac seemed distracted.

"Who cares?" He waved Matt off. "He's trashed."

"You look nice," I said before I could stop myself, taking in the way his shirt pulled tightly across his biceps and shoulders. Freaking baseball players always had the best arms.

"You always look nice," he fired back, and I felt my face get hot.

I was pretty shocked that we were standing face-to-face and not tearing each other's throats out like we'd been doing all the other times before this one. And I'd been looking forward to—and dreading—this moment since he'd left that flower in my car.

"I like your hair." His fingers reached out and grabbed some of my newly dyed silver strands, twisting them around as he stared.

At some point during the last two weeks, I'd found myself craving some sort of drastic change. My hair seemed like the easiest thing to control and manipulate, so I'd gone to the store, picked out a box of silver permanent hair dye, and done it myself, praying that it would look good. I had no idea how much I'd love it.

"The color really suits you," he added.

I found myself at a loss for words. I—Sunny Jamison, who

rarely got flustered to the point of being unable to speak—couldn't find a single syllable to utter in this moment. I knew I was supposed to be angry with him still, but I was struggling to hold on to that particular emotion.

A loud crash caused us both to startle and break away from one another. We looked around, and Mac spotted the chaos before I did, his head shaking with his disapproval. Matt was on the floor.

"Shit," Mac mumbled. "I gotta go handle that," he said, giving my shoulder a quick squeeze. "Do not go anywhere," he insisted before hurrying off and leaving me alone.

I wasn't sure what to do. *Should I stay put and wait for Mac to come back, or should I wander the house and see if I know anyone else here?*

Feeling unsure and uncomfortable, I decided to go walk around instead of staying in one place like a loner with no friends.

Wandering a crowded house filled with drunk athletes on the prowl might have been a mistake, considering that I was doing said wandering alone, but at least I was sober. I got stopped every few feet by random guys offering me a drink. Instead of taking one from any of them, I kept moving, not stopping until I got into the backyard, where a pony keg sat, unattended. It was shocking that no one else was outside when this was usually the place to be at these parties.

I moved toward the steel barrel and poured myself a cup of ...*foam*.

"It's out," a voice sounded from somewhere behind me, and I spun around quickly to see Colin stalking my way.

"Already?" I asked even though the answer was obvious.

"We might have started a little too early," he said with a grin. "But you came! I knew you'd come," he said before pulling me into a tight hug. "Your hair looks sick," he said, and I was surprised that he could even see it in the dark.

I liked Colin. He was always so laid-back and happy, and the text messages from earlier had swayed my decision.

"Thanks. And, well, you did threaten to kidnap me if I didn't show up tonight."

"It was a necessary evil," he said seriously, and I gave him the side-eye. "What? It was. It is. It's pertinent that you and Mac work your shit out."

"Ooh, pertinent, eh? Big word," I teased.

"You have no idea what he's been like lately," Colin added, sounding stressed.

But he was right. I didn't have any idea because I hadn't freaking talked to or seen Mac since the morning he'd changed my tire.

"And I think it's because of you."

"Me? What did I do?"

Colin shrugged. "Beats the hell out of me, but you have to fix him, okay? He's broken now."

Before I could overanalyze what he had said or ask him anything else, a group of people appeared from the side of the yard, carrying something between them, and Colin cheered in response.

"Excuse us," a random male voice boomed as they tossed the empty keg out of the way and replaced it with a new one.

And just like that, the backyard went from empty to

packed, and I was uncomfortable again. I was a walking contradiction—hating being alone in my apartment because I was scared to death, but dying to get away from all these people at a party. *What the heck is wrong with me?*

While Colin was distracted, I decided to head back into the house and look for Mac. Once I was back inside, I realized that Mac was nowhere to be found, and I had no idea where he was. Maybe I should have stayed out there with Colin until he found me.

I kept scanning the packed rooms, looking for his long, surfer-like hair and sexy frame before someone tapped me on the shoulder three times. When I turned my neck, my eyes instantly crashed into Mac's hazel beauties, and my entire body relaxed in his presence.

"There you are," he said with a half-grin. "I was looking for you."

I coughed out a breath. "For little ole me?"

"Yep," he said, his hand suddenly on my bare lower back, and I instinctively leaned into it, loving the way his rough fingers felt against my skin there.

The thought of super-gluing his hand to my body crossed my mind, and I had to stop myself from laughing out loud.

He whispered into my ear, "I told you not to move."

Before I could come up with a witty retort in response, a brunette female stepped between us, forcing Mac to drop his hand. I wanted to kick her in the teeth for making that offensive action happen, but then her hands ran down the length of Mac's chest, and I wondered if it was the first time she'd touched him or not. I suddenly envisioned myself doing much more than just punting her.

"I've been looking for you all night, Mac." She was practically drooling as she said his name, and I wanted to vomit all over her bare legs.

"I've been here," he responded, but it wasn't flirtatious or even entirely friendly.

I'd honestly never seen Mac be anything less than charming, especially to girls, and him rebuffing her made me feel good.

"Want to go to your room?"

"No," he said before gesturing in my direction. "I was talking to Sunny, and you interrupted."

Tall girl gave me a quick glance before dismissing me. "Well, I'm here now, so you can talk to me instead."

"Wow," I said loud enough for her to hear me, but she didn't even look in my direction.

"That's pretty rude," Mac added, and I couldn't stop the laugh that bubbled up and out of my mouth.

"I can be anything you want me to be. I've heard all about you, Mac. You're legendary. I want to be a part of it." She batted her eyelashes and licked her lips.

"No, thanks," Mac said, trying to maintain his composure, but I could tell that she was pushing his buttons, and it was pissing me off to witness such blatant disrespect.

"But, Mac." She reached for his chest again, and I saw spots.

"Seriously? He said no. Can't you hear?" I ripped her hands off of his chest and gave her a slight jab.

"Mind your own business, twat," she spat, looking me up

and down, her lips twisting, as if my very presence disgusted her.

"Did you seriously just call me a twat? What are you, seven?" I asked forcefully, my need to defend Mac and not myself fueling my ire. "And he obviously isn't interested. A concept you can't seem to get through your thick fucking skull," I growled.

"Mac's always interested." She looked at him like he was a piece of meat who had no opinion or say over his own body. "Aren't you, babe?"

She clawed his shoulder and tried to hold on, but he wiggled out of her grip. Before he could make another move away from her, she pressed her lips against his, and I stood there, my mouth falling open in shock. I watched as Mac unattached her from him with force and wiped at his mouth with the back of his hand.

"Are you joking right now? Who does that shit?"

"What?" The girl feigned shocked by his rejection as she continued to bat her fake lashes at Mac. "I thought that's what you wanted. You kiss everyone, right?"

"He said no. Multiple times!" I yelled, and before I could stop myself, I shoved her hard enough to make her lose her balance and fall flat on her ass.

Oops.

"You bitch!" she screamed at me as she struggled to get up, but her shoes were too tall, and she stayed on the floor instead.

"Mouth rapist," I shouted back before Mac had his arms wrapped around me, holding me back because I was coming.

Absolutely. Unglued.

"Come on, Cujo," he whispered in my ear, pulling me away.

I noticed that we had drawn a little too much attention to our situation. It only surprised me because the music was so loud and everyone was usually too caught up in their own world to notice anything happening outside of their little bubble. But I guessed that tossing someone to the ground might cause a commotion.

I had no idea where Mac was dragging me off to, but I didn't care. I was happy to get away from the drama, the unwanted attention, and the girl who had refused to take no for an answer. I wasn't paying attention to where we were walking, my eyes still filled with rage, but Mac pulled me into a bedroom before shutting and locking the door behind us.

SWEET, BROKEN BOY

Sunny

"I REALLY HOPE this is yours." I looked around the space, taking note of the size, and realized that we were in Chance's old room. Which was now Mac's.

There were piles of clothes on the floor and baseballs randomly scattered all over the place. A single wood bat lay across the desk, covering a closed laptop and a dark blue notebook.

Mac sat down on the bed and put his head in his hands. Blowing out a long, slow breath, he looked up at me, his light-hazel eyes weary. "Thanks for that, Sunny."

I moved next to him to sit before hopping right back up and pacing. I was too amped up to stay still. "Girls shouldn't treat you like that," I said as fire raged through my veins. I wanted to rip that chick's hair out in clumps. "You know that, right, Mac?" I suddenly had a feeling that he didn't.

"But I created this, you know? 'The playboy baseballer who hooks up with a different girl every night,' " he said, using his fingers to make air quotes before glancing up at me, his bright eyes locking on to mine before looking away in defeat.

"It might be a part of who you are, but it's not all you are." I stopped pacing and took a few calming breaths before dropping my body next to his once more and doing my best to stay put. Placing my hand on his thigh, I continued, "And even if you are a giant flirt and hook up with girls all the time, that doesn't mean you don't get a say in the matter."

He wasn't listening to me. I could see it in his eyes, his body language. Mac was lost in his thoughts.

"It's my fault. I did this to myself," he mumbled to himself.

We girls went through this kind of thing all the time—blaming ourselves for the actions of others. We'd been subliminally taught to question every single thing from what we wore to what we said. Did we smile too much? Did our body language contradict our words? We broke down every single aspect of what we had done to deserve whatever it was that had happened to us, that'd wronged us. Because society had basically told us that people wouldn't take us at our word. They wouldn't believe what we said, just because we said it. They'd look at everything else to make it our fault. It was ironic to see it happening to a guy.

"No, it's not. And you did not. You said *no*, Mac." I emphasized the word *no*, but he still wasn't looking at me. Reaching for his chin, I gripped it softly and turned him to face me. "You said *no*. You have every right to say no regardless of how many times you've said yes before."

"Thanks." He was so quiet that I wasn't sure I'd actually heard it or made it up.

I let go of his face, and he focused on his hands in his lap.

"Sunny, I'm really sorry about this summer. And that first party. And hell, I'm sorry about all of it. I haven't been nice to you, and I know that, but I couldn't seem to stop. I have no excuse, but I really am sorry."

I was taken aback. I hadn't expected him to actually apologize or own up to what he'd done without being confronted about it. If I'd brought it up, most guys would have played it off like they had no idea what I was talking about or made up a hundred excuses as to why they had been too busy to return a single text message when everyone knew the truth—we made time for the things we wanted. And sending a text took literally two seconds.

"Thank you," I said, accepting his apology because it was one of the things I knew I'd needed from him.

"That's it? You forgive me?" He actually brightened up a little, his hands unclenching.

"I mean," I started, "I still have questions. And I don't like how you treated me."

He put a finger to my lips, stopping me. "I know. I really do know. And I'm not sure how to make you believe me, but I am sorry. I wish there were another word or something else I could say. I'll keep saying it if that's what you need. I'll tell you I'm sorry every day for a year if it helps."

A small laugh escaped my lips with his offer. I believed that if I told Mac I needed that daily apology, he would give it to me. I wasn't sure exactly what I required, but since he'd opened the door to this conversation, I decided to go for it. We were going to have to address it all sooner or later. I just hadn't expected it to come up tonight, during a party.

"Can I ask why you did it then? Why you ignored me this summer and why you've been mean since?" I hoped he couldn't hear the hurt in my voice, but I had done a shit job at hiding it.

Mac's gaze leveled me. His eyes were so intense, filled with so many things I couldn't even begin to read or understand. All I could do was stare back and wait for whatever insight he'd give me.

"Our phone call that night," he started, and I was instantly back in that moment, "I told you so many personal things."

"You did," I agreed, hoping that I didn't sound like I was judging him for it.

"I felt stupid after." His eyes pulled together, and he looked like he was in physical pain.

"Why? Why would telling me all that make you feel stupid?" I hated that he felt dumb about that conversation when it had made me feel anything but.

After we'd hung up, I'd felt so close to Mac, and I loved it. He had sounded so burdened, and I wrongfully assumed that talking to me had eased the weight he'd been carrying. I'd figured I'd made him feel better, not worse. So, hearing him say that he felt badly almost made me wish I could take the call back and that we'd never had it in the first place. *Almost.*

"Because I was so ..." He paused, staring up at the ceiling before bringing those beautiful hazel-colored eyes back to mine again. "I was so weak that night, Sunny. I was upset. And jealous. And angry. I'd never said half the shit I said to you to anyone else before. Ever."

My hand moved to his thigh, and I squeezed it, feeling the

muscles in his leg flex. "That's usually a good thing, Mac."

"Not for a guy like me."

He swallowed hard, and I had no idea what he was talking about. To be honest, I was a little too scared to ask. Now, I was the one feeling foolish.

"Are you worried that I'll tell someone what you told me?"

He shook his head. "Nah. You would have already done that by now if you were going to."

A quick huff escaped me. "That's not very reassuring."

"In case you haven't noticed, I have trust issues." He tried to play it off like it was a joke, but he was serious.

"I've noticed."

"So, that's why I pulled away this summer. It fucking killed me to ignore you, and I knew I was doing the wrong thing—I need you to know that. But I convinced myself that I couldn't let you in any deeper. I had to stop myself from reaching out to you almost every day," he explained, and my heart physically ached with his words. "And then whenever I saw you, I felt dumb and ashamed and embarrassed. And I thought that was all you saw when you looked at me too."

Good Lord. This guy ... is ... killing ... me.

Mac closed his eyes before blinking a few times. "Some dumb, weak guy who practically cried on the phone with you one night because he hadn't gotten drafted and he felt sorry for himself."

"Mac," I said his name, and my voice cracked. I was getting emotional. "I never, not once, thought of you or saw you that way. Being able to talk about your emotions is a strength, not a weakness. Any guy can shove his emotions down and pretend they aren't feeling them, but it takes a bigger man to admit when he's sad or not okay. I got off the phone with you that night, knowing I had never felt closer to anyone in my life."

"Really?" he asked, sounding completely surprised.

"I'd never wanted you more," I admitted, feeling vulnerable and embarrassed myself. Being this honest was more than a little terrifying.

He softly shook his head, like this was almost too far-fetched for him to comprehend. "I figured you were as repulsed by me as I was."

Oh dear. My poor, sweet, broken boy.

Colin was right. Mac needed fixing. Or maybe he just needed some good old-fashioned loving.

"Can we change the subject?" he asked, and I knew that I'd do anything Mac needed me to in that moment. He was hurting, and I wanted to stop it. "Just for a little bit."

I'd had no idea that tonight would go this direction, but I didn't want it to end. I'd never been in this position with a guy before, having conversations that felt like they were life-changing somehow. I hadn't had a serious boyfriend since high school. Looking back, I realized that relationship hadn't been half of what this was, and Mac and I weren't even together.

"Yep. What should we talk about instead?" I shifted on the bed and tried to think up another topic of conversation that might make him more comfortable and lighten the mood.

"Why'd you pick silver?" he asked, reaching out for my hair and running his fingers through it.

"I liked the way it looked on the box. It was either this or this really pretty ice blue. Maybe I'll do that next." I smiled.

"Don't. Keep it silver forever. I'm obsessed. It's my new favorite color."

"Oh yeah?" I asked with a smile.

"Definitely. What's yours?"

"My what?"

"Favorite color. I told you mine. What's yours?"

"Yellow," I blurted out before I said it was the color of his eyes when the light hit it or something equally as embarrassing.

He smiled. "Of course it's yellow. The color of the sun. Just like your name. Just like you. All bright, happy, and warm."

I held my breath and pretended like his response hadn't just shocked the hell out of me when he gave me his answer, "Aside from your hair color, my other favorite color's blue. But not like baby blue or the crayon. Dark blue. Like the ocean in places where it's really deep. You know what I mean?"

Leave it to Mac to give a complicated answer.

" 'The ocean in places where it's really deep,' " I repeated, my mind conjuring up an image of a deep-sea fishing trip I'd tagged along on with my dad once before. I remembered seeing the varying shades of blue in the water and thinking how incredible it was that the ocean could look so different from one side of the boat to the other. "It suits you. That color."

"Does it?" he said, his mind still somewhere else, and I wanted to pull him back into the room with me. I was thinking how to do just that when he asked out of nowhere, "What do you want to do?"

"Huh? Like right now or when I grow up?" I arched a brow toward him, and he gave me a crooked smile.

"When you grow up," he said in a teasing tone that I found myself enjoying even though I hated the answer I was about to give him. "What do you want to be?"

I swallowed hard, wondering if he'd look at me differently once I admitted the truth. "I don't know," I said with a shrug.

"Really? You don't?" He sounded so surprised, and it made me feel like some sort of disappointment to someone other than myself.

"No. Why does that surprise you so much?" I asked a little defensively. I hated this topic because I was no closer to an answer at the end of my college career as I'd been at the beginning of it.

"Because you seem like the type of girl who has it all together. I just assumed you knew what you wanted and were halfway there already," he explained, and while I appreciated his view, it couldn't have been more inaccurate.

"I feel like I'm the only person who has no idea what she wants to do with her life. And I hate it." I spilled my truth onto the floor between us as my eyes started to water. This topic always made me emotional, and I did my best to pull it together. I felt like an idiot for not knowing, not even having an inkling of an idea as to what I wanted to spend my life doing.

"You're definitely not the only one."

"Well, you know exactly what you want to do."

"Yeah, but it's not the same."

"How is it not the same?"

"Because what I want is a long shot. What happens if I don't get drafted? Don't get to play baseball for the rest of my life? Then what?"

My heart cracked with his words. I knew how much baseball owned him and how badly he wanted a future in it.

"Don't say that." I tried to sound reassuring, but I had no idea what it took to make that dream a reality. I knew bits and pieces from living with Danika and hearing Chance talk about it last year, but I'd never been completely invested.

"I'm not trying to be negative. I'm being realistic. There's a good chance I won't get drafted. Then what? Outside of playing baseball, I have no idea what I want to do."

He sounded so sad. Like the very idea of baseball not being in his life took a part of his soul away and left him empty.

"At least you have a goal. Something you're working toward."

He nodded slowly. "Okay, I'll give you that. What are you majoring in?"

Mac wanted to steer the conversation away from him and back toward me. I hated it because I wanted to hear more about him and less about me and this particular topic.

"I was undecided when I got here, and then when they forced me to pick a major, I still had no idea what I was interested in. So, I just picked communications."

Mac laughed, and I shot him a look that could kill.

"I'm not laughing at you," he said, holding one hand in the air. "You're just so adorably honest. Have you noticed that no one ever talks about or admits this kind of shit?"

"Yes!" I practically shouted my response. "Why do you

think I feel so alone and avoid this topic if I can? And social media doesn't help. I always feel less than. Like I'm so far behind all of my peers, it's not even funny. Everyone looks like they have it all together and knows exactly what they want and how to get there, and I'm sitting here, floundering, without a clue of what even interests me."

He angled his body toward me, his knee brushing against mine, and I tried like hell to concentrate on anything other than the fact that his bare skin was touching my own. But when his hand reached out and intertwined with mine, I was a lost cause. I melted right then and there, and he damn well knew it.

"Mac," I breathed out, but it was too late.

His lips were on mine, his mouth opening and his tongue finding its way inside. We'd kissed before, but this was different. Last time, it had been all fun. This time, it felt like it meant something.

He kissed me with precision, his movements slow and sensual. I felt like I was dying and being brought back to life each time his tongue touched mine or he moved his mouth in a different position, claiming my lips once more.

Kissing this version of Mac was like a dream, and I never wanted it to end.

BREAKING ALL MY RULES

Mac

Kissing Sunny was like kissing a fucking goddess. Every single thing I did with her, I did with care. There was no rushing the moment. No slobbering tongues or teeth clashing against each other in a frenzy of mouths opening and closing too quickly. No. Every movement was intentional. Every swipe of the tongue and bite of the lip elicited more emotion than I'd ever experienced before.

And Sunny kissed me like she meant it. She poured every emotion and feeling that existed inside her body into mine, and I took it greedily, wanting more. So, it took every ounce of willpower I could conjure up for me to pull back from her, breaking our fused mouths. I would rather kiss Sunny until it killed me.

What a way to go.

"Wow." Sunny's soft voice forced my eyes to open, and I was thankful that hers were still half-closed as she was lost in the moment.

"Yeah. So, um, what, uh ..." I stumbled on my words and scooted slightly away from her magnetic pull and the way her tiny frame fit in my hands so perfectly. "What were we talking about before you kissed me senseless?"

Her beautiful blue eyes opened fully as she looked at me. Her silver hair shone, and if I'd thought she was beautiful before this moment, she was even more so now.

"Me? Pretty sure you started it," she said before quickly adding, "I think you were apologizing for not doing that the second you saw me weeks ago, but I could be wrong."

That made me laugh. "You're not wrong. I was an idiot. I should have kissed you the minute I saw you outside my bedroom door. I'm sorry I didn't."

Her eyes closed, and she swayed slightly. "You can say that again."

"I will." I reached out and touched her cheek. "I told you I'd say *I'm sorry* a hundred times if you wanted me to."

She cleared her throat. "No. You said three hundred sixty-five times, to be exact. But who's counting?"

God, she was fucking adorable. And I was a mess. A mess who wanted her in every way and knew that once I had her, I'd never be able to let her go.

"You're right. I did promise every day for a year." I gave her a wink.

"I might not get tired of hearing it," she teased.

"I guess we'll see," I played back.

"Words are one thing, Davies; actions are something else entirely," she said, pulling out the last-name card.

"Oh, last-name use. You must really mean business."

"I'm just saying that it takes zero effort to *saaaay* all the right things. The real effort is in the action. The doing. The following through." She tried to sound all nonchalant about it, but I knew there was conviction behind her statement.

"I know. You want me to mean the things I say to you. And I do. I'll show you," I said, and she smiled so big that her whole face lit up. I got lost, just looking at her. "But you know what? I think we were actually talking about your major," I reminded us both as I tried to sound like I wasn't picturing her with no clothes on, waiting naked for me on my bed. *What a fucking sight.*

I kept staring at her lips, all swollen and begging me for more even though they were currently frowning. She did not want to talk about this subject.

"You're majoring in communications, but you don't want to be a communicator?" I asked like a smart-ass, and she leaned over to swat my shoulder.

"Why did you bring that back up? Now, I'm depressed again." She pouted.

"I'm trying to help."

"How?"

"Well, I'm helping you pick out your future profession," I said with confidence, like this should be easy and could be decided on a whim in my bedroom. "I do remember you baking some fantastic-tasting cookies once or twice before. Think you might want to do that someday?"

Her mouth twisted into a small snarl that didn't suit her face, and I wondered how that question had garnered that reaction from her. "I don't think so. Danika used to say that all the time, too, but I bake for fun. I think if it was my job and I was forced to do it, it wouldn't be fun anymore."

I nodded along with her assessment because it was logical and made perfect sense. I had thought along the same lines before in regards to baseball, but I knew it wasn't really the same thing. Playing ball was already work, and I considered it my job. I'd been on a sixteen-year interview that was finally coming to an end.

"I get that."

"Really?" Her expression shifted, her snarl gone. "Danika always told me I was crazy and that if I loved something, I should do more of it. She never understood how I couldn't want to bake for people."

"I mean, she's not wrong about loving what you do. But baking is a hobby for you. You do it because you want to. And you do it whenever you want. Everything's on your terms right now. It would completely change if it was your everyday job. Nothing would be on your terms."

"Exactly!" she said, her eyes wide. "I would be baking because I had to. And I'd be fulfilling orders because people made me and were relying on me to bake the perfect cookie. I don't think I'd like it. I think I'd be miserable, being told I had to bake every single day." She started fanning herself. "Is it hot in here?"

I huffed out a small laugh. She was getting riled up for all the wrong reasons. "All right. No cookie store for Sunny. I can see that now."

"Nope." She shook her head once, her chin high. "No store."

"But you'll still bake for me, right?" I batted my eyelashes at her and gave her a small pout.

She reached out, her hand still able to touch my face even though I'd moved away from her. "Always."

I swallowed around the lump in my throat as so many emotions swirled around inside me. I wanted to run into her arms, and I also wanted to run away as fast as possible.

A knocking sound both relieved and irritated me as I averted my gaze from Sunny and toward my bedroom door.

"Expecting guests?" Sunny asked with an uncomfortable look on her face.

"Mac. Open up." The voice hit my ears like a sledgehammer.

I thought for a second that I might actually throw up. Hayley wasn't someone I wanted Sunny around, but I didn't know how to avoid this confrontation or make Hayley go the fuck away without opening my door.

"Who is that?" Sunny asked, trying to be calm with the fact that some girl was at my door, but she was struggling.

"My ex."

Sunny looked at me, her face paling slightly. I wasn't sure what to do or say exactly, but I knew I'd messed up when she pushed herself off my bed and stood up.

"I'll just go." Her tone was a mixture of too many things that felt like tiny pinpricks to my heart.

I was hurting her without even trying. I didn't want her to leave, but before I could tell her to stay put, Hayley started pounding again.

"Mac!" Hayley yelled.

I walked to the door and opened it, Sunny right behind me. I felt the disappointment rolling off of her in waves.

"Finally," Hayley breathed out in annoyance before even noticing that Sunny was trying to move past her and failing. Hayley was blocking her escape.

"What do you want?" I said, pissed off that she was at another baseball party when I'd specifically told her not to come anymore. I was going to have to tell all the guys that she wasn't allowed in our house. "Why are you here? Spit it out."

"I thought that you could help me."

"Help you?"

"Yeah. With our class." She propped out her hip. "I know you got an A on that quiz, and I failed it."

Before I could say anything, Sunny started talking, "Sounds like a personal problem. Not sure why you're making it Mac's. Now, can you please move, so I can get the hell away from whatever this is?" Sunny wagged her finger between me and Satan's soul mate.

"Who the hell are you?" Hayley gave her a once-over, like Sunny wasn't worth her time, and that single look snapped me out of whatever idiotic trance I'd momentarily fallen under.

"It clearly doesn't matter," she answered Hayley's question but stared right at me as she said the words.

"You said it, not me," Hayley snarled.

Sunny let out a sound of disgust before shoving her out of the way, almost making Hayley lose her balance. Twice tonight, Sunny had been a badass when it came to other girls being bitchy to her.

I started to go after her when a hand gripped my shoulder, stopping me short. "Let her go. She wants to leave."

"No," I argued. "I don't care if you fail the class. Now,

leave me the fuck alone and stay away from me," I said before slamming my door and running after Sunny like a madman with no agenda, no plan, and no idea what the fuck I was doing.

PICK A PERSONALITY

Sunny

I GRUMBLED THE entire way out the front door and toward my car, my keys jingling in my nervous hand as I fought back tears of frustration.

What was I thinking, just forgiving and kissing Mac like that?

And then his ex-girlfriend showing up in the middle of it all! It was like a bad movie I couldn't stop watching, but it was my life we were talking about here, not some poorly written screenplay for the masses.

The fact that she was the girl I'd seen walking out of Mac's room that night wasn't helping things. The way he had chased after her should have told me everything I needed to know. They had history, and it showed. But now that I knew exactly who she was, it irritated me even more. Because whenever I'd seen that girl on campus or at other parties over the years, she'd always acted like a complete snob. She had an entourage that followed her around like she was royalty or something, and I remembered her "accidentally" knocking a tray of food out of someone's hand once in the student union. Basically, the chick was a bitch. And Mac had liked her, dated her, called her his girlfriend.

The look on his face when he'd heard her voice almost made me sick. *Why were guys rendered stupid whenever it came to a pretty face and a nice body? Didn't they want more?* I shook my head as I stalked through the warm night air, convincing myself that they didn't. Guys didn't care if you were funny or smart or kind; if you weren't a total smoke show, they moved along. All they cared about was having the hottest girl on their arm regardless of whether or not she had a heart. And that female back there was a heartless harpy—I'd bet money on it.

"Sunny!" The sound of my name in Mac's voice made me slow down and eventually stop.

I turned around to see him running toward me.

"Sunny, wait," he said again, but I'd already stopped moving.

"I am waiting," I said, my tone coming out a little bitchier than I'd meant it to.

The gravel kicked up under his feet as he reached me, and he leaned over, his hands on his knees as he sucked in a couple breaths.

"Overdramatic much?" I asked as I watched his arms flex. *Curse Mac Davies and his ridiculous biceps.*

"I couldn't make it out of the front door, so I had to sprint around the back and hop the fence to get you before you left. And I ran to the other parking lot first," he explained, and I felt like a jerk.

But why was he chasing after me when he had Giselle

Bunch-whatever back in the house, waiting for him?

"Did I forget something?" I asked because maybe I'd left something in his room and he was just being nice and bringing it out to me.

"Yeah," he said before leaning close. "Me."

Before I could ask him what the hell he meant by that, his lips were on mine again, his tongue instantly crashing against my own as he claimed me. It wasn't sweet and gentle, like back in his bedroom. This kiss was all-consuming and owning. He was trying to tell me who I belonged to. I could barely stand, half-expecting my knees to buckle at any moment.

Kissing Mac was that intense. All that existed was the air we shared as the rest of the world fell silent.

Mac hesitated for a second, and I broke the kiss completely.

"I thought—" I started to say, but he put a finger on my lips to stop me. He seemed to like doing that.

"You thought wrong. I don't want her."

I took a step away from his heat and his body to clear my head and regain focus. One of us needed to be in control. "You sure looked like you wanted her," I said bitterly even though he hadn't sounded like it. He had been mean to her.

"Did I?" He cocked his head to the side and studied me.

"You should have seen your face when you heard her voice."

He reached out, his hand cupping my chin, and I let him. "I was surprised. That's all. She keeps showing up, and I can't seem to make her stop," he explained.

"What exactly are you trying to say, Mac?" I pushed, and

he dropped his hand.

Because if he was trying to tell me that he wanted to be with me, then I was going to force him to say the words out loud for both of us to hear. This time, there would be no taking it back or pretending that it didn't happen, like he had last summer.

So, I waited.

Waited for him to confess that he wanted me the same way I wanted him. Waited for him to admit to what I'd instinctively known was true since last year. I'd been patient when I wanted to push. I'd given Mac space when I wanted to smother him. I had done everything right when it came to a guy who was scared of committing and getting his heart broken.

At least, I thought I had. It suddenly dawned on me that maybe Mac was more messed up than I even knew, and maybe he didn't need me to play it safe. Maybe he needed me to push and fight and show him that I wanted more than just a one-night stand or a fling. Maybe Mac needed to know that he was worth more to me.

"Mac?" I asked because he had grown quiet, too quiet.

"I don't want Hayley. I need you to know that."

"You said that already." I tried to encourage him to keep talking, but he didn't, so I stepped toward him, reached for his hand, and held it. "Mac, I like you."

His face tilted up, and his eyes met mine. Even in the dark, I could see them boring into me, searching.

"I like you too." He said the words like they caused him physical pain.

"Then, do something about it." I pushed even harder even

though I knew it was making him uncomfortable.

"Damn, Sunny." Mac spoke my name like he couldn't believe I'd just come right out and challenged him. "Throwing down the gauntlet."

"It's a curse," I said, referring to my straightforward nature.

He shook his head. "Nah. It's not a curse. There's nothing bad about you." He sounded so serious, and all I wanted to do was laugh.

"You barely know me," I fought back, and his face twisted.

"Don't say that." He sounded agitated. "I know you. I know parts of you. I know your favorite color's yellow and that you have no idea what you want to do with your life and you think that makes you behind everyone else, but it really just makes you normal. I know that you're kind and a good listener who gives stellar advice; you have crazy killer legs, a gorgeous body, and this fucking silver hair." He reached for it like he'd done so many times tonight. "It might be the death of me. Either that or your cookies."

I fought back the tears again because Mac seemed to press every emotional button in my body. "I want to be with you. I want to at least try," I confessed before my heart started raging like a wild animal inside my chest. Every thump against my rib cage reminded me of what I'd just done and what I'd just offered up.

"So, now what?" he asked, sounding a little unsure, and I wasn't certain that what I'd just told him required that kind of response.

Doesn't he want to be with me too?

"What do you mean?"

"What do we do now? How do we do this? We started something here tonight," he said, and I laughed, cutting him off.

"We started something here way before tonight."

I watched as he nodded in the dark, contemplating whatever thoughts were going on in that head of his.

"We did."

"And I'm not talking about the summer," I clarified because in my opinion, what was happening between us had started happening last year at the same time Chance and Danika were getting together.

"I know."

"Maybe one day, you'll tell me why you started avoiding me last year then. Every time Chance came over, he said you wouldn't come. But he also said that you wanted to."

He closed the space between us, touched my face, and kissed me softly. I hadn't expected it. Every kiss with Mac was like being transported into another world, where there were no crickets chirping, no breezes blowing, and no partying classmates yelling.

"I have a feeling that I'll tell you anything you want to know, sweet girl. And that makes you dangerous for a guy like me."

I leaned up on my tiptoes and kissed him another time. "I don't want to be dangerous," I whispered against his mouth, my lips brushing against his.

His brow arched. "You don't? I thought girls liked that

kind of shit."

"Some girls probably do. I'm not one of them."

"What do you want then?"

"To be the place where you're safe," I said genuinely.

He looked instantly triggered as he took three steps away from me, breaking all contact and leaving me feeling whiplashed.

"I don't have any safe places." His tone turned defensive, his anger only masking his hurt.

I knew his reaction had nothing to do with me, but it was hard not to take it personally.

"Then, I'll be your first."

There was so much more to Mac, lurking under the surface, and I had no idea what I'd find if I kept digging.

"Why? Why do you push so hard, Sunny? What are you fighting for?"

"You, you big dummy!" I practically shouted. "I'm fighting for you. Because I like you. I want to be with you. I can't pretend like that phone call last summer didn't happen. I've thought about it a hundred times. You opened the door that night, and now, I want all the way in." I confessed way more than I'd meant to. "Ugh, why do you make me say these things to you?"

I felt so stupid, laying my emotional truth out in the open for him to see, judge, and analyze. Giving a guy like Mac my heart was possibly a bad idea, but right now, I couldn't seem to stop myself. This would either be the biggest mistake of my life or the best thing I'd ever done with it. Love was always worth the risk, and I'd played it safe for too long, always selling myself short and taking less than I deserved.

The only way to get through Mac's walls was to break them down. And I held the fucking jackhammer.

"I don't know how you do it," he breathed out. "You're so honest. You always say exactly how you feel."

"That's not true," I countered because it wasn't. "Not always."

"I'm a mess." He sat down on the ground and put his head in his hands, pulling at the strands of his hair before looking up at me. "I come from a fucked up family. I have some serious issues I'm still trying to work through. You don't want to get involved with me."

I sat down and faced him, our knees barely touching. "Everyone has issues, and no one's family is perfect. No matter how hard they try to pretend otherwise. At some point in your life, you have to let someone in."

"I did once." I knew Mac meant his ex-girlfriend, and I stopped myself from asking a million questions about exactly what had happened between them even though I was dying to know. "Didn't work out so well that time."

"Sometimes, we choose people who are bad for us. But that's usually where we learn the most."

"I didn't want to learn all that." He sounded so sad.

The night had taken such a drastic turn, and I had no idea how to get us back on track.

"Come home with me," I blurted out, and he looked right through me, saying nothing while he slowly shook his head. I pulled out the big guns. "I'll bake for you."

"Salty cookies?" His eyes lit up while the rest of him

looked so defeated.

He was a sitting contradiction, and I couldn't stand it. I wanted to help him, to make him feel better, even if it was short-lived.

"Anything you want," I said with a smile because I meant it.

If Mac wanted me to bake him fifteen different types of cookies tonight, I'd do it for him.

He pushed up from the ground, and his hand reached for mine, lifting me up with little effort. "Lead the way."

CAN'T SAY NO TO HER

Mac

I SHOULD HAVE stuck to my guns when I first said no to her. I should have stood up, told Sunny good night, and walked back into the baseball house and away from all of her beautiful goodness. But I couldn't do it. The offer of baked goods was just a bonus, one that had pushed me over the proverbial edge. I would have gone with her anyway, even without the cookies.

I was beginning to think that I'd follow Sunny Jamison anywhere she wanted me to. And that was a dangerous line for me to cross, giving in to someone who could crush me without trying. The craziest part in my mind was that she clearly had no idea how I felt about her. Not that I blamed her necessarily, considering the fact that I was more up and down than a fucking amusement park ride.

Telling her that I didn't want Hayley the devil had been one thing. Telling Sunny that I wanted to work through all of my issues and try to be a normal human being with her was another. I wasn't sure I could do it. Like, I wasn't sure I was emotionally capable of handling it. And the last thing on earth I wanted to do again was hurt her.

Sunny was too pure. Too good. Too honest. She deserved someone as equally amazing as she was. A guy who could give her everything she craved without being a fucking basket case about it.

"Oh, thank God," she breathed out as we reached what I assumed was her car.

"What?"

"There was a car parked up my ass earlier. I was afraid we wouldn't be able to get out."

"I would have picked up the car and moved it," I said with a grin, and she laughed.

"You can't just pick up a car," she said between giggles.

"So, you don't think I'm strong enough?" I asked, flexing my muscles in her direction. "I'm offended."

"No, you're not," she said before hitting a button and unlocking the doors. "Offended, I mean. Not that you aren't strong enough. I'm sure lifting cars is totally normal." She smiled as I slid inside the passenger seat and waited for her to get in.

"Gotta be honest, Sunny," I said as she buckled up and started the engine, her blue eyes meeting mine. "I'm really looking forward to those cookies."

She laughed again, and it filled me with something I couldn't place. A kind of happiness in knowing that I was the one bringing that smile to her lips. I planned to keep doing it for as long as she'd let me. Or until I messed it all up.

Why—why—are my thoughts so self-destructive? I fucking annoyed myself.

"I'm glad I can make you happy."

"Also," I began before making sure my tone was as serious as my intention, "thank you for taking care of me tonight. And for sticking up for me."

I'd never had someone come to my defense before. Usually, people stood by and watched shit happen, but no one ever did anything about it. Especially when it was happening to a guy. Everyone always assumed that we men could take care of ourselves and we didn't need an entourage to have our backs. And while we might not always need it per se, it'd sure felt nice to have tonight.

"Anytime," was all she said in response. I watched as she focused less on me and more on the road in front of us. "But I did lie a little earlier."

Her admission caught me off guard, and I felt my entire body tense with her words. *What has she lied about? Was the car moving slow enough that I could open the door and jump out if I need to?*

"About what?" I asked, my voice practically shaking.

"The cookies. I mean, I made some already this afternoon. I meant to bring them tonight, but I forgot. They'll still be good though, I promise," she overexplained, and I instantly relaxed.

"Jesus, Sunny, you scared the shit out of me."

"Why? What did you think I was talking about?" She sounded so surprised.

"I have no idea. But not your damn delicious cookies."

I really was more messed up than I'd realized with trust issues and relationship fears lingering right below the surface. They weren't even buried deep, hidden underneath layers of ego or false confidence.

Nope.

My issues were ready and waiting to bounce out at a moment's notice. Give them an opening, and they were taking it. I shook my head to myself, wishing I could snap them away but knowing it was no use. Life didn't work that way, no matter how badly you wanted it to.

Blowing out a soft breath, I leaned back against the headrest as Sunny gave me a quick look and a soft smile, but she didn't ask me what was going on even though I knew she must have wanted to.

The rest of the short drive was spent in a comfortable quiet, aside from the radio playing pop music in the background. At least, I thought it was comfortable. I couldn't be sure how Sunny interpreted it, but I hadn't felt the need to say anything to break up the lack of words being spoken.

There had been plenty of times in my life when silence felt not only deafening, but also downright strangling. I couldn't breathe in the quiet.

This wasn't one of those times.

It seemed crazy to be so relaxed, but then I remembered that Sunny always seemed to have that effect on me. When my world was in chaos, she gave me calm. Even tonight, I'd gravitated toward her over all others. Every second that I was taking care of Matt and getting him settled in his room, my mind was on her. And while it hadn't shocked me that I left Hayley standing there alone in order to chase after Sunny, I knew that it'd surprised both of the girls in that scenario.

Running to Sunny hadn't felt like a choice. It was a necessity. And even though it was the right thing to do, I wasn't the guy who always did the right thing. Especially when Hayley was involved. I might have hated her, but that only meant she still got to me.

"We're here." Sunny's voice broke through my inner diatribe, and I turned to look at her before reaching out and touching her face.

"You ground me," I said before I could even think about what I was admitting. It was one hell of a confession. One that carried a lot of weight.

"Yeah? Well, you make me crazy," she said with a grin before adding, "in a good way."

"There's a good kind of crazy?" I cocked an eyebrow at her before reaching for my seat belt and unfastening it as she opened her door and stepped outside.

She leaned back into the car, her eyes sparkling as she said, "I think when it comes to you, there is."

I got out and followed her toward the double glass doors of her apartment complex. I watched as she scanned her key fob across a small flat pad. A loud click sounded, and I pulled one of the doors open and held it as Sunny walked through, my eyes scanning her ass without shame.

She paused mid-step, so I could catch up to her. I'd fallen ridiculously behind for no good reason other than ... that ass.

"Are you looking at my butt?" she asked, her hand on her hip, mouth slightly agape.

I thought about lying for all of two seconds before admitting, "Yeah."

She laughed out loud, and it echoed around the halls. "At least you're honest. Come on." She reached for my hand and pulled me so that I was next to her. "It's right up here." She jingled her keys as she pointed.

We stopped in front of a door that had a doormat that read, *Probably at Target.*

Pointing at it, I asked, "Big Target fan?"

"Is that a trick question?"

I shrugged. "I guess it's a girl thing."

Shoving her key into the lock and twisting, she scowled at me, refusing to let me in as she took a step inside. "Victoria's Secret is a girl thing. Sephora is a girl thing. Target is an *every person* thing."

Hands up in the air, I pretended to surrender. "I guess *big fan* was an understatement."

"Take it back, or you can't come in," she flirted.

I laughed, but she was serious. Sunny was going to make me stand outside her door for the rest of the night if I didn't confess my love for that damn store. Even though we both knew that if I wanted to grab her tiny waist, kiss her senseless, and force my way inside, I could do it. But like a good vampire, I actually wanted to be invited in.

"Fine, fine. It's a good store. One-stop shop. Everything you need, no matter your gender."

"Exactly. I'm glad you see things clearly. You can come in now." She stepped to the side, and I rushed in before she changed her mind.

I looked around at her apartment, trying to take it all in. It was exactly like the one she had shared last year with Danika with the exception of the kitchen being a little bit smaller. That was literally the only difference.

"How do you like living alone?"

"I hate it," she said without taking a breath.

"Really?" I sort of laughed at that. I hadn't meant to, but I couldn't stop it from coming out. It wasn't what she'd said but how she'd said it.

"Don't laugh at me. I'm not built to be by myself all the time." She walked into the kitchen and started fumbling around as I took a seat at the table before noticing the plate filled with cookies sitting in front of me, taunting me, just begging me to rip open the cover and shove them all in my mouth.

"Danika mentioned that to me," I said as I pulled my eyes away from the cookies and pretended like I had the ability to be patient.

"I miss her so much," she admitted before appearing at my side, reaching for the plate and disappearing with it.

SHE TOOK THE COOKIES!

"I miss them too," I confessed. "It's stupid, I know, but I really miss having Chance here. It's not the same without him."

"It's not stupid to miss your best friend," she said.

I heard the sound of the microwave turn on, and I had no idea what was going on in that kitchen.

The microwave beeped, and before I knew it, Sunny was placing a warmed-up chocolate chip cookie and napkin in front of me before taking a seat across from me with her own cookie. "Careful. It's hot. So, why would it be stupid?"

"Huh? Oh, to miss Chance? 'Cause I'm a guy. I don't know. We're supposed to be tough and all nonemotional and shit. Right?"

"I think we both know that's not true." Her blue eyes ghosted straight through me, and I felt a sense of calm again as she broke off a piece of her cookie and plopped it into her mouth. "And you want to know something?"

"Of course." I took a giant bite of mine, crumbs falling everywhere. I was pretty sure I'd moaned, but I was too caught up in the combination of chocolate and salt to care.

Sunny giggled. "Good?"

"Delicious. I don't know what it is about your cookies."

"I told you before, it's the sea salt flakes." She shrugged. "It changes everything. Makes it better for whatever reason. But as I was saying"—she inhaled—"I think it's incredibly sexy when a guy is in touch with his emotions. And can talk about them."

I knew she was referring to the phone call. Everything seemed to circle back to that damn call. Sunny was giving me the green light to keep opening up to her, basically letting me know she not only wanted it, but she also liked it.

"It's just weird how quickly it all changes. How fast college has flown by, you know? Chance was just here, and now, he's a professional baseball player, and I'll barely get to see him anymore."

"Maybe you'll get drafted for the Mets too," she offered, her silver hair catching the light.

I knew she was only trying to be positive, but it felt like she'd dropped a boulder into the pit of my stomach. I couldn't breathe around it.

"Hey, are you okay?" She reached across the table and put her hand on mine. "Mac, I didn't mean to upset you."

I pulled my hand away. "I know you didn't."

I was going to be sick. Reaching for my stomach, I placed my hand there, willing it to calm the fuck down. The last thing I wanted was to throw up the cookie I'd just eaten all over her table.

"Talk to me," she pleaded, but I didn't know what to say.

If I said the thoughts that were currently spinning around in my head, it might make them real.

What if saying them out loud makes them come true?

I looked into her eyes, and I could literally feel her concern for me. Sunny genuinely cared, but this was all too much, too fast. I suddenly felt overwhelmed with my feelings for her and my fear for the future, all swirling together in one giant pot of messed up shit.

I'd never done this before, not even with my ex. Hayley never wanted to talk. At least, not in any real capacity. The one time I'd admitted to her that I was scared I wasn't good enough to get drafted, she'd told me to stop being a pussy and that she never wanted to hear me admitting weakness again.

I would have been way more shell-shocked if I hadn't grown up in the same kind of environment my whole life—being talked down to and disappointing those closest to me with every decision. So, after Hayley's declaration, I shut my fucking mouth and never brought it up again. She'd dumped me anyway, throwing my fears back in my face as her reason for doing it, so that hadn't worked out well in the end.

Pushing up from the table, I swallowed the bile threatening to come up. "I need to go."

"What? Mac, no. Don't leave. You just got here."

"I'm sorry, Sunny. I just … can't do this right now," I said as I started for the front door with no idea or plan, just the fact that I needed to get the hell out of there before I passed out. I felt like I couldn't breathe.

"I'm scared too, you know." Her voice stopped me dead in my tracks. I wasn't sure what she meant.

"Of what?" I managed to get out between labored breaths. *Am I having a panic attack?*

"Everything. You. Us. This. The future mostly."

I wanted to tell her that she wasn't the only one. That, for some of us, the future wasn't some beautiful, open book filled with options and variables and choices and free will.

I should have reassured her or comforted her somehow, like I knew she would do if the roles were reversed and it was me admitting those things.

But I didn't. I couldn't. Instead, I pulled her front door open, walked through it, and closed it behind me, desperate to get away and leaving Sunny to do the one thing she hated … be alone.

WHAT THE HELL JUST HAPPENED?

Sunny

I FOUGHT THE urge to run after Mac and drag him back into my apartment, kicking and screaming if I had to. I'd clearly struck a nerve or triggered him somehow, and I hated that I was letting him walk away without at least trying to work through it. I knew that he was sensitive about getting drafted, but I hadn't understood just how much it affected him until he looked like he was about to throw up.

It hurt, watching him walk out my door, but Mac Davies was a runner. I'd already figured that out last year. So, I let him go. And then I kicked myself for it because even though Mac liked to run away, there was a part of him that needed to be chased. I sensed it even if he didn't.

Grabbing my keys from the counter, I tore open my door and slammed it hard behind me without meaning to as I looked left and right, not knowing which way he had gone.

"Oh my God, can you stop with the slamming doors already?" A head popped out from next door; jet-black hair with bright green stripes, pulled into a ponytail, accompanied a frowning female face.

The girl with the hair lives right next door to me? I was too preoccupied to be excited.

"I'm sorry. I didn't mean to," I apologized. "I'm Sunny. I live right here," I overexplained as I pointed toward my front door.

"Gathered that much," she said, her tone sarcastic as she took a step inside the hallway and stopped the door from closing with her foot. Her clothes reminded me of something Billie Eilish might wear, all edgy and punk-like. I looked at her with appreciation, knowing that I could never pull off an outfit like that. "Are you looking for the disgruntled baseball player?"

"How'd you know?"

She didn't look like the kind of girl who cared about athletes, let alone even knew who they were. But then again, this was the Fullton State baseball team, and Mac was ... well, he had a reputation whether he wanted one or not.

"Everyone knows who Mac Davies is."

"Did you see which way he went?" I needed to get to him before he called for a ride and I missed my chance.

"Lovers' quarrel?" She picked at her nails, pretending not to be interested. She was though.

"What? No. We're just friends," I stumbled over my words, making them sound like a lie.

"Even I know that Mac doesn't have friends who are girls, and I couldn't care less about the guy. Unless you're doing his homework or writing his papers for him, which can't be right because Mac's smart and gets all *A*s," she waxed on.

I wondered how she knew that Mac got all *A*s in his classes. Even I hadn't known that. I couldn't get distracted with her though because I was running out of time.

"Just tell me which way he went. Please."

Her thumb jerked to the right, and I took off running.

"Thank you!"

"The name's Rocky, by the way!" she yelled toward me, and I shouted back, "It fits you." She looked like a Rocky, and I was going to make her my friend—but not until after I found Mac.

I hit the exit door with my arms extended, and it flew open, smacking with a loud crash into the wall of the building. I was like a tiny bull in a china shop. Or maybe more like a top spinning out of control.

"Mac!" I yelled his name into the night air, hoping that wherever he was, he might hear me and stop leaving.

The parking lot had plenty of streetlights that illuminated the space, but outside of it was pitch-black. Mac could be anywhere, and I'd never even see him. With my luck, he was probably in a car, halfway back to the baseball house by now.

I stopped running and blew out a long breath before shouting one last time, "MAC!" realizing that I was probably waking up the whole apartment complex.

"Sunny?" I heard him say my name like a question from somewhere in the distance.

I headed the direction I thought it had come from, my eyes focused straight ahead in front of me. A hand reached out and grabbed my calf, and I almost screamed with the contact. Mac was sitting on the ground, between two cars. My heart pounded against my chest.

"Mac," I breathed out and immediately sat down. I thought

I might fall to the ground anyway; he'd scared me so bad.

"You were looking for me?" He sounded so wounded, so caught up in whatever was going on in his head that he couldn't comprehend the idea.

"I thought about letting you leave. That maybe you needed space to work out whatever was going on in there." I leaned forward and gently tapped his forehead with my finger. "But I couldn't stand it."

His eyes pulled together. "Couldn't stand what?"

"Leaving you alone." There were other things I couldn't handle as well, like the thought of him feeling depressed or thinking that he was alone. "I didn't want you to think that I didn't care."

"I know you care, Sunny. You care too much," he said.

I interrupted him before he could say anything else, "There's no such thing."

He let out a gruff laugh. "Yeah, there actually is."

"Oh, really? Give me an example then," I pushed.

For as much as Mac liked to run away when things got too heavy, he also had a tendency to open up as well.

His body shifted as he pushed himself to sit up straighter. "You."

"Me? I'm your example?"

"Yeah. You give way too much of yourself without getting anything in return."

"You say that like it's a bad thing." I felt myself getting a little defensive. "Being selfless isn't a negative quality."

"It can be. If you let people walk all over you or take advantage of your kindness."

Shaking my head, I disagreed. Maybe Mac saw me that way, but I didn't. "But I don't."

"But you would." He reached out and put his hand on my bent knee. "You would give everything to me even if I never opened up and gave you any more than I did last summer. You'd still turn the world upside down in order to help me."

I started feeling more than a little uncomfortable. Mac was seeing me in ways I wasn't sure I'd ever even seen myself before. But in this particular scenario, he wasn't wrong.

"You're right. I would. But it's not like I'd do that for just anyone. I don't walk around, lighting myself on fire to keep everyone else warm."

"Exactly," he said, sounding satisfied as he pulled his hand away, and I was confused until he continued, "You care too much for me, and I haven't done a damn thing to deserve it."

Clearing my throat, I fought back, "Well, that's your perspective, and you don't get to decide."

"Decide what?"

"Who I care for and how." I was being stubborn. Arguing just for the sake of doing it.

"No, I guess not," he agreed, and it surprised me. "I'm just saying, be careful who you go to bat for. Make sure they're not only worth it, but that they'd also do the same thing for you."

"You're so frustrating," I groaned before pushing myself up from the dirty street and brushing myself off. Pacing in small steps, I ground my teeth together as I searched for just the right words. Halting to a stop, I turned to face him. "Get up," I demanded.

His mouth turned into a sexy little grin, and I snarled in return as he did what I'd asked, his body suddenly towering over mine. "I'm up."

Poking a finger against his chest, I started in on him, "You care about me too. Whether you want to admit it or not, you do. You wouldn't be here tonight if you didn't." I poked at him again. "And another thing"—*poke*—"you're not the only person on this planet with issues, okay?" *Poke.* "I get it, Mac. For whatever reason, you don't think you're good enough. For me"—*poke*—"or for baseball." *Poke.*

His body adjusted quickly away from my stabby finger. "Stop poking me. Damn, that shit hurts."

"Come back inside. Don't leave. Not like this. It's stupid." I expected him to disagree immediately, so when he didn't, I kept explaining, "We don't have to talk anymore. But we can if you want. We can watch Christmas movies. Or you can give me a hand massage," I suggested while shaking out my fingers.

"Christmas movies? Now?"

"It's scientifically proven that all things Christmas bring joy, no matter the time of year. The lights and magic give people hope, and they're sixty-five percent happier than they were before they started watching."

He laughed again. "Scientifically proven, eh?"

"Fine. No. But who doesn't love watching *Elf*? 'Have you seen the toilets?'" I started quoting the now-classic Will Ferrell movie.

"'They're ginormous!'" Mac said back with a gorgeous smile.

God, he really was something else, and I was a total goner.

"See? You're already happier."

I watched as he took a step toward me, but I held my ground, refusing to back away. His hands cupped my face as he leaned down and kissed my mouth. I opened, allowing him to take me, the feel of his tongue sending me into sensation overload.

"You're too good for me," he whispered before kissing me again.

"Stop saying that."

"I'm fucked up, Sunny." He sounded so convinced of what he was saying. As if him believing it would make me believe it as well.

"We're all fucked up."

"You're not." He wrapped his arms around me and held me tight as I laughed, my body shaking against his. He was so large, so much bigger than I was, and I felt cocooned by him. I wanted to wrap myself up in his body and wear him like a coat.

"You mean, aside from being too nice to you?" I asked with a grin.

"I'm sorry," he apologized. "One of my go-to defense mechanisms is to push people away."

"Oh, believe me, I've noticed."

"Let's go back inside," he suggested, and I reached for his hand and held it tight.

No matter how hard Mac tried to push me away, I wouldn't leave him.

MORE CONFESSIONS

Mac

"I SEE YOU found him." A voice echoed in the hall, and I swiveled my head to see a punk rock–looking chick with crazy hair glaring at me. Glaring.

Do I know her?

"I did. Thanks for the help," Sunny said with a smile before introducing us. "Mac, this is my neighbor Rocky."

"Rocky? Interesting name."

"My parents were big fans of the movies. And they wanted a boy. Lucky for them, I liked it too," Rocky explained.

"The movies or the name?" I asked with a chuckle.

"The movies are trash. But I love my name."

Honestly, the name fit her. She looked tough enough to kick my ass.

"Well, it's nice to meet you. You'll look out for my girl when I'm not around, yeah?" I said without thinking twice, and Rocky's frown turned up noticeably. "She doesn't like being alone," I added.

"Hey." Sunny stomped her foot and forced a frown.

"Your girl, huh?" Rocky looked directly at Sunny.

"Thought you two were just friends?" she mimicked.

"Don't listen to him," Sunny said with a grimace. "He hit his head. Doesn't know what he's saying."

"No, I didn't," I argued playfully and watched as Sunny brought her hand up and smacked me upside the head with it. "Ow!"

"See? Brain malfunction or something. Gets information wrong."

"You two are weird." Rocky shook her head. "I'm going back inside now. I'll talk to you later, Sunny."

"What about me?" I pretended to pout as Rocky closed the door without playing along. "She hates me. Your new best friend hates me," I said as I followed Sunny down the hall toward her place.

"She's not my new best friend," she bit back before adding with a laugh, "but she definitely hates you."

"How can anyone hate me?" I whined.

Sunny patted my head as I walked through her front door. She closed and locked it behind us. "Poor baby. I'm not sure how you'll survive this rejection."

"You joke, but I'm not kidding. I'm seriously crushed right now," I said, putting a hand over my heart.

Sunny waltzed into her kitchen, and before I knew it, a cookie was sailing in the air toward me. "Here. Eat your feelings."

I scrambled but caught it without mutilating it into a million tiny cookie pieces. "You could have killed it! You can't just toss your cookies at me without any warning."

She started giggling, her cheeks turning red as I realized

what I'd said.

"You have a dirty mind. Who knew?"

She shrugged and took a bite of a cookie herself. I watched as she chewed, her eyes closing as she savored every bite. Her mouth worked so slowly that it looked like she was making love to the damn thing. My dick got hard instantly.

"Stop eating it like that."

Her eyes popped open and grew wide. "Like what?"

I adjusted the bulge in my pants, but it was too late. "Like it's the best thing you've ever put in your mouth," I said, feeling insanely jealous.

Jealous! Of a fucking cookie!

"Who says it isn't?" she sassed.

I dropped my own cookie on top of the table as I stalked toward her, my steps brisk. Rounding the kitchen corner, I pushed my body against hers, one arm snaking around her waist, the other firmly behind her head. She stepped back, and I let her until we hit the wall I had been aiming for, so we couldn't move any further.

Looking down at her petite frame, I wondered how my body felt to her. "Do you feel that? What you do to me?"

She swallowed hard, her lips parting as her eyes stared at my mouth. "I feel it," she tried to say, but the words came out in a seductive whisper.

"I want to be the best thing you've ever put in your mouth," I said before taking her lips and plunging my tongue inside.

She tasted sweet, like sugar and chocolate, and I couldn't get enough of her. My hand fisted her hair, pulling at the long silver strands and wrapping them in my fingers. Her hair was so soft. Her mouth warm. I wanted to dive into this girl and never come up for air again.

"Mac," Sunny breathed out, her hands wrapped around the back of my neck, pulling me harder as her hips started grinding in small circles against me.

Jesus. This girl was going to kill me if she didn't stop moving like that. Or I was going to explode in my pants and embarrass the hell out of myself à la *American Pie*.

I stepped away from her hot little body, my hands gripping her arms so she couldn't move with me. I used all of my strength to keep her at a distance. "Sunny." Her name was a plea as she stared at me, her pink lips swollen and more than lust in her eyes.

"Yes?"

"We need to stop."

Disappointment flashed in her eyes before she put on a brave face. "Oh. Okay. Yeah, you're probably right," she agreed even though I knew that she wanted me just as badly as I wanted her.

"It's not you. It's just ..." I flinched, feeling insecure, vulnerable, and downright terrified.

She wiggled out of my grip, the spell between us officially broken as hurt coursed through her. She wore her feelings on her face, and I was gifted at interpretation.

"You don't have to explain." Her words sliced right through me.

"But I want to try." Closing my eyes, I blew out a breath before opening them back up and staring at the ceiling for a second. "Can we sit?"

Nodding, she moved wordlessly to the couch and sat down. Tossing my cell phone onto the coffee table in front of us, I sat close enough that our legs touched but kept the rest of my body parts to myself... for now. I wasn't sure exactly where to start, but Sunny deserved an explanation. One second, I'd wanted to shove my dick in her mouth and die from pleasure, and then the next, I had pushed her away, telling her I couldn't.

"I know you have a lot going on in that head of yours," she said with a small smile. "But it's late, and we can do this some other time."

She was giving me an out. I knew that I could take it, but things would never be the same. Eventually, I'd end up telling Sunny all of this anyway, but who knew when? I hated feeling like such a colossal screwup.

Why do I have to have so many complex feelings and emotions? Why can't I just fuck my way through college like everyone thought I was doing anyway? The consummate player. The only one to rival Fullton State legend Jack fucking Carter—aka Chance Carter's dad and my baseball coach.

I fought back a laugh. If they only knew. Apparently, Coach Carter's reputation had been based on actual events, whereas mine were all rumors and hearsay. No one knew the truth about me, but everyone acted like they did.

"Mac," Sunny said my name, drawing my eyes to her lips, "we can just watch a movie or something."

Sunny would let me put this away and bottle it up if that was what I chose to do. And, man, that decision could be so easy to make. It was what I'd done my whole life—shoved things down until they suffocated me. I'd learned from the best. When my mom had started feeling depressed, she never talked about it, even when I begged her to. She kept everything locked up tight in a vault she sealed with vodka and long afternoon naps. When she was awake, she lived in a state of fierce denial, isolating everyone around her—most of all, me.

All I wanted was to feel understood. I needed to be told that it wasn't wrong of me to live my own life and make my own decisions. I never wanted to follow in my dad's footsteps, but no one seemed to give a shit about that. There were hundreds of times when my mom should have taken my side, but she never did. And even though I knew it was because she was afraid of my father, I secretly hated her for it.

So, when it came to Sunny, I longed to be better and give her more than the shitty hand I'd been dealt. I knew she deserved it, and I wanted to try.

"Hayley," I started, diving headfirst into my personal hell.

Sunny's blue eyes narrowed as she snarled, "Your ex-girlfriend I'm assuming?"

"Yeah. How much do you know about what happened between us?" I asked because I knew how quickly word had spread after she dumped me. It'd felt like the entire campus had heard within five minutes of it happening. Granted, it was three years ago, but Sunny would have been here at Fullton at the time.

"I'm not sure. I mean, I heard some things about her breaking up with you, but I never knew what was the truth or not. And I didn't go to many baseball games back then, so I wasn't there when it allegedly happened."

"Did you only start going to games once Danika met Chance?" I asked even though it seemed too far-fetched to be true. You see, everyone went to our baseball games even if you knew nothing about the sport. We were the Fullton State team to watch. If you picked one sport to support, it was ours.

"No, but I went to more games once they were together. I've gone to a handful over the years but not that often or anything."

"Why not?"

She laughed. "I didn't have a reason to go to the games. It's not like I had a boyfriend on the team. Plus, you guys play a lot. That's a big commitment."

I smirked. "True. We do have a shit-ton of games."

"Tell me what happened." Sunny's expression turned thoughtful, her eyes inquiring, as she was desperate to hear this tale.

In order to tell her about Hayley though, I had to go back in time even further and fill her in on things I'd never told any other girl before. Ever.

"When I came here as a freshman, it was my first taste of real freedom, you know what I mean?" I asked, wondering if she'd felt the way I had when I got here. Maybe she had already been able to do whatever she wanted during high school, so college hadn't been that much of a transition for her. I had no idea.

"Of course. We don't live with our parents anymore. We can go grocery shopping at two in the morning if we want to, and no one can tell us no! We can get Taco Bell at midnight.

Or doughnuts at four a.m. when it opens and they're still warm."

"I'm sensing a trend here," I said, as everything she'd just mentioned revolved around some sort of food or snack.

"I wasn't allowed to do those things when I lived at home. But I can now. See? Freedom."

Smiling, I couldn't disagree. "That is freedom."

"But it's not what you're talking about, is it?"

"Not the same, no."

"Okay. Go on. I'm listening," she encouraged.

"All right. So, my dad, uh," I stuttered, but it was too late to stop, "he isn't the easiest guy to get along with. We have nothing in common. He's very controlling. And he runs with a certain kind of crowd back in Arizona. That's where I'm from."

"I knew that part. Arizona, I mean. Are you from a crime family?" She was serious, and I looked at her like she was insane. "They totally have crime families in Arizona, right? That's where they all go to 'retire.'" She used air quotes around the word.

Laughing, I shook my head. "A crime family? You've been hanging out with Danika for too long. No, I meant, rich people. My dad runs with all the bigwigs in our area. Politicians, CEOs. That kind of thing. He works in taxes and finance. Handles a lot of big money."

"Ah, okay. That makes more sense," she said, tucking a leg up underneath her, and I wondered how girls could sit that way and be comfortable.

"When I was in high school, I was a scared kid."

"What do you mean?"

"I was nothing like I am now. I had no confidence," I said even though my confidence had tended to elude me more often than not lately. "I was terrified that everything I did would get back to my dad somehow that I literally did nothing but play baseball and sit at home with my mom. Granted, she was drunk most of the time."

Her eyes pulled together. "I'm so sorry."

"Don't be." I didn't want Sunny's pity, and I hated that look I saw in her eyes. "Don't feel bad for me, Sunny. It is what it is. The hand I was dealt—or whatever you want to call it."

"I can still think it sucks," she bit back, her tone a contradicting mixture of defensive and soft.

"Yeah, you can think it sucks, but I can't change the past. Anyway, when I got here, I was super naive. I thought I knew what to expect, but holy shit, I had no idea."

She kicked her leg back out as she reached for a blanket hanging over the back of the couch that I hadn't even noticed before and wrapped herself in it like a burrito. "Do you want one?" she asked, already moving to stand up.

"No, I'm good."

" 'K. Go on. In what way were you surprised?"

How can I word what I mean exactly and not make it come out wrong?

"The girls. I had no idea that it would be like this. I mean, I'd heard things, but I always thought they were an exaggeration or blown out of proportion. There was no way the things that I'd been told about this school could be real."

"Honestly, someone should come here and conduct a study on female behavior and the baseball team. I'm sure their minds would be blown."

"Right? At home, the girls all thought I was weird, and they stayed clear of me. It's because I never went out or did anything social. But here, all anyone knew about me was that I was on the baseball team. And apparently, that was all it took. That was all I needed to be some big man on campus without even doing a damn thing. It was exhilarating for someone like me."

"I still can't picture you being some antisocial homebody," she said, like the idea was purely comical and unbelievable.

"You can't even imagine it?"

"No." A laugh escaped. "I see you like this"—she waved her hand toward me—"running the show. Making all the decisions. You have rules for the girls in your life, Mac. RULES! That's not someone who isn't confident or cocky as hell."

"Rules because I'm insecure and scared to death," I admitted a little too quickly, and it was too late to take it back.

"Hard to believe." She shook her head, and I knew it was because she was so inherently honest. And when you were that kind of a person, you thought that everyone else was too. If you told the truth, you assumed everyone told the truth.

"Anyway, when I got here, I was completely overwhelmed by all the attention. I met Hayley really early on in the semester. Pretty much right away. I couldn't believe that a girl who looked like that was even giving me the time of day," I said before feeling like I'd put my foot in my mouth. "I don't mean anything by that, Sunny. I think you're gorgeous, and I don't know why you're talking to me either."

"Stop it." She put up her hand. "I know this isn't about me right now. I'm not taking it personally, I promise. Go on."

"I couldn't believe that she wanted me. Hayley could probably have any guy on campus—or in Los Angeles for that matter—and here she was, choosing me. I was so dumbstruck by her looks. How beautiful I thought she was. And how genuine. I really thought she loved me. I believed all her lies," I said, feeling like an idiot all over again.

"So, what happened? How did things end?"

I thought back to the day. I still remembered every detail vividly. It was burned into my memory, pictures I wished I could erase but knew I never would. They'd always linger somewhere in the back of my mind, waiting to come out and ruin my day whenever I was inadvertently triggered.

"I was a freshman. We already had a starting first baseman, but I still played a few innings sometimes. I had a bad game. Played like I'd never touched a baseball before in my life. It was embarrassing. Truly. I made two errors at first. Instead of moving my foot off the bag to actually catch the damn ball, I tried to stretch, thinking that getting the out was the most important thing when catching the ball was."

Sucking in a breath and then blowing it out, I continued, "I just played bad. Bad enough that I was worried I'd never get the chance to start at first base again for the rest of my time at Fullton. After the game, Hayley was waiting for me in the stands, a scowl on her face. I wondered why she was mad at me or what I'd done. There were still people around too. Families of the players, my coaches, my entire team, and some fans. She yelled that I had embarrassed her in front of everyone. Asked how I could do that to her. Said I made her look bad, stupid even. She said that I was never going to get drafted and she was an idiot for even thinking that I might have a shot. That she overheard the scouts talking and they'd said I didn't have what it took. What a waste of time I'd been when she could have been focusing on someone else. Someone who was actually going to play professional ball, not a loser who was going nowhere, like me."

I sucked in a breath and tried to rid myself of the memories that were playing on the big screen in my mind. Reliving that moment was humiliating and made me feel about two inches tall.

"So, why is she all in your business again? I mean, if you're so bad at baseball, why does she keep coming around?" Sunny asked, her tone vicious and accusatory. I knew it wasn't meant for me, so I found it downright endearing.

"She thinks I'm getting drafted. Apparently, she followed my stats this summer."

"Ohh." Sunny let out a disgusted laughing sound. "So, you're good enough for her again. I get it."

I wasn't sure what to say.

"I want to kick her ass," Sunny growled. "If I see her walking on campus, I'm going to *accidentally* trip her. Or maybe I'll not-so-accidentally shove her into a tree, face-first."

"Damn, killer. I'd tell you to go for it, but she's not worth it," I said, meaning it.

"It's just ..." Sunny sucked in a quick breath before blowing it back out. "That's a horrible story, Mac. Seriously horrible. Who does that? I hate her," she snarled as she looked over my shoulder and avoided eye contact.

I liked seeing her all riled up on my behalf. It was hot as hell and made me feel good. "You all fired up like this is doing something for me." I smirked, hoping I wasn't ruining the mood.

Her head snapped back to me, the silver strands swaying with the movement. "Yeah? You like seeing me upset?"

I swallowed hard. "I like seeing you mad at her. For me. It feels nice," I barely said the last sentence out loud because there were so many emotions in the room that it was hard to breathe.

"I think if the roles were reversed, you'd be pissed for me too," she said.

I sank deeper into the couch as the scenario played out in my head, knowing she was right.

"I'd make him wish he'd never met you." The words sounded honorable, but I was fucking serious. The thought of any guy doing that to Sunny made me beyond angry. "Shit," I breathed out.

"What?"

"Is that guy me? Is that what I did to you? Did I treat you like that?" I asked, wondering if I needed to kick my own ass or not right now. *Was Sunny trying to tell me something without coming right out and saying it?*

Sunny's eyes widened as she reached for me, her soft hand stroking my cheek. "No, Mac. No. It's not even remotely the same thing. She was supposed to be your teammate, and she worked against you. She was your girlfriend. She should have supported you in your dreams, not helped tear them apart."

"So, you're not mad at me then?" I tried to clarify.

"Was I mad that you'd ignored me this summer when I thought we'd started something potentially amazing? Yeah, I was. Was I mad at how you'd treated me this year before tonight happened? Again, yes. But obviously, not mad enough to not forgive you because here we are."

"I really am sorry."

"I know."

"Do you think you'll ever forgive me?"

Her lips formed the sweetest smile. "Only if you promise not to do it again."

My heart sank because I knew that I could never make her that promise. "Which part?"

"I don't even know." She shrugged. "The disappearing, I think. Don't disappear on me. And the being mean. I don't like it when you're mean to me. It feels awful. Promise me those things."

My defense mechanisms had become my go-to habits. And habits were hard to break, even when you wanted to. If Sunny had realized that, she'd never have asked me to promise her this, knowing that I'd mess it all up without trying or meaning to. Screwing up was easy for me. Making things right took work.

"I promise," I said, knowing damn well it was a lie.

IT ALL MAKES SENSE

Sunny

MAC WAS UNCOMFORTABLE again. We had been in such a good place, and then something had shifted. I sensed it, but I didn't want to push like I had been.

Mac had given me so much more than I'd ever expected. I couldn't believe the things that he had confessed to me tonight. I always assumed that he was messed up from life in some way, but I had no idea the depths of it or where any of it had come from.

"Can I get some water?" he asked, and I realized that I'd been an extremely bad hostess, not offering him anything to drink this whole time.

Hopping up from the couch, I said, "I'll get it," before he could get up himself.

I walked into the kitchen, grabbed more cookies, and a couple of bottles of water for us. I placed everything on the small coffee table and sat back down, remote control in hand as I turned the television on and lowered the volume. Background noise was always nice, but I did it mostly so that Mac would have the option to stop talking without making it uncomfortable for him. I was basically letting him know that it was okay to relax without saying it out loud.

He reached for a cookie and inhaled the entire thing while I watched him with wide eyes. He chuckled as he swallowed the last bite. "What?"

Grabbing one of the bottles, he twisted off the cap and took a long swig. I did the same with the other bottle before putting it back on the table and leaning back into the couch.

He snatched one of my throw pillows and tossed it on my lap. Staring down at it, I watched as he maneuvered himself on the couch, his head suddenly lying on the pillow ... *in my crotch*. Instinctively, I started playing with his hair. Running my fingers through the light strands and scratching my nails against his scalp. I swore he started purring.

"If you keep doing that, I might fall asleep."

"I can think of worse things." I stared down at him, memorizing his features in case he disappeared on me again even though he'd just promised he wouldn't.

"Hayley was my first." His hazel eyes stared up at me as he waited for my reaction.

I wasn't getting what he was trying to say.

My stomach muscles tightened, and his head bounced in response.

"Wait, what? Really? You were a virgin when you got here?"

"I told you, the girls at home thought I was weird. I never had a girlfriend before. That was why I was so enamored with Hayley. And why I believed she really liked me when she didn't. I had no real relationship experience. And my parents are so fucked up; I still have no idea what's normal and what isn't."

With every sentence, Mac revealed more than he probably intended to, and I savored every morsel, every tiny crumb, storing it in my head to process and think about later. There was a part of him that was attached to Hayley and always would be. It wasn't really a choice or something he could control. For whatever reason, our "first" got a sacred spot in our heart that never went to anyone else. It was a reserved space that no one else could quite reach or replace.

I understood that even though I still wanted to kill her for being such an evil witch. Mac hadn't deserved that. Hell, no one did. Except maybe that Logan guy who had been on the team a couple years ago, who had done all that shady shit to Cole Anders. Hayley and Logan would have made a perfect couple. Maybe I could set them up.

"Is that when you made up the rules?" I asked, assuming that after the debacle with Hayley, he didn't trust anyone again, and hence his rules for hooking up with girls had come to fruition.

"Not quite," he said, putting up a finger because, apparently, there was still more to this particular story.

The fact that he had been a virgin when he got here and that Hayley was his first made every single thing make so much more sense. Why he'd had that look on his face when she showed up at his bedroom door earlier tonight.

God, was that just a few hours ago? It feels like a lifetime.

"After she broke up with me, I went a little crazy," Mac started to explain, and I refocused my attention and thoughts back on him. "I basically fucked anyone who let me. But doing that only made the girls clingy. And I wasn't trying to open my heart back up. I was just trying to fill in the cracks."

My heart squeezed and promptly began pumping out jealous beats. Even though I hadn't known him at the time, I still hated hearing about this. I was already attached, and the idea of him giving himself to any girl who wasn't me made me queasy. It was irrational, but it was how I felt. At one time, Mac had fucked anyone who walked, but when it was our time, he had pushed me away.

"Girls get clingy because we usually have some feelings for the people we're giving our bodies to. It's kind of the way we females operate," I said even though I knew that wasn't even remotely true. Not *every girl* thought or felt that way about sex.

But I did. I was not the kind of person who could do it with someone she wasn't into. Making out was a different beast altogether. I'd kiss anyone without a second thought and go on my merry way, never to think about it again. But giving my naked body and all of its parts to a guy I didn't actually like? Never gonna happen.

"Yeah. I learned that real quick. It made things hella worse for me, so I stopped fucking around and made the rules instead as a joke one night."

I adjusted my body a little, but Mac stayed firmly planted in my lap.

"Wait. You haven't had sex since you started the rules?" I asked, already sensing the answer.

"No."

"I knew it," I breathed out, and he rolled over so that he was facing my chest. I felt the warmth of his breath through my shirt and against my skin.

"Knew what?"

"I knew you weren't sleeping around. There are always rumors, but I never believed them."

"Why?" He shifted again. "Why didn't you believe them?"

"Because I'd never seen you disappear, sneak off, or come out of a room with a girl at a party before," I started to explain. "I don't know. They just seemed like bullshit."

"Thank you, Sunny," he said as his eyes closed, and he seemed to get lost somewhere deep in his head.

"For what?" I asked.

"For believing in me when no one else does."

I fought the urge to lean down and kiss him, unsure of what to say in response. I started running my fingers through his hair again, replaying the things he'd just said.

"You said you started the rules as a joke?"

His eyes opened. "Yeah. I was messing around when I spouted them off that first night, but the girl didn't even flinch. She was completely agreeable, like what I was saying was perfectly logical, even though we both knew it was beyond ridiculous."

I watched as he swallowed, his Adam's apple bobbing.

"Hey," I interrupted. "I agreed to those rules once too, ya know."

He laughed. "Yeah, but I'd perfected them by then." He waved a hand in the air, blowing me off. "You should have heard the ones at the beginning. It was some crazy shit. Shit no girl with any self-respect should ever agree to."

"Are you saying I have no self-respect?" I started questioning how he saw me and how I saw myself and wondered if I'd done something wrong by agreeing last year.

"Sunny, no. The rules now are basically about getting on the same page from the get-go. They aren't disrespectful. At least, I don't mean for them to be. It's more about expectations, so there's no disappointment or hurt feelings. And it sounds really messed up, but when I started them back in the day, it gave me a lot of power. For the first time in my life, I felt like I had some kind of control." Mac's pain ran deep, and it hurt me, just sensing it. "I sound like an asshole, right? You want me to leave?"

He sat up, and my legs felt like they might float off the couch. Like the only thing grounding me to the furniture was the weight of his body.

"No. I mean, I don't want to like what you're saying, but you make it really hard when you explain it all so logically. Your reasoning makes sense to me."

"You don't think I'm crazy? Should be locked up somewhere to think about my actions?" He tried to joke, but I knew a part of him was serious.

"You're not crazy. I get why you did it. But I do have to ask you something," I said, wishing I could take back the words the second they left my mouth.

"What?"

I was embarrassed, but it was too late to turn back now. "Do you look at me differently for agreeing? For saying yes to your rules that time last year?" I wondered if he thought all the girls who had agreed to his arrangement were foolish, myself included.

His hand reached out and cupped my chin, holding it tight. "That would make me a hypocrite. I can't make up a list of rules and then think less of you for agreeing to them."

"I mean"—I kept my face firmly in his grip—"you could. But you don't? You're sure?"

"I could never think less of you," he said seriously, and suddenly, his lips were pressed against mine, his tongue sweeping across my lips before moving inside my mouth.

This kiss was pure decadence. Like every second that passed between us was meant to be savored and worshipped. Mac was a master with his mouth, and I couldn't help but want it all over my body. If he kissed like a god, I could only imagine the way he did everything else.

Moaning, I pulled away, my eyes fluttering open to look at him. He looked like a Southern California surfer, born and raised on the sand, even though I knew he was from landlocked Arizona. He was like the boy next door, if the boy next door was gorgeous with the body of an athlete and arms you constantly wanted to grab just to make him flex.

Mac gave me a quick peck before grabbing the pillow, fluffing it up, and lying back down in my lap, facing the TV. I reached for the remote and turned up the volume to give us both a moment to collect ourselves or to get lost in something else for a while. The night had been so serious, and I wanted to lighten it up.

His arm started flailing around on my body, smacking my stomach, and I laughed. "What are you doing?"

"Where's your hand?" he asked, still smacking around in search of it.

"Here," I said, shoving my arm toward him.

He grabbed my hand and placed it on top of his head. A request without words.

"You want me to play with your hair some more?"

He nodded his head, and before I knew it, I was doing as he'd asked. I wasn't sure how much time had passed, but he started breathing heavy as his chest rose and fell in perfect rhythm.

Mac Davies had fallen asleep in my lap.

NO DAYS OFF

Mac

I STARTLED AWAKE, my body jumping and jerking as I opened my eyes and wondered where the hell I was before sitting up and cracking my neck. The television was on, some infomercial trying to sell the world's best knives that never needed to be sharpened. Ever. Self-sharpening knives. *Cool.*

Swiveling my head, I looked behind me to see Sunny's tiny body curled up on the couch, taking up as little space as possible. *Shit.* I'd fallen asleep here. Reaching for my phone, I checked the time before pocketing it. It was after four in the morning, and I fought the instinct to slip out the front door and escape without making a sound. I knew it would be a dick move, so I forced myself not to make it. I'd already made so many when it came to this girl.

I scooped Sunny into my arms, her silver hair spilling over as I walked into her bedroom and laid her on top of her bed before figuring out how to unmake it and tuck her inside. I stopped myself from laughing at the amount of throw pillows she had when her eyes fluttered opened.

"Mac? What time is it?"

"Early."

"Are you leaving?"

"Not yet," I said, moving the comforter off and placing it on top of her.

Before I knew it, I was taking off my shirt and hopping into the bed right next to her. I wrapped an arm around her waist and tugged her tight against me, noticing how perfectly she fit there. Like she had been made for my body, and how good it felt scared the shit out of me. Her body was so warm and soft, and her hair smelled like the beach—coconut, I thought.

The last thing I remembered was breathing in the scent of it before my alarm blared to life at six a.m. sharp. Patting my jeans, I quieted it, not ready to get up yet, and even though Sunny stirred, she didn't fully wake. She moaned something unintelligible before backing her ass into me, and I fought the urge to start grinding my morning wood against her, creating a problem I wasn't quite ready to solve. But damn, she felt so good against me.

My alarm started up again, and I realized I'd hit Snooze instead of Dismiss. Irritated, I took it as a sign that I should probably head back home to the baseball house and deal with whatever shit was waiting for me there. Most likely a trashed house and passed-out teammates all over the place. All I knew was that no one had better be in my bedroom.

Tossing the covers off my body, I pressed my feet to the floor and held my head in my hands before cracking my neck and stretching.

"You're leaving, huh?" The sound of Sunny's groggy

voice pulled me out of my thoughts.

I hadn't meant to wake her.

"Morning, gorgeous," I said without thinking as I leaned over and planted a peck on the side of her head and then another on her cheek. "I have to go work out, hit, and take some ground balls."

"But it's Sunday."

"No days off," I said, letting her know how serious I took my sport.

If I didn't do something baseball-related every single day, I felt like a slacker. Like I was basically telling the baseball gods that I didn't want it bad enough and to give my spot to someone else. Someone who was willing to put in the work. An athlete who wanted it more than I did. And there wasn't anyone who wanted this more than me. So, I had to prove it. Seven days a week.

"No days off," she repeated without judgment, like the words were soaking into her skin as she processed them and my mindset.

"It's not an excuse, and I'm not trying to get away from you. This is my last season playing here. I have to give it everything I have. I can't quit now."

"I get it." She rolled over and faced me, her hand reaching out for my cheek. "I understand. You have to fight for your dreams."

Her smile was soft, her body warm, and part of me wanted to crawl back under the covers and hold her all day. But I couldn't.

"And I'm running out of time," I said again, the honesty

spilling from my mouth before I could stop it.

"Do you want me to drive you home?" she asked as she started to sit up, rubbing at her eyes with her fists.

"It's okay, babe. I'll call a car."

"But I can take you. Really."

"Go back to sleep. I'll call you later," I insisted before standing up, tucking the sheets tight around her so she couldn't move, and pressing another kiss to her forehead.

"Mac," she said my name like a promise, and I stared at her, taking in the silver strands of her hair spilling all around her pillow. It looked like stardust. "We're good, right? You and me, I mean."

My skin heated with her question. She was nervous, and I didn't blame her. I had been more than a little wishy-washy, and she was right not to trust me even though I knew she wanted to.

"Yeah, Sunny, we're good."

"Good." She smiled like she couldn't help it as she nuzzled back into her pillow. "I want to be with you, so let's just do that, okay?" she said through a yawn as her eyes closed, and I wasn't sure if she would remember that later or not.

She made it sound so simple, us being together. Hell, maybe it was for all I knew. Maybe it could be. Maybe simple was exactly how it was supposed to be.

Flinging open the door of Sunny's building, I stepped into the crisp morning air and bit down on one of the two cookies I'd taken with me. A little sugar would wake me right up. And since I was about to be wide awake, there was no sense in going back to the baseball house to do nothing but sit around and wait for one of them to drag their asses out of bed. Plus, the walk from the apartment to the baseball house was a little far, and I wasn't feeling it.

But Sunny's place was within easy walking distance to campus, and I decided to head over to the field house instead. The weight room would most likely be empty at this time, which was honestly how I preferred it. After I worked out, I'd text the guys and tell them to meet me for ground balls and tee work. They might still be passed out, but there was a slight possibility that Colin would be awake by the time I was done working out. If he wasn't, I'd do whatever I could on my own.

I pressed in my personalized code on the panel on the door, and the sound of it unlocking echoed in the otherwise empty space. Pulling the door open, I breathed out a sigh of relief that no one else was in here. Don't get me wrong; I liked my teammates, but I loved working out alone.

I went through my conditioning routine, which had been strictly planned out for me, focusing on explosive movements and speed. Anything that might boost my chances for the draft, I was willing to try. Anything legal, that was. I wasn't down for any sports-enhancing drugs or "safe" steroid. Not that they hadn't been offered to me in the past because they had, but I wasn't willing to risk getting kicked off the team and ruining my chances for good. Plus, I was scared that once you started something like that, how the hell did you stop?

Grabbing my phone, I turned off my music app and sent a group text to Colin, Dayton, and Matt. Colin responded, saying they'd be here in twenty.

I took my time re-racking the weights and wiping some

equipment down before I made my way toward the team fridge. It was always stocked, never empty. Ever. Which I knew would not be the case if we shared it with the football team. Thankfully, they had their own training facility and fridge stocked with food, so they left ours alone. All I was saying was, those guys knew how to eat. And they were always hungry.

I finished off the bottled ion-positive water I'd been drinking during my training and grabbed a post-workout drink to help hydrate and soothe my muscles. Taking a few long breaths to slow my heart rate down, I pulled on the fridge door and scanned the items inside. Deciding to forgo the usual protein shake—I'd had too much liquid already—I grabbed a bar and a hard-boiled egg instead. Cracking the egg on the small counter, I laughed to no one as I tried to peel the fucking thing. Why were the shells such a bitch to get off?

Sitting down on a bench, I waited for the guys to show up, no sounds at all around me, except my own.

Both doors flew open, slamming into the walls behind them, and I looked up to see Colin fresh-faced and Matt looking like hell.

"It's too early for this shit," Matt groaned as he moved his sunglasses on top of his head, over his hat.

"You wanna start or sit on the bench, Transfer?" I asked, pretending like I had any idea what Coach Jackson's plans were for Matt.

"Fuck you," he said, sliding his sunglasses back over his eyes. "And stop yelling."

I looked at Colin and let out a quick laugh.

"Someone's a little hungover," Colin said as he gripped Matt's shoulder and gave it a slap before giving me a fist pound in greeting.

"How are you not?" Matt asked Colin, seriously questioning how he was the only one who felt like death while the rest of us were okay. "And where were you anyway?" Matt directed the last question at me.

"What do you mean, where was I?" I started to ask before adding, "You don't remember falling, do you?"

"Falling?"

"I picked your ass up and tucked you in bed." I shook my head, and he looked at me like I was crazy.

"That didn't happen," he argued.

"Oh, it fucking happened," I emphasized, and he looked at Colin for confirmation.

Colin nodded.

"Shit. Well, thank you for taking care of me." He sounded so disappointed and sad. "I won't get that hammered again."

"You will," both Colin and I said at the same time as Matt walked to the cabinet and pulled out something for his headache.

"But Matt's not wrong. Where did you go? One second, you were there, and then I saw Hayley at your door, looking around, but no you," Colin added with a smirk, and I struggled to remember exactly how I'd left things when I went and chased after Sunny. All I could think about was getting to her.

"Please tell me Hayley was not in my room."

"She was," Colin said, his smirk turning into a frown. "But I made the bitch leave. Hope that was the right call."

Colin had been on the team when Hayley dumped me in front of everyone, so he knew our history and hated her for what she'd done.

"Thank you. Definitely the right call."

"She was pissed." He gave me a salty smirk. "I kinda enjoyed making her feel like shit."

Matt raised his hand in the air like he was in class and wanted to be called on. "Hayley's that super–smoking hot chick, right? Why do we like embarrassing her? What am I missing?"

"That's a story for another time. Here," I said, tossing a drink filled with electrolytes at him. "Drink that, and let's get to work."

"Does this have anything to do with Operation Sunny-Mac?" he said, and I pounded my chest with my fist as I coughed, remembering that he had said that last night as well.

"Operation what?" I asked, my eyes wide, no idea what the heck Matt was talking about.

"Operation SunnyMac?" he said the words again, only slower this time and more like a question. "Maybe I'm making it up. I don't know what I'm saying."

Matt waved me off, Colin looked at me and shrugged, and I let it go.

AFTER TWO HOURS outside, my stomach was grumbling, and

my body was sore. I was starved and dripping with sweat. It was well before noon, but it was already hot as hell outside. Welcome to fall in Southern California. It wasn't quite as hot as it was in Arizona, but the air was wetter here, and it felt heavier somehow.

"I'm so hungry," Matt said.

I nodded as we headed back inside toward the locker room. "Me too. Do we have any food at the house?" I asked.

Colin laughed. "After last night? I highly doubt it."

"Let's go to the store then. I'll buy," I said, patting my pocket like it was filled with cash when it was actually empty.

Dick Davies never gave me cash, only a credit card that I was to charge everything on—from groceries to baseball equipment and even my bar tabs. Something about write-offs and expenses that I only partially understood, mostly because I didn't care.

"You know, you never answered about where you ran off to." Colin nudged against my shoulder, acting like he knew something even though he wasn't coming out and saying it.

"Oh yeah. Did you hook up with Sunny or what?" Matt asked, and I felt my blood pressure rise. "I think I remember seeing her there last night. It's all kind of a blur. But does she have"—he stopped, holding his head between his hands—"silver hair now?"

"It doesn't matter what she has," I snapped. "She's off-limits." I practically bit his head off without meaning to.

"You already told me that," Matt said, sounding annoyed as we walked into the locker room and toward our stuff.

"Just making sure you remember."

Matt held up one finger. "Stay away from Sunny, the silver-haired goddess," he said before adding another finger. "Being mean to Hayley the smoke show is okay."

I laughed slightly before punching his shoulder. "You're an idiot."

"Why?" he whined. "That's what I've learned so far."

"Did you leave with her?" Colin asked again, a little too excited and clearly pushing me for info.

"Why do you care so much?" I pinned him with a glare, wondering why he was so concerned about Sunny and what I had—or hadn't—done with her. I didn't like it, but before I could say anything else, Coach walked in.

"Hey, guys." Coach Carter came into view with our other roommate Dayton trailing behind him, his eyes tired.

I hadn't even realized that Dayton was out here, throwing, but it made sense. He was as serious about baseball as I was.

"How long have you guys been here?" I asked.

"About forty minutes," Dayton answered as he took his hat off and wiped at his forehead. His face was red, and he looked like he might pass out as he grabbed a towel and walked to the sink to get it wet.

"I'm actually glad you're here, Coach," I said, looking at my best friend's dad. "Can I talk to you?"

"Of course," he said with a shrug.

The guys all gave me weird-ass looks. They had no idea what I was up to, and while it wasn't odd that I wanted to talk to Jack Carter, my best friend's dad, it was strange to do it here and now because he was the pitching coach, and ... well, I wasn't a pitcher.

I gave a nod toward the locker room exit before grabbing an extra drink I had and tossing it at Dayton. "Drink this before you die."

"What's up? Heard from Chance lately?" Coach Carter asked as we walked away from the group of guys, leaving them to whisper.

"I texted with him the other day. He seems really happy," I said, and Jack's face lit up.

He was one of the proudest and most supportive dads I'd ever met. I couldn't imagine.

"He does, doesn't he? I think it's that girl of his."

"I think it's everything," I said, hoping I didn't sound jealous or envious even though I was a little of both.

"Yeah, you're probably right," Coach agreed as the bright lights hit us. We were back outside, clear of any prying ears. "So, what'd you want to talk about?" He stopped walking, his arms folding in front of his chest as he looked down at me.

I decided to dive right in. I needed to know what the reality was this season and how hard I needed to push myself and in what capacity. Did I even have a shot? "It's about my future, Coach. As far as I know, there aren't any scouts asking Coach Jackson about me. There doesn't seem to be any interest, and I know that, usually, by now, if there were, I'd have some idea about it. Right?"

He pondered what I'd asked him, taking his time to formulate a response, and all it did was feed my nerves.

Was he wondering how to break the news to me that I didn't have a future in professional baseball?

"Mac, all I can tell you is that some guys have scouts

following them the second they get into college. Other guys don't. Hell, most guys don't. It isn't a death sentence for you, so don't give up. Just because it seems like you aren't on anyone's radar right now, it doesn't mean that's the truth. We don't always know what the scouts are up to. Coach Jackson and I will make sure your name gets out there, but you have to do the work. You have to make a name for yourself."

"I know." I swallowed hard before continuing, "And I've been doing all the right things, but should I be doing more? What if everything I'm doing just isn't enough?" I shifted my weight and started biting the back of my thumb. "You can tell me, Coach. I can take it. Just be honest."

I squeezed my eyes closed and waited for him to say that I didn't have what it took. I expected to hear it.

He clapped my back instead, forcing my eyes to open. "You're quick on your feet. You have the speed and a good eye at the plate. But you don't hit for power, and sometimes, that's all the teams are looking for in a season, you know?"

I knew he was right. There were so many nuances that went into each professional team. It was a business after all, and they had specific things they needed that changed after each season.

"You're a solid hitter, always getting on base and rarely striking out, which is impressive but not always enough. Look, Mac, I'm going to do my best to fight for you this season, but in the end, it's not up to me. And every other coach out there is going to be pulling for his own guys too. If you want a different perspective on things, you can always talk to my brother. I know he'd be willing to answer any questions you might have, and he knows way more about what's going on behind the scenes than I do."

Jack's brother, Dean Carter, was a sports agent—specifically, baseball. He was one of the best, and we all wanted to be repped by him. I knew that Dean was regularly in touch with the scouts and had firsthand knowledge on what they looked for and who they were currently looking at.

Nodding, I decided that maybe talking to Dean would be the right move.

"I might take you up on that. Thanks, Coach."

"I know it's hard, Mac," he started to say. "To be a senior and to feel like it's your last chance. When Cole was here, he told me that he always felt like he was running out of time. He said every day was like racing against a ticking clock that he couldn't stop. It haunted him. Just like I'm sure it's haunting you. And every other senior on the team who wants to keep playing after this year ends."

I felt instantly sick as my stomach churned.

The accuracy of what he'd said, of my old teammate Cole's words, were too much. They were fucking debilitating.

"Yeah. I don't know how to get that out of my head, and I'm afraid that if I play like I'm running out of time, I'll play desperate. And that will lead to errors."

"Desperation is the enemy of confidence," he said, and I stayed quiet. "It eats away at it until there's nothing left."

I knew he was right. Baseball was a mental game, and if your head got messed with, it was hard to recover. Every single time you were up to bat, the pitcher was trying to crush your spirit. It was a silent battle between you and him with every pitch he threw. And only one of you won. You either hit his pitch or he struck you out.

And each time you stepped onto the field, the batter or the base runner was trying to mess with your head to get you to screw up. Bobble a ball, make a throwing error, read the play wrong—the game had multiple outcomes, and you had to know them all.

Basically, once someone was in your dome, it was really easy to let them stay there. Some lucky players had the ability to shake things off like they hadn't even happened and move on. But most of us were affected by a bad at bat or an error on the field. We carried it with us into the following innings, like shoulder weights we couldn't drop. *Rattled* was the term we ballplayers used.

And I'd been rattled on more than one occasion. I knew it was a negative attribute for me as a player, and I wished I could let things go when I screwed up, but it was hard. I spent my time replaying what I'd done wrong, overanalyzing it to the point of exhaustion, but I made sure I never repeated the same mistake twice. It was a shitshow inside my head, and that was a bad thing.

"You okay?" Coach Carter cut through my thoughts, and I realized I hadn't heard anything he'd said.

"Just overthinking everything." I tried to laugh, but it came out strangled, and he offered me a strained smile.

"There's only so much you can control, Mac. There will always be a pitcher who wins the battle against you at the plate. Throws that curveball a little out of your reach and you go down swinging. And a hitter who slices it just right when you're in the field and you miss making that great catch. All you can do is be the best player you're capable of being. And be willing to get better."

"Thank you," I said, my head nodding in agreement even though my biggest takeaway from that entire conversation was, *I was right.*

There were no scouts asking or looking at me. If they were, Coach would know. And he would have told me. After the summer I'd had up in Washington, I'd figured I'd have at least one or two bites, but per usual, I was still hanging on to hopes and dreams that clearly weren't fucking holding on to me.

AND SO IT BEGINS

Sunny

I EVENTUALLY DRAGGED myself out of bed, thankful that I could still smell Mac in the air around me. Leaning back down, I smashed my face into the pillow he'd slept on and breathed deep as the memories of last night crashing into me like a dream.

But it wasn't a dream.

Mac had stayed the night. And it wasn't just to get into my pants. He hadn't even remotely gone there, and normally, I might have questioned what had gone wrong because guys usually at least TRIED to have sex with me but not this time.

Not with him.

Part of me wished instead of Mac leaving this morning, he'd stayed in bed with me, and then I could have spoiled him with pancakes and eggs and breakfast in bed, but once he'd told me *no days off*, I'd refused to argue or try to convince him otherwise. Mac needed to feel like he was giving baseball all of his time and energy, and as much as I wanted some of it as well, I was weirdly okay with taking a backseat.

It wasn't like he had blown me off for another girl or

anything. Hayley's face flashed in my mind, and I felt sick to my stomach, wondering if she had waited for him to get back to the baseball house all night long or not. The idea of her being anywhere near him made me violently angry, especially after learning what she'd done. I wasn't the type of person who usually walked around, hating on other girls, but this one deserved it. She'd humiliated someone I cared about. And even if I hadn't known Mac, what she had done was still horrible.

My phone rang, and my stomach flipped as I wondered if it was him, hoping it was. Disappointment panged for a second when I realized that it was only my mom. I walked back into my room and pulled open the curtains to let light flood in.

Plopping back down on my bed, I answered, my lips instantly curving into a smile when I heard the dogs barking in the background. I wasn't sure why, but my mom's self-imposed chaos always made me laugh.

"You really don't have to save every dog, you know?"

"If I don't, who will? Plus, Sun, you should see them! Oh my gosh, I have the fluffiest, waggiest Labs here right now," she said in a funny voice, and I knew she was probably smooshing their faces while she talked.

"You're going to drive Dad to drink."

"Your father loves me. And he basically asked me to become a crazy pet person when he opened up a vet clinic! I mean, what does he expect? I'm only so strong," she explained, and I decided that I couldn't argue with her logic even if I wanted to. There would be no point.

"So, what's up?" I asked, reminding her that she'd called me.

"Oh. Chloe! Get out of the sink! Seriously! Out, out!" she yelled, and I heard things clatter in the background.

"Mom!" I shouted, wanting to get her attention.

"Maybe I did bring too many home," she said in a hushed whisper. "I don't want them to hear me and get their feelings hurt."

Slapping my palm to my head, I dragged my hand across my face and waited for her to tell me whatever it was that she'd called for. At this rate, we'd be on the phone until dinner.

"Mom!"

"Sorry, sorry. Okay. I was calling about Thanksgiving."

"What?" I shook my head because it was still well over a month away. "It's not even Halloween yet."

"I just wanted to make sure you were planning on coming home still."

"Where else would I go?" I asked because I hadn't missed a single Thanksgiving at home since moving out. I even brought Danika home with me every year. It had become a tradition of sorts between us.

"I don't know. Maybe Danika's? I was just asking since you two used to always come here and you always called it *your* holiday," she reminded me.

Danika and I'd started claiming the day as *ours* freshman year. No boys, no boyfriends—including her ex, Jared—and no other friends. Just us. And we looked forward to it each year. I hadn't even thought about it yet because it was still so early, but I was sure once November 1 rolled around, I'd have gone through withdrawals or something.

"Oh, well ..." It hadn't occurred to me that I could go

somewhere else ... not actually go to my parents' for a holiday. But now that she'd brought up Danika's name, I wondered if seeing her was even possible. That would be awesome, and now, it was all I wanted to do.

"Oh, what?" my mom snarked, calling me out.

"I don't know, but now that you mention it, I kinda want to go see her."

"I knew it," she snapped, making a clicking sound over the line.

"You brought it up!" I shouted playfully. "And it's not like I won't be home for Christmas. I'd never miss Christmas."

"I know you wouldn't. And that's why I wanted to ask. Because if you go to Danika's and your sister goes to Todd's, I might convince your father to take me on a cruise." She sounded excited even though we both knew that the chances of it actually happening were slim.

"How are you going to do that? You know Dad doesn't like to leave his patients, especially during the holidays."

"Well, Miss Smarty-Pants," she started, "I've been talking with the pet hospital so that we can work on recommending our patients to one another. A symbiotic partnership that serves us both. If we go on a vacation, our patients can go to the hospital if they have an emergency. Your father is not supposed to be on call twenty-four hours a day. No other vet clinic does that."

I knew all of this. It was the one point of contention in my parents' relationship. The fact that my father worked way too hard and cared way too much. He would forgo anything for himself if it meant that his patients were in good hands—aka his own.

"I think it's a good idea. If you need any help convincing Dad, I'm in."

"I knew I could count on you. Your sister agreed too. I've already started secretly plotting," she said, whispering again.

I wondered what she was up to. "What have you been doing?"

"Telling the patients that if it's after hours, they should call the hospital instead of your father. That they're already up and running and equipped to handle any emergency. I even had your sister update the website."

"And Dad has no idea?" I asked because once he found out, he was going to be pissed.

"Not yet, but he is getting suspicious, I think. He keeps complaining about how quiet it's been at night lately with no phone calls."

"Hmm," I said because my dad was smarter than that. "Careful, Mom. You're gonna get caught."

"Hush. Don't put that out in the universe. Think about my Mexico cruise instead."

Another crash in the background, followed by a howl and incessant barking, let me know what was coming next.

"Sunny, gotta go."

And just like that, the call ended. I laughed, shaking my head to no one but myself as I thought about how crazy my mom was but how much I loved her. I hoped that when my dad found out what she had been doing, he wouldn't be too upset with her and would understand that she was only looking out for him and the clinic's best interests. Eventually, he'd have to stop being on call anyway. It wasn't realistic, long-term.

Opening the Calendar app in my phone, I set a reminder to myself to call Danika and talk about the possibility of having Thanksgiving together. Obviously, the *no boys* rule would be thrown out the window, but maybe Mac and I would be in a good enough place that we could go see them together. I felt my cheeks flush at the idea and how badly I wanted it to happen.

I WANTED TO head over to the campus bookstore and look at all of their stuff. I'd never ended up checking it out that one time because I ran into Mac when I was trying to avoid him. After a quick shower, I tossed my silver hair into a messy bun and headed out my front door, slamming it way too hard instead of simply closing it like a normal person.

Rocky instantly appeared in the hallway. "Didn't your mama ever teach you how to close doors?" she chastised.

"What if I said no?" I questioned, and she smiled. At least, I thought it was a smile.

"Where are you off to? Is that hot baseball player still in there?" She gave a nod toward my now-closed door.

"You think Mac's hot?" I asked, assuming that someone like Mac wouldn't even be on someone like Rocky's hot-boy radar. He didn't seem like her type.

"For a jock," she explained, "but I'm not interested, so don't worry."

Laughing, I finished locking the dead bolt and met her in the middle between our respective apartments. "I'm going to campus. I want some stuff from the bookstore, and they're having a sale. They have cute clothes sometimes."

Her nose crinkled, and I noticed a small stud piercing that I hadn't seen last night.

"Cute clothes?"

"You know, like Fullton State sweatshirts and hoodies. Pens and pencils with the school name on it. Little notebooks and stickers," I continued explaining, but her face only grew more confused. "I have school spirit, okay?"

"Uh-huh. Someone has to make sure you don't buy all the Fullton State Baseball shirts. I'm coming with you," she informed me, like I didn't have a choice in the matter, but at least now, I knew she was a student there too. Or at least, I assumed she was.

"Do you even go there?" I questioned, feeling a little stupid for asking, but the truth was that she could go to one of the other schools nearby.

Fullton State wasn't the only university in the vicinity, and so far, I hadn't seen her leaving her apartment once to head in the same direction as me.

"Does it matter?"

Her response caught me off guard.

"I guess not."

"What if I said no?"

I shrugged. "I don't know."

She tossed me a look over her shoulder. "I go to school there. I'll be right back."

As she disappeared behind her own door, I stood and waited for all of ten seconds before she reappeared.

"I'm ready. Just needed to turn off the TV."

"Aren't you going to lock your door?" I asked, freaking out that she would just leave it unlocked without a second thought. *What if someone comes in while we're gone?*

"No."

"Do you live alone?"

"What do you think?" she asked, her tone almost comical.

I took stock of her demeanor as we walked toward the parking lot. "Yesss?" I said, dragging out the word because I had no idea if she lived alone or not, and how was I supposed to know just by looking at her?

"Yes. It's easier."

"What is?"

"Living by yourself. Keep up, Sunshine."

"How is it easier?" I asked, hoping she wouldn't bite my head off.

Rocky was a little aggressive. Or maybe it was the fact that her edges seemed more than a little rough.

"No one gets mad if you leave dishes in the sink. Or don't take out the trash. Or for doing whatever the hell you want to do," she said as I pointed at my car door and unlocked it with the remote. Rocky pulled the passenger door open. "You don't have to take anyone else's opinion into consideration for how you choose to live."

I listened as I walked to the driver's side of my car, but I couldn't really relate. It hadn't been like that with Danika and me when we lived together. It had been easy but probably because we had similar ways of living. I might have felt differently if all we'd done was argue and fight over things, like Rocky had talked about.

"Baseball player sit here?" Rocky asked as she fumbled around with the seat to raise it. I hadn't even noticed how far back Mac had reclined. "Why do guys always put the seat back as far as it will go? I've never understood that."

"You're weird," was my only response.

"Thanks. You are too," she said, and I smiled.

"Taking that as a compliment," I tossed toward her and started driving.

"I meant it as one."

Rocky switched the radio station from the pop channel it was on to an alternative one and then turned the volume up without asking. I glanced at her, but she was expressionless. Most people wouldn't touch someone's radio without asking permission, but I was quickly learning that Rocky wasn't most people.

"I like your hair, by the way," I said, and she pulled at the short strands, twisting a bright green one between two fingers.

"Thanks. I'm getting tired of it though. It's been this color for too long. I was thinking blue next," she said.

I wondered how people could color their hair like that and not have it fall out. I had been scared to death to try the silver.

"Do you color it yourself?"

"Yep," she said, popping the P. "I like your new hair too. It's way better than the blonde."

"Thanks," I said as we pulled into the short-term parking lot nearest the bookstore, and I searched for an open spot. "It's a madhouse," I breathed out. "Why is it so crowded on a Sunday? I'll never find a space."

"We should have walked," Rocky said, and I choked on a laugh.

"You don't really seem like the walking type." I motioned toward the unlaced combat boots on her feet.

"I walk. And they can be tied, you know."

"Well, we should have walked then."

"Nah," she disagreed before pointing a finger straight ahead. "Look."

I watched as brake lights appeared, followed by the white reverse lights, and the car started to back up. Stepping on the gas, I threw both of our bodies into our seats with the force. No one was going to beat me to that spot.

Putting on my blinker, I waited patiently for the car to shift out of reverse and move forward before I started ahead. Before they could get out of my way completely, a white BMW sped in front of them from the opposite direction, cutting them off, and pulled into the empty space. They'd almost caused an accident. And they had taken my damn space.

"Are you kidding me?" I honked my horn and then laid on it like a madwoman, half-convinced I might never stop honking. I was pissed.

Everyone, except the driver, piled out of the car, acting like nothing had happened, like they hadn't just stolen the spot I had been patiently waiting for and like I wasn't blaring my car horn at them. Moving behind their car and blocking them in, I put my own vehicle in park before opening the door and hopping out, ready to confront the driver.

"Hey. I was waiting for that spot."

The driver's door opened, and out stepped Hayley, Mac's ex-girlfriend, looking unaffected and bored.

"Figures it would be you." I tried to sound tough as I stopped myself from clawing out her extensions and shoving them down her throat.

She looked down her nose at me, like I was nothing, before pushing her sunglasses back up on her face. "Why are you talking to me?"

"I was waiting for that spot, and you know it," I said, losing what little cool I had left. "Now, get back in your car and move out of my way."

Hayley huffed out a laugh. "Parking for peasants is around the corner somewhere." She wagged a finger in the air.

"Where's the parking for bitches then? That's where you should be," Rocky said, suddenly standing by my side, empowering me even more.

"Nice hair. Your mom color it for you with a crayon?" Hayley bit back, and her group of cronies giggled.

"Nice tits. Your mom buy them for you at the discount store?" Rocky cocked her head to the side, studying them. "I think they're uneven."

Hayley looked down at her chest, her mouth agape, and I let out a loud laugh as her friends gasped and immediately went to work, reassuring Hayley that her boobs weren't lopsided.

Hayley's face reddened, but before she could formulate a

response, I stepped toward her, feeling insanely justified in my anger. "Move. Your. Car."

"Or what?"

That was the million-dollar question. *What the heck am I going to do if she doesn't move it?*

"Do I look stable to you?" Rocky asked, her eyes narrowing.

Hayley actually looked uncomfortable for a millisecond before regaining her composure.

"Why don't you call off your girlfriend, sweetie?" Hayley said in my direction. "Or should I call Mac and tell him to come fetch his pet?" she asked, holding her cell phone in the air, and my stomach dropped at the mention of his name.

"Like he'd answer your calls. He hates you."

Her perfectly made-up lips curled into a smile as she lifted her sunglasses on top of her head. "Oh, honey. The last thing Mac feels for me is hate, and we both know it. He chased after you last night because he felt sorry for you. But he's been chasing me for the past three years because he's in love with me. He's not going to stop until he gets me back. You never really get over your first love, don't you agree?"

My insides twisted with every foul word that spilled from her mouth. I didn't want to believe them, but I wasn't *that* secure in whatever the hell Mac and I had started. Her venom had done its job. It injected itself inside of my bloodstream and floated around in there, making me question everything. Maybe Mac really wasn't over her regardless of what he'd said to me. Maybe he never would be.

"The guy I saw last night definitely wasn't in love with

you or even thinking about you," Rocky said. This girl was quickly becoming my new favorite person.

"I don't expect you, of all people, to understand. Nice to see you found someone more your type to play with," Hayley bit back.

I looked at Rocky, wondering what she meant. *Do they know each other?*

"I'll tell you later," Rocky all but whispered.

"Tell her now, sister," Hayley said.

I almost lost my balance as I looked between the two of them, horrified. They looked nothing alike, but neither did me and my sister. No one knew that we were related until we told them. And even then, they still questioned it.

"You're not my sister," Rocky snarled.

"Not anymore," Hayley said as she palmed her phone and pressed a button before holding it up to her ear. "Heyyyy, babe," she cooed, and I knew it could only mean one thing—she'd called Mac, and he'd actually answered. "Your little friend from last night is here, giving me a hard time. Put her in her place, love, or I'll do it for the both of us."

Ending the call, she stared directly at me, and I wondered if she'd faked the whole thing. Maybe she hadn't called Mac at all. Maybe he hadn't really answered. I was just thinking how I wouldn't put it past her to lie when my phone vibrated in my back pocket. Pulling it out and looking at the screen, I noticed one unread text from Mac.

Pressing on the notification, it read, *Why are you with Hayley? Get away from her, Sunny. I mean it.*

The blood drained from my face. *He's defending her?*

After everything he told me that happened between them, he's telling me to get away from her?

"Good luck with that parking spot, peasant," Hayley said with an evil grin as she locked arms with her group of heathens and walked away without another word.

"How do you know her?" I asked Rocky the second they were out of earshot.

"We used to be in the same sorority," Rocky begrudgingly admitted.

I swore my eyes bugged out of my head. "You were not in a sorority."

Rocky didn't seem like the kind of girl to join anything, let alone the most feminine girl club on a college campus.

"It didn't last long. I moved here, not knowing anyone, and stupidly thought joining a girl gang would be fun," she explained, and I hung on every word. "Spoiler alert: it wasn't."

"Not to be a bitch, but," I started, and she focused her dark eyes on me, her black eyeliner winged to perfection, "you don't seem like their type."

I knew that most sororities were known for certain things on campus, and they tended to recruit girls who fit their agenda, whether it was being one of the hottest or smartest girls at school or coming from a rich family.

Reaching both hands into her hair, she shook it around. "Is it the hair?"

Laughing, I made a face. "Among other things," I said, looking down at her still-untied combat boots and baggy, oversize cargo pants.

"I looked a little different as a freshman. I hadn't started coloring my hair yet. But you're right; I definitely did not check all the boxes on their checklist. But joining made my mom happy."

"So, what made you leave?"

"I overheard Hayley one day saying that I was a freak but that they needed me for my GPA. The rest of the girls agreed, calling me unstable and shit. So, I went out and dyed my hair black and purple that afternoon, hoping it might give Hayley a heart attack the next time she saw me."

"Obviously, that didn't work"—I made a face—" 'cause she's still alive and all."

"Yeah, but boy, was she pissed. It was worth it."

A car horn honked, and I'd forgotten all about the fact that I was blocking not only Hayley's car in her space, but someone else's as well.

"Are you leaving?" I asked the person honking, and he nodded. "If anyone tries to take that spot, I'm going to war."

Rocky saluted me. "I'll stand guard."

After nabbing that space, I got out and locked the doors, my wheels still spinning about learning that Rocky had been in a sorority with Hayley and the fact that Mac had texted me, clearly taking Hayley's side. "Can I ask you something?"

"No," she said, and I let out an uncomfortable laugh. "I'm joking. Ask away."

"Were you around when Hayley started dating Mac?"

Rocky's eyes pinched together. "Not when they were together, no. But I remember her talking about him."

"Talking about him how?" My curiosity was through the proverbial roof. I wanted to know every single thing about this topic. I didn't trust Hayley, and if I was going to be with Mac, I needed to know what my enemy was capable of.

"Hayley always has her eye on someone. She plots when it comes to guys. Makes lists. Mac was on that list. She has a reason for everything she does, Sunny. She's calculating and calculated."

I swallowed hard around that tidbit of knowledge. "Good to know," I said, but I wasn't sure I meant it. I wasn't sure at all.

THE BASEBALL GODS HATE ME

Mac

I'D FALLEN INTO a dark hole after my talk with Coach Carter this morning. I got like that sometimes, where I just wanted to be left the fuck alone so I could think. I didn't want to talk it out, analyze my feelings, or break down what Coach had said into bite-sized pieces so I could digest it and work through it all.

No.

I just wanted to fucking sulk and feel sorry for myself. And be jealous of everyone else who had already gotten what I was still trying to get. I couldn't help it. I compared myself to other players, feeling like I was just as good as they were, if not better. If they had gotten drafted in their junior year, then why hadn't I?

But baseball wasn't that easy, and I knew it. It wasn't a black-and-white situation. There were unspoken rules and metrics and so much that went on behind the scenes that none of us could even fathom from the outside. We all knew that Major League scouts ranked us on five things—our running speed, arm strength, fielding and footwork, hitting, and hitting for power—even though no player *ever* had all five things going for him. The typical player excelled in three of the five categories ... sometimes only in two.

I hated when I got this way, all stuck in my head and bitter. And although I knew that the negative thoughts would eventually fade, while I was in the thick of it, it was really hard to pull myself out of it. See, when you found something that made you feel valuable, the last thing you wanted to do was give it up without a fight.

My phone rang, and I saw Hayley's name flash on the screen. I debated on not answering it, but I was in such a fucked up mood anyway, I figured, *Why not?* And I instantly regretted it.

She mentioned my friend from last night, and I knew immediately that she was talking about Sunny. My sweet fucking angel of stardust and light. Hayley sounded vindictive over the phone, and my protective instincts flared to life. Sunny needed to get the hell away from her.

I had no idea what Hayley was truly capable of, but I didn't trust her as far as I could throw her. Maybe even less. So, when she basically threatened Sunny, I freaked out and sent her a text, telling her to get away from Hayley and leave her alone. It was the first thing that had come to my mind, and I'd sent it without a second thought. Sunny didn't respond, but I saw that she'd read it and hoped like hell she'd listen to me.

"Davies!" A loud knock on my bedroom door irritated me.

"What?" I grumbled, refusing to move out of bed.

"I'm coming in," Dayton said before opening my door and hitting the light switch.

Groaning, I covered my eyes with my hat, willing the light to turn itself back off.

"You haven't come out of your room in hours. I just wanted to make sure you weren't dead."

Slowly removing the hat, I gave him a head nod. "I'm not dead. Just a little tired."

"Don't bullshit me, man. I saw you talking to Coach Carter. You've been in a bad mood ever since. What happened?"

I pushed to a sitting position, pressing my back against the wall. "Nothing. I just asked him a few questions, and he gave me the answers."

Dayton's face pulled together, and his eyes narrowed. "I know you're stressed because it's our senior year. Cole was the same way, remember? And look what happened for him."

I'd thought about Cole Anders a thousand times since I'd landed at the airport for my last year here. I remembered how shaken up he had been about having to come back to the field as a senior. At the time, I'd thought he was overreacting … making a mountain out of a molehill, so to speak, but now, I completely understood how he'd felt.

"You think I'm not worried?" Dayton asked, his expression as sour as this conversation was turning.

A sick laugh ripped from my throat. "You're a pitcher. You'll be fine."

Major League teams drafted guys like him the most because they needed a lot of pitching on their staff at every level. My being a corner infielder made my chances even slimmer. Maybe a team only had an opening for one first baseman. Or maybe they thought someone who played second base would be a better fit at first instead because he had a stronger, more powerful bat. I had a different set of rules to abide by in order to be deemed "good enough for scouts to watch and follow," all because I played first base.

"Dude, come on," Dayton disagreed, knowing that his getting drafted wasn't a guarantee the way I was acting like it was.

"I know. I'm sorry." I shot him a look. "I'm just freaking out and feeling bad for myself."

"I get it. Trust me, I do." He looked around the room like he was seeing it for the first time. "But you're a good player, Mac. And you keep getting better every season."

I perked up a little, gripping his words and holding on to them like a life preserver. "You really think so?"

"Yes! Every year, you get stronger, faster, and more confident on the field, and it shows."

He hadn't mentioned my batting. And if we were being honest, the plate was where I tended to struggle the most—and not because I wasn't a great hitter. I just wasn't the guy who was going to slap out ten home runs a season. Or any home runs, honestly. I got on base a lot, rarely struck out, walked often, but if you needed me to hit for power, it wasn't going to happen. And that wasn't necessarily a good thing even though my stats looked great on paper.

Swallowing hard, I gave him a smile. "Thanks, Dayton. I needed that."

Waving his fingers toward himself, he closed his eyes and grinned. "Now, give me some."

"You're going to be our Friday night starter this year. You don't need shit. You're gonna kill it," I said, and I meant it.

Dayton had been working with Coach Carter to hit his spots and be as accurate as possible with his pitches. He was hard as hell to hit when he was *on*, and I knew that once he got drafted, he would just keep getting better.

"Thanks. Now, get out here and eat dinner with your boys. Matt made some mac-and-cheese thing that's actually pretty good." He gave his stomach a pat. "Kinda nice that he can cook."

My stomach growled in response. "No shit? I'll be right out." Dayton turned to leave but not before I stopped him. "Thanks for coming in and checking on me."

"You'd do the same for me," he said.

And I knew that; of course I would. Always. We were teammates, brothers, two seniors fighting for our last chance to get it right, knowing that all we could continue doing was give baseball our hearts and hope like hell she didn't break them.

I WOKE UP the next morning, feeling a hundred times better. Sometimes, a good sleep was all I needed to get out of a shit mood. As I stretched, I reached for my phone, realizing that Sunny had never texted or called me last night and I'd completely forgotten to call her, like I'd promised. I'd been too busy wallowing in my own self-induced misery to think about anything other than myself. She was probably pissed. I planned on finding her today, hearing exactly what had happened between her and Hayley, and then apologizing to her ... *again*. I had a feeling that I was going to find myself fluent in groveling whenever it came to this girl.

After a hearty breakfast, the guys and I all piled into one car and drove toward campus. I hustled toward my building up in the distance. I still had ten minutes before class started, but I knew that wasn't always enough time when you were a baseball player at Fullton. We got pulled in all different directions, and what should be a quick walk across campus never was. It could turn into a fifteen-minute flirting and picture-taking session without warning.

With my head down, I yanked open the door to the four-story building and walked inside. Taking the stairs two at a time, I ignored the girls grabbing my arms and calling my name as I walked toward the right classroom number on the third floor. Spotting it up ahead, I slowed my pace and waltzed through the open double doors. Fullton didn't have a lot of theater-type lecture classes, but this was one of them. There were about two hundred seats that framed a small curved stage up front. An actual real-life stage. I'd never been in a classroom like this in all my years here.

As I looked around, I noticed a few girls staring in my direction, smiling and smacking their lips together; some were even pointing their phones at me. Not wanting to give anyone the wrong idea by sitting next to them, listening to them flirt the entire time, I'd been changing my seat each time I came to class. I breathed out a sigh of relief when I noticed one of the guys from the basketball team sitting in the far corner of the room. I made my way toward him, and he tossed his hand in the air when he noticed me approaching.

"Mac, my man. Thank God. How are you?" he asked, and I slapped his hand before giving him a knuckle bump and sitting down next to him.

"I'm good. How are you, Harvey?" I asked, calling him by his last name.

"I was worried no one I knew would be in this class. You see the size of this thing?" He sounded overwhelmed and a little nervous.

"Did you just transfer in?" I asked because he hadn't been in here until now. Or at least, I hadn't seen him before.

"Yeah. Today's the last day to drop and add. Another class of mine was not going to work if I wanted to play this season," he explained, and I nodded along in complete understanding.

"Glad you're in here. Let me know if you need any help," I offered, and he actually looked a little relieved.

"Thanks. How does the professor teach in this thing?" he asked, still clearly bewildered by the size of the class. "Do they shout the entire time?"

"She wears a mic," I explained.

Harvey leaned his head back and blew out a breath toward the tiled ceiling. "Ohh, that makes sense."

"Excuse me."

The familiar voice hit my ear like a two-by-four to the face, and I turned to see Hayley the devil standing there, staring down at the two of us.

You have got to be shitting me.

"Can I sit there?" She pointed at the open seat next to me, and before I could tell Harvey that I'd kill him if he said yes, he was standing up and letting her pass, staring at her ass as she walked by.

"Sure you don't want to sit here?" He patted his lap, and she gave him the world's fakest grin.

"I'm sure, basketball player. Baseball's more my thing anyway." She bit her lip, and Harvey clutched his heart like he was in pain.

"You wound me with your words," he said.

I shot him a look that should have killed him on the spot but didn't. He obviously didn't know my and Hayley's history, or he wouldn't have gotten up for her.

"There are, like, a hundred other seats in this class. Why can't you sit in one of them?" I snarled toward her as she sat down. Shifting my body away from hers, I practically leaned on Harvey's shoulder like a love-struck teenage girl.

"Damn, bro." Harvey laughed under his breath and gave me a slight shove.

"I want to sit near you." She tried to sound sexy, but she was fucking annoying. A point I'd thought I'd made clear the night of the party.

"I'd rather you didn't," I said rudely. "I want nothing to do with you."

Everything I'd told her the other night wasn't because I was drunk or for any other reason she might have concocted in her head. I'd meant every word I said.

"Come on, Mac," she said before putting her hand on my shoulder, and I glared at it. "Don't be like that. I just got into this class, and imagine my surprise, seeing you here. It's fate."

"It's fucked," I spat. "Sorry, man." I sat up straight and looked at Harvey before rising to my feet. "I gotta move since Satan here won't." I thumbed toward Hayley, who sat there with a shocked look on her face as I gathered my shit.

I refused to sit next to her for a single minute, let alone an entire sixty-minute class.

"Wait up," Harvey said as he grabbed his backpack and followed me down to the middle of the auditorium, leaving Hayley alone in the back, where she could drown in her own misery for all I cared. "What was that all about? She's hot as fuck."

"So's the Devil, and I'm pretty sure they're related," I said.

He busted out laughing right as our professor entered the lecture hall.

"What's so funny? Anything you'd care to share with the class?" the professor asked through the microphone on her jacket, her voice booming throughout the theater.

Harvey started choking, smacking his chest, while I sat there, mortified that the teacher had called him out like that.

"Okay then, let's get to it," the professor said, moving on, and Harvey and I were quiet through the rest of the class.

EX FROM HELL

Sunny

MAC NEVER CALLED me last night, like he'd promised. And when I never responded to his shitty text, demanding I stay away from Hayley, he never sent another. I'd spent the whole night trying not to be mad at him, but I was. I felt stupid for falling for his bullshit again.

And now, here I was, standing twenty feet away from Mac and Hayley, watching them with equal parts interest and fire-breathing jealousy. And I wasn't the only one. The two of them together had created a bit of a scene. I noticed quite a few people paying attention to their interaction, watching their every move like they were afraid to miss something good.

I had been walking from class toward the commissary for some coffee when Mac's figure caught my eye. I knew it was him from just a glance, and I planned on continuing my quest for caffeine, but when I saw Hayley with him, I stopped walking and started watching. For such a big campus, it felt like some sort of sick sign for me to run into them like this. Almost like the universe had wanted me to see them together. I fought the urge to leave but felt rooted in place even though the scene was making me sick.

When her hands gripped his arms, I wanted to run over there and rip them off. My breath caught in my throat when Mac did it for me. He pulled out of her grasp and looked down at his arms like they were on fire. He flailed around like an animated figure, pointing and shaking his head at her. And each time she took a step toward him, he took a step back.

"Told you she had a plan." Rocky suddenly appeared at my side, eating a banana and watching my nightmare unfold before our eyes.

"She makes me ragey," I said, balling my hands into fists, wondering how Rocky had found me in the first place. This morning, I seemed to be running into everyone I normally never saw.

"She has that effect," she said before finishing off the fruit and holding the peel with two fingers. "You should go over there."

I whipped my head in her direction. "What? No way. Why would I do that?"

Rocky shrugged. " 'Cause it would be fun to watch you put her in her place."

After giving her a playful shove, I second-guessed myself the second she turned toward me with an unsure look in her eyes. I threw both hands in the air. "Sorry. I was just playing. Don't shove me back," I said, thinking that she might send me into the next zip code.

She laughed and was about to speak when a loud bang echoed out of nowhere, quickly followed by another. Rocky instantly fell to the ground, her hands covering the back of her head.

What the hell?

I frantically looked around, noticing everyone else in various states of alarm. Some people had started running, and others were searching for the location of the sound, seemingly frozen in place.

I was one of them. Frozen yet searching.

"Rocky?" I looked down at her and realized that she was shaking like crazy. "Rocky, are you okay?" I got nervous, wondering if she had gotten hurt somehow and I just hadn't seen it.

She looked up at me, her eyes glossed over with unshed tears as she extended her hand. "What was that?"

Checking around once more, I saw that someone had kicked over a metal construction barricade. It was lying on its side, still reverberating from the impact. Reaching for her hand, I pointed in the direction of the downed piece of equipment just as two guys ran up to it and tried to get it to stand back upright.

She wiped at her eyes and tried to control her erratic breathing. "I thought it was a gun," she said.

I realized in that moment that it had actually sounded like one. We unfortunately lived during a time when someone bringing a gun to school was an absolute possibility even if you never thought it would happen to you.

"Sunny? Rocky?" It was Mac. He yelled our names as he jogged across the pavement toward us. "That scared the shit out of me. Are you two all right?"

"It was just a barricade," I said, trying to sound like it was no big deal. "You can go back to your ex-girlfriend." I waved a hand toward Hayley, who was staring intently in our direction, looking like someone had pissed in her Cheerios.

"Fuck Hayley," Mac said sharply. "Rocky, you good?"

He wrapped an arm around her and pulled her to her feet. She was unsteady, and he instinctively held her tightly against his body, basically holding her up as she continued to tremble uncontrollably against him.

She shook her head, her breaths catching. "Do you think one of you could take me home?" She started crying, clearly shaken up.

Before this moment, I wouldn't have believed that Rocky was scared of anything.

"I don't have a car," Mac said before I could respond.

"You ... can drive ... mine," Rocky offered in between sobs.

"I've got her," I interrupted. "Go back to whatever it was you were doing, Mac. I can handle this," I snapped at him even though he had shown everyone watching that he didn't want Hayley. Apparently, I was angry anyway.

I pulled Rocky out of his grip and took her in mine. Before I could lead her away, a hand was on my shoulder, stopping me.

"Sunny, there's nothing going on between me and Satan," he said, and I would have laughed if I wasn't so worried about Rocky's emotional state.

"I need to go," I insisted, gripping Rocky tighter than I meant to, and she whispered, "Ow," under her breath.

"I'm coming with you," Mac said, and before I could

argue, he had Rocky in his arms again. "Which way's your car, beautiful?" He was trying to distract her, and I thought it was working until she pointed her finger toward the parking lot and I noticed how violently her hand was shaking.

We walked together, the three of us in relative silence. Mac and I shared confused looks as the tears fell from Rocky's eyes without stopping. We searched for her car. She pressed the key fob, and we listened for the sound of her horn.

"It's right there." She nodded toward an old red Mustang before dropping the keys into Mac's open hand.

"That's your ride? You're even more of a badass than I thought you were," Mac said with a grin, and Rocky tried to smile but couldn't.

I watched as Mac placed her in the passenger seat and buckled her in. He looked like he'd done this before, taken care of someone who couldn't take care of themself. We both raced toward the driver's side even though Mac had the keys.

"I'll drive," he said before pulling up the seat so I could get in back.

"Do you even know how?" I asked because I knew that he didn't have a car here but I didn't know why.

He smirked. "Do I know how to drive? Yeah, babe, I have my license and everything," he teased before helping me into the backseat. He waited for me to put my seat belt on before he even turned the engine over.

Billie Eilish blared through the speakers, and Mac instantly turned the volume down to almost nothing.

Rocky was in a world of her own, her tears still falling with abandon whether or not she wanted them to. I wanted to talk to her, ask her if she was okay, but I decided to wait until we got her into her apartment. I sensed that she needed to feel like she was in a safe place, not on the road or out in the open. It took us no time at all to get to our complex, and by then, Rocky could walk on her own without me or Mac assisting her, although Mac refused to leave her side, just in case.

"I'm sorry, you guys." Rocky blinked rapidly a few times, looking like she was embarrassed or ashamed by her reaction.

"Don't apologize," Mac said reassuringly.

"Yeah. I'm just glad we were there. Are you okay?" I asked as I opened the main building's door, and we trekked down the long hallway toward both of our apartments.

She nodded before changing her mind and shaking her head instead. "Not really," she started to explain as she opened her front door and held it open for us to follow.

Her apartment was the exact same floor plan as mine, but she barely had anything in it. Nothing decorated her walls with the exception of a pair of elaborate and large cast iron candelabras, which were absolutely stunning, framing the patio doors. They looked like something stolen straight out of a real-life castle, and now, all I wanted was to see them lit.

Rocky blew out a long breath as she walked into her kitchen and filled a glass with water from a pitcher in her fridge. Mac and I watched her down the entire thing before she looked at us, her eyes still glassy and swollen.

"I was in a shooting," she said.

I felt my heart drop. I couldn't even imagine how terrifying something like that must have been even though I'd thought about it before. You couldn't live in this day and age without having it at least cross your mind once or twice.

The tears started falling from her eyes again, but I wasn't even sure she noticed.

"I was a senior in high school. My brother came home from college for the weekend because he wanted me to go to some Halloween haunt thing with him at the local amusement park. You know what I'm talking about?"

She focused on me as I said, "Yeah. Like at Knott's Berry Farm out here?"

"Exactly." She sniffed and wiped at her face with the back of her hand. "We both love scary movies and stuff," she said with a slight laugh. "Anyway, we were in line for a ride when the shooting started. At first, you don't have any idea what the sound is because your brain is so focused on the fact that it's something that doesn't belong, and it doesn't process what it might actually be."

The sound of her voice was enough to make me break down in tears myself, just from listening to her.

"I remember that shooting," Mac said, sounding as heartbroken as I was.

"You start making excuses to explain what you're hearing. Like maybe it was a ride or a special effect or fireworks or something. You never once think it's a gun. At least, I didn't. But then everyone started running toward us. I mean, swarms of people like you can't even imagine, all running the same direction, screaming that there was a shooter." She refilled her glass and took a small sip. "My brother grabbed my hand, looked me in the eyes, and told me to run. I'd never heard that tone in his voice before. There was all this smoke from the smoke machines, and it was, like, pitch-black. I mean, none of the normal lights were on because it was a Horror Night thing, but they never turned them on. Not even while someone was shooting. They kept us in the dark to fend for ourselves as we tried not to die."

I gripped the side of the counter for balance, knowing that Rocky was reliving this moment in excruciating detail as she explained it to us, and I hoped like hell her brother hadn't been killed.

"We ran, hearing the pops behind us, around us, everywhere. The girl next to me fell, and to this day, I have no idea if she tripped on something or if she got shot because I couldn't fucking see anything, you know? My brother said we couldn't stop until we got outside. No matter what. He never let go of my hand. Not even when we were both so coated in sweat that we shouldn't have been able to grip anything, let alone each other."

More tears fell, and she wiped her eyes with the back of her sleeve and started sucking in small breaths. "So, that's why I got so scared today. I thought there was another shooter. And I haven't been this triggered in a long time."

"Is your brother okay?" I asked, remembering all about that shooting and how unbelievable it was that it'd happened at an amusement park. It emphasized the fact that absolutely nowhere was safe anymore. Not when someone had it in their mind that they wanted to kill people. All it took was a gun and some ammunition.

"Yeah. I mean, he has flashbacks, and we both get triggered by loud noises and crowds. The biggest change for him though was that he used to like to hunt, and now, he hates it. He can't be around people shooting, or he freaks out. See, I've always *hated* guns, but now, I'm *scared* of them too."

"I can't even imagine going through that," Mac said as he swallowed hard, looking and sounding completely emotional by Rocky's account of events. "I don't think I'd ever leave my house again."

I assumed Mac was exaggerating, but I thought Rocky appreciated the fact that he was trying to make her feel more normal.

"It was really hard at first, being around people I didn't know. Like, all of a sudden, I didn't trust anyone anymore. We pass by hundreds of strangers in a day, and before that, I never once thought that one of them might pull out a gun and try to shoot me. But after, it's all I think about."

My mind reeled. Rocky was saying things that I'd never really dived deep into before. And she was right. We wandered through life, passing people on the streets, on campus, in a bar, at a restaurant, and we never once thought that anything bad was going to happen because of one of them. We had this innate trust for strangers because we trusted ourselves.

"It makes sense," I said, hoping she felt understood. "There is a level of trust we have while doing everyday things. We trust that no one will try to murder us while we're doing them. And that was broken for you."

"Definitely. I mean, if you haven't been through something like that, you can't even begin to understand what it's really like. I thought I was going to die. And there's nothing that prepares you for that level of fear or for all the feelings that come after it starts to sink in."

"I'm really sorry you went through that. I can't believe you were there." I wiped at my eyes because my own tears had started to fall just as Rocky seemed to be pulling herself together.

"That's why I joined the sorority," Rocky said with a half-grin.

Mac perked up. "Wait. You were in a sorority?" he asked with the cutest expression on his face.

"Don't get too excited, buddy. It wasn't my idea. My mom had pushed for it. She said that if I was going to move down here and go away to school after everything that happened, she wanted to make sure I had friends," Rocky explained with a twisted laugh. "Clearly, she didn't know how sororities work."

"They aren't always the nicest of girls," I said even though I'd considered rushing one once or twice over the years. It was the females like Hayley who had stopped me. I never wanted to be associated with that kind of *mean girl-esque* crowd.

"Understatement of the year." Rocky guffawed. "I mean, depending on which one. They aren't all bad."

"I don't mean to cut this short—and I'd stay here all day with you if I could, Rocky—but I have to get back to school. Coach will kick my ass if I miss any classes, and he'll make me run until I puke later."

"I can drive you guys back to campus," Rocky offered, but Mac and I both said, "No," at the same time.

"No, really, it's okay." I rounded the corner into the kitchen and gave her a hug, whether she wanted one or not. I didn't think she hugged me back, but I didn't care. "Rest. Call your brother. Do whatever you need to do. I'll come check on you later, all right?"

"Does that mean she's getting fresh cookies?" Mac asked.

Rocky's eyes lit up. "Cookies?" She looked marginally happier than she had a moment ago.

"Sunny makes the best cookies you've ever tasted. Better hope she brings some when she comes to check on you. Matter of fact, I'd be *unwell* for, like, weeks if I were you," he said with a grin, and I walked back toward him and swatted his shoulder. "Why are you always hitting me?" He pouted.

I didn't answer him. "I'll see you later, Rocky. You'll be okay if we go?"

"Yeah. I'm all right. Thanks, you guys. Seriously. I don't know what I would have done if you hadn't been there. But now, I want cookies, Sunny, so I'll just be sitting here"—she clasped her hands together under her chin—"waiting like a sad puppy for a treat."

"You won't be sorry." Mac sauntered over to her, pulled her into a hug, and planted a kiss on her cheek. "I feel protective over you now," he said.

She rolled her eyes. "Oh jeez. Here we go. Take him away." She gave Mac a shove in my direction. "Please. Bye, Baseball Boy. Pretend we never met."

"Not a chance," he said, and I laughed as I had to practically force him out of her front door.

"I'll ignore you in public," she yelled.

I quickly closed the door behind us, so Mac couldn't turn around and head back inside to argue with her.

"Come on. I need to stop at my place real quick."

CLEARING THE AIR

Mac

I LOOKED AT Sunny and asked, "She wouldn't really do that, would she?" referring to Rocky ignoring me in public. I wasn't sure my ego could take the hit.

"You're so sensitive," she said, which wasn't really an answer.

"You know this about me already," I whined as we reached her front door, and she unlocked it. *When did I turn into such a pussy?*

"I still can't believe Rocky was in that shooting," she said, clearly changing the subject as she tossed her keys on the kitchen table and walked into the kitchen. She started pulling out things like flour and sugar from the cupboard and talking to herself. "I can't imagine how scary that must have been," she added but kept her focus on counting and measuring the ingredients she had started lining up. She started making a list for whatever was missing from her recipe, but mostly, she was trying to avoid talking to me.

"Me neither," I agreed before silently willing her to stop whatever it was that she was doing and pay attention to me.

Forget beating around the bush, I wanted to get right to the heart of the matter and clear the air, which, I had to admit, was very unlike me.

"Sunny," I said her name, and she dropped what was in her hand. "Can we please talk about what you think you saw earlier? With Hayley?"

Sunny's body flinched. It was subtle, but I noticed.

"I don't know what I saw." She tried to sound nonchalant and unaffected, but she was upset.

"You saw two people talking. Well, you saw Satan talking and me trying to get her to shut the hell up and leave me alone," I said, hoping she believed me.

She swallowed noticeably, her eyes avoiding mine, and I hated whenever she did that. It was one of her tells, and that was how I knew she was more upset than she was letting on.

"What are you thinking? Just tell me, so I can fix it."

"I'm mad at you," she said instantly, and I swallowed hard, feeling a little uncomfortable with the direct outburst.

"I know. I'm sorry I didn't call you last night." I wasn't sure exactly what to tell her about that. *Did she really need to know how big of a basket case I was and that I had been wallowing in self-pity all night before forcing myself to fall asleep with the help of some melatonin?*

"Why didn't you?"

"I, um ..." I hesitated, my mind spinning. "I had a talk with Coach yesterday that upset me, and I was in a bad headspace for the rest of the day," I answered honestly and held my breath, waiting for her response. Maybe she would realize I wasn't worth all this trouble and cut her losses.

"Mac." Sunny walked from the kitchen and toward where I stood. "It's okay if you have a bad day. But just give me a heads-up. It's not that hard to send me a text, saying you just need to be alone or whatever." She sounded frustrated. "Just freaking communicate with me. I can't take the silent treatment."

"It goes against my nature," I spat out before realizing what I'd even said. It was the truth though even if I'd truly never put the pieces together before now. "I'm just used to keeping everything to myself."

Sunny closed the distance between us and wrapped me in her arms. She held me tight, hugging me, and I had to force my hand to stay on her lower back and not drop to her ass.

As she pulled away, her face looked pained. "I want you to tell me the hard stuff. That's what I'm here for."

"You're going to have to remind me of that. Probably pretty often." I tried to lighten the mood, but the smile she gave me didn't reach her eyes.

"I'm mad about that text you sent me too." Her eyes pulled together, and I'd almost forgotten all about that.

I pulled my baseball hat off and scratched at my head. "I freaked out when I heard you were with her. Or near her. I don't trust Hayley, and I have no idea what she's capable of when it comes to other girls," I explained, hoping I didn't sound like a liar. "She's poison, and I didn't want her to get in your head."

"I read the text differently. I read it like you were telling me to get away from her because I was the bad guy or something," she said, and I hadn't even realized that she could interpret my message any other way than I'd meant it.

That Hayley was evil.

I shook my head. "No. I didn't mean it like that. I meant that Hayley's horrible, and just knowing she was near you after what happened the night before ..." I stumbled all over my thoughts. "I don't know, Sunny. She's just bad."

"I think between the text and then not hearing from you at all," she started before continuing, "and then seeing you with her this morning ... I don't know. My mind went places I didn't want it to go." It made so much sense, all the things she was saying. But Sunny had taken my silence wrong, I thought, because she said, "I don't want to be your second choice," and it nearly broke my damn heart.

"You're *not*," I emphasized, hoping she believed me.

"If you're not completely over her, I need you to tell me. I can handle it. But I can't handle being second place to her. Or any other girl. I want all of you, Mac. Not just the parts left over."

Her words were hard for me to accept, but as insecure as I could be about some stuff, Sunny apparently was too. Obviously, I hadn't made myself very clear.

"I am over her. And you're not my second choice. You're my only choice, Sunny. I only want to be with you," I said.

"Just to be clear," she started, and I had to stop myself from laughing. This girl was going to kill me. "You're not into Hayley? At all?"

Why were girls always asking the same questions in different ways?

"Not even if my life depended on it," I answered without

taking a breath. "Literally."

"Okay. Sorry. It's just that she said you were still in love with her and had been chasing her for the last three years," Sunny added, and I started grounding my teeth together as my anger raged.

"What? Sunny, she's a fucking liar. See? That's exactly what I'm talking about."

I walked to the patio doors, opened them, and stepped outside. I needed some fucking air. Sunny was at my side within seconds, her long silver strands blowing in the breeze.

"She lies. She's pissed because I don't want her back. This morning, what you saw? That was me telling her to stay the hell away from me. She'd transferred into my class."

"She what? Transferred in?"

I gave a frustrated wave as I leaned against the privacy railing. "I don't know if she knew I was in the class or not. But when she saw me, she sat next to me."

Sunny snarled, "And what did you do?"

"I moved."

She laughed. "Okay."

"Okay?"

"Yeah. I believe that you don't want to be with her."

"Thank God," I said because I might have completely lost my cool if she had said something to the contrary. "Do you believe that I want you?" I asked.

Her cheeks instantly started to color. It was fucking adorable, the way that my words affected her.

She shrugged. "Maybe."

"Maybe, huh?" I reached for her and tugged her body

against mine. "You're mine, Sunny Jamison," I said with a smirk before claiming her.

Those fucking lips would be the death of me. I reveled in the taste of her tongue and how it moved inside my mouth. I wanted to press pause on the clock and have my way with her, savoring every inch of her perfect, little, petite body, but I knew Coach would have my ass if I skipped class already.

"Well, if I'm yours," she started, but I knew what was coming out of her mouth next, so I took the words from her.

"Then, I'm yours. I know."

She bit her bottom lip, her face practically glowing. "It's about damn time," she said before grabbing the back of my neck and pulling me down, the wind picking back up on the patio where we stood. Her tongue swept inside my mouth again before she moved to my neck and started biting.

My dick hardened instantly, and my breath caught in my fucking throat.

"Sunny," I tried to talk, but it had been so long since I'd let anyone get this close to me. It felt like years since I'd actually wanted to be with a girl the way I was dying to get inside her. "You have to stop."

"I don't want to."

She was tempting me, pressing all of my buttons, and so I pulled my phone out and checked the time. I had thirty-five minutes before my next class started. It wasn't ideal, but it would be worth it.

"This isn't going to be my best work, but you asked for it," I said before scooping her into my arms and carrying her back inside.

"We have to rush?" she asked as she started kicking off her shoes and reaching for the button of her shorts.

"We have about twenty minutes before I need to get back to campus."

"Okay," she said, but she didn't sound dejected or unhappy.

"I wanted to take my time with you." I let her know that I hadn't planned for our first time to be this way.

"It's okay. The first time is always a little awkward anyway, right?"

She gave me a face, and I nodded in agreement because she was right.

No matter how sexy and perfect we wanted our first time with someone to be, it rarely worked out that way. Fucking was one thing; it didn't necessarily require caring or feeling. But this was different. At least, it was for me.

We undressed ourselves and stood there, drinking each other's naked bodies in. I wasn't sure where to look first or what to focus on ... everything about her was so beautiful. I liked it all. I wanted to map every inch of her out and commit her curves and muscles to memory.

"You're so beautiful," I said, and she blushed, moving her hands to cover up her private area.

"And you look Photoshopped"—she laughed—"like that one movie said." She walked to me and ran her hands down my ab muscles and then moved up to my shoulders, her finger tracing an imaginary line down my bicep to my forearms. "You're so sexy," she breathed out, and that was all it took.

Grabbing her hard, I pushed my lips against hers and

claimed her mouth. I was rough, my hands kneading and squeezing her ass as she moaned into me, our tongues dancing against each other. My hand moved of its own accord, my fingers itching to get inside her. When I reached her most sensitive area, I teased her clit for only a second before plunging inside. I wasn't gentle, and I had given her no warning. Her hips jerked away from the contact, but she was soaked. Already so fucking wet for me, and I hated that we were on a time limit.

"Fuck, Mac," she moaned, her voice filled with pleasure, and it only stroked my ego even more.

I continued finger-fucking her before adding another finger inside. She was so tight, but I wasn't surprised. Sunny was petite, so it made sense that her pussy would be too.

"I hate that I can't eat you until you scream," I breathed out, my dick so hard that it hurt. "Fuck it. I can at least get a sample."

"What?" she started to ask, but it was too late.

I was on my knees as she stood above me, her hands fisting in my hair as I took my first lick of paradise.

Whatever Sunny was made of, I couldn't get enough. I wanted to throw her legs around my shoulders and feast until her body gave out. And then eat some more.

"I'll be back," I whispered to her girl before standing up to my full height, Sunny's mouth wide open from the pleasure I'd been giving her.

"Get on the bed." I pointed, and she practically jumped on the damn thing.

Fumbling through my shorts for my wallet, I pulled out the

emergency condom I always kept in there, just in case. I carried one unexpired latex glove, figuring it was all I would ever need.

"No glove, no love," I said, and Sunny giggled.

Rolling on the condom, I looked into Sunny's eyes, feeling all of her emotions in the air between us.

"Ready?" I asked, and she nodded.

"Please," was all she said.

I moved my dick toward her entrance, a little nervous that I might hurt her. Not because I was walking around with some elephant cock between my legs, but because Sunny really was tiny. Two of my fingers inside her had felt like a stretch, and I damn well knew my dick was bigger than two of my digits.

I pressed inside slowly, careful not to go too quick. But when she started moving her hips down to make me get all the way in, I lost it and shoved myself inside. She gasped, her eyes watering.

"Did I hurt you?"

"It's okay," she said before I started moving in and out.

My dick was being strangled by her tight hold, and I actually worried for a minute that I might come in two more seconds. But the more I moved in and out of her, the more she loosened up, her body becoming a slick vise that felt fucking incredible around me and some of the pressure relieved.

"Sunny, you feel out of this world," I said, and she started running her finger across my bottom lip.

I licked at it before she plunged it in my mouth, and I started sucking. Her eyes rolled in the back of her head as her entire body moved with mine, her hips doing this thing that drove me crazy. It felt like Sunny had a cliff inside her and I kept jumping off it. The sensation was overwhelming.

"Sunny, I can't," I started to warn her that I was about to lose it even though I didn't want to. Not yet. But my hips refused to listen to my mind as they started pounding into her harder and faster.

"Yes, Mac. Fuck me. Just like that," she said, raising her hips off the bed, making me hit that cliff again. "Harder," she demanded, and I listened like a good boyfriend and pounded her into the fucking pillows at the top of her bed over and over and over again.

I was on the edge, on the verge, and before I could let her know I was going to come, I released inside the condom and pushed out two more shuddered thrusts before collapsing on top of her. Breathing hard, I propped myself up on my elbows, so I didn't smash her.

"I'm sorry it was so fast," I apologized, but she looked so sated and peaceful.

"It was the perfect first time." She gave me a lazy smile, but I knew she was lying.

There was no way I'd satisfied her, but I planned on remedying that the next time. Then, she would mean it when she called it perfect.

"Uh ..." I rolled off of her and sat on the bed. I felt like a jerk, leaving Sunny right after having sex with her. "I hate to do this and run"—I thumbed toward her door as I pushed up to stand and noticed the way her eyes lingered on my abs before lowering to my dick and staring—"but I'll be right back. Then, you can continue admiring me," I said, and she laughed.

I really needed to take this condom off before it fell to the floor all on its own and made a mess. By the time I came out of the bathroom, Sunny was already dressed, her bed made, and the ride-share app she showed me on her phone let me know that she'd already called a car.

"You're the best," I said as I quickly pulled my clothes on.

She giggled, pressing a kiss to my neck before moving her lips to my cheek and eventually back to my mouth. "You're mine, Mac Davies. And don't you forget it," she said before swatting my ass.

"Not a chance in hell I'd forget, babe."

And just like that, life started to feel a little less lonely and a whole lot better. Sunny turned out to be the easiest thing I'd slid into since my first home run in pony ball. It was crazy how good she felt and how quickly I'd found myself needing her in my life.

And as more time passed, that girl became my best friend and someone I didn't think I could ever live without. She supported me like crazy, never got mad when I needed to put baseball first, and seemed to understand me in ways no one else ever had. I felt like for the first time in my life, I finally knew exactly what Cole and Chance had tried to tell me.

When you found the right girl, you held on for dear life and didn't let her go.

LIFE IS GOOD

Sunny

THINGS WITH MAC and me got on track rather quickly. Once we finally gave in to what we both knew we wanted, our hearts lined up perfectly for it, everyone else be damned—*I'm looking at you, Hayley.* Everything about our relationship was ... *really. Freaking. Good.* Sometimes, I worried that it was falling into place a little too easily, but I knew that was only my fear talking. For whatever reason, I'd stupidly assumed that relationships came with a certain level of chaos, and without it, you were doomed, living in some fairy tale where it could all come crashing down around you at any moment.

Mac started opening up to me—without my pushing—and I took everything that he gave, anxious to learn more about what made my man tick. He talked about his parents, and I tried to hide my shock every time he told me something that his dad had done or said over the years. It was crazy to hear how he was treated when I had nothing but the opposite experience with my own family. If Mac had had a tendency to lie or exaggerate, I would have thought he was making the stories up—they were truly that awful. But he wasn't a liar, and it broke my heart to know that he had grown up in such a dysfunctional environment, where his opinion didn't matter.

He spent quite a few nights here at the apartment with me, which helped calm my nerves about being alone and also kept me sexually spent. That man's appetite for me was on another level. But I welcomed it because I'd never been so desired before. Mac made me feel like the most beautiful girl in the galaxy, not just our planet. And if he wanted to work out his frustrations on my body or show me all the ways in which he craved me, I was here for it.

Other times, he went to the baseball house alone, or we went together. I never blamed him for wanting to hang out with his teammates, and the last thing I wanted to do was take him away from them during his last season. And even though it was a little bit of an adjustment, knowing that I came second to all things baseball, for some reason, it didn't really bother me. What bothered me at times were all the other girls.

No one could believe that Mac had settled down, even when they saw us together on campus. Some girls would cast us shocked looks and shake their heads in disbelief. Others couldn't have cared less. It was a weird reality, being thrown into this universe all of a sudden. One second, I had been Sunny Jamison, typical senior, and the next, it felt like the entire student body knew who I was and was judging me for it.

I remembered Danika going through a similar thing after she'd gotten together with Chance. I thought it had been worse for her though because Chance never gave any girl the time of day, so everyone wanted to know why she was so special.

Whereas my boyfriend had made out with half the campus. It was a little embarrassing to know that he'd kissed some of the girls we walked by on a daily basis. I hated knowing that I shared my boyfriend with so many random females.

And then there was the social media aspect. I saw the nasty comments after he posted a picture of the two of us together, confirming our exclusive status. The remarks got so downright mean that he turned them off and begged me not to look anymore. But I was a curious beast and couldn't stop myself even if I tried. It was hard not to care what other people were saying about you, especially when they didn't even know you.

Of course, most of the comments were about my looks. How I wasn't *hot enough* for Mac or how I was *too skinny* or how I dressed *slutty*. And my favorite: *Who told this bitch that she looked good with silver hair?*

Not all the comments were mean though, and I appreciated that fact. Some girls wrote some really nice things, complimentary and kind. But it was the nasty ones that stuck in my head the most and made me feel insecure. It was all worth it though if it meant I got to be with Mac. That didn't mean that my jealousy never reared its ugly head because it definitely did. And Mac was always patient and understanding, apologizing every single time for putting me in the position in the first place.

"I'm sorry I've made out with half the school," he said one night when I was in a particularly ornery mood.

"I mean, I was one of them, so I get it. But now, every time I catch a girl looking at me sideways, I think it's because she hooked up with you, and then I imagine it, picturing the two of you making out and I can't stand it."

He grabbed my hand and looked me right in the eyes. "I can't change any of that. I swear, if I could go back in time and take it all back, I would."

I knew that he meant it. He was genuinely sorry for the pain it caused me. But I'd known all of those things before I fell for him in the first place, so it wasn't right of me to keep throwing his past decisions in his face.

When my phone rang one evening, I knew it was Danika without even looking. Her personal ringtone blared from the other room, and I practically kicked a chair and broke my toe, trying to reach it in time.

"Hey, I've been meaning to call you!" I shouted into the phone, breathing hard.

"I mean, I have to hear from Chance that you and Mac can't get out from under each other long enough to come up for air? What the hell is that?" She pretended to be pissed, but I knew she was happy for me.

I'd told her all about Mac and me finally working our issues out and deciding to be together, and she'd told me she knew it was only a matter of time before we pulled our heads out of our asses. But then she'd gotten busy with moving back to New York after Chance's season ended and building the new branch of her dad's business that we hadn't been talking as much as usual. The time difference never helped either.

"I know. I've been a bad friend, but listen," I started saying, hoping she'd shut up long enough for me to get this out, "it's about Thanksgiving."

"You mean, OUR holiday? The holiday that was created

for me and you? That Thanksgiving?"

I laughed. "Yes, that one."

"Okay. What about it?"

"I was wondering what you thought about Mac and me coming there for it? I mean, I haven't asked Mac yet. And I have no idea what your plans even are, but my mom mentioned it a while back, and I can't stop thinking about it, but I keep forgetting to ask you."

"Oh my gosh!" she literally yelled into the phone, and I had to pull it away from my ear. "YES! Do you hear me? We're staying in New York for Thanksgiving and having it with my dad. And then we're all going to California to see Chance's family for Christmas. So, YES! YES! Come out! Stay with us. Now, you have to because I'm so excited, I can't see straight!"

"What if Mac says no?" I asked, and Danika guffawed super loud.

"He won't. But if he does, you come anyway! You've never been here. It will be so much fun. And I'm dying to show you the office, so I can offer you a job and make you come work with me. And it's Thanksgiving! In New York, Sunny! I'm going to book you a ticket, so you can't say no." Danika was talking a mile a minute, and I swore I heard computer keys typing in the background. I wouldn't put it past her to book me a ticket before we hung up the phone.

"Danika! Let me talk to Mac first. And I need to tell my mom to make sure she's really okay with it. But I'm so glad you said yes."

We were both so freaking riled up that we couldn't stop

shouting our responses to each other.

"I'm so happy! I'm going to plan it all out. Now, go do what you need to do. I need to find Chance, tell him the news, and then jump his bones."

"I give you this news, and he gets the reward?" I asked with a laugh.

"Well, I'm not jumping your bones, so yes! If I'm excited, he gets to hear all about it. While I'm on his penis."

Rolling my eyes, I sucked in a breath. "Being with Chance has changed you. You're a foul-mouthed little hussy now."

"I know. Isn't it great?"

"It's something all right."

"Go away. Find a flight. Convince Mac to come with. And then send me all the details," she said before ending the call, and I stared at the phone in my hand, looking at a blank screen.

I guess that answered that question. I was going to New York for Thanksgiving!

I shot my mom a text:

ME: BIG APPLE TURKEY DAY IS A GO! MY FINGERS ARE CROSSED FOR THAT CRUISE OF YOURS TO MEXICO.

MOM: CONSIDERING THE FACT THAT I'VE ALREADY BOOKED AND PAID FOR SAID CRUISE, I'M GOING, NO MATTER WHAT.

ME: DID YOU TELL DAD YET? MY BET'S ON NO.

MOM: SMART ASS. BUT, NO.

Her response made me laugh. I wouldn't put it past her to drag my dad, kicking and screaming, all the way to the port if she had to.

MOM: IS MAC, YOUR *HOTTIE-WITH-THE-BODY BOYFRIEND*, GOING TO NEW YORK WITH YOU?

ME: I HAVEN'T ASKED HIM YET BUT I'M HOPING HE SAYS YES.

MOM: JUST IN CASE YOU'VE FORGOTTEN, I STILL HAVEN'T MET HIM. AND IF YOU DON'T BRING HIM TO ME SOON, I'LL JUST GO TO HIM.

ME: WHAT? YOU'LL GO TO HIM?

MOM: THEY HAVE THIS THING CALLED THE INTERNET. IT SHOWS HIS BASEBALL SCHEDULE AND EVERYTHING. I EVEN KNOW HIS COACHES EMAIL ADDRESS. I CAN GO TO HIS PRACTICE AND CHEER FOR HIM UNTIL HE HAS TO LEAVE THE FIELD AND COME INTO THE STANDS JUST TO SHUT ME UP.

The lady was incorrigible. And embarrassing.

ME: OMG! MOM! I'LL BRING HIM HOME SOON.

MOM: THAT'S ALL I NEEDED TO HEAR. :)

I just needed to run all that by Mac first. Working through his fears to be with me was one thing, but meeting my parents was something else entirely. That felt like a big step. *What if he isn't ready to take it? Or what if he hates the idea because his own parents are so messed up?*

I knew just how to get him to at least consider it, so I started pulling out all the ingredients necessary to try a new cookie flavor. I wasn't above bribing my boyfriend if I needed to. And a lemon and white chocolate concoction was just the way to do it.

After the cookies were done baking, I looked at the clock. Mac's practice had ended an hour ago, and he'd sent me a text, letting me know he'd come by after he showered and grabbed some stuff from his room. I knew he'd be here any minute now. He usually convinced one of the guys to drop him off, but sometimes, I picked him up instead even though he hated it. He'd said he felt like a loser without his car, having to ask people for rides all the time. I understood what he was saying, but no matter how many times I told him it wasn't a big deal, he still cringed whenever I offered. Mac said that he should be the one picking me up and not the other way around.

I grabbed a few lemon delights and put them on a paper plate to bring over to Rocky, but when I opened up the front door, I almost ran smack into my sexy-as-hell boyfriend.

"Babe! I almost dropped these!" I said as his arm snaked around me, holding me tight.

He kissed me, and I really almost dropped the plate.

"Hi," he said with a smile. "Where were you going with my cookies?"

"Who said these were for you?" I teased, and he blocked the doorway, so I couldn't get out.

"Who are they for then?"

"Fine, they're for you. And Rocky. I was just bringing some over. Wanna come?" I asked, and I swore he got even more excited than he just had been.

Mac loved Rocky.

I'd grown closer to her in the past month, but I could tell that the situation at school that day had really rattled her. She hadn't been fine since then even though I knew she wanted to be and tried to act like she was. She stayed inside more, and I heard the sound of her door locking whenever she left. She never used to lock her door.

Mac tossed his bag to the floor, and we headed toward her apartment. I knocked on her door right as Mac took the plate out of my hand.

"You can't take credit for these," I whispered.

"Watch me," he said as the door flew open.

"Baseball Boy. Sunshine. And cookies?" Rocky flipped her hair and opened the door wide enough for us to walk through. "Come in."

We followed her lead, the three of us heading into the kitchen before Mac hopped up onto the counter and pulled me between his legs.

Rocky peered at the plate, eyeing the cookies before bringing them to her nose and inhaling. "Lemon?" she asked as she lowered the plate.

"With white chocolate chips," I said, biting my bottom lip, hoping that she liked lemon. I never even asked.

"I'm excited to try these," she said before breaking a piece off and putting it in her mouth. "Sunny. Damn. These are …" She swallowed without finishing her sentence and promptly shoved the rest of the cookie in her mouth. I swore Mac whined audibly. "I'm sure you have your own cookies at home, Baseball Boy. I'm not sharing," she said around a mouthful of crumbles.

"You like them?" I'd never made them before, so I liked the feedback.

"They're incredible. Sounded like a weird combination when you first said it, but it totally works. Why does it work? I have no idea. But it does," she said, breaking off another piece. "I can't believe you don't want to start a business, doing this."

"I know. I know," I groaned, not wanting to get into this again.

Rocky and I had talked about my baking on numerous occasions. She said all the same things that Danika always had, but nothing ever changed my mind. I had less than zero interest in baking for other people, and no amount of conversation about it could make me feel otherwise. It apparently sounded crazy from an outsider's perspective but not from mine. I knew in my heart that it wasn't the right move for me.

"I'm glad you two are here. I need to tell you guys something," she said, and my stomach dropped.

I had an inkling what was coming next, but I wasn't sure that Mac did. His body tensed, his knees pressing into my sides harder than they had been a second ago, and I wiggled for him to loosen his hold.

"Spit it out," Mac said when Rocky had stayed quiet for too long.

"I'm going to move back home when the semester ends."

Rocky had talked on more than one occasion about moving back, and even though I wanted to beg her not to go, I knew I had no right to do that. I wanted to support whatever made her feel the most comfortable and safe. Plus, I had zero clue what it felt like to live through what she had and then go on each day, pretending not to be affected by it.

So, I wasn't surprised by her news. I stepped out of Mac's vise grip to check on him. He looked devastated, which was ridiculous, but I honestly thought he was more attached to her than I was. Rocky looked at me and then looked at Mac, and she stuck out her bottom lip to match the pout currently on his face.

"You'll be okay, Baseball Boy. I'll have Little Miss Sunshine here put me on speakerphone during your games, so you can hear me cheer for you, okay?"

"Promise?" He sounded excited as his pout lessened.

"Promise," she said before he hopped off the counter, grabbed her, and hugged her tight against her will.

"I'm going to miss you," he said.

"Ugh," she groaned. "This is why I don't tell you things."

He stopped hugging her, holding her by her shoulders. "Why? 'Cause I like you and don't want you to move? I know, I'm such an asshole."

Rocky sniffed and wiped at her nose. "No. Because you'll talk me out of leaving, and I really need to go."

Whoa. I didn't see that coming.

"We're not going to talk you out of it. Of course we don't want you to go, but we want you to be okay more than anything else," I said, hoping that she knew how much we cared about her.

"I feel like I failed you," Mac huffed out, his arms crossing over his chest.

"This has nothing to do with you, Mac." Rocky never called Mac by his real name. "There isn't anything you could have done. I'm just not feeling safe on a general day-to-day basis. That stupid fucking barrier thing falling really messed me up."

"You'll stay through the semester though?" I asked, if only

to confirm it so I knew how long we had with her. I was a little bummed she wouldn't be here to go to Mac's games with me, but that was just me being selfish.

She nodded her head. "I'm going to try."

"Okay, well"—I reached for Mac's hand and intertwined my fingers with his—"we'll let you go. Come over if you want more cookies. No way this guy's eating them all."

He let out a crazed noise. "Sounds like a challenge to me."

"Sounds like a stomachache to me," Rocky bit back, and I shook my head.

It was always like this with the two of them—constant banter. It was exhausting.

"Come on. I'll see you later." I gave her a sad smile, and she thanked me for the cookies as we walked out.

"I'm so sad that Rocky's bailing," Mac said once we were in the hallway, and I wondered how long he was going to sulk for.

"Come eat some cookies. Plus, I have something to ask you." I gave him a smile, hoping to put him in a better mood.

NO MORE SURPRISES

Mac

I COULDN'T DEAL with any more surprises tonight, so I really hoped that Sunny's question was something good. The smile on her face gave me more than a little hope even though I had no idea what she was up to.

Rocky leaving really bummed me out. It was stupid, but I did feel like I'd failed her somehow. I knew it wasn't logical, and Rocky wasn't my responsibility, but I hated that she felt like her only option was to go back home.

Then again, if I'd gone through a shooting where I thought I was going to die, I might not have ever had the guts to leave my own room, let alone move out and live alone. Rocky was the definition of a badass, and maybe that was why it hurt so bad. I felt for her, and naturally, I wanted to fix it.

Sunny brought me over a giant plate of cookies while I sat on the couch, my mind still in a Rocky-filled fog. Snapping out of it, I forced myself to think about something else. That was easy—baseball.

Practice had been great today. I felt good on the field. Better than I'd felt in a long time. I belonged there, and I knew it.

Coach had even mentioned that some scout had asked about me. And even though he wouldn't tell me who it was, it was still a good sign. Things were looking up.

Which always made me a little apprehensive. Everything I'd ever wanted in life always felt like a struggle. Mostly because I seemed to be working against Dick Davies. If I wasn't following his plan for me, then I was letting him down. The guy had tried to talk me out of playing baseball my entire high school career, reminding me that I was just wasting my time and taking small digs at my ability whenever he could.

"So, I wanted to talk to you," Sunny started, and I almost choked on the cookie I'd just put in my mouth.

"Are you breaking up with me?" I asked quickly as nerves filled me. I had no idea why my mind had instantly gone there, but it had.

There were days I waited for Sunny to tell me I wasn't worth the hassle. That the other girls and their fucking rude comments were too much for her to take. Not to mention that I really had hooked up with a ridiculous number of girls at this school and Sunny had to face that fact every single time she walked across campus or entered a classroom.

My past was in her face. I wouldn't blame her if she was sick of dealing with it.

"What? No. Never." She looked at me like I was insane and moved on like I hadn't just asked that question in the first place. "It's about Thanksgiving."

My stomach instantly settled. "Oh. Yeah? What about it?" I sucked in a few quick breaths and stared at my girl. *How did I get so lucky?*

"We haven't talked about the holidays. Do you go home for them?" she asked tentatively, and I realized that she was tiptoeing around something.

"I don't usually go home for Thanksgiving. I just stay here. Go to Chance's house. But I guess this year ..." I just realized that Chance wasn't here anymore and he was probably going to be with Danika.

Maybe Sunny was going to ask me to go to her parents' house instead. I would agree in a heartbeat. I still hadn't met them yet, but from all of Sunny's stories, her mom sounded insane. In a good way.

"I thought we could go to New York and have Thanksgiving with Chance and Danika if you wanted?" Sunny blurted out, like keeping that idea inside for one second longer might have made her explode if she didn't say it out loud.

Her whole face was happy, but I noticed that she was holding her breath, waiting for me to say something in response.

"Hell yes! When did you plan this? I definitely want to do that. Does Chance know?" I reached for my girl and pulled her onto my lap, her silver hair falling all around us.

She looked at me and shrugged. "I don't know if he knows. But I talked to Danika earlier, and she's so excited. I just didn't know what your plans were. I figured you went home for Christmas, but I wasn't sure what you did for Thanksgiving."

I swallowed at the mention of my going home to Arizona. I hated it every year but felt obligated, of course, to go back during Christmas. Plus, leaving my mom alone with DD made me sick. I had to give her some reprieve and check in on her.

"I do go home for Christmas. But then I come right back 'cause baseball starts."

"So, you want to go?" Her tongue stuck out as she grinned at me. "To New York? With me? For Thanksgiving?"

"Definitely." I leaned forward and kissed her. "You know," I said, "I've never been there before."

"Me neither! I can't wait!" She leaped off my lap and did a little dance around the living room, shaking her ass and hips as she thrust her arms into the air like a lunatic. "I have to call Danika, okay? Or I can just text her."

"I'll buy our tickets," I said, pulling out my wallet and credit card from my dad. At least he was good for something.

"You don't have to buy our tickets. I mean"—she stopped dancing and cocked her head to the side—"I can pay for my own."

"Dickhead Davies said I'm to use this for all things. I'm sure that includes first-class airfare." I waved the credit card around, and Sunny looked uncomfortable.

"I don't know. Are you sure? What if he cancels them?"

I laughed. "He won't even notice until we've gone and come back, I bet. But he would never cancel the tickets. That would be potentially embarrassing, and DD does not like to be embarrassed."

"If you're sure," she said between typing on her phone.

"I'm sure."

My girl squealed. "Okay. Danika said we're all set. Just to let her know what we end up booking and she'll take care of the rest."

I waved Sunny over, and she sashayed her way back to the couch and sat down next to me. We both had the calendars up on our phones as we looked at the dates and decided when to leave and come back.

"Are we staying with them?"

"Yeah. They're at Chance's parents'. I guess they own a flat there or something. I don't know what they're called."

"Ah." I nodded because that rang a bell. "I think Chance told me that once. They have a condo."

After we agreed on the dates, I booked us two roundtrip tickets. I knew that I could have gotten us coach seats, but I decided that I didn't care enough what my old man thought and ordered us first class instead. Plus, I wanted to fly my girl in style even if I wasn't paying for it.

"We're confirmed." I forwarded the confirmation to Sunny's email address and watched as she opened it, noticing the seat class.

"This is going to be the best vacation ever." She launched herself into my arms, and I caught her easily.

"Are you happy?" I placed a small kiss on the tip of her nose.

"Very." She licked her lips as she stared at my mouth.

"Show me how much," I said as I stood up from the couch with her still in my arms and headed toward the bedroom.

FIRST CLASS TO NEW YORK

Sunny

I DROVE US to LAX for our nonstop flight to *NEW YORK CITY!* To say I was enthusiastic would be the freaking understatement of the century. I couldn't stop bouncing in my seat, even with Mac's hand on my thigh. He kept laughing at me and shaking his head, but he couldn't blame me. Not only was I getting to see my best friend, who I missed terribly, but I was also going to New York with my boyfriend.

I'd never done anything like this in my life. The most vacationing my family had ever done was camping at the local beaches on the weekends. They were always fun, and I enjoyed them, but they weren't New York. And I'd definitely never gone anywhere with a boyfriend before.

We parked the car, grabbed our luggage, and headed into the busy airport. It was an absolute madhouse inside, kids running amok, their parents looking way more stressed than happy. I glanced at Mac while we waited in line to check our luggage, and he seemed to have the same expression on his face that I assumed I had on mine.

"Are you as excited as I am?"

He leaned toward me. "Maybe even more."

He winked, and my stomach flip-flopped. His shirt was pulled taut against his shoulders, his arms looking like they ached to be set free, and I swore I could spend hours simply admiring his body.

"Are you checking me out?" he asked, and I felt myself blush.

"I can't help it. Look at you."

He grabbed me hard and started kissing me for everyone at LAX to see. The old man behind us cleared his throat, making Mac stop.

"Have you seen yourself lately?" Mac whispered in my ear, and I used his arms to steady myself.

Kissing Mac always made me weak in the knees. One of these times, I was going to fall to the floor in a puddle, and he'd have no one to blame but himself.

After checking in and making our way through security, which took two hundred years, we sat in the fancy airport lounge, eating mini sandwiches and drinking at the bar. First-class perks were insane and unnecessary, but I was enjoying myself anyway.

"We should head out soon," Mac said as he finished off his sandwich and reached for a cookie I hadn't seen him grab earlier.

I eyed the delectable-looking treat and watched as Mac took a giant bite before covering his mouth with a napkin and wiping his face.

"Did you just spit it out?"

"It's hard. And dry. And"—his face twisted with his

disgust—"it's gross."

I smiled smugly, feeling proud of myself for no reason whatsoever, except the fact that my boyfriend thought my cookies were better than the super-fancy ones at the airport lounge.

He slid the remainder of the cookie toward me. "Try it."

"Why? You just said it's gross."

"Just do it," he insisted.

I broke off a small piece, which crumbled against my fingers, and tossed it in my mouth.

"It's either a day old or they baked it too long," I said with a shrug.

"But it's not good."

"It's not good," I agreed.

"Yours are so much better. These people don't even know what they're missing out on," he said as he hopped out of the chair and extended his hand to help me out of mine.

Mac must have kept us in that private lounge until the last minute because the instant we walked up to our gate, they started boarding first-class passengers. Nerves and excitement raced through me as I texted Danika one last time, letting her know we were getting on the plane. The flight attendant greeted us with a smile as she welcomed us aboard. I must have looked like such a newbie, my eyes wide and my mouth dropping open when I saw the size of the seats.

"This is crazy," I whispered toward Mac, who was smiling as he followed behind me, his hand on my hip.

He'd probably flown first-class a hundred times, but I'd only walked past it and not really paid attention because I wasn't sitting there.

I moved into the seat closest to the window and moaned as soon as I sat. I swore it hugged me, the cushion all plush and soft. There was a blanket waiting for me to unwrap and just ... so. Much. Leg. Room. The seat in front of me was nowhere near the rest of my body, and I knew that even if they reclined all the way, they still wouldn't hit my knees. This was a far cry from the seats in coach.

"I could really get used to this," I said as Mac buckled his seat belt.

The smiley flight attendant appeared in our row. "Can I get you two something to drink before takeoff?" she asked.

I looked at Mac, a little unsure, and he ordered for us.

"We'll just take two champagnes," he said, and she disappeared.

"I can't with this," I said, and Mac reached out, taking my hand in his and squeezing. "I mean, I knew it was fancy up here but champagne?"

"Wait until you see the food," he said, and I grabbed my stomach.

I was still full from all the mini sandwiches I'd inhaled earlier.

"Why'd you let me eat so much?" I whined. "I'm little. I don't have that much room in me."

"I just want you to enjoy yourself." He smiled so sweetly, and I wanted to launch myself into his arms and hug him.

I loved this side of him, all caring and considerate, wanting me to be happy.

"What's that face for?" he asked, his eyes pulling together.

"I was just thinking about how lucky I am."

"You and me both," he said right as the flight attendant returned, carrying a tray of champagne and other drinks.

She handed us each a flute before disappearing again.

Mac and I clinked our glasses together and said, "Cheers," at the same time before taking a sip.

I guessed it was good, but I knew nothing about champagne. Mac downed his in one gulp, and I stared at him with wide eyes. I wasn't even sure I could finish mine, let alone down it the way he had.

The flight was uneventful unless you counted the sheer amount of food and snacks they plied us with throughout. Even though I was stuffed, I still took what they offered anyway, storing the bags of chips and individually wrapped cookies in my purse for later. Mac just smiled at me, seemingly enjoying my level of crazy.

When the plane landed, I shot up in my seat, dying to get off and see Danika.

Mac looked up at me, that gleam in his hazel eyes, and smirked. "You're so cute when you're excited."

"Oh, please, like you aren't just as excited to see Chance," I teased, but he was still firmly in his seat, his seat belt wrapped around his middle as he made no move to stand.

"Get up. I want to be the first ones off," I said as I looked around at the other people in first class, who were still seated. I must have looked insane to them.

"Sunny," Mac said, his voice soft and low, "sit." His hands grabbed my hips as he tugged me onto his lap, and I did as he'd asked. "Stop squirming," he added, making me feel like a petulant child.

After we got off the plane, I wanted to run through JFK Airport until I reached Baggage Claim, where Danika was waiting for us, but Mac forced me to walk, holding my hand tight and yanking me back like a dog on a leash whenever I got too far ahead.

"Come onnnn," I whined and looked back at him, but he only smiled and gripped my hand harder.

He enjoyed torturing me, and he knew it.

When I spotted the sign for Baggage Claim, I started hopping up and down, and Mac let go of my hand. I took off, speed-walking like a lunatic until I rounded the corner and spotted Chance and Danika craning their necks impatiently.

Danika shouted, and before I knew it, we were both running toward each other, arms wide open.

"Oh my gosh, I've missed you so much," she said as we hugged and bounced around.

"Me too."

"Your hair," she said as she grabbed it, admiring each strand.

"Do you like it?"

"I love it! I mean, I saw the pictures, but it's so much prettier in person."

"Thanks. I'm sort of obsessed with it," I admitted because I'd already colored it more than once. I'd felt myself growing a little bolder, buying that icy-blue color the last time, but I had gone with the silver again. I really liked it.

"Now, where's that man of yours?" she asked, looking around me for any sign of Mac.

"I might have sort of run here and left him behind." I turned around as well.

He couldn't be that far behind.

"There he is," Danika said with a smile as she pulled me over to where Chance stood, taking pictures of us with his cell phone.

He reached down and gave me a huge hug, lifting me up in the air, and instead of fighting back, I allowed it.

"Are you guys hungry?" he asked as soon as Mac walked up, and they embraced.

"I don't think I could eat another bite." I grabbed my stomach. "But he might be hungry." I thumbed toward Mac.

"I'm good for now," Mac said before wrapping an arm around me and walking toward our correct baggage claim carousel.

The airport was as packed as LAX had been, but I could tell just by looking around that we weren't back home. Everyone was dressed for winter in coats and beanies. I'd brought some hoodies with me, but I didn't even own a jacket. Hopefully, Danika had an extra one I could borrow.

The four of us made small talk while we waited for our suitcases to drop down the chute and make their way toward us. Apparently, our bags got unloaded before anyone else's because within no time, I spotted them. Another perk of flying first class, I figured. Mac pulled both of them off the belt, and he and Chance lugged them through the crowd as I followed Danika's lead. I had no idea where I was or where we were going.

"We have a car waiting outside," Danika said.

I looked at her like she'd lost her mind as she sent off a quick text. "What do you mean, a car waiting outside? Like an Uber?"

"No. My dad has a driver. We don't really drive here. I mean, people do," she started to say before Chance interjected.

"But she doesn't."

"So, you have a car and a driver, and he just takes you everywhere?" I asked again, feeling like we'd stepped into some alternate universe where people were just chauffeured around all day like royalty.

"I borrowed my dad's. Usually, we take a cab. Sometimes, we take the train."

"But it's fucking hot," Chance said, and I wondered what he meant.

"What's hot? The train?"

"Yeah. The subway. Not all of the cars have air-conditioning, so you run the chance of being a ball of sweat by the time you get off."

Everything I knew about New York I'd learned from TV shows or movies, so even though Chance had made the subway sound unappealing, I still wanted to experience it. There was no way I was leaving here without having gone on at least one ride.

We stepped outside of the double doors, and the blast of cold air hit me right in the face. I shivered, wrapping my arms around my middle.

"Holy fuck, it's cold," Mac said, and I looked at him, agreeing.

"Here's the car," Danika said right as a black SUV pulled

up and stopped.

The four of us piled into the back, Danika and me in one row while Chance and Mac sat in the two captain's seats. The driver took our bags and tossed them into the trunk before getting into the front seat and buckling up. It all felt very fancy, being driven around in a big black car with tinted windows darker than what was allowed in California. As he navigated the unfamiliar-to-me streets, Danika pointed out the names of the neighborhoods even though it was too dark for me to see them clearly.

The drive was longer than I'd expected, but the moment the lights of New York City finally came into view, I started tearing up. I'd never seen anything like it before. I'd been to San Francisco once, but it was nothing like this. New York had so many tall buildings, all lit up, just begging to be looked at and admired.

"Are you crying?" She nudged her shoulder against mine as I wiped at my eyes.

"Maybe. It's so pretty," I said as I stared in awe.

There had to be a hundred structures all stacked around each other, vying for the same space. It was mesmerizing.

"Wait till you see her," Danika said, and before I could ask who she meant, she pointed out the other window in the opposite direction.

In the distance, I spotted a statue with her arm in the air, her fist holding a single ball of light. "Oh my. Is that the Statue of Liberty?" I asked before leaning forward to hit Mac's arm. "Look, babe. Look!"

Mac laughed. "I am looking. Pretty cool."

"It never gets old," Chance added with a grin of his own as we all craned our necks to stare out the windows as she grew smaller with each passing second.

"New York is amazing," I said with a fascinating grin.

"You haven't even seen anything yet." Danika smiled. "I'm so glad you guys are here."

"Me too."

"Mostly, I'm glad you two finally figured your shit out." Danika pointed as she ping-ponged her stare between me and Mac.

"Yeah, it's about time," Chance added, and Mac just lifted both hands in the air.

"You're one to talk," I reminded them both because it wasn't like them getting together had been some easy feat. "If I remember correctly, it took you both a bit to figure your own shit out as well."

"Yeah," Mac backed me up, and the four of us busted out laughing.

The car continued driving through the busy rush of the city, and I found myself even more fascinated than I'd just been moments ago. Yellow taxis rushed by, horns honked, and there were so many people outside, walking around, even though it was damn near freezing. New York bustled with life.

We finally stopped outside of a building in what I assumed was a neighborhood. I didn't know; New York was different. One second, we were on a street lined with fancy boutiques and bougie stores, and the next, there wasn't a single store in sight, except a Dunkin' Donuts.

"We're here. Thanks, Francisco," Danika said as we

hopped out of the car, and he moved to get our luggage from the back.

"Call me if you need me to take you anywhere," he said, a thick accent permeating every word.

"We're good, but thank you."

I stared up at the mile-high building. "We're going in there?"

"Twenty-third floor," Chance said with a grin, and Mac laughed.

"Shocking."

"Why? Why is that shocking?" I asked, wanting to be let in on whatever joke I wasn't getting.

"That was my dad's number. Twenty-three. He said that when he and my mom looked at this place, he took it as a sign that it was on the twenty-third floor," Chance explained, and I thought that was cool.

"I would have thought the same thing. About it being a sign," I added as we started heading inside.

"Once they toured it though, they fell in love. Wait till you see the views."

We walked into the building, the door opened for us by an honest-to-goodness, real-life doorman. I'd thought they were only in the movies, but here we were, being greeted by one.

Stepping inside the brightly lit lobby, I noticed another person sitting at a desk.

"Good evening, Mr. Carter, Miss Marchetti. Are these your guests from California?" he asked as he slid out from behind the giant desk and tipped his hat.

"Marcel, this is Sunny and Mac," Danika introduced us,

and he shook our hands.

"I'm here if you need anything. Here's a guest key, so you can access the pool and fitness center," he said, handing me a key card.

"Thanks," I squeaked out, but my mind was racing. *Pool? Fitness center?* This wasn't a hotel, but it had all the earmarkings of one.

Marcel walked us toward the elevator and pushed the button for us. Once it arrived, he stepped inside, pressed the button for floor twenty-three, and stepped out, waving as the doors closed.

"This isn't a hotel, right?"

Danika laughed. "No."

"But there's a pool and a gym?" Mac asked, clearly as bewildered as I was, which made me feel a little less stupid.

"Yeah," Danika said. "We're in a more upscale neighborhood."

"And," Chance started to talk, "My dad wanted my mom to be safe. They lived here when he played for the Mets, so he was on the road a lot, and there were some issues with fans. He didn't want her somewhere without a doorman and a lobby. And having a gym and a private park meant that she could work out and do some things without being harassed."

"That's actually really sweet." I thought about how that sounded exactly like something Jack Carter would want for Cassie.

"Anyway, we're here," Danika interjected as the elevator stopped its upward ascent.

Once it dinged, we all stepped off and into the hallway.

When we reached the front door, Danika opened it, and my eyes instantly went to the floor-to-ceiling windows, noticing the views Chance had mentioned.

I walked right for it, realizing that there was a balcony outside. "Can I?" I asked, and Danika was at my side instantly, pulling open the slider and stepping into the cold air with me.

"You need a jacket," she said.

"I don't even own a jacket," I reminded her.

"I have one. It might be huge on you though."

"It's okay," I said, not caring how big the thing was as long as it kept me warm. "This is incredible." I looked around at all the lights and listened to the sounds of the cars as I took it all in. "What am I looking at?"

"Basically, the Upper East Side."

"Well, whatever it is, I love it."

She giggled as the guys stepped outside, and my body was instantly enveloped in Mac's arms. I leaned into him, appreciating his warmth.

"This view is sick." Mac sounded almost starstruck.

"It's crazy, right?" I nudged my head against his.

"The buildings. There're just so many," he said, literally stealing the words from my mouth before he started yawning.

"Tired?" Chance asked, covering a yawn of his own, and before I knew it, I swore all four of us had done it.

"A little," Mac admitted even though we should have been wide awake since we lost three hours, traveling here. "Why is flying so exhausting? All I did was sit the whole time."

"You should try to get some sleep, so you can adjust to the time difference. It's not real jet lag, like traveling abroad, but still," Danika mentioned, and we agreed even though the last thing I wanted to do was sleep.

As we started to head back indoors, Danika grabbed my arm, stopping me. "You two look really happy."

"We are."

"And things are good? There's no drama or anything?" she asked.

I was sure she was expecting the answer to be yes because we both knew that Fullton State had its fair share of tabloid-worthy dilemmas whenever it came to their baseball players.

"Not really. I mean, aside from his ex, but she's all talk, I think."

I hoped it was true. But really, all Hayley had been was all bark and no bite. She was jealous and competitive, but that was as far as her ire went. She had no real power.

"I'm so happy for you."

"Thank you." I smiled, feeling like I'd just said the same thing to her not that long ago.

"Who would have thought that you'd be the one to tame the player?" She offered a laugh as the realization hit me.

Is that what I've done?

"The same people who thought you'd nab the elusive Chance Carter." I laughed back.

"Touché."

Once we were through the door and back inside, I looked around, noticing the framed J. Carter jerseys on the walls and bookshelves lined with photographs and at least twenty random jars filled to the top with quarters.

"What's with all the quarters?" I asked out loud as I leaned down to look at one.

"Don't ask," Chance said, and that was the end of it.

"Okaaayy then." I made my way to the kitchen, and even though I could tell it was dated, it still looked brand-new. "Hey, do we need to go to the grocery store tomorrow?" I asked.

Danika shook her head as she held on to Chance. They looked so comfortable here, together, like they'd always been this way.

"I already got everything. My dad's bringing some fancy wine from Italy. And I might have gotten all the ingredients you'll need to bake us some cookies." She sounded a little terrified of my reaction, and that made me giggle. The last thing I knew I did was scare Danika in any way.

"Sounds good then. I'll bake us a cookie cake." I was actually excited to have something to do. Not that I hadn't planned on helping, but baking always calmed me.

"And I'll try not to ruin Thanksgiving dinner. Just so it's out there." She pointed at each of us. "I have no idea what I'm doing, and I've never done this before."

"We don't care. We're just happy to be here."

"Speak for yourself," Mac said from over my head as he walked up behind me. "I care. I need food to function. You gotta feed me, Danika."

Chance looked around for something, found a sweatshirt, and tossed it at Mac's head, which almost hit me instead. They both took off running, chasing each other around the living room, dodging between the couches and coffee table like children.

Danika and I stepped closer to each other, eyeing our boyfriends as they stomped around, clearly not caring if they woke the neighbors.

"I know you're dying to go do things, but everything's closed for the holiday. We'll start exploring first thing Friday morning, okay?"

Her words relieved me. I was going crazy, being in New York but not getting to experience it. "I can't wait."

"Can't wait for what?" Mac reappeared at my side, breathing heavy and sweating. "Can't wait to see our room?"

"You're such a guy," I pretended to complain as he wiped his forehead on my shoulder. "Did you just wipe your sweat on me?"

"No." He looked around with a guilty expression. "Now, I need a shower."

Chance was just as sweaty as Mac but was already downing an entire bottle of water. "Yeah, you do."

"You guys have the master." Danika wagged her eyebrows at me, but I was confused.

"Why do we have the master bedroom?"

Chance made a disgusted face as he finished off the bottle. "Because my parents used to live here. I am not sleeping in that bed. Or doing anything else in it either."

"Thanks for that visual." I shook my head, wanting to get rid of the idea of anyone's parents doing it—I didn't care how hot they were.

"You're welcome. Better you than me." He walked to the sliding glass door and locked it, a clear sign that we were all going to bed.

"All right, we'll see you two in the morning. There's bottled water in your room. Tons of food in the pantry if you get hungry in the middle of the night and need a snack," Danika explained before giving both Mac and me a hug. "I'm so glad you guys are here."

Mac moved behind me and started pushing me toward the bedroom by my waist. "We're going to bed now," he yelled, and I knew that sleeping was the last thing we were about to do.

A NEW KIND OF FRIENDSGIVING

Sunny

ONCE I'D FINALLY gotten it out of my head that we were in Chance's parents' old bedroom, in the bed they used to sleep in, I gave myself to Mac. I resisted in the beginning, more than slightly weirded out by the whole thing even though the sheets and pillows were brand-new. It took a little effort on Mac's part to get me in the mood. Mostly him diving between my legs. Once his tongue had licked at me, I'd started seeing stars and stopped thinking about anything else, except how good it'd felt to be ravished by him.

When I woke up the next morning, the bed was empty. I heard voices coming from the other room, so I hurried out of bed, brushed my teeth, and stepped into the living room, still wearing my pajamas. Everyone was up and dressed already.

"Why'd you let me sleep so late?" I whined as they all sipped on coffee.

"It's only a little after eight," Mac said before walking over to me and giving me a kiss.

I was visibly relieved, and I swore I heard Danika sigh as she poured me a mug of something and slid it toward me.

I gave her a look, and she smiled. "Sorry, but you two are so cute; I can't stand it."

"Yeah, the cutest," Chance teased, and Mac grabbed me by the hips and pulled me against him.

"I'll show you cute," he said as he kissed me hard, his tongue instantly in my mouth.

Even as I tried to pull away from him, he wouldn't let me. I laughed against his mouth, completely embarrassed, but he held on.

"Okay, we get it," Danika yelled, smacking her hand on top of the counter, and Mac finally released me.

"Good God," I said, swatting his arm and wiping at my mouth. I'd laughed through half of whatever that was.

"So, it might actually snow later," Danika said.

I wanted to scream in delight. "Really? Snow in New York for my first time here? What could be better?"

Danika frowned. "No snow," she said seriously. "It's usually warmer this time of year."

"I want it to snow. I want all the snow!"

"Me too," Mac said with a grin that matched mine.

Danika shot Chance a look, waiting for him to back her up, but he only shrugged and sipped at his coffee. "I want the snow too."

"Ugh, you Californians."

"Hey," Mac started to argue, but Danika waved him off.

"Close enough, Arizona."

"Fine," he relented.

"I'm going to go get dressed and send my mom a text. Happy Thanksgiving." I grinned from ear to ear, still ridiculously excited just to be here.

"They're on that cruise, right?" Danika asked, and I nodded. "It's still pretty early there."

"I know, but I'm afraid if I don't send it now, I'll forget later. And, oh! She sent me this picture yesterday that you have to see." I ran into the room, grabbed my phone, and jogged back out. I turned my cell around, so Danika could see my mom and dad sipping on drinks with umbrellas in them, my mom's hair blowing like crazy.

"Your dad actually looks happy."

"I know. She did good," I agreed, thankful that my dad had said yes instead of arguing. I couldn't wait to hear all about it when they got back. Maybe they would start taking more vacations now, but I wasn't convinced.

"Who's watching the dogs?"

"My sister. Who else?"

Danika giggled. "Your mom and those dogs."

"Tell me about it," I tossed over my shoulder as I headed back into the bedroom to finally get dressed.

After I finished, I marched into the kitchen, determined to help. Danika had a ridiculous amount of food spread out all over the granite countertops. The boys must have been banished because they were sitting on the couch, watching the Thanksgiving Day parade on the TV.

"Wait!" I shouted, and everyone focused on me. "That parade is here!" I pointed at the television. "Can we see it from the balcony? Did they go by already?" I ran to the sliding glass door, unlocked it, and pulled it open before leaping into the freezing cold air, my head craning from side to side to see around the buildings and into the streets.

The view was so different during the day. Long gone were the lights that had adorned each floor and windows. Replacing them were tall gray buildings, void of any color. Even the trees on the streets below were bare. Not a stitch of green in sight. But it was still unlike anything I'd ever experienced before. And we were right smack dab in the middle of it all. It looked like we were living in the clouds; we were up so high.

Mac wrapped his arms around me and planted a kiss on my neck. "It's cold as shit out here, babe."

"I know, but can you see them?" I asked, too focused to care about the weather.

"The floats?" he asked, stepping around me and leaning forward on the balcony railing. "No. Can you?"

Danika poked her head out of the open door but didn't step all the way out. "You can't see them from here. They go around the other side of the park. The west side. We're on the east."

"Fine." I pretended to pout. "But I know they're there," I shouted to whoever as Danika disappeared.

"Come back inside," Mac whispered against me. "Or get a jacket."

"Okay, Dad," I teased.

He narrowed his eyes at me. "You don't want to get sick, do you? We just got here."

He shook his head at me with disapproval, and my eyes grew wide. If I got a cold while we were here, I'd be so mad at myself.

"You're right," I agreed quickly and ran inside.

Mac followed, closing the door behind him before trying to chase me toward the kitchen. "I'm what? Say that last part again."

"Back to your couch." Danika pointed at Mac.

He stopped mid-step. "But I—"

"Couch. No boys in the kitchen."

Mac gave Danika a wiseass grin. "Don't hate the sound of that."

Typical male.

"Okay, I'm ready. How can I help?" I asked, and Danika's shoulders sank as we stared at the ridiculous amount of food that she'd bought that we still needed to prep and cook.

"I honestly have no idea. Why didn't I order in? I'm going to ruin our holiday," she said, and we both started laughing.

"We'll figure this out. It can't be that hard. Right? I mean, everyone does it," I said, and she gave me a crazy look.

"We should probably start drinking. I think it will help."

I glanced at the clock on the microwave. "It's still morning."

"So?" She looked past me and into the living room. "You guys want a beer?"

Both boys' heads turned quick. "Yes," they shouted like she might take the offer back.

Twisting off the caps, she walked to the couch and handed them each one. Chance grabbed her, pulled her down, and gave her a kiss before thanking her. Her cheeks turned bright red. Still. After all this time.

"I have some Lambrusco," she said like I had any idea what that even meant. "We can drink that and pretend to be civilized." She opened up one of the cupboards and pulled out a bottle before going to another cabinet and grabbing two of the smallest wineglasses I'd ever seen.

"Why are they so small?" I reached for one and studied it, spinning it around with my fingers.

"We drink Lambrusco in tiny glasses. I don't know why!"

I dug inside one of the drawers, searching for a bottle opener. "Yes," I said as I pulled it out and handed it to her.

She opened and poured the wine, and we swished it around inside our little glasses. I had no clue what we were doing, but I did it anyway.

"We're letting it breathe," Danika said in a thick, fake British accent.

"Oh, yes, darling. It must breathe an ample amount of time before we devour it," I added, my accent as bad as hers.

We eventually finished off the entire bottle of wine, and all we'd done was make even more of a mess in the kitchen. Potato peels were in the sink, but we hadn't sliced or diced them yet. The turkey was sitting in some turkey cooking thing that Danika had started calling his bathtub because neither one of us could remember the name of it. The fresh-bread stuffing was still sitting in a bag, waiting to be made. There was asparagus on the chopping block. The oversize rolls were in the fridge. And the two of us were hammered.

"I think our girlfriends are drunk," Mac said, suddenly standing in front of me, his hazel eyes looking all dreamy.

"When did you get here?" I asked as I reached out to run my fingers across his face. "You're so hot."

Mac started laughing, and Chance appeared out of thin air.

"Are you two magic? How do you just appear like that?" I asked, snapping my fingers.

"They didn't just appear," Danika explained, her words slower than usual. "They walked. From the couch. You know"—she pointed over to the couch where the parade was done and some football game was playing instead—"over there."

"I think you two had better slow down, or we won't have anything to eat," Chance said, sounding all reasonable and annoying.

"You'd two better slow down or ..." Danika mouthed off back, but when she couldn't think up a retort, she started giggling instead. "Crap. We drank too much."

"It's the little glasses! They seem so harmless," I complained.

Mac handed us each a bottle of water. "Here. Drink these. You girls need any help?" he offered.

I shook my head. "No. We want to do it. Go away." I shoved at him, but his stupid, strong body refused to move. "Out of the kitchen." I kept shoving. He kept staying put.

Giving me a quick kiss, he grabbed another beer and left like a good boy. Even with my blood now made of wine, I knew I could make my cookie dough, so I went to work, mixing and measuring and trying to stop Danika from eating it all. I swore I swatted her hand at least twenty times, but nothing stopped her.

"I'll double the recipe, and then I'll bake half of it and leave the other half in the fridge for you to eat, okay?"

"Can you quadruple the recipe, so I can freeze some and

have it forever?" She sat in a barstool for a second and gave me a funny look. "I need more water."

"Are you going to be sick?" I asked, suddenly concerned.

"No." She waved me off. "I just need to stop being so buzzed. Why won't it go away?"

"We need more bread," I suggested, and she nodded furiously before hopping up, grabbing a fresh loaf and some butter.

With whatever luck and magic we'd pulled out of our asses, Danika and I ended up making a pretty decent Thanksgiving meal. I had no idea how much time had passed. The day blurred. She grabbed the turkey and his bathtub from the oven just as the doorbell rang.

My head shot up as I wondered who might be here before I remembered that it was her dad. "I'll get it!" I ran to the door, pulling it open and giving Ralph Marchetti a giant hug before he knew what hit him. "Hi, Other Dad!"

"Hey, other daughter," he said back with a huge grin as he stepped inside. "It smells incredible in here."

Chance and Mac stood up from the couch, walking over to Ralph, and they each shook his hand.

"Happy Thanksgiving," Ralph said, giving them a firm shake.

"You remember my teammate Mac, right?" Chance asked, reintroducing them to one another.

"First baseman," Ralph said, and I noted how Mac's entire face lit up.

"Yes, sir. It's nice to see you again," Mac said, sounding extremely polite and professional. It was so hot.

"You too. Excited for the season to start?" he asked, and I had forgotten how much of a baseball fan Ralph Marchetti was.

"I can't wait," Mac said, and I couldn't wait either.

I was looking forward to watching him play, knowing that he was mine when he stepped off that field.

"You'll be great," Ralph said, sounding confident before he looked at Chance. "Have you talked to your parents yet?"

"Not yet. I sent my mom a text this morning, but she hasn't called yet."

"I'm excited to go out there for Christmas," Ralph said as he pulled five bottles of wine from a bag he carried. Danika's and Chance's families had blended so easily without any kind of awkwardness. They all got along great, like they were always meant to be together.

"Dad, why'd you bring so many?" Danika asked, her eyes wide as she spooned the mashed potatoes into a giant bowl.

"We don't have to drink them all today, sweetheart," he said, giving her a hug and a kiss on the cheek. "But you should always have wine at the house."

"They've had enough wine already," Mac teased, and my jaw dropped.

"Hey! That was hours ago!" I complained as I reached for one of the bottles and opened it before setting it on top of the dinner table.

Everything was almost ready.

"Dad, will you carve the turkey? I have no idea how to do that, and I'm not going to even pretend to try," Danika asked, and Ralph started rolling up his sleeves.

Dinner went off without a hitch. The food was not only edible, but actually good too. The five of us sat at the table, rubbing our stomachs, as the TV played low in the background. Danika and her dad talked about the new business division Danika had started, both of them incredibly excited and proud, which made me excited and proud as well. It sounded really interesting, and when Danika said I'd be the perfect fit to work there with her, I blew it off, not thinking she was really serious even though she'd mentioned it before.

And when they started talking about Chance's baseball with the same level of pride, it amazed me how at home it felt, being here with them. I'd thought that it might feel a little weird, being away from California and my own parents for the first time, but if anything, it was the exact opposite. I liked it here. And it seemed like Mac did too. He looked more relaxed than I'd seen him in a long time. Maybe getting away from Fullton and the stress of the upcoming season was good for him. Or maybe it was just seeing Chance. I wasn't sure what it was, but it made me happy.

After the dishes were cleaned—by the boys no less—and everyone was on the couch, watching more football, I pulled my cookie cake out of the oven, the smell permeating the entire apartment. Everyone, who just moments before had said they'd never eat again, was suddenly salivating at the mouth, begging for a piece. It was funny what dessert did to people's appetites.

"You should get this one to come work with us," Ralph mentioned to Danika as he dragged me into a hug at the end of the night.

"I'm trying," Danika agreed.

I smiled, not knowing if they were serious or not. The idea entered my head, and I wondered if it was something I could do and be good at. I still had no clue what interested me, but I refused to rule this out. That would just be plain stupid.

"It was great to see you, Sunny. Hopefully, it won't be the last time. Good luck with your season, Mac. And I'll see you two later. Love you, kids," he said, and I almost teared up at the endearment. He'd said he loved them both.

Goals.

After Ralph left, the four of us plopped onto the couch in a food coma and didn't move for hours. At least, it felt like hours. But when Danika reminded us that tomorrow was a big day filled with sightseeing, my heart started racing.

"It's time for bed then. I want it to be tomorrow already," I said, and she laughed at me. "I mean it. Come on, Mac," I practically whined, and he begrudgingly stood up, said good night, and followed me into the bedroom, where we were too full to do anything but sleep.

THE BIG APPLE

Sunny

I'D SET THE alarm on my phone the night before for eight a.m., not wanting to sleep in any longer than necessary. I refused to miss a single moment of seeing Manhattan. When I opened my eyes, I pulled myself from the bed and looked outside. A fresh coat of snow covered the ground.

"Mac! Mac, wake up. It snowed!" I ran back to the bed, shaking his shoulders as he rubbed his eyes and forced them open.

"It really snowed?" he asked, his voice groggy but still incredibly sexy.

"Come look." I pulled at him, ripping the warm covers from his body.

"Dang, woman." He grabbed me and held me tight. "Now, you have to keep me warm. My own weighted blanket."

"Please look." I pouted, and he tapped my nose with his finger before telling me he'd do anything I asked. I might have melted, but I was too excited to notice.

We both speed-walked to the window and looked outside.

"It's so pretty," I breathed out, and he agreed.

"We're gonna freeze though," he added.

I frowned. I wasn't built for snow.

"Let's go see if they're up," I suggested, meaning Danika and Chance. I hoped they were awake and not still in some sort of food coma from last night.

"I have a better idea." He playfully smacked my butt, and as much as I wanted to have sex, I wanted to go explore more. But I couldn't tell Mac that and hurt his precious ego.

"After we see the sights. I promise."

He shook his head. "Go see if they're up. I'll be right out."

Mac didn't have to tell me twice. I practically threw the door open and ran out into the living room.

"Yay! You're up!" I shouted when I saw Danika standing in the kitchen, holding her head between her hands.

"Don't yell," she said.

I groaned out loud. "No, you cannot have a hangover. Not today of all days." I was going to be so upset if Danika felt bad all day and didn't enjoy being out and about.

"I'll be fine. I just need some caffeine."

As if on cue, the coffeepot gurgled to life and started brewing.

"Did you take anything?" I pushed, wanting her to be in perfect health for our first day of exploring.

"I just did." She leveled me with a look. "Sunny, it's okay. I just have a little headache."

"Did you see the snow?" I clapped, and she blew out a breath like the weather annoyed her. Or maybe it was the clapping.

"Ugh. No. How bad is it?" she asked as she made her way

toward the balcony door, opening it and stepping outside as a gush of cold air whooshed inside. She looked down and around before giving herself a nod. "It's not much. We should be fine," she said as she stepped back indoors. "Tell me you brought sensible walking shoes, or our first stop will be at a store."

"I brought some Adidas and a pair of Madden boots," I said, hoping that was good enough. I didn't own anything other than them and a bunch of sandals and flip-flops.

Danika pivoted her head from side to side like she was hitting an imaginary ping-pong while she thought. "Wear the boots. But if your feet start hurting, let me know."

"Okay."

"Is there anything you want to see?" Danika asked as she sat back down in one of the barstools after pouring out four mugs of coffee even though neither boy had come out of their rooms yet.

"I thought you were going to show me everything." I started to pout as I pulled out the stool next to her and sat just as both guys walked out, fully dressed and ready for the day. It wasn't fair that it took guys ten seconds to get ready when us girls had to adjust our whole appearance before we could even leave the house.

"I am," she reassured my overactive brain. "But I was just wondering if there was anywhere that was a must-see on your list."

"Morning," Chance said as he planted a kiss on Danika's cheek and stood across the counter from us. He reached for one of the mugs, poured something weird and green in it, stirred, and took a sip.

"I want one too," Mac said as he kissed the side of my head before joining Chance at his side of the kitchen instead of sitting down.

"What are you girls talking about?" Chance asked, and Danika told him that we were trying to plan the day.

I interrupted, "I want to see Central Park. And what's that famous hotel that's in all the old movies?"

"The Plaza?" she asked.

I snapped my fingers excitedly. "Yes! The Plaza. And, um ..." I paused, trying to think of where else we could go, but I was drawing a blank.

Mac leaned across the counter between us. "Not to be a downer or anything, but I'd really like to go to the 9/11 Memorial. If no one else wants to go, I can go alone," he started.

I swallowed hard as the images from that day flooded my mind. None of us were old enough to remember when it had happened, but every year on the anniversary, the same horrifying pictures and videos were repeatedly shown that it felt like we had been.

"I want to go," I said.

"Me too," Chance agreed. "I haven't been yet."

Danika looked sad, and I wondered if her dad had known anyone who died that day or not. "Of course we'll go. It's important. You should see it."

"Not today though," Mac interjected. "Just at some point before we leave, okay?"

"Is that big tree up yet?" I asked, meaning the one they showed on television every year.

"The Rockefeller Center Christmas Tree?" Danika asked, shaking her head. "It doesn't go up until December. But I think Macy's decorated their Christmas windows already. You have to see them. You'll love them, Sunny. I wonder what the theme is this year," she kept talking to herself, and I found myself getting emotional.

New York was filled with so many familiar things that had been made famous by television shows and movies, and now, I'd get to see them all in real life. It was surreal even if I wasn't sure exactly why, and I wondered if this was how people felt about Los Angeles when they visited for the first time.

"We should eat something light here. Then, we can walk over to Central Park. That could take hours. We can go into The Plaza Food Hall for lunch. And then we can swing by Times Square and the Macy's windows. How's that sound?" Chance asked, sounding like a New York native already.

"I forgot about Times Square," I said, smacking my hand on top of the counter like a little kid. "How could I forget about that?"

"Go get dressed. Wear layers, Sunny. I have a jacket for you. Maybe two pairs of socks," Danika directed. Clearly, she was feeling better already.

"Two pairs of socks?" I complained. I'd never worn two pairs of socks in my life. *What if my shoes don't fit over them?*

"Trust me," Danika said. "Your toes will thank me."

I got ready in record time, not wanting to waste a single minute of daylight. My head was spinning as Mac walked into the master bathroom, where I was finishing up the last of my makeup.

"It's freezing outside, babe."

"You came in here to tell me that?" I asked him with a smirk because we'd already been told how cold it was. Or at least how cold it could be. Multiple times before we arrived.

"Yes. And to see if you were almost ready."

"I've been in here for, like, ten minutes."

"I know, but"—he looked at me in the mirror and bit his bottom lip—"I just want to get out of this apartment and go see everything."

I smiled big before turning around and wrapping my arms around his massive shoulders. "I love that you're as excited as I am."

"I totally am." He leaned down and pressed a kiss to my lips before smacking me hard on the ass. "Now, hurry up, gorgeous. Let's go see the city."

I SWORE WE walked by ten pizza places on our way to Central Park, each one claiming to be the best. I had no idea what the difference was between them; they all looked the same to me. Mac and I walked hand in glove-covered hand behind Danika and Chance, who led the way. The air was crisp and cold, but the wind made it bitter. Thank God Danika had had an extra beanie and scarf for me to wear. And the two pairs of socks? She had been absolutely right.

I was grateful when the wind finally died down. It made

the cold bearable.

Central Park was absolutely enormous. I knew that people always said it was big and that they had concerts there and stuff, but I'd had no idea it was as large as it was. It was so much more than any *park* I'd ever been to back home. Whenever I thought of that word, I imagined a playground and basically an oversize lawn in my mind. This was like a hundred of those. Maybe more. And apparently, we hadn't even walked half the length of it, and I'd already seen a zoo, a couple of lakes, multiple baseball fields, and an ice-skating rink! I thought I could spend the entire day walking around Central Park and still not see it all.

Mac grabbed and kissed my frozen lips constantly, spinning me around and dipping me like we were dancing. He made Central Park romantic. I thought we were both swept up in the magic of it all. The holiday, the snow, adventuring together.

"Come on, you two," Chance yelled, and I realized that we'd fallen back pretty far from the two of them.

Mac pulled my hand as we ran to catch up, making sure not to slip on any ice or snow.

"If you two don't stop kissing every five seconds, we'll never see anything," Danika scolded us like a pair of naughty teenagers.

I offered a nonchalant shrug. "Probably not gonna happen."

"Definitely not gonna happen," Mac agreed as he kissed me again.

A burst of snow exploded around our faces, and I realized

that Chance had tossed a snowball at Mac's head.

"Better run, Carter!" Mac shouted as he bent down to make a snowball the size of a freaking beach ball and threw it with both hands.

Chance easily maneuvered out of the way, and Mac saw the error of his ways.

He quickly made a new, much smaller ball of snow and threw it like a freaking Major League pitcher. It hit Chance right in the back as he tried to move to miss it but was struck anyway.

"Damn, that hurt," Chance said, throwing a snowball back at Mac but aiming for his pants.

"Hey! No hitting the goods," I demanded as Danika and I watched them and took pictures with our cell phones.

"Sorry, Sunny," Chance apologized as the guys chased each other around like they'd done in the apartment the first night.

"Is this what it's like to live with boys?" I asked.

Danika let out a stifled laugh as she looked around at the small crowd forming, watching them. "How would I know?"

"Can we please go now?" I yelled, hoping they'd stop running around long enough to realize that they were creating a scene.

Both of them stopped, snowballs in hand as they looked at one another with matching mischievous grins.

"Oh no," Danika yelled and put her hands up. She realized what they were doing before I had a chance to put it together.

"Don't you dare." I started backing away from Mac, who was walking toward me way too quickly.

The two of them smashed their last remaining snowballs on top of my and Danika's heads at the same time, the snow falling all around our faces and sticking in our hair.

"Sleep with one eye open, hotshot." Danika glared at Chance, who was now begging for her forgiveness behind eyes filled with laughter.

He wasn't sorry, and we all knew it.

Mac didn't even pretend to apologize as we continued walking. We stepped out of the trees, and the most stunning building was right in front of us.

"Is that …" I started to ask, but I wasn't sure.

"The Plaza," Danika said with a smile. "Isn't it beautiful?"

"It's unreal," I said, staring at it.

I wasn't sure how to explain it in words, even to myself in my head, so I pulled out my phone and took a few pictures. But none of them did the structure any justice at all.

"How do people take pictures that make it look as amazing as it really is?" I asked no one in particular as I took turns between staring at the picture on my phone and at the building in real life.

"Wait till you see the inside," Chance added.

"What are we waiting for?" Mac asked. "I'm starving. You sure they have food here?"

"There's a whole food hall downstairs," Chance said.

"Like a food court?" I asked, and Danika shook her head.

"Not really. It's not like something you'd find in a mall. It's more like Harrods in London," she explained, and I chuckled.

"Oh yeah, of course. Harrods. In London," I mimicked,

bringing out the fake accent again.

"Sorry," she complained. "I just don't know how else to explain it. You'll see."

The Plaza Food Hall wasn't at all like a mall, even though there were various shops there. It was definitely more upscale, and you could either dine in or do your shopping for that night's meals. It was incredible. I ate cheese I'd never heard of before and had fresh pasta made from scratch, which was unlike anything you could buy at the grocery store.

The woman had told me, "No preservatives," since it didn't need to last on a store shelf, I guessed.

There were insanely fancy desserts that looked almost too pretty to eat. But I ate them anyway. And even they tasted expensive.

"This is how the other half lives," I said as I bit into a dark chocolate cupcake and moaned.

"It's definitely pricey but also worth it," Mac said, pulling out his dad's credit card once again to pay for the cupcakes and macaroons.

"Worth it 'cause you're not paying?" I teased, and he leaned down to lick the chocolate off my lips.

"No. Worth it because it tastes amazing."

I nodded in agreement, and Danika asked if I wanted to see parts of the hotel that we could access. That was a definite yes, so off we went, upstairs to see whatever the staff would let us look at. And it was beyond my wildest imagination. Crystal chandeliers, marble columns, gold leaf highlights, murals on the walls, and fresh rose arrangements *everywhere*. The Plaza screamed class and European style. I wasn't sure we had anything even remotely like it back in LA. If we did, I'd never seen it before.

When we finally walked outside, the sun was setting, and the wind had picked up again. The last thing I wanted to do was walk more, but I wasn't going to mention it. We'd spent so much time doing so little, but somehow, I still felt fulfilled.

"Should we see the Macy's windows or Times Square?" Chance asked Danika, and she placed a finger against her lips, as if pondering.

"I think we should visit Times Square tomorrow. Windows tonight," she suggested, and we all agreed.

We waited in line to see them. Apparently, it got more crowded once it was dark, but Danika said there was most likely a line all day. But I didn't care because just like everything else I'd seen today in this magical city, they were marvelous. The theme was all about believing in the magic of Santa. Each window had a different word and an intricate scene that went along with it. I couldn't even begin to guess how many hours had gone into creating each display, but it seemed worth it when I saw the sheer amount of people waiting just to look at them. And they all seemed so happy.

"I can't believe they do this every year." I nudged Mac's shoulder, and he held me tighter as he pointed out one of the elves moving in the background.

"What a cool job, right?"

"Can you imagine creating this much joy for people year after year?"

"Nope. I'm nowhere near that creative," he said, and I laughed. I wasn't either.

After we looked at all the windows, the temperature continued to drop, and my feet were sore from standing all day long—and not because my boots were bad. I knew my feet would have hurt no matter what I was wearing on them.

"You guys ready to go home or ..." Danika asked, stopping at the end of the question because I knew she didn't want to make us leave if we weren't ready.

"I'd love to take a hot bath," I said, and she oohed at me.

"Yes! That sounds so good. And we can grab a pie on the way home for later," she said.

I threw my head back. "A pie?"

"Pizza. She means, a pizza," Chance interpreted, and I nodded even though I wasn't even remotely hungry.

"We still have a fridge full of leftovers," I said, reminding everyone about all the turkey sandwiches waiting for us at home.

"True," Chance said. "Maybe pizza tomorrow," he suggested instead.

Danika agreed, "That's better anyway. Tomorrow, I'll introduce you both to the best pizza you've ever eaten. You'll never be the same."

I couldn't wait. It was our last full day in the city, but I tried not to think about it because I didn't want to be sad. We definitely hadn't booked a long enough trip.

Next time.

NYC IS FOR LOVERS

Mac

WHEN DANIKA SUGGESTED taking a cab back to the apartment, I almost bit her head off with my enthusiasm. The idea of traipsing around *any-fucking-more* made me want to curl up in a ball and die. Not that the entire day hadn't been unbelievable. This city was a fucking gem. I loved it. But I was tired of walking around in it.

And I wasn't the only one. Everyone was exhausted.

Whether it was the number of miles we'd hiked throughout the day, the cold, or a combination of the two, the four of us could barely keep our eyes open past nine as we sat on the couch, trying to watch a movie. We called it a night and headed to our rooms to crash and do it all over again tomorrow.

Once again, I was too tired to do much else but sleep. My girl was going to start thinking I didn't love her. And I did, by the way. I knew it. Hell, I'd known it. But I still hadn't said it.

I'd started falling for her that night on the phone last year. But I fell even more the night of the party, where she defended me more than once, stood up for me, and showed me that she had my back when people were trying to stomp all over it. And

I'd been falling more and more every day since.

I couldn't imagine not having her in my life. It would be like trying to live without the sun—no pun intended.

As I held her in my arms, her tiny body tucked up against mine, I fought the urge to confess my feelings. I planned on telling her. I'd been planning on telling her since the minute we stepped into the airport back in LA. But I wanted the perfect moment.

THE NEXT MORNING, I woke up, and my arm was numb. Freaking out, I looked down and noticed Sunny fast asleep, her head using my bicep as a pillow. I slowly pulled it out from under her, not wanting to wake her up but needing to get some blood flow circulating. The tingles started immediately, followed by the flutter of my girl's eyelids.

"Morning," she said.

I leaned down to press a kiss to her cheek. "Morning."

"What time is it?" Her eyes closed again as I reached for my phone to check.

"Six thirty," I said, and she groaned. "I'm going to see if Chance wants to go to the gym. I need to work out, and I'm sure he does too."

"Okay."

"Stay here until I get back," I demanded, knowing she probably wouldn't listen to me.

"We'll see." She opened her eyes and grinned before snuggling into the covers, tempting me.

I thought about diving underneath and making her scream until we woke the neighbors, but talked myself out of it.

"When I get back here, you'd better be ready," I warned.

"For what?"

"Your man."

She laughed. "I'll see you when you get back then, all sweaty and sexy."

"You like that, do you?" I asked, rolling on top of her and pinning her beneath my body.

She nodded. "Mmhmm."

"Fuck waiting. I want you now." I leaned down and took her mouth, begging her to open up even though I knew she was probably freaking out about not having brushed her teeth yet. I couldn't care less. I missed her body and being inside her.

Her legs fell open, giving me all the invitation I needed. I pulled my boxer briefs down and kicked them aside before reaching between her legs and running my fingers down her pussy. Even through her thong, I could feel the heat. Moving her panties to the side, I let my finger trace the length of her, stopping right at her entrance. I made small, slow circles at first before I pushed inside, her slickness coating me. She was so wet and ready.

"Damn, babe."

Her hips bucked and writhed against my finger as I fucked her with it, begging me for more.

"Mac. Please."

She moved faster against me, and I pulled out, grabbed her

panties, trying to move them out of the way.

"Get these off," I demanded as I grabbed a condom and rolled it on as fast as I could. If I didn't get inside her, I thought I might die.

Her hand reached for me, and she played with my balls before gripping the base of my cock. Even around the condom, her touch felt incredible.

"Get inside me," she begged, her lips parting as she watched me.

I held my dick as I moved to her entrance and pushed inside. Each time was more perfect than the last. Moving slow, I worked my way in as deep as I could go, and she arched her head back and moaned, letting me know she loved it as much as I did.

"Feel good?"

"Fuck yes," she breathed out, and I almost came, just from the way she'd sounded.

Her hips moved in time with mine, letting me reach that deepest part of her with every thrust. It was too fucking good.

I leaned down, taking a nipple in my mouth, sucking and nibbling. Her back lifted from the bed as she pulled at my hair, and I moved to the other nipple and did the same. I grabbed and kneaded her tits as she repeated my name over and over again, sending me close to the edge.

Her nails dug into my back, and she dragged them down, the pain sending waves of pleasure through me. I moved my mouth back to hers and kissed her like my life depended on it. Thrusting in and out of her tight little body, I knew it was only a matter of time before I came. Without warning, she moved her legs, wrapping them around my lower back, and suddenly, I was hitting places I never knew existed before now. I couldn't stop if I wanted to.

"Yes, Mac. Yes," she moaned, her legs pinching around me in a vise grip, and I found myself fucking her so hard that I thought I might hurt her.

I came quick, releasing so viciously that it wouldn't shock me if I tore the damn condom. With one last shudder, reality crashed into me, and I pulled out quicker than I ever had before just to check. When I glanced down, everything looked to be in the right place.

"You okay?" Sunny asked, her breathing heavy.

"Thought I might have torn it," I said, and her eyes widened.

"It didn't, right?" She looked worried.

"No. All good," I said as I got up and walked with my hand on my dick toward the bathroom to get rid of it and triple-check. "Phew."

After flushing, I strutted back into the bedroom, where Sunny was propped up, waiting for me.

"It's not that I don't want kids," she started to say, and I stopped walking and cocked my head to the side as I stared at her, wondering where this was headed. "I mean, I don't want kids now. Or anytime soon," she continued to clarify.

I breathed out in relief. I was nowhere near ready to be a dad. And who knew when I would be? "We're on the same page, babe," I reassured her as I grabbed some workout clothes.

I shot off a text to Chance, telling him to wake up, and he

responded immediately, saying that he was waiting for my sorry ass. Kissing Sunny bye, I tucked her back into bed and pretended to hit the gym with my best friend.

When Chance and I returned about an hour later, the girls were already dressed and ready, which was a nice surprise. I didn't mind waiting for them, but it was our last day in Manhattan, and there was still so much we wanted to see and do.

"The 9/11 Memorial first, I think," Danika was saying as Chance and I raced each other, chugging a glass of orange juice.

I won.

Barely.

"Please tell me we don't have to walk there," I complained, sounding like a chick.

"Hell no." Danika looked at me like I was crazy. "That's far. We'll take the train."

"She means, the subway," Chance interjected.

"Cool. Let me go shower real quick, and then I'll be ready to go," I said, and Chance shot me a look.

"Race you," he said before taking off, running toward his room, and I sprinted toward mine in response.

Were we always so competitive?

After the quickest shower in the history of the world, I got dressed and didn't even tie my shoes before running into the living room. Chance was sitting at a barstool, sipping a mug and tapping his fingers on the countertop, like he'd been waiting hours for me to get there.

Punching his arm, I shook my head. "How long?"

"Just got out here." He laughed.

"I swear you two weren't like this last year," Danika said.

"I think this is how they show their love," Sunny added, and I considered that maybe she was right. We hadn't been this childish when we lived together.

We all grabbed coats and gloves because it was still cold as shit outside. But nothing was going to stop me from seeing this memorial.

We walked the short distance to the subway, and I was impressed as hell when we entered a whole new world underground. There were empty booths, kiosks, newspaper stands, and people rushing every which way. It was like an entire city existed underneath the roads above.

The four of us bought MetroCards from what was basically a vending machine before swiping them and walking through a turnstile to even more chaos. There were so many people running and darting around others in their rush to get to wherever they were going. I gripped Sunny's hand even tighter, not wanting her to get run over.

I followed Danika down, down, and even further down until I was convinced that we couldn't possibly go any lower. We rounded a corner, and another world opened up. The smell of stale air hit my nostrils, and I noticed how warm it was. There were multiple tracks littered with trash, and steam was billowing as people waited for their trains to arrive, completely oblivious to anything else, except their cell phones.

"I'm loving this." Sunny gripped my arm, her eyes filled with wonder. "Even the trash," she said, and I laughed.

"What are you two whispering about?" Chance leaned toward us before putting a hand in the air. "No. Don't tell me. I probably don't want to know."

Our "train" arrived in no time, and I assumed that we'd have to stand. Once we got on though, Danika found four seats for us, and we took them right as the doors closed and the train took off. There were multiple stops and starts with people getting on and off in clusters. I was just about to stand up to offer my seat to a pregnant woman when Chance beat me to it.

When we reached our stop, the four of us exited and followed a steep set of stairs back above ground. It was bright as hell, and I shielded my eyes until they corrected themselves.

"This way." Danika continued to lead us in the proper direction, and I had no idea how she did it.

I was so fucking turned around that nothing made sense. Where we were looked different than where we'd been, but that literally meant nothing to me.

We kept walking, my eyes taking in all the buildings as my steps slowed. It was almost like I sensed we were close.

Sunny pulled on my hand. "You okay?"

"Yeah," I said as I stared up at the tall, looming tower.

"It's right up here." Danika pointed ahead.

The second we crossed the tree-lined threshold, the whole atmosphere seemed to shift. This part of the city felt heavy with what had once been. Or maybe it was just me. As we made our way toward the footprints of the old buildings, which were now water features outlined with everyone's names, I sucked in a somber breath, feeling the weight of it all.

It seemed unreal, but I'd seen the pictures. I'd watched the videos. It had really happened.

Sunny wrapped an arm around my middle and leaned her

head against my shoulder. "I wonder what the roses mean," she said, pointing to a single white rose sticking out of someone's name carved into the stone.

"It means it's their birthday," Danika answered, and I hadn't even known she was next to us.

"Today is their birthday?" I turned to ask, and Danika nodded. "They do this for each person's birthday?"

"Yep."

"That's beautiful," Sunny said, her voice sounding as emotional as I felt.

Danika left to follow Chance, who had started to wander to the other side of the memorial.

I tried to process exactly what we were looking at, but there was no way to truly comprehend it all. Wrapping my head around the sheer size of the buildings felt impossible. This city had lost so much. The whole country had. And it made me fucking ache, just thinking about all the people who never got to go home again when all they'd done was show up for work that day.

And maybe it wasn't the right time, but at this sacred place, where so many people said *I love you* for the last time, I wanted to say it for the first time.

"Sunny," I tried to say her name, but I choked. "Sunny," I tried again, and she turned toward me, her silver hair reflecting the light, looking like a damn angel.

"Yeah?" Her expression tightened as concern for me spread through her features.

She sensed that I wasn't okay. I reached out for her, needing her touch, and she walked past my hand and into my arms, pressing her head against my chest, where I held her.

"I love you," I whispered, and I felt her breath hitch as she pulled away from me to look me in my eyes, wondering if she'd heard me right or not. Cupping her chin with my fingers, I repeated myself, "I love you."

I leaned down and planted a kiss on her lips, hoping like hell she'd say it back because I'd never felt more vulnerable in my entire life.

"I love you too." She wiped at her eyes as the tears fell, and when the snow started to fall as well, it felt like a sign from above.

Or a blessing.

Or whatever you wanted to call it.

But I took it as approval.

The rest of the day, I was on cloud nine. Knowing that Sunny loved me made me feel whole, complete. I'd always assumed that I'd stay broken forever, not worthy of being truly loved by anyone outside of my mom. But Sunny made me feel like all of that couldn't be further from the truth. She made me feel deserving.

The four of us sat in a small pizza shop, eating the best pizza I'd ever had.

"You were right," I said as I copied Danika and folded my slice in half, watching the grease drip out the bottom. "This is the best pizza I've ever had."

"Told you," Danika said as she swallowed. "And before you ask, it's the water."

"What is?" Sunny inquired, her nose red from the cold.

"Why it's so good. It's the water here."

Chance just shrugged. "Just agree with her," he said, and she punched him in the shoulder the same way Sunny always did to me.

"I really want to show you the office, Sun," Danika said as she finished off the last of her pizza. "Do you want to see it?"

Sunny's eyes instantly met mine, as if she was unsure of what to say in response. I gave her a smirk, letting her know I thought she should go without saying the words.

"Yes. I'd love to. But what are the guys going to do?"

Chance stood up and wiped the crumbs from his jeans. "I'm going to take you to the Tavern. And the girls can meet us there after they're done."

"Sounds good," I said, clapping my man on the back.

"Okay." Sunny grinned, looking excited as she walked over to me and gave me a kiss. "I'll see you later."

The girls walked out the door and disappeared out of view.

"Tell me this tavern has food."

"We just ate pizza."

"One slice, dude. We had one slice," I complained. "I'm a growing boy."

"It has food. Let's go," he said.

I braced myself for the cold as we headed outside. Just as I was about to suggest we take the subway, Chance's hand was in the air, and he was hailing a cab.

"Where is this place?" I asked, not that I would have any idea where it was once he told me.

"Walking distance from the apartment," he said.

I was relieved. I liked the idea of being close to the house. When we finally got there because traffic in Manhattan was a bitch, the place was practically empty. The dark wood gave off a casual, old-school vibe, and I suggested we sit at the bar, but Chance pointed at one of the high-top tables in the back.

"So we won't have to move when the girls get here," he said.

I nodded. "You're right. My bad."

We ordered drinks and food from the bartender and then moved to the table.

"Food will just be a few minutes," the bartender said as he slid our beers toward us.

"So"—Chance took a sip of his drink while he looked at me—"you and Sunny seemed extra smooshy today."

I grinned, wishing I could stop myself but I couldn't. I didn't even make fun of his use of the word 'smooshy.' "She loves me," I said, sounding like an excited little kid.

"Did she actually say that, or are you just assuming?" He was being a smart-ass, but I would have done the same thing if the roles had been reversed. I probably had when they were.

"She told me."

"Good for you, man. She's a good girl," he said, taking another swig. "Are you ready for the season?"

I cleared my throat. "Yeah. Gonna give it my all, and hopefully, it will be enough."

"I know it's hard," Chance said, but the truth was that he didn't know. There had never been any question as to whether or not he was going to get drafted. Everybody, including ESPN, had known that he would even if Chance acted like it wasn't a sure thing. He was just being modest.

"No offense," I started, "but I don't really want to talk about baseball right now."

I wondered if he was as surprised as I was by my admission. Chance and I always talked about everything, especially baseball—and I rarely avoided that subject. I'd eaten, lived, and breathed baseball for as long as I could remember, and now, I didn't even want to talk about it.

"Okay. I get it. But I'm here if you need me."

"I know you are," I said as I took a drink of my beer and swallowed. "Your dad said that same thing. Offered to hook me up with your uncle in case I had more specific questions."

"My uncle would have insight that my dad wouldn't."

"I know." I nodded. "But I'm not sure there's a point."

"What do you mean?"

"I don't know what your uncle would tell me that I don't already know. No matter what he says, it won't change the way I play," I explained.

Chance nodded. "And you don't want anything he says to get in your head."

"Exactly."

"Anything new with your old man?" he asked. Another touchy subject.

"Not really. Same old Dick."

"But you and Sunny are good?" He circled back around to the one topic I was actually willing to talk about in greater detail.

"Yeah, we are. I'm just stupid for not making it official with her last year." I smacked my hand on top of the table. "Why didn't you tell me?"

Chance laughed and leaned back. "No, no, no. Don't even go there, buddy."

"What?" I feigned innocence as the bartender appeared with our food.

The size of the fish on my plate made me laugh. It was huge. I grabbed a way-too-hot French fry and dropped it back on the plate.

"I did tell you last year." He shook his head at me. "And then you stopped going over there with me just so you could pretend like you didn't have feelings for the girl."

"You should have tried harder then," I said, blaming him.

He rolled his eyes. A signature Chance Carter move. "Well, it worked out anyway."

"No thanks to you," I offered with a smirk before grabbing a fry again and blowing on it so I could finally eat it.

Both of our phones vibrated on top of the table at the same time.

"Girls are on their way," Chance said, telling me what I'd just read myself in a text message from Sunny.

"What else are we doing tonight?" I asked because I knew we wouldn't sit at home on our last night in the city. I broke apart a piece of my fried fish and watched the steam billow out of it. At this rate, I'd never get to enjoy my fish and chips.

"I'm pretty sure Danika got tickets for the Empire State Building, so we could all see it at night."

"Oh." I blew out a breath. "I forgot about that place. That sounds sick. Have you been?"

He slowly shook his head. "No. Not yet."

"It wasn't enough time," I started to say before

elaborating, "being here, I mean."

"I know. Do you like it though?" he asked before taking a giant bite of his burger.

"Yeah. I actually like it a lot. You?"

"I always loved it here as a kid, but I think I like it even more now."

"You think you two will stay here then? You'll never go back to Cali?" I wondered as I finally took a bite of my fish, and the flavors exploded in my mouth. "Damn, this is good."

He held up a finger as he finished chewing and swallowed. "We've talked about it. We both want a place in California, but for now and the foreseeable future, our home base will be here."

"Well, it makes the most sense, right?" I asked.

The New York Mets had drafted Chance, and even though he was still playing in their farm system at the moment, we all knew he'd be in the Major Leagues within five years. Which meant that he'd have to live in the area. And Danika was working for her dad, who owned a big real estate firm here as well. The two of them being in Manhattan was logical.

"Yeah. But I still want a place back home. Even if we never technically live there again."

I went to say something in response but was distracted by the silver-haired goddess walking through the door. The smile on her face the second her eyes found mine made my fucking heart melt inside my chest. She loved me. I could see it in the way she looked at me.

I stood up from my chair to greet her, pulling her into my arms for a kiss that showed her just how much I'd missed her while she was gone. When it came to this girl, everything in my life felt right, even the fucked up parts that would have wrecked me before. All of the pieces—especially the jagged, broken ones—were less painful as long as I had her by my side.

I only hoped I made her feel the same way.

BACK HOME

Sunny

OUR LAST NIGHT in New York had been magical. We'd spent the evening on top of the Empire State Building, freezing our asses off but making some incredible memories. There were still so many things we hadn't gotten the chance to do or see, but that only made me more determined to come back again. But hopefully, when it was warmer.

When Danika and Chance dropped us off at the airport, I had to stop myself from crying. I had no idea when I was going to see my best friend again, and this trip had been more than I ever could have expected. I'd always assumed I'd think Manhattan was cool, but I'd had no idea that I'd love it as much as I did. Not to mention, the little detour we had taken yesterday to see her office that turned into more of a sales pitch really. Danika had offered me a job and told me to think about it, but now, it was all I could envision. Working here. With her. In this city.

But where does that leave me and Mac?

"Can you see yourself living here?" Mac asked me once we were alone in the airport, and it rattled me, like he was reading my mind somehow.

I wondered if Danika had mentioned something to him about the job offer, but I knew she wouldn't do that without telling me first.

"I don't know that I'd be any good at it, but I'd love to try." I laughed, and he seemed to know exactly what I meant.

"You'd get used to it. I can totally see you here."

"You can?" I was so shocked. "I mean, New York is so different from California, and I've always been such a SoCal girl," I overexplained, wanting to hear more about why he thought I belonged here.

"You've always been a bright light, babe. But here, you're a fucking spotlight."

My cheeks turned red, and I covered my mouth with my hand at his compliment.

"I could see you here too," I tossed back, and he grinned.

"I like it," he said, and that made me happy. "A lot. Hey, did Danika offer you a job yesterday?" he asked, and I almost started coughing.

"I mean ..." I wasn't sure what to say. "I guess, technically, she did."

He didn't look surprised or upset. He looked happy. "What'd you say? Is it something you're interested in?"

That was the million-dollar question. "It sounds exciting, but I don't know anything about real estate or rich people, so I'm not really sure."

"I bet you'd be great at it," he said, sounding so freaking supportive that it was almost pissing me off.

We'd just said we loved each other, and now, he was

pushing me away, encouraging me to leave California and him and come here.

"Why do you think that?" I asked with a snotty tone.

"Because you're honest. And people, particularly rich ones, don't like to be jerked around. Especially when it comes to their money and investments," he explained, but I was still frowning. "Hey, why are you mad?"

"You want me to move here?"

He leaned toward me and reached for my hand. "Sunny, I want you to be happy. And if coming here and working with Danika would make you happy, then yes, that's what I want."

"Without you?" I asked, getting emotional because I no longer looked at my life as separate from his.

When I saw my life down the road, I saw him next to me. I had no idea where we were, but we were together. What if he didn't see the same thing?

"Hell no, not without me." He looked like I'd slapped him. "I'm just saying"—he rubbed his thumb across the top of my hand—"if you're interested in working here with Danika, then you should say yes and at least give it a try. You and I will figure the *us* part out when the time comes. But I'm not going anywhere. I'm not leaving you."

"Unless you get drafted," I said, the words sliding right out.

If Mac got drafted, he could end up anywhere, and I wouldn't be able to follow him the way Danika had with Chance. They'd gotten lucky with the way things had fallen into place for them.

"We can cross that bridge later. But don't you dare give up

on this opportunity because of me and my dreams. That's all I'm saying." He kissed the side of my head, and I leaned into the crook of his neck and closed my eyes. "I love you."

"I love you too."

Mac was being supportive, and I was taking it all wrong. So, I took a deep breath instead and decided to let it go for now. There was nothing to figure out this second anyway. Danika had said my job offer was good until I died, and we wouldn't know anything about the draft until June. There was no rush to make a decision before we landed back at LAX. I needed to chill out.

I DROPPED MAC off at the baseball house, and we kissed for longer than usual as we said our good-byes. New York had been so sweet to us. I'd never forget hearing Mac say that he loved me for the first time under the falling snow, in such a hallowed place. It was funny how hard it was to hold those words inside, but once you finally said them, they came out all the time.

And it shouldn't have, but it felt weird, being back home. California was hot, still shorts weather, and it was such an odd thing after just being in the snow, where the atmosphere was so completely different than it was here. I felt like I finally understood what Danika had always tried to explain to me when she lived here. She'd said New York had a distinct vibe, but it'd never made sense before. My head couldn't even comprehend how they could be so unique from one another, but they were.

I missed it already.

I'd never missed a place before.

Parking my car, I pulled my suitcase out of the trunk and wheeled it toward the doors of my building. I noticed Rocky's Mustang in the lot with the trunk open. It looked like she was either putting things in her car or taking them out. When I walked into the hallway and rounded the corner, I almost ran straight into her.

"Oh. Sunny, you're home," she said, looking tired. Maybe it was because she wasn't wearing any makeup. "How was New York?"

"Hi." I gave her a hug. "It was incredible. Are you coming or going?" I noticed that her hands were empty, so maybe she was unpacking after all.

She gave me a soft smile. "I can't stay. I just came back to get my things."

"You're moving back home?" I asked, sounding sadder than I'd meant to. I didn't want to make her feel any worse than I knew she already did.

"I went back for Thanksgiving, and it was so nice. I didn't realize how much I was just trying to prove a point by being here. Either to myself or everyone else." She pursed her lips together before continuing, "But in proving how strong I was, I wasn't dealing with what had happened. Being here alone just let me ignore it and push it away, but it didn't help me get any better."

"I didn't realize," I said, feeling guilty. Obviously, I'd noticed that day in the quad had rattled her, but I'd wrongly assumed she'd pull out of it. That it had only been a minor setback in the grand scheme of things and she just needed a little more time. I felt stupidly naive.

"I want to get better, Sunny. I used to be a really happy person," she said with a laugh, like it was a silly thing to say but it wasn't. I could see it. "I just want to be happy again."

"I want you to be happy too."

And even though I really, really, really didn't want her to go, I did want her to be okay. Her emotional health most definitely outweighed my own selfish reasons for wanting to keep her here.

And that was when it hit me like a ton of bricks. The stark realization of how I felt about Rocky's state of mind and how Mac had said he felt about mine. Him wanting me to be happy, accepting this job with Danika, was more important to him than anything else. He was willing to put his feelings and wants aside for the greater good of my future and my happiness. It was the most selfless thing a person could do for another.

"Can you tell Baseball Boy I said bye?"

"He's going to be devastated he missed you," I said, tempted to pull my phone out and call Mac so he could see her in person before she took off.

"He'll get over it." She looked at the floor before focusing back on me. "Oh, I almost forgot to tell you!"

"What?" I wondered what had gotten her so excited.

"Hayley's gone," she said with a shit-eating grin.

"No way. What do you mean, gone?" I asked because I knew she only had to finish out this semester before she graduated. "Did you do something to her?"

Rocky blew out a harsh breath. "I wish. No. She got into a skiing accident. Broke both of her legs. She's finishing the semester online."

"How do you know all this?"

"I follow that bitch on all her socials. Gotta stalk your enemies." She gave me a nod, and I stood there in shock. "I need to go. It's already later than I planned."

"You were going to leave without saying good-bye?" I asked, feeling a little hurt.

"I wrote you a note. It's under your door. And I was going to text you later," she said, like that made everything better, but honestly, it kind of did. Rocky didn't owe me anything.

We hugged one last time, and I watched as she left before I made my way into my apartment. I sent Mac a quick text to let him know that Rocky was gone and that Hayley was broken. He called me immediately and pouted—about Rocky, not Hayley. And even though we had originally planned on staying at our own places tonight, he told me to "hurry up" when I asked if I could come over instead.

NONE OF THE guys were at the house when I got there, and Mac and I were so tired from our bodies being three hours ahead that we got into bed early.

I'd brought Rocky's note with me, so Mac and I could read it together. It was short and sweet, basically thanking us both for caring about her and that she was sorry she couldn't stay. She said she wished she'd met us sooner, but now that she had, we weren't getting rid of her that easily, no matter where we lived. That last part made Mac happy.

"She's one of the fiercest people I've ever met," Mac said after I folded the letter in half. I realized then that he felt connected to her somehow. "It's her attitude and the way she doesn't back down when life throws her a shit sandwich. She isn't going down without a fight. I respect that, you know?"

I couldn't stop the smile that stretched across my face. "You should have seen her that day with Hayley," I said, and he gave me a confused look. "When Hayley called you and you told me to get away from her," I added, and his face fell. "Rocky was amazing. If she hadn't been there, I don't know what I would have done, but for every crappy word that came out of Hayley's mouth, Rocky made her choke on it."

Mac clapped his hands together. "You never told me that. I wish I had seen it."

"It was pretty epic."

"Sounds like it." He seemed lost in his head for a moment, imagining the scene he'd missed out on.

"You're tough too, you know." I wanted to remind him that he had also done things that required strength, albeit in a different way. It wasn't easy, going against your parents' wishes and carving out a life they never approved of or supported. "You defy your dad every day you stay out here and step on that field."

He huffed out a small breath. "It's not the same."

I knew that he didn't see his actions the way I did.

"It still takes strength. A lot of people wouldn't be able to do it. And I respect you for it," I added that last part at the end because I knew Mac hadn't felt respected for most of his life.

"If you don't fight for yourself, who else will, right?" He gave me a small smile and a kiss before lying down, his eyes closing the second they hit the pillow.

I WOKE UP the next morning to the sound of dishes crashing in the other room and Mac not lying next to me. After getting dressed, I pulled open the door and peeked around the corner. Matt was standing in the kitchen.

"I heard a rumor that you do all the cooking in the house," I said, and he jumped about twenty feet in the air.

"Sunny. Hey! I didn't realize you were here." He walked over to me and gave me a quick hug.

"Hands off my girl, Transfer," Mac's voice boomed, and Matt immediately raised his hands in the air.

"Where were you?" I asked Mac as he wrapped me in his arms and nuzzled into my neck.

"Shower. I came out, and you were gone," he said.

I hadn't even heard the water running.

"Where's everyone else?" I asked, meaning Colin and

Dayton.

"I'm sure they'll be out any second," Matt said as the toaster dinged. "They smell the food and come running."

"I don't run," Colin appeared, wiping his eyes with his hands. "Sunny." He smiled so big.

Out of all the guys in the house, Colin was definitely my favorite. Maybe it was because when it came to Mac, he had been on my side from the beginning, and he seemed to want us together. I always appreciated the support.

"How was your Thanksgiving?" he asked me.

"It was the best. How was yours?"

Colin shrugged. "Decent. Whatever. It wasn't New York—that's for sure."

"Yeah, thanks for the invite," Dayton added as he entered the room and pulled his baseball hat low. "I'm jealous you hung out with Carter. How is he?"

I stayed quiet, knowing that last question wasn't meant for me.

As the guys caught up and talked about Chance, Matt slid a plate of food in my direction. "I kinda wish I'd been here last year, so I could have met the guy."

"Oh, you mean, Chance?" I asked.

"Yeah. They all worship him, and I feel left out."

That made me giggle. "He's not that great," I said playfully.

His brows shot up. "Really? He's not?"

"No. He is. I just wanted to make you feel better."

He snapped his fingers. "I knew it. You know what would make me feel better?" he asked.

I got a little uncomfortable, not knowing what might come out of his mouth next even though Mac was only a few feet away. He wasn't paying attention.

"Whaaaat?" I asked, drawing out the word.

"These cookies I keep hearing about. That's the other thing they won't shut up about. But I've never seen them. Are they real?"

"They're real. I'll bring you some later this week."

"Really? That'd be great, Sunny. Thanks." He forked food into his mouth and chewed with a smile.

We all sat there, eating and talking, while Dayton and Mac seemed caught up in something private between them. I made a mental note to ask him about it later.

Colin moved his plate next to mine and leaned on the counter, staring at me. "I'm so glad that Operation SunnyMac worked," he whispered like he didn't want anyone to overhear, but I assumed that everyone had already known about it.

"What was that all about anyway?" I asked, intrigued.

"Just about you two getting together."

"That's it?"

"It needed to happen."

"So, what was the big plan then?" I asked because the last time I'd checked, no one had helped us work through our issues and figure it all out, except Mac and me.

Colin blushed. "There wasn't one."

I choked and laughed at the same time. "You had a code name for us, but there was no plan?"

"It's just what I called you guys. It was obvious you liked each other. And he was so mopey that I couldn't take it anymore."

"Well, it's a good thing we worked it out, huh? Thanks for all the non-help." I smacked his arm.

"Hey," he complained, and I realized that Colin wanted some of the credit. "I helped. I kicked Hayley out that one time and told her she couldn't come back."

"Did you hear what happened to her?" Dayton was suddenly back in the conversation.

"Yeah, she broke her legs in some skiing accident in Mammoth," Colin offered nonchalantly. "She won't be back."

"She did? Damn," Matt said. Clearly, this was news to him.

Then again, had Rocky not said something to me, I wouldn't have known either.

"I'm glad she's gone," I said before I could stop myself.

The guys started oohing and aahing like I'd said something that was a low blow, but that girl was the biggest drama bitch queen I'd ever met. And even though I knew Mac wanted nothing to do with her and she was no longer a threat in my eyes, her presence had still irritated me. I was glad we wouldn't be running into her on campus anymore.

"We all need girls like you, Sunny," Colin said with a grin, and I saw Mac shoot him a look that could kill.

"Speak for yourself. I want to be single as a Pringle." Matt tossed his dish in the sink, and we all started laughing, even Mac.

"We need to go," Mac directed, and the guys all started moving around frantically. He definitely ran this house. "I'll catch a ride with my girl. See you guys at practice."

Mac's hand was on my lower back as he pushed me toward his bedroom, where all of our things were. I palmed my car keys, and we headed out, the other three guys piling in Dayton's car at the same time.

Once I parked at school, Mac sprinted to the driver's side and opened the door for me before helping me out. He seemed to get even sweeter with time.

As we walked on campus, holding hands, I saw the numerous glances in our direction, but they didn't seem as mean-spirited as usual. There were no narrowed glares or snarls on faces. People simply seemed more curious than anything else.

"It's calmer than I thought it would be," I said as he walked me toward my building even though his class was clear on the other side of campus.

"What is?"

"Just being with you. It was pretty hellish for Danika the whole time." I remembered all the crap she'd gotten from other girls after she started dating Chance.

"Well, I think dating a Carter is a different experience altogether."

Mac was probably right, but I wasn't going to admit to anything that might make him feel less than.

"I wouldn't change a thing."

"Me neither." He kissed me in front of the entrance to my building. "I love you," he said as he pulled one of the doors open and held it for me to walk through.

"I love you too," I said before he turned around to hustle toward his own class.

Mac Davies still loved me. And I was never going to get

tired of hearing him say those words to me. Ever.

END OF THE SEMESTER

Mac

THE LAST FEW weeks had flown by. Time seemed to do that once you were in a routine. Sunny and I both missed New York, which was insane because we'd barely gotten to know the place. We argued one night that maybe it was Danika and Chance that we missed and not the location. But when we both started shaking our heads at the thought, we knew we were wrong.

It was definitely both. Our best friends and the place.

I'd been dreading the semester ending since the day it'd started. I was one step closer to my last season of playing baseball at Fullton State and hopefully getting drafted. It would all come down to the next few months. I'd been working my ass off in the weight room and on the field. I'd never felt more prepared to tackle a season than I did right now. But it wasn't all up to me, and I wasn't sure if that made things better or worse.

Winter break also meant that I had to go back home to Arizona. And even though I wasn't going back for very long, my stomach was in knots, just knowing I had to go at all. No one should feel that way about their home. Home should be what Sunny had once said—safe, comforting, and welcoming. My house was none of those things.

"I'm going to miss you so much." Sunny sniffled against my neck.

It was the longest we were going to be apart since we'd started dating, and I hated the idea of leaving her. I wanted to be by her side all the time. She anchored me and gave me peace. It was an incredible feeling to know that while other parts of my life might be shaky, she and I were solid. There was something about having a stable relationship that made all the other shit bearable ... even if it still sucked.

"I'm going to miss you too. But I'll call you every day, okay?"

"I freaking hope so," she said as she swatted my arm and growled. She actually growled at me.

"Why'd you hit me? You're always hitting me." I pulled my bag out of the backseat of her car and slung it over my shoulder.

" 'Cause who wouldn't call their girlfriend every day? That's what you're supposed to do."

"Babe." I couldn't help but laugh as I reached for her chin and held it in my grip before planting a kiss on her luscious lips. "I'll be back before you know it."

She shook her head. "It's not that." Clearing her throat, she looked up at me, her blue eyes shining like freaking sapphires. "I mean, yes, I'm going to miss you so much that I don't even want to think about it. But I'm worried."

The last thing I wanted was for Sunny to worry about me.

I could take care of myself. I'd been doing it for years. "Why? What are you worried about?"

She bit the back of her thumb, stalling. "I'm worried about your dad. What if he doesn't let you come back?"

I wanted to reassure her and tell her that Dick Davies couldn't stop me if he tried, but the same question had definitely entered my mind. There was always the possibility that Dick wouldn't *allow me* to come back to Fullton. Not that I'd listen, but that threat was still there.

"Nothing is stopping me from coming back for the season," I ground out, determined, channeling my inner Rocky. "Or for you."

A small but still worried smile formed on her lips. "Okay. But you'll tell me if things go sideways, right? I'll come get you."

She'd offered to come get me. The fact that this girl loved me that much was so fucking overwhelming at times. *What did I do to deserve her?* I wasn't sure I'd ever stop asking myself that question.

"I love you so much." I grabbed her and pulled her into my arms, holding her tight.

"I love you." Her breath was hot against me. "You'd better go," she said, pulling away, and I glanced back at the inside of the airport, thankful that it wasn't too crowded.

"I'll text you when I land," I said before walking inside and leaving my heart in the front seat of her car.

I FELT SICK to my stomach for the whole flight, which was only an hour. Not even enough time to formulate a plan—and I always needed some sort of plan. Letting my guard down around Dick wasn't an option, and he never came unprepared. The only slight sliver of hope was that maybe he wouldn't be the one picking me up, but I knew that was a long shot.

Dick Davies loved to verbally destroy me, and he rarely missed an opportunity. So, imagine my surprise when I finally stepped into Baggage Claim and saw a man I didn't recognize, holding a sign with my name on it.

"I'm Mac," I said as I walked up to the stranger.

"I'm Curtis. Your dad sends his regards. Do you have any luggage?"

"Just this." I motioned toward the bag slung over my shoulder.

"Follow me," he said, and I did as I had been told.

Once we were outside, he walked into the closest parking lot and pointed at a blacked-out Mercedes G Wagon. He opened the rear passenger door for me, and I got in before firing off a text to Sunny, letting her know I was here and that I'd call her later.

There was so much I'd been keeping inside recently. My fears about the upcoming season. Coming here for the holidays and all of the familial expectations that went along with it. I was required to play a part, to show up and be the prodigal son who couldn't wait to come work for the company, but I wasn't sure I could do all the faking this year. I hated the lying.

"Hey, Curtis, do you know where my mom is?"

I wondered why she hadn't come to pick me up, but I knew that it was already late enough in the afternoon that she was probably too drunk to drive. It made me angry with her, and I hated being mad at my mom. I felt like a piece-of-shit son for judging her drinking when I knew that it was her way of coping.

Still, her choices pissed me off.

"I believe Mrs. Davies is at home," he answered, and I couldn't tell if he knew about her situation or not. He honestly didn't sound like he did. But he could just be a good actor. My dad would hire nothing but the best in order to protect the family reputation.

Curtis turned the wrong way, and I sat up straighter, growing uncomfortable with each second that passed.

"You're not taking me to the house?"

His eyes met mine in the rearview mirror. "He asked me to bring you by the office."

Fuck. The dog and pony show was beginning earlier than usual.

DD typically waited until the company holiday party to tote me around and force me into uncomfortable conversations. But apparently, not this year.

"I'll wait here," Curtis said as he pulled into a designated parking spot in front of the large building.

Maybe this trip to the office was going to be short and quick. If DD had planned on keeping me here all night, he would have sent Curtis away and driven me home after.

I left my bag in the seat and walked inside, pressing the elevator button for the fifth floor. I could find my dad's office with my eyes closed, but when the doors opened, DD was standing there, waiting for me.

There was no hug. No smile. Nothing that indicated he was even remotely pleased to see me. Typical DD, the eternal asshole. He gave me a once-over, clearly disapproving of my casual attire, but I hadn't known he was bringing me here. Had I known, I wouldn't have changed anyway, so fuck him.

"Follow me." He started speed-walking, and I practically had to break out into a light jog to keep up with his pace.

He walked me into an empty office with floor-to-ceiling windows on one of the walls. The room was massive, already fitted with a couch, a TV mounted on the wall, and an attached washroom.

"This is yours," he said with a flick of his hand.

"My what?"

"This will be your office when you start in June," he said, ignoring the fact that the draft was in June and the last thing I wanted was to ever come work here, baseball or not.

I swallowed around the newly formed lump in my throat. "I thought I was starting in the mailroom?" I asked sarcastically, giving him the wrong idea that I was actually interested in this shit.

"Oh, you are." He leaned toward me, his tone menacing. "But no son of mine can stay at the bottom for long. It's all for show. Formality, you see. That way, no one can complain that you didn't pay your dues." He sounded so proud of his plan.

"When's the Christmas party?" I asked, completely ignoring everything he'd just said. The same way he pretended like my future in baseball didn't exist.

"Tomorrow night. You'll be expected to show up with me and your mother and not leave before we do," he said, as if I didn't already know the rules.

It was the same thing year after year. *Arrive at the party as a family, smile, pretend that we can all stand each other instead of wanting to rip each other's throats out. Leave your cell phone at home. Be excited about the company and your future in it. Ignore all questions about baseball.* Try not to look as dead on the outside as you feel on the inside. Smile. Lie. Smile. Pretend. Smile. Fake it. *Don't make me look bad. Don't embarrass me.*

"Don't you have something you'd like to say to me?" he asked, his power trip firmly in place as he leaned up against the desk that was supposed to be mine in a matter of months.

"Um, I'm not sure." I had no idea what he was waiting to hear from me.

"How about *thank you*?" He waved an arm around the office like he was presenting me with the world's greatest gift.

"For what?"

"For what?" he repeated, pushing off the desk and stalking toward me. "For providing you with a future that you clearly cannot provide yourself on your own. What would you even be without me?" he snapped, as if he'd ever given me a choice.

It was truly a wonder how I'd gotten to go to Fullton State in the first place and play baseball.

"I want to see Mom," I said, hoping that he'd let me leave

and that showing me this office was the only reason he'd made me stop here in the first place, that there wasn't something else up his sleeve.

"Good luck with that," he said with a groan.

"What is that supposed to mean?"

"She's probably asleep. She's never awake anymore."

My jaw clenched. "How would you even know? You're never home."

His finger was in my face instantly. "Watch your tone, boy. You think you know everything, but you don't know shit."

"Can I go now?" I pretended to be unmoved by his behavior, but he intimidated the hell out of me. I hated how I still felt like a little kid his presence.

"Ungrateful asshole. Leave," he said, and I took off before he changed his mind, hating that I'd have to see him later that night.

MY FAVORITE PERSON IN ARIZONA

Mac

"**M**OM!" I SHOUTED as I walked through the front door, unsure of where I'd find her, if I'd find her at all.

DD hadn't been wrong when he said she was probably sleeping, but there was a chance she might be awake. She knew I was coming home today.

"Mac?" Her voice sounded quiet and soft as she pulled open one of the bedroom doors and stepped out of it, fully dressed. It made me happy to see her up and alert. "I'm so glad you're home."

"Hey, Mom." I walked up the stairs and gave her a hug, smelling the faint hint of alcohol on her breath. She didn't seem even remotely hammered, but the scent still deflated me. "How are you? You look nice," I complimented, and she seemed so genuinely happy with my words. I wondered when the last time was that she'd heard something nice.

"I'm hanging in there." Her hand cupped my face as she gave me a kiss on the cheek. "How are you? You look so handsome. Now, tell me about this girl of yours." She linked her arm in mine as we navigated down the stairs together.

I had almost forgotten that I'd texted her pictures of Sunny and me during Thanksgiving while we were in New York. She wanted more information, but I told her that I'd fill her in when I came home. Mom had accepted that response and never pushed me, but I'd sent her pics all weekend.

"She's amazing, Mom. You'd love her," I started to say before she interrupted.

"I really like her silver hair." She smiled as she fiddled with her phone before turning it around to show me. It was a picture of Sunny and me on top of the Empire State Building at night, her hair blowing around in the wind.

"I like it too," I agreed before being struck with an idea. "Do you want me to video-chat with her, so you can say hi?" I asked, and she looked so pleased.

"I don't look very nice." She started messing with her hair, trying to tame the unruly, unbrushed pieces.

"You look perfect," I said even though she did look a little bit like a hot mess. Sunny would never say a word, and I figured that since she might never get to meet my mom, this would be a nice gesture for both of them.

"Let's sit at the table." I redirected us to the kitchen table, and we sat side by side as I pressed on Sunny's name.

Her face lit up my screen as she answered immediately. I swore it hadn't even gotten the chance to ring twice.

"Sexy boyfriend. How's Arizona?" she asked.

I made a face, willing her to stop. I never knew what might come out of that girl's mouth.

"Hot. My mom's here." I tilted the phone, so my mom's face was in the frame before Sunny could say anything else that might embarrass me.

"Oh." Sunny looked flustered. "Hi, Mrs. Davies. Sorry I called your son sexy. But I mean, I guess it's your fault anyway. You made him," she kept running off at the mouth, and if she were near me, I would have kissed her lips just to get her to stop talking.

My mom laughed. I hadn't heard that sound in I didn't know how long. It felt like forever. Years even, although that couldn't have been right. Her laugh was like a punch in the gut, a reminder of how miserable she'd become.

"Hi, Sunny. I was just telling Mac how much I like your hair," my mom complimented.

Sunny started pulling at the strands. "Thank you. It was something new I tried this year, and I'm sort of obsessed. I love it so much."

"So, are you at home with your family too?" my mom asked.

Sunny nodded. "Yep. My parents, my older sister, and a thousand dogs," she explained.

My mom touched the screen, as if she could reach Sunny through it. "Why so many dogs?"

"Well ..." Sunny tried to figure out what to say, and I told my mom that Sunny's parents owned a vet clinic. "Yeah. So, my mom basically fosters all these dogs that need their forever homes. It's only temporary, but she doesn't know when to stop. There are literally eight giant-sized dogs at our house right now. THERE ARE EIGHT DOGS HERE, MAC!" she yelled to reiterate.

I'd always wanted a dog. And if my memory was accurate,

my mom had wanted one, too, but DD had said our house wasn't made for animals. The floors were too easily scratched, the couches too expensive to be torn, and he didn't want his suits covered in hair.

I remembered trying to convince him one year, but DD had not relented. Once his mind was made up, that was it. There would be no changing it, no talking him out of his decision, no chance of a compromise. DD said our home was not a democracy and I needed to know my place. Something about if I learned how to take direction now, it'd be easier for me to deal with having bosses in the future. Like the possibility of me being my own boss was completely out of the question.

My dad was a fucking asshole.

Sunny and my mom had continued talking while I was zoned out, and only the sound of my mom laughing again at something Sunny had said snapped me out of it.

That sound.

How could such a genuine melody cause me so much pain?

It only made me hate my dad more. He'd taken so much from us—joy, hope, laughter, our choices. And we'd, what ... allowed it? Accepted it? Perpetuated it?

"Mac?" Sunny was repeating my name, and I shook my head to focus back on the phone that was now in my mom's hand.

"Sorry, babe. I was in my head for a second."

"It's okay. I was just telling your mom that she needs to come out for a game when the season starts." Sunny sounded so excited, and I looked at my mom to try to read her expression, but I couldn't.

My mom had come to my games in high school but only when DD was out of town. I'd learned at some point during my junior year that if she came up to my games without his permission, he'd punish her. He canceled her personal appointments so that when she showed up, they wouldn't have her in the books and couldn't possibly squeeze her in. He always knew what she was doing and was one step ahead.

He'd gone so far as to shut off her credit cards once, but when that only proved to be an embarrassment to him and his name because it happened in front of a lot of people, he never did it again. Instead, he simply hid her cards from her, so when she went to use them, they were missing from her wallet. Apparently, my mom looking like a forgetful lunatic wasn't a source of shame for him. He played the victim card.

Poor Dick Davies. Look how unstable his wife is. How does he deal with her? everyone whispered instead of the other way around.

I tried to reassure my mom that it was okay that she didn't watch me, but it wasn't. It made me just as angry with her as I was with DD. Every other player on the field had at least one person watching them and cheering them on. But not me. And, yeah, I felt fucking sorry for myself because of it.

"Do you think you'll be able to come out?" Sunny asked. "It's his last season playing here. And he's really good," Sunny continued her sales pitch.

My mom shifted in her seat, a fake-as-fuck smile plastered on her face. She was incredibly uncomfortable.

"Hey, babe. We gotta go," I said, cutting the conversation short and tossing my mom a life preserver so she didn't drown all alone.

"Oh. Okay. It was nice to meet you, Mrs. Davies," Sunny shouted because I had grabbed the phone and was walking into another room.

"I'll try to call you later, but things are a little tense here," I explained, and her eyes pulled together. I could tell she was worried.

"At least text me if you can't call, okay?" she suggested, and I agreed before ending the call and heading back into the kitchen.

My mom hadn't moved an inch. She was sitting in the same chair with her hands folded as she stared at the table.

"Mom." I put my hand on her shoulder, and she turned her head toward me.

"She's really sweet," she said, meaning Sunny.

"Yeah, she is."

I sat down next to her again, and she faced me.

"Mac, I hope you know that I want to come see you play," she began to explain, but I knew what was coming next. It was the same thing she always said.

"But you can't. I know," I finished the sentence for her.

She put her head in her hands and started shaking. "I wish I were stronger. You needed me to be stronger."

"Mom," I said, feeling small, "I never understood why you couldn't stand up to him before. But I understand now."

Sunny and I had talked about it a little bit once, and she gave me a perspective that I had been too pissed to ever see clearly in the past. I'd made everything about my parents' relationship this black-and-white thing, but Sunny showed me all the shades of gray. She made me see my mom's side instead of just my own. I'd been so mad, but she had been right.

"How——" She sniffed. "How do you understand now?"

"Because he's a controlling asshole who gets off on making us feel less than," I explained before adding what Sunny had taught me. "But I get it now—that you feel stuck. And powerless. And you've been with him for so long that you don't know how to get away."

"I stopped working when you were born," she said.

I never knew that she'd worked before I came along, which was stupid and naive of me to think that my mom never had something of her own. The reality was that I'd never asked. I always assumed she liked the lifestyle DD provided.

"I don't have any property or assets. None of this is in my name." She waved a hand around in the air, indicating our massive estate.

"But it is though. Your marriage assures that. And he couldn't have built his little empire without your support. He would still have to take care of you and provide for you. He'd have to give you alimony," I argued, but she had to know all of that already.

"He'd make me sorry for leaving. For embarrassing him publicly," she said, and I realized that DD treated us both the exact same way. Like pieces of property. Pawns. And he ruled not with an iron fist, but with fear.

"You need to stop drinking," I insisted out of nowhere, like the very concept should be that easy.

But if my mom wanted any semblance of life going forward, she needed to actually participate in it and stop numbing away her days. She had to regain control of her senses, and that was impossible to find at the bottom of a bottle.

"I never used to drink, you know. Not a drop. I hated the taste of it." Her eyes got that faraway look in them, and I leaned closer, invested in the words I'd never heard before. "But eventually, I started looking for ways to cope." She swallowed hard, and I knew she was talking about coping with him doing things, like canceling her appointments and hiding her credit cards. "Drinking made me numb. And being numb was so much better than being angry."

I hated that I understood her perspective, but I did. Understanding felt like I was saying what she had done was okay when it wasn't. I'd needed her, and she'd chosen the bottle over me. Although, in essence, she'd chosen herself over me. Neither option made me feel that great.

"What did you do before I was born?" I asked before elaborating, "For work, I mean. You said you used to have a job. What did you do?"

"Oh, I worked at the bookstore on Main," she said, and I knew exactly where she meant. It was the only bookstore in town. "I was the event planner there. I set up signings for all the local and visiting authors. I was the one who got all the big-name writers to come to town and hold events here. It was a really significant deal at the time, and I was so proud."

"Did he make you stop?" I asked, wondering if DD had forced her to give up her job once I came along.

"No, but I couldn't keep working there full-time and take care of you." She stood up from the chair, grabbed a glass, and filled it with water.

"People do it all the time," I said even though there was no point. That part of our history had come and gone, and it couldn't be changed now. My tone of voice sounded way more judgmental than I'd wanted it to. She was going to get defensive if I made her feel stupid or bad about it.

"You're right. But I didn't want to. I wanted to be home with you. And your father agreed and supported that decision. He wasn't always the way he is now. He used to be kind," she started to defend him, but I didn't want to hear it. "I wouldn't have fallen in love with a monster," she added.

I realized that I'd been seeing him that way for years without even considering that he used to be someone else. But the truth was, I didn't care.

It was hypocritical of me to accept the reasons why my mom had changed but not want to do the same for my dad, but it was how I felt. I couldn't give a shit if he had once been a decent human being because he was no longer that person. All that mattered to me now was who he had become. He seemed to relish in being cruel.

"Mom, you don't want me to work for him, do you?" I had no idea why I'd asked that particular question in this particular moment.

And I could tell that she was caught off guard.

"I don't. But only because you don't want that. I just want you to be happy."

"Have you ever told him that? Have you ever tried to make him see reason?" I asked, desperate for her to be on my side for once. I needed her to fight for me because it wasn't working on my own.

She sat back down next to me and reached for my hand. "Oh, honey. It took everything in my power to convince him to let you go to Fullton State. That was one hell of an argument that went on for weeks," she said before looking right into my eyes. "I just don't have any fight left in me for anything else. And he wouldn't allow it anyway."

It was my mom who convinced my dad to let me go and play baseball there? All this time, I'd had no idea how it'd happened. I always thought she was sitting here, drunk, feeding me to the fire, but she was trying to save me from it.

"Mom"—I shook my head as I gripped her hand—"you don't have to stay here. You can leave. Come back to California with me. You can stay with Sunny. She'd love it."

She looked away from me and pulled her hand from mine. "I'm not ready to do that, Mac. I appreciate what you're saying. It's sweet. But I'm not quite there."

Even though I hated her response, it was honest. She could have placated and fed me some bullshit line, but she hadn't. She'd told me the truth, and I had to respect that.

The sound of one of the garages opening caused us both to stop talking and stare at each other in silence. DD was home.

Story time was officially over.

MERRY CHRISTMAS TO ME

Mac

I'D REVEL IN all the information my mom had shared with me the other day as I took long drives in my car. I never had a particular destination in mind. I simply liked being on the road, driving. Something I never got to do in California. Plus, it might be shallow, but I really missed my fucking car.

With the windows down, the music blasting, and my mom's words in my ears, I would think about why it had taken us so long to have that conversation. Maybe it was because she was sober-ish or because I was finally old enough to listen instead of fight back. But now that we'd talked, I felt closer to her than I had in years. We'd reached a silent understanding, and instead of being angry with her like I usually was, I found myself blaming her less and loving her more.

When I'd called Sunny to fill her in on everything, she had practically burst into tears on the phone. She was so overjoyed to hear that I was mending fences while I was home. She'd said she was proud of me and wished she were here.

I was grateful she wasn't.

I never wanted Sunny to step foot in this fucking house.

But when she sent me an X-rated voice message after seeing a picture of me in my tux for the holiday party, I started second-guessing that idea. I decided that she could be here as long as she was underneath me or on top of me or her legs were wrapped around my shoulders, cutting off the circulation to my head. Only under those circumstances.

"You almost ready?" My mom poked her head inside my bedroom and saw me fidgeting with my tie. I knew how to tie one, but I always made it crooked. She walked over to me, reached for it, and fixed it. "There."

I looked in my full-length mirror and nodded. "Thanks," I said before giving her a once-over. "You look gorgeous."

My mom was wearing a floor-length red gown with deep slits in the front. Her auburn hair was done to perfection, not a single hair out of place, and her makeup looked like she belonged on a magazine cover.

"Thank you." Her eyes softened with my words as she pressed a kiss to my cheek. "You look debonair. Did you send Sunny a picture?"

"I did."

"What do you kids call them? Self-something?" she asked, and I knew she couldn't be that out of touch with reality. Then again ...

"Selfies," I corrected.

She nodded, her mouth forming a big, "Ahh."

"Let's go," DD shouted from the bottom of the stairs. He sounded like he was outside already.

"Such a gentleman," I said sarcastically.

She gave me a disapproving look. "Mac, don't. Just

behave. It will make tonight easier."

I groaned but said nothing back. She hated putting on a show as much as I did, and I only had to do it once a year. My poor mom had to do it constantly.

The holiday party was a nightmare. And I couldn't even get any solace from my girlfriend since I wasn't allowed to bring my cell phone inside. Texting her all night would have been a thousand times better than being here and pretending to give a shit while watching everyone kiss DD's ass.

All the higher-ups in the company eventually introduced themselves to me and told me they couldn't wait until I was officially a part of the company. They all seemed to be under the impression that I had a firm start date when I'd never agreed to shit. Unless you counted the deal that I'd signed when I was eighteen—and we knew that Dick certainly did. To be honest, the whole night felt like a sales pitch, filled with old guys faking excitement at me coming on board, telling me how great my old man was and how fun it was, being rich. They were so out of touch with reality that I wanted to rip my hair out and throw a tantrum. I almost did, but my mom stopped me.

She had done her best to stay sober during the event, but when I noticed her doing shots at the bar, I walked over and paced her before it got out of control. I hadn't done it for my dad's sake, but for my mom's. I knew that DD would have punished her once we got home, and living with him was punishment enough for anyone.

"It's not worth it," I whispered toward her as she put the glass down.

She smiled at me. It was big and fake. "I hate this more than anything," she admitted, and I could relate. "And he's been putting on the charm for the ladies all night long."

I turned around to see what my mom was talking about, and it didn't take me long to see what she meant. DD was standing next to some girl who was definitely younger than him, his hand touching her lower back every few seconds. I couldn't be the only one who noticed. Maybe he was just flirting, or maybe he was a cheating prick. I had no idea, but I'd never seen him with anyone else before or heard any rumors about him with other women.

"Doing shots alone at the bar will only make you look bad. Not him." I wanted her to see it from a different viewpoint. "They'll say that he's flirting with other women because you're a drunk. No one knows the side of him that we do. They don't see it."

She swallowed and sucked in her cheeks. "You're right. I always forget that they don't know."

"Don't let him win," I said, taking her arm in mine and leading her to the dance floor.

"You're the only person who makes this all bearable," she said as we danced, and I felt the same way.

Without her here, I'd have left the second we showed up, consequences be damned.

CHRISTMAS MORNING HELD about as much charm as any other day. I dreaded getting up and pulling myself out of bed. There wasn't a pile of presents waiting underneath the tree anymore. Hell, half the time, there wasn't even a tree at all. But ever since I'd moved out of the house, DD said that paying for me to go waste my time at Fullton State was present enough, so what else could I possibly need?

He was right though. I didn't want or need shit from him.

My only saving grace was the money that got automatically deposited into my bank account each month. My mom's parents had set up some sort of trust for me before they died, and I'd been getting money since I was fifteen years old. I had to reach out to a financial advisor if I ever wanted to access any of it, so I tried not to touch it, knowing that at some point in the future, I was going to need it, and it was going to save me. For now, as long as I played by DD's rules, he still let me use the credit card in my name. But I knew that one bad move by me, and that would get cut off faster than I could blink an eye.

A swift knock on my door let me know that my mom was up.

"Breakfast," she said.

I told her, "Okay," as I fired off a quick text to my girl, wishing her a merry Christmas. When there was no immediate response, I left my phone on my nightstand and padded downstairs.

The least I could do was not leave my mom alone with DD while I was here. The smell of food slammed into my senses before I hit the last step.

Mom's cooking?

"That smells incredible," I said as I walked into the kitchen, noticing my mom at the stove, making pancakes and frying up eggs.

DD sat at the table, a newspaper covering his entire face, as if waiting to be served. As I pulled out the chair to sit across from him, he folded the paper and put it down, his eyes narrowing in on me.

"Did you have a nice time at the holiday party?" he asked.

It was the first time we'd sat down together since the big soiree.

I shrugged my shoulders, sick of lying just to appease him. "It was whatever," I said, knowing it might piss him off.

"*It was whatever?*" he mimicked. "Stop acting like a child, Mackenzie."

"What?" I argued. "It was boring. It's always boring."

"Well, you'd better get used to it because there's a lot more where that came from once you join the firm."

I cleared my throat and cast a concerned look toward my mom, who gave me a small shake of her head, warning me not to push his buttons.

"Dad, look," I started.

He pressed his elbows onto the table. If he were wearing a tie, he would have started messing with it. The sign that I was frustrating him.

"Look at what? What a gift I've given you? What a screwup you are? What an ungrateful, unworthy son you are? Tell me, Mackenzie, what exactly am I looking at?" The words flew out of his mouth without any effort. He didn't have to stop and think about what names to call me or what to say. They lived right there, on the tip of his tongue, just waiting to come out and decimate me.

Normally, the blunt force of his words would have done their job. Not today.

"Richard"—my mom sounded so wounded—"it's Christmas."

"So?" He slammed his hands on top of the table with so much force that his glass started to wobble. I silently wished it would fall. "Christmas means what? That we pretend he isn't coming here as soon as he graduates? That he doesn't have a responsibility to uphold? That he didn't sign a contract?" he shouted, each question growing in volume. "When you start working for the company in June—" he started, launching into the same lecture he'd given me a hundred times before.

Baseball didn't factor into his mind at all. The draft wasn't even on his radar. What I wanted never mattered.

"I don't want to work for you," I said in a calm tone, but his face turned an unusual shade of red as I said it. "I don't know why you can't accept that. I have zero interest in your company or having a job there."

"That's non-fucking-negotiable, and you know it," he yelled, slamming his fist on the table again. His glass did topple this time, spilling the contents all over the floor.

"Dad—" I tried to sound reasonable, but there would be no reasoning with the man.

"You signed a contract. We made a deal. You will abide by the terms of said agreement," he chastised me, acting like some deranged business partner.

"I was just a kid. I wanted to go play baseball. I would have signed anything you asked me to." I started to get emotional. I was tired of playing nice. Tired of tiptoeing around the fact that the last thing I wanted to do on this fucking planet was work for or with him.

"Just like your mother. Always leading with your emotions instead of your fucking brain."

"Why would you want to force me to do something I don't want to do?"

"Force you? I'm giving you a gift. God, Mackenzie, you can't even see the opportunity I'm handing you. Other kids would kill for this much money and influence, and all you do is disrespect it. You've been that way since you first held a bat in your hands. I never should have allowed it. Ruining your life for a game. A game you aren't even that good at." He tossed the last words like an arrow, sending them straight into my soul. They burned on contact, killing a part of me.

"You really hate me that much?" My heart ached with the realization as I pushed to a stand.

"Yes!" he screamed, and I almost passed out from the shock, but at least he'd admitted it. "You ruined everything!" he kept yelling, and I had no idea what he meant. "You were supposed to be like me. But instead, you're just like her," he screamed the words like they disgusted him as he pointed at my mother, who was watching the two of us through terrified eyes. "Chasing dreams in your head instead of money, like two fools. You're nothing but a disappointment, and I hate that you're my son. Anyone would have been better than you."

"Shut up! Just shut the hell up!" I yelled.

He stood up and threw his chair away from his body. It hit the floor with a crash. He stalked over to me, and I stood firm, but I was scared to death. I'd seen Dick mad before, but I'd never seen him downright murderous, the way he looked right now.

"Watch your ungrateful fucking mouth," he spat as he spoke.

I refused to back down. I stood my ground and puffed out my chest. "What are you going to do? Hit me?" I taunted.

He'd never once gotten physical in the past, but he looked like he was about to lose what little self-control he had left.

"Do it then. Since you hate me so fucking much! Since I'm the worst thing to ever happen to you!"

I wanted him to do it. At least that way, I'd have a valid enough reason to leave and never come back.

"You always have to have the last word, don't you? You can never just shut your fucking mouth and listen. Maybe this will finally shut you up." His fist hit my jaw with so much force that it sent me flying sideways.

I'd basically asked for it, but I couldn't even gather my wits around the enormity of the surprise I felt.

I covered the side of my face with my hand. It never even crossed my mind to hit him back. I was too paralyzed by the realization of what he'd just done.

And then he did it again. I thought he might have broken my jaw as blood dribbled out of my mouth and onto the floor.

"Richard!" my mom screamed.

I shook my head to regain focus, making sure he didn't go after her next. I might have stood there and taken him hitting on me, but I'd kill him if he touched her.

"This is all your fault," he shouted at her. "If you could have actually kept the other one instead of killing it, maybe he would have been worth a damn! Instead, all you gave me was this." He waved a disgusted hand in my direction. "You two deserve each other." He stomped away and slammed the front door so hard that it bounced open and closed repeatedly before staying open, the sunlight streaming in.

My mom ran to my side. "Mac, are you okay? I'm so sorry." She started crying.

"What was he talking about? What other one?" I asked, still clearly in shock.

"I was pregnant when you were ten. I lost the baby. He's never forgiven me," she explained.

I hadn't known that.

Why the hell hadn't I ever known that?

This family was filled with secrets, and we were so damn dysfunctional because of it.

"I'm sorry that happened, Mom. I never knew."

She walked to the freezer and pulled out an ice pack before handing it to me. "We never told you."

I thought back to my childhood and remembered when things had started to change. Every ounce of happiness seemed to get sucked out of the house all at once, but I never knew why. Mom cried a lot. Dad started spending all of his time at the office. I guessed that was when it all happened.

I held the ice pack to the side of my face and winced. "Has he ever done this to you?" I asked, and she shook her head rapidly.

"No. Never," she said.

I believed her. DD had never even threatened to hit me before, which was why I was still so horrified by what had just occurred. And as much as it killed me, I had to go.

"I can't stay here, Mom."

"I know," she said, her body shaking. "Hold on." She put up a finger and disappeared upstairs before coming back with something in her hand. She shoved a wad of cash into my palm and closed my fingers around it. "You know he'll cut off your card. I don't want you left with nothing. It's all I have right now."

Opening my palm, I looked at it, the stack of bills. There had to be at least five thousand dollars there. I could tell from the weight and the thickness. "Mom, I don't need all this. Keep some. Keep half. More than half."

"No. It's okay. I have more in a private account your father doesn't know about. That's just all the cash I have on hand," she explained. "I want you to take it. And go. You need to be gone before he gets back." She sounded downright terrified.

"I can't just leave you here." I started to get nervous at the thought.

Now that DD had crossed the line into physical violence, what was going to stop him from doing it again? To her?

"You can, and you will." She sounded so firm and strong. "Right now. Get your things, then take your car, and go. I'll call you later. Don't worry about me. I'll take care of myself."

I shook my head. I was unwilling to leave. "Come with me."

"It will only make things worse," she explained, but it

sounded like some sort of sick justification for staying.

I tried to blink the tears away, but it only made them fall instead. I felt sick to my stomach, not knowing what the right answer was or what I should do. All I wanted was to get the hell away from this house and never look back, but I couldn't stomach the thought of abandoning her.

"Should I call the cops?"

"No," she answered so fast. "No cops."

I knew that calling them would only make DD even angrier and that she would pay for it, but doing nothing felt so wrong.

"Mac, look at me," she insisted, and I did as she'd asked. "Go get your things and pack up your car. Get on the road before he comes back. I don't know what he's capable of anymore."

That admission woke me up. "I'll never forgive myself if something happens to you," I said as she followed me up to my room to help me pack my crap.

"Listen to me." She grabbed my shoulders and turned me to face her. "None of this is your fault. And nothing will happen to me. I need you to go. I need you to trust me."

Filling two duffel bags with everything I wanted and needed because I knew I was never coming back, I hustled downstairs and into the garage, where my car waited.

"You're sure?" I asked her one last time.

She nodded her head. "I'm your mother. It's my job to protect you. Let me do the one thing I've been failing at lately."

There would be no changing her mind. No convincing her to leave. She was stubborn but determined. And at least she hadn't been drinking. I could tell that much. I gave her a massive hug before telling her I loved her. And then I got into my car and left her there, praying like hell she'd be okay.

How was I going to get through this without completely falling apart?

After I pulled out of the gates and drove far enough away from the house, I swerved to the side of the road, opened my door, and threw up a mixture of whatever was in my stomach and blood from my mouth.

Giving Arizona one last glance in the rearview, I stepped on the gas and got on Interstate 10 toward Los Angeles. I was never coming back here.

HE'S HERE

Sunny

WHEN I OPENED up the front door that Christmas evening, I almost couldn't believe my eyes.

"What are you doing here?" I was so shocked to see Mac standing there. On my parents' front porch. With a couple of duffel bags in his hands. "How'd you know my address?" I asked, my questions coming out in rapid fire before he had a chance to answer.

Mac held up a red envelope and I immediately recognized the writing and the Jamison return address stamp in the upper left-hand corner. "My mom sent you a Christmas card? How did she get your address?" I narrowed my eyes to look at where she'd sent it. "She sent this to the baseball house?" I stopped myself from laughing because it was official, my mother was insane.

"You know, I've been calling and texting you all day," I said, my tone coming out more annoyed than I'd meant, but I had been worried.

He never responded to a single text after the one he sent in the morning, and his phone kept going straight to voice mail.

I'd had a bad feeling all afternoon.

"My phone died. I forgot to charge it last night, and then I didn't have a charger and figured it was better if I left it off. I'm sorry." He looked at me, his eyes red and swollen, like he'd been crying.

Is that a bruise on his jaw? Is his face swollen? It was hard to tell underneath the yellow porch light, but something wasn't right.

"Did you drive or fly here?" I asked because there was no BMW in the driveway or in front of the house, and I knew that was his car from home.

"I drove. It's a long story. I'll tell you later. Can I come inside?" he asked, looking completely worn out.

"Sunny, who is it?" my mom yelled in the background, and I turned around to see her walking toward me, wiping her hands on an apron. She recognized Mac immediately, and her face broke out into a smile. "Oh, it's that hottie-with-a-body boyfriend of yours." They still hadn't had the chance to meet in person.

"Mom," I said through my embarrassment, but Mac looked entertained.

"Well, don't leave him outside. Bring him in. Mac, come in, come in," she said, moving me out of the way.

MY MOM HAD PUSHED ME OUT OF THE WAY TO GET TO MY BOYFRIEND.

And that was when all hell broke loose. The dogs. All eight of them rounded the corner at once and made a beeline toward the front door.

"I'm sorry," my sister screamed as she chased behind them

in some lame attempt to corral them, but it was only making them run faster. They thought she was playing.

"So, this is my family." I pursed my lips as I stopped the dogs from getting out the front door as Mac made his way inside through the massive group of jumping and tail-wagging animals.

"Oh yeah, he is hot. You were right, Mom," my sister said, and my mouth dropped wide open.

The fact that my older sister and my mother had discussed the level of my boyfriend's hotness was beyond awkward.

"Can you two please not?" I was so embarrassed, but Mac seemed okay with it all. Of course he was. He lived for this kind of stuff.

"No, no. Don't stop on Sunny's account," he said.

I could tell he was trying to be his usual charming self, but something was definitely off.

No one else would have noticed, but I knew him better. The smile that didn't quite reach his eyes. The way his body language wasn't as comfortable in his own skin as usual. He was tense and uneasy. Not to mention the fact that he was here, at my house, on Christmas night when he was supposed to be in Arizona for three more days.

"Oh my. What happened to your face?" my mom asked, her tone worrisome, and I realized that I had been right.

There was a bruise. And there was swelling.

"Mac," I said, already assuming the worst.

He'd told me once before that his father never hit him, but I had an eerie feeling that was no longer the truth.

"Car accident," he said to my mom. "I hit the air bag."

It was a lie. One that could easily be bought and sold, but I could tell by the way he'd said it that it wasn't true. He squeezed my hand, letting me know that he'd tell me what really happened later. In private. And I let it slide because this was his first time meeting my family, and if he was here on Christmas, things must have gotten really bad for him at home.

"Those things seem so dangerous even though they apparently aren't. But everyone I know gets banged up when they go off."

My mom got ahold of the dogs, and they seemed to calm down once we all walked back into the living room, where they each had their own bed and treats waiting. The fire was burning in the fireplace, the tree was lit but was bare underneath, and we had just been cleaning up the table from dinner.

"Are you hungry?" I asked at the same time as my mom, who was still looking at Mac like he'd hung the dang moon, even with all the bruising.

"Hey there. I wondered what all the commotion was." My dad walked into the kitchen with a smile, holding a beer.

The cruise my mom had insisted they go on had seemed to do wonders for him. He was more relaxed than I'd ever seen, willing to share his patients with the emergency hospital, like my mom had recommended, instead of taking them all on by himself. He was even sporting a tan. I wasn't sure I'd ever seen my dad tan in my entire life.

"You must be Mac. Want some ice for that fight you clearly lost?" he teased.

Mac offered a tense chuckle as he reached for my dad's hand and gave it a firm shake. "Hi, sir. That would be great actually. And maybe some Advil?" he asked, and it hit me that he was in pain. And he'd driven over five hours to get here.

"Call me Mr. Jamison, please," my dad said, and right when I was about to complain, he started laughing. "Just kidding. Call me Mark."

"Apparently, my family has turned into a bunch of comedians," I said with a shrug, feeling like Mac had just walked into the Twilight Zone and he didn't even realize it.

"Can we fix you a plate?" my mom asked before waving her hand around. "Oh, I'm making you one anyway. Have you eaten? Doesn't matter," she kept talking, answering her own questions, as she started pulling everything out of the fridge that we'd just put in it.

"I have to go over to Todd's. His parents are waiting," my sister announced as she held a bunch of presents in her arms for his family. Her boyfriend had stopped by in the morning to have breakfast with us, and now, it was my sister's turn to go to his place for dessert. "I'm sorry I can't stay. It was nice to meet you, Hot Mac."

"Oh my God," I groaned out loud. "For the love of everything holy and good. Stop calling my boyfriend hot."

"Bye, Hideous Mac," she said instead, and I rolled my eyes. "Sorry you're so ugly," she said as she headed out the front door and it slammed behind her.

"I had no idea your family was so funny," Mac said with a smile before he winced and stopped.

"Neither did I."

"Come sit," my mom directed as she grabbed Mac by the shoulders and maneuvered him to the dining room table.

"There's some of everything," she said, pointing at the multiple plates of food she had prepared. "But you don't have to eat it all."

"Thank God you don't have to eat it all," I imitated as my mom walked out of the room and gave us a little bit of privacy.

Before long, she reappeared, setting up one of the dog gates at the entrance to the room. "They won't leave you alone if they know you're in here with food."

"Thank you," Mac said as he slowly cut at the turkey.

"You don't have to eat this, babe," I said reassuringly.

"I am hungry, but ..." he started to explain before putting the food in his mouth. Within seconds, he was spitting it out and holding the side of his face. "It hurts to chew," he said, his eyes closing, my heart breaking.

"Here." I spun the plate around, so the mashed potatoes were facing him. "This is soft. I'll go get you some more." I whirled in my seat, but he put his hand on top of mine to stop me.

"Just stay here with me," he said, and I nodded, maneuvering my legs back under the table to stay put.

"Do you want to talk about it?" I asked because I had to know what had happened. My imagination was working overtime.

His hazel eyes looked so drained of life. "I need to charge my phone. I have to call my mom," he said before saying anything else, and I nodded, holding my hand out so he could put his phone in it.

"I'll be right back." I took his phone up to my bedroom and plugged it in.

When I came back down and sat next to him, he was picking at his food, almost like he was trying to find things that would be mushy enough to eat without causing him pain.

He took a few more bites of his mashed potatoes before reaching for the bowl of applesauce. "This is really good," he said after taking a giant spoonful.

"It's homemade."

"No shit?"

"No shit," I repeated, wanting to touch the swelling on his cheek with my fingers but not wanting to hurt him.

Without warning, Mac launched into what had happened at his house this morning. I sat there, listening, trying to keep my emotions in check and biting my tongue the whole time as he told me every pain-filled detail. But I was horrified. And shocked. I had no idea what to say or how to help. I'd never been in this kind of a situation before.

"Is your mom okay?" was all I asked once I thought he was finished talking.

"I don't know, but I'm worried sick," he said.

"I'll go get your phone." I ran back upstairs to grab it, knowing that it wouldn't even remotely be fully charged yet, but it would be enough to send a text or call.

"Here." I handed it to him, and I'd noticed there were over thirty text messages waiting to be read. I knew that half of those were from me. "I might have gone a little crazy earlier when I couldn't get ahold of you," I admitted, feeling like a possessive girlfriend, but I'd been worried.

"It's okay. I like your crazy." He patted my hand before clicking on the Messages app and pulling them up. His body instantly released some of its tension. "She left the house before he got back," he said, his eyes instantly watering, and I watched as he tried to wipe the unshed tears away, not wanting to cry in front of me.

"So, she's somewhere safe then?"

"I'm going to call her real quick," he said, his fingers frantically scrolling and then pressing buttons before he held the phone to his ear.

"Mom. Yeah, I'm okay. I'm at Sunny's."

Pause.

His eyes found mine, and he stared right at me while he listened. He sucked in a breath. "I know. He reported the car stolen. The cops were cool. Are you okay? You did? Let me know if you need me to come get you or anything. I know. Mom, I know. Yeah. I love you too. Don't tell anyone where you are. Call me anytime. Bye."

I only heard his side of things, but it filled in a lot of the blanks and questions I'd had since he arrived.

He ended the call and held his phone tight in his hand, like he couldn't bear the thought of letting it go.

"Is she okay?"

"Yeah. She's at a hotel under a fake name while she figures out what to do next."

"What do you think she'll do?"

He looked down at his food and slowly shook his head. "I honestly don't know."

We spent the rest of the evening on the couch, watching old Christmas movies with my parents and the dogs. At one point, Mac was on the ground with them, his arm wrapped around a giant Lab while a rottweiler sat in his lap.

"I always wanted a dog," he said, and my mom proceeded to try to talk him into taking one ... or three. "Thank you, Mrs. Jamison, but I don't have the time. Baseball starts in a week," he added, and my heart started racing.

This was what we'd been waiting for.

All of Mac's hopes and dreams were riding on this upcoming season. And we wouldn't even know if his hard work had paid off until the end of it. If anyone deserved a chance at happiness, it was Mac Davies. But if I'd learned anything at all this year, it was that people didn't always get what they deserved. And that sometimes, life threw you a shit sandwich and expected you to be grateful for the meal.

GIFTS & GOODIES

Sunny

MY PARENTS WERE ridiculously cool and calm when it came to our sleeping arrangements. They had no issues with Mac sleeping in my room and in my bed, even though my dad did say, "No funny business under my roof."

Mac was respectful, shook his hand, and reassured him that he would never do that. My mom winked at me, and I huffed out an annoyed breath.

"Take her away, please," I said to my dad as I gave my mom a slight shove.

Once we were in my room, Mac looked around, taking in all the boy band posters that still lined my walls and pictures of me with friends. Why was it that our childhood rooms stayed that exact way we'd left them?

"Your room is so you," he said as he leaned down to look at some old pictures of me from high school.

"I'm taking that as a compliment." I moved to my bed and fluffed the pillows up against the wall, so I could lean up against them.

Mac reached into one of his duffel bags and struggled to

pull something out.

"Is that my present?" I asked, noticing the familiar wrapping paper still firmly in place.

Mac and I had exchanged presents before he left for Arizona, and we weren't allowed to open them until Christmas Day. No exceptions.

"You said we were going to open our presents together. Did you already open yours?"

I softly shook my head. We had promised to do it over video chat.

"It's up there." I pointed toward my dresser, where the small box waited, still tempting me. "I had to hide it."

He smirked. "Why?"

" 'Cause I wanted to open it so bad! I made my sister keep it until this morning. It's been torture," I admitted because the present was the size of a jewelry box, and I was coming out of my skin, waiting to see what was in it.

"Open it." He gave a slight head nod toward the gift, and I jumped off the bed and grabbed it.

Carefully peeling open the wrapping paper, I sighed when I saw the familiar Tiffany blue box underneath. I'd never gotten anything from Tiffany's before, but I still knew exactly what it was, based on the familiar teal-blue color alone.

My jaw dropped as I looked at Mac, who sat there, watching me with all of his attention. I tore through the main box, and there was another smaller one inside. Taking it out, I opened it to see a gorgeous necklace with a massive yellow stone and a tiny silver bee sitting on the edge of it. It was stunning.

"Mac," I said because this had to be expensive, and neither one of us had a job.

"Do you like it?" he asked, clearly wanting my approval.

"It's gorgeous, but it's too much," I said.

He shook his head. "It's not enough." He took the box from my hand, and I turned to face the mirror on my wall. Undoing the clasp, he wrapped the necklace around my neck and fastened it before stepping to the side.

My hand instinctively went to the gemstone, touching it as I stared at my reflection in the mirror. It was beautiful, and it did look really nice on me. "What is the stone? Do you know?"

"Yellow quartz. It's from their Love Bugs collection. They had other colors, but I wanted to get you the yellow one. I know it's obvious since your name is Sunny and all, but it suited you the most and it's your favorite color," he explained.

I loved hearing all the thought he'd put into buying me this gift. He hadn't just walked into the store and picked out the first thing he'd seen.

"When did you get it?"

"When we were in New York."

My jaw dropped open again. "What? When?"

We had been together almost every waking moment, so how had he found time to go to Tiffany's without me noticing? *And how did he go there without me?*

"I told you Chance and I were working out. We went to Tiffany's instead. Apparently, that's where his dad bought his mom's engagement ring," he added with a smile before wincing again. "I just wanted to look around. I wasn't sure I'd even like anything there, but then I saw that collection and couldn't walk away."

I swallowed hard as he kept talking, hoping he hadn't noticed.

"What's the matter?"

He'd noticed.

"It had to be expensive. Your dad—" I started to explain when he cut me off.

"I bought it with my own money. I have a savings account," he said.

I hadn't known that. I'd thought that all of his money came from his father, and I'd hated thinking that his dad had "technically" bought me this.

His response visibly relieved me, making me more willing to accept the gift even though it was still way too much. But he'd bought me jewelry!

"Thank you. I love it. It's so beautiful." I kissed him softly, almost forgetting about his jaw, but he pushed me away.

"I can't. It hurts. I'm sorry."

"Don't apologize. Do you think you should go to the doctor?" I asked, suddenly more worried than I was a second ago.

"No. I don't think anything's broken. Just sore. It will heal on its own."

"Okay. But if it gets worse, we'll go, right?"

"Yeah, babe. We'll go if it gets worse," he said, purely to placate me, but I allowed it.

"Now, open yours. It's not expensive or anything." I started to feel a little stupid because my gift couldn't compare to his. It had barely cost me a thing.

He tore through the wrapping paper, leaving bits and

pieces of Santa all over the floor of my room in a messy pile. When he noticed that it was a book, he looked at me with a confused expression before he opened it. Each page was filled with baseball articles featuring Mac Davies, going back as early as I could find them online. The first one was when he was ten years old and had made the local all-stars team.

I had at least one article that mentioned his name every year since. I'd searched for weeks, printing out every single thing I'd found on him and basically putting together a glorified scrapbook, like most parents would have done for their kids but I knew that his hadn't.

He flipped through the pages, his fingers running across each column and picture that showed his name and face. "This is all about me?" He sounded like he'd never even known the articles existed in the first place.

"Yeah. From ten years old until this past summer. I'll add this season's, too, once it starts," I explained, and he still looked bewildered.

"You did this for me?"

"Yes. Do you hate it? Do you think it's stupid?" I asked because maybe he thought it was dumb. Maybe the last thing he wanted was a book filled with all of his accomplishments for him to look back on. I wasn't sure.

"I think it's amazing. I've never even seen these before," he said as he continued turning each page carefully. "This must have taken you days."

"Weeks," I teased even though it was true.

He'd played on so many different teams throughout the years that finding them all had been a pain in the ass but totally worth it.

"No one has ever done anything like this for me before, Sunny. Thank you." He looked up, his eyes glassy as he pulled me into his arms.

"You really like it?"

"I love it." He gave me a kiss on the cheek, his lips barely able to form a pucker.

When he started to yawn but flinched from the pain, I held him.

"Let's get ready for bed," I suggested, and he nodded.

We both walked into the guest bathroom, and I brushed my teeth while he basically attempted to eat toothpaste. Brushing hurt, moving his mouth hurt, opening his jaw hurt, and swishing any kind of liquid was out of the question.

Once we changed into appropriate sleepwear with parents in the house, I turned off my light, and we crawled into bed. Mac had to lie on his back since being on his side caused him more pain.

If I wasn't so desperate to make him comfortable, I'd be more focused on plotting his dad's murder. But Mac feeling better was at the forefront of my mind. I just wanted my boyfriend to be okay.

"Want to tell me what happened to your car?" I asked as we lay in the dark, suddenly remembering the one-sided conversation with his mom from earlier.

"I was driving here. I got pulled over. Car had been reported stolen," he explained like he was giving me the CliffsNotes version, but I wanted more information.

"Why'd you get pulled over?"

"I was speeding."

"How fast were you going?" I asked, wondering if he had been driving as desperately as I knew he'd felt.

The mattress shifted as he moved his pillow around. "Eighty. It was too fast. I knew better. My car's a cop magnet."

"So, what happened then?"

He inhaled quickly before blowing out a long breath. "The cop asked if I knew why he pulled me over. I said yes. He asked for my license and registration. When he came back, he asked me to step out of the car."

"Were you scared?" I imagined how terrified I'd be if a cop asked me to get out of my car.

"No," he said matter-of-factly. "He told me that the car had been reported stolen by a Richard Davies, and then he asked me if I knew him." Mac let out a sick-sounding laugh. "I told him that was my dad and that we had an argument and I took off."

"I can't believe he reported your car stolen," I said, still surprised by each new piece of information I'd learned.

"I can. Anyway, the cop actually asked me if he did this to my face."

"Oh, wow. What'd you say?"

"I said no."

"Do you think he believed you?"

"I'm not sure. But he told me that he couldn't let me go with the car because whenever he stopped someone, he called it in, and now, it was on record in the system and blah, blah, blah." He stopped clarifying, but I knew what he was saying. The cop would have gotten into trouble if he'd let Mac leave with a stolen car. "He said that if this were any other situation, I'd be arrested and charged with vehicle theft. But he had some discretion in the matter, and technically, he was only required to bring in the car. Not me."

"So, he let you go." I reached out and searched for his hand before finally finding it. It was at an awkward angle, but I took it in mine anyway and held on tight.

"Yeah. We actually moved off of the freeway and into a restaurant parking lot. He let me get all of my things out of the car before he called a tow truck. And then he made sure I got a ride to your house before he took off."

His thumb started drawing lazy circles on top of my hand. I loved whenever he did that.

"Where was this? How far away were you?"

"About an hour out. The ride-share guy wasn't too happy, but I gave him a big cash tip."

"Where's your car now?"

"Some impound lot. I don't know. I don't care."

"And you're just going to leave it there?"

"It's not mine anyway. And I don't want it. I don't want anything from him anymore."

We stayed quiet after that, listening to nothing but the sound of our breathing.

"I'm sorry all this happened," I said, not knowing what else to say, but wanting to say something. I felt so out of my element when it came to this kind of parental drama and horror. I couldn't relate on any level.

He reached out for me and pulled me onto his chest, his fingers running through my hair. "Thank you for being here. I don't know what I'd do without you."

I felt the tears rush to my eyes with his words. Mac hadn't had to come here, to my parents' house. He could have gone to the baseball house, to Coach Carter's, or to one of his teammate's instead. But he'd chosen me. I knew how big of a deal that was for him ... for us.

When his world had started crashing around him, he had driven straight to my arms. Literally. As that realization and the weight of the day finally hit me, I couldn't stop the tears from falling. I'd been holding it all in, and now, in the dark, I didn't have to anymore.

"I love you, Mac."

The arm that held me gripped me tighter in response. "I love you too, babe. Never leave me."

"Never," I said in my most confident tone, making a promise I had every intention of keeping.

I should have known that, eventually, Mac wouldn't feel the same.

NEW YEAR, NEW ME

Mac

I'D SPENT THE last few days holed up in Sunny's house with her parents. They made it ridiculously easy to feel like I belonged there even if all their attention was a little uncomfortable. I wasn't used to being taken care of. The way they fawned all over me, fed me nonstop, and made sure my face healed properly with constant ice and Advil. Plus, I got to play and walk the dogs whenever I wanted, which made me insanely happy. I couldn't believe I'd never had a dog before, and now, all I wanted was one. Or five.

Nah, just one.

Sunny made a good point one afternoon while we were walking two of the dogs. Dayton was already at the baseball house, a good week before we had to report in for baseball, and I was considering going back too. But Sunny suggested that I stay away from Fullton until at least the bruises faded. They were almost gone, but a nice purple hue still shaded part of my jaw toward my mouth.

When she offered to cover it up with makeup, I told her, "Thank you, but no chance in hell."

She said that people would buy the *car accident and air bag* story, but that it would lead to a lot of questions and unwanted attention, especially as long as I couldn't eat solid foods, which I was still struggling with. My jaw fucking ached, and the force of my dad's blows had caused some of my teeth to loosen. They were tightening back up on their own though—something I'd had no idea that teeth had the ability to do, but I was grateful for it. I couldn't imagine if my teeth had fallen out.

When Sunny also added that my coaches would freak out when they heard about the accident and demand to see me, interrogate me, and possibly sit me out if they thought it was in my best interest, I realized that staying out of sight until I had to report back for practice was a necessity. The last thing I needed was my coaches worrying about my family situation and my state of mind regarding it. Especially now that I'd handled it. I'd left. There was nothing to work out, analyze, or discuss.

I talked to my mom about once a day. She was still hiding out in the hotel under a fake name, refusing to leave until she figured out what she was going to do. I could tell that her resolve was weakening with each day that passed. I thought she felt trapped and knew that she couldn't live in a hotel forever. It wasn't realistic. DD would eventually find her, if he hadn't already. At some point, she would have to check out and face her future head-on. I thought the idea terrified her. She'd been living a certain way for so long that she'd grown used to it.

I tried not to be mad at her, but it was hard. I knew that if she went back to DD, I'd have to cut her out of my life, too, and the thought alone gutted me. Sunny kept telling me to have a little faith in her and give her time, but the truth was, I didn't have faith in her to do the right thing even if I wanted to. I just ... didn't.

When we walked back into her parents' house, we let the dogs off their leashes, and the other six jumped up, wanting a turn.

"Being a dog walker's a full-time job," I said as I hooked another dog up to the leash I was still holding.

"You guys don't have to walk them all," her mom said as she rounded the corner, hands on her hips. "I'm making you an assortment of mushy foods, Mac. I found a blog online!" She sounded so excited, and it made me smile. Which still hurt too.

Was my face ever going to stop aching with every movement?

"We'll be right back. These are the last two," Sunny said as we turned around to head right back out the way we'd just come in, the necklace I'd given her reflecting the sunlight. It looked so beautiful.

I held Sunny's free hand as we walked our dogs with the other hands.

"I know I said you shouldn't go back yet, but I only meant the baseball house," Sunny started to say, and I wasn't sure what she meant.

"What?" I asked, hoping she'd clarify.

"We can go back and stay at my apartment. I just didn't think you should see anyone while your face is still"—she waved a hand toward my face—"you know."

"No. Tell me, babe," I teased. "What's my face like?"

She stuck her tongue out but didn't answer.

"So, you're ready to leave?" I asked, surprised but happy. I didn't think she'd want to leave.

"Hell yes, I'm ready." She laughed. "I love my parents, but I also love my privacy with you."

Privacy sounded nice.

"I'm ready whenever you are. It's up to you," I said, and I felt sort of relieved. Which made me feel like a dick. All her parents had done was be incredible to me, and here I was, dying to get away from it all.

WE ENDED UP leaving that night after dinner. Sunny's mom sent us home with Tupperware filled with various soft foods for me, and Sunny promised to bake me cookies and let me eat the dough.

When we stopped at the grocery store, I got everything I needed for a week's worth of protein shakes and so many eggs that Sunny suggested we buy a chicken instead.

Little smart-ass.

Then, we went to her apartment and spent the next five days in between the bedroom and the kitchen. Eating, fucking, and hiding out from the world. I finally felt like myself enough to remind my girl just how much I constantly craved her. I buried myself in her, making love and fucking her until she begged me to stop. Her body was spent, her legs were sore, and just when she thought she couldn't possibly take me again, I dived between her legs and ate her out instead. She pulled at my hair and told me how good it was and how much she loved me, wearing nothing, except the yellow necklace I'd bought her.

THE DAY BEFORE practice started, I packed up some of my stuff, and she dropped me off at the baseball house with a kiss and a smile. I loved my girl, but I needed my boys now.

This is it.

Do or die.

Now or never.

Shit or get off the pot.

Thank God my face had finally healed. Not a single discolored bruise remained, and I was able to eat solid foods again, so I wouldn't have to answer any questions from my roommates. When I walked through the front door, the guys practically tripped over themselves, trying to get to me at once.

"Dude, we missed you," Colin said with a big bear hug.

"Missed you guys too," I said even though I really hadn't technically missed them, but I did like being around them.

"Ready to get this season started?" Dayton asked, and I nodded before tossing my bag toward my bedroom door.

"Beyond. You ready, Transfer?" I gave a nod in Matt's

direction.

He grinned. "I just want it to start already."

"Careful what you wish for," Colin said with a grimace. "You'll be hating practice and workouts soon enough."

"What do you mean?" Matt suddenly looked nervous.

I clapped his shoulder. "We practice hard. Our weight sessions are brutal. Coach makes us run with tape over our mouths, so we can learn to breathe right," I said, and Matt looked like he might pass out. It made me laugh. "We get pushed to the brink. But that's why we're the best."

Fall practices were one thing, but now that we were in season, it was a different set of rules altogether. Weights at six a.m. sharp, even on travel days, unless it conflicted with our flight. Practices daily, except on game days. Batting cages after field work. Games four to five times a week. Not to mention, any travel and games away from home. It was a brutal load to carry when you tacked classes on top of it all.

But it was all worth it. Just for the chance to go pro after it was all said and done.

"You'll be okay, dude," Colin said, and I realized that I'd just freaked Matt out.

"Hey, it's fine. You got this. If Coach Jackson didn't think you could handle it, you wouldn't still be here," I said, hoping it would make him feel better.

But then he bent over at the waist and had his hands on his knees while he breathed in and out. I shot the other two guys a look, and they both shrugged.

"What do you mean?" Matt asked and looked up at me, still bent over.

"He would have cut you in the fall," I answered like he was an idiot because that was exactly what would have happened.

Coach Jackson never fucked around. If you weren't cut out for Fullton State Baseball, he wouldn't waste your time or his. Players had been dropped from the program during fall before—good players too. And none of us ever knew about it until it was too late and the guys were long gone.

"So, I'm good then?" Matt righted himself.

"You're still here, aren't you?" Colin said. "Now, stop freaking out and pull it together. You can't act like this tomorrow," he warned, and Matt nodded, but I could tell that he was nervous.

"I almost forgot." I snapped and walked back over to my bag, unzipped it, and pulled out a container. "Sunny baked for us."

Before I even had the words out, all three of them were surrounding me, trying to pull the box out of my hand. I almost dropped it to the floor, but I knew Sunny would kill me if she found out.

"Give them to me!" That was Dayton. He sounded like an animal.

It made me fucking laugh, so I let go, and Dayton looked around the room, thrusting his fist in the air like he was victorious in battle. Peeling open the lid, he pulled out two cookies and handed the container to Colin next. Matt whined but waited his turn.

"You have the best girlfriend," Colin said as he inhaled one of her creations.

"I know." I smirked, knowing that there was a whole other box of cookies in my bag, just for me.

THE NEXT MORNING, my alarm woke me up at five thirty on the dot. I tossed the covers off my body and stepped into the shower, turning it on cold. It was fucking miserable, but the cold water had been proven to wake up your senses, improve circulation, increase your metabolism, and help your body heal quicker. I always felt more alive and awake after a freezing shower.

All four of us met in the living room, each of us grabbing a banana as we headed out the door. The semester wasn't starting for a couple more weeks, but for us, this was day one of the season. My last season. Dayton's last season.

When we walked into the weight room, Coach was waiting with a list of workouts he had broken down by player and position. We checked the pages for our names and went to our respective areas to start training.

Two full hours later, I was drenched in sweat and exhausted. I grabbed a protein bar and a protein shake from the fridge. If I downed it all too fast, I'd puke, so I nibbled at the bar first before inhaling the rest of it.

Coach told us to meet him at the field at one. We were free to go until then. The four of us piled back into Dayton's car and headed home to crash. I sent Sunny a text, telling her I loved her and that I'd call her later, and then I passed out with my phone in my hand, still sweaty and gross.

Practice that day was a little rough, to be honest. We had kinks to work out with the new starters. They were still learning Coach's signals and our hand calls even though they should have had them memorized by now. We looked like a team who had just come off a ten-month vacation and not touched a ball the entire time. Coach Jackson looked like his head might explode.

Thankfully, I had my shit together and only got yelled at once. When Coach split us into teams so we could play against each other, I was excited to hear him tell me that I was batting leadoff. When I stepped up to the plate to face Dayton, we both grinned at each other and tried not to laugh. Coach Carter told Dayton to strike me out, and Coach Jackson told me to knock his head off.

It was surreal but probably not unlike playing pro ball when you faced off against people who were your friends off the field. You both wanted to win the "battle at the plate." I knew that Dayton wanted to get me out, just like he knew I wanted to hit the shit out of the ball.

So, when the first pitch curved at the last second for a strike, I shook my head as I stepped out of the batter's box and gave him a look. He'd been working on that pitch during the entire off-season, so I should have known it would be the first one he threw. Stepping back in, I crouched into position, the weight of the bat feeling nice against my shoulder. Dayton pulled his arm back, and I lifted the bat from my shoulder right as the ball made its way toward me, my eyes locked on. I swung, and the bat made contact with the ball, flying into left field with a bounce. I made it to first easily, my team cheering wildly.

I'd won that round.

But there would be a lot more.

SENIOR SEASON

Mac

THE SEASON WAS in full swing, and Fullton State was having an okay year. We weren't as good as we had been last year, but that was to be expected when you lost a third of your team. Those who had been drafted or graduated left a lot of positions to be filled.

Guys you expected to step up and kick ass sometimes disappointed you and couldn't pull through. Or if they were killing it in the field, their hitting wasn't as strong. It was tough, finding players who were great at both—playing defense and offense.

Sunny came to all my home games. There was nothing like glancing up in the stands and seeing her silver hair swishing around as she smiled and cheered for me. That girl made me feel so loved. And fucking invincible. Like I could do anything as long as she was by my side. I missed her like crazy whenever we left for our away games, but she was the perfect fucking girlfriend—supportive and understanding.

Her parents even came to some of my games, which was awesome. Her mom never brought any of the dogs though, which was the exact opposite of awesome. They made me feel like family. I appreciated that and never took it for granted.

Personally, I'd been having a killer season. My numbers had never been better.

Coach Jackson even pulled me aside after the game to let me know that someone was asking about me.

"A scout?" I clarified.

Coach rolled his eyes so hard that I thought they might stay in the back of his head. "Who the fuck else would ask about you, Davies? My mom?"

"I'm just excited, Coach," I explained, hoping he wouldn't think less of me.

"Take your excitement somewhere else. I just wanted you to know." He sent me away with a flick of his wrist.

When I walked out of the locker room and made my way up the stairs, Sunny was waiting for me with a smile, like always.

"Coach said a scout was asking about me," I said, unable to keep that information to myself for a second longer.

"Well, it's about time," she said, pressing her lips against mine before we started walking toward the parking lot.

I couldn't have agreed more.

I honestly didn't know what else to do to get their attention. I couldn't have been playing any better. My first base was solid, and my hitting was consistent. I had the least amount of strikeouts on the team. And the most walks. My fucking eye was impeccable at the plate. But I had zero home runs, and I knew that was working against me. The fact was, I wasn't a power hitter. I never had been, and most likely, I never would be. I just wasn't that type of hitter.

"I talked to your mom today," Sunny said.

I stopped walking for a second to give her a surprised look. "You did?" I asked. "What'd she say?"

Sunny and my mom had started talking recently after they exchanged numbers. My mom was in the process of filing for divorce and leaving DD. I was happy for her, but I couldn't shake the worry that lived in the back of my mind because of it. I'd never forget the way he'd snapped on me at Christmas. If he did it once, he was capable of doing it again. Even if it wasn't his normal MO. I just wanted my mom away from him already, but I should be thankful she'd found the strength to leave in the first place. I knew it was hard for her.

I still hadn't talked to him. And he never reached out to me to apologize. Not that it would matter. I was done with him for good. But there was a part of me that wanted him to be sorry.

"She wants to come out for a series," Sunny said.

I pressed my lips together and reared my head back in shock. "Wow. A whole series?"

"Yeah. Do you care when she comes? I'll just plan it with her and figure out all the details. Unless you don't want me to," she offered.

I was relieved by the idea of her handling all of that.

"That would actually be really helpful. I don't have the time to deal with that right now."

"I figured," she said with a smile, her necklace bouncing against her chest as she walked. "She and I will get it all planned out, and then I'll let you know."

We reached her car, and I grabbed her by the back of the neck, pulling her to me. "Thank you. I really appreciate it."

"I can't wait to meet her!" she practically shouted.

I wanted to tell her to lower her expectations. That my mom wasn't like hers.

"She might be drinking," I mentioned because I wasn't sure if her trying to stop had stuck or not. Sometimes, when I talked to her, she sounded okay, but other times, her words slurred.

"She's sober. She told me." Sunny smiled again as she unlocked her car and slid inside.

"Why do you know more about my mom than I do?" I teased.

" 'Cause we text every day."

"Every day?" My eyes grew wide, and Sunny laughed as the engine roared to life.

"No, but I text her during your games and send her pics. So, it feels like every day."

I hadn't realized that they communicated that often. *Sunny sent my mom pictures of me playing baseball?* It was all too surreal. But better late than never, I guessed.

BASEBALL SUCKS

Sunny

I DIDN'T KNOW everything there was to know about baseball, but I understood it well enough to know that Mac was having a phenomenal season. He started every single game at first base and was batting leadoff, which meant that he hit first in the order.

He'd had only three errors at first base the whole season so far. And after Coach had told him that there was a scout asking about him, it was all Mac had needed to hear to stay in a positive headspace. Every night after his game, he was so happy and excited about how he'd played. There was nothing like seeing him feel good about himself when he was on that field.

I went to every single home game. There were about two million fifty-five thousand of them, but I was always there, in the stands with the other girlfriends, cheering on our boys.

It was amazing when his mom came out for a big weekend series and stayed at the hotel on campus. Mac played incredible, and she looked like she'd had no idea that he was that good. Maybe she hadn't. It was nice to meet her in person after all I'd heard. She looked healthy and was officially two-months sober. My parents had wanted to come down and meet her, too, but I'd forced them to give Mac some time alone with his mom, and they'd begrudgingly understood.

I thought it was for the best. When Mac said the light was coming back into her eyes, I knew that my sweet, broken boy was finally healing.

"This is so much fun," his mom said from our seats behind home plate.

Mac had gotten us a pair of reserved seats for the weekend, so we weren't sitting in the student section.

I looked at his mom as she wiped the tears away. "What's the matter?"

"I missed out on this for so long. I could have been watching him play for years," she said, clearly regretting all the time that she'd lost.

"At least you're here now," I said, hoping to ease some of her guilt.

"He doesn't hate me, does he?" she whispered toward me, her eyes filled with regret and pain that her only son might not like her.

"No." I placed my hand on her arm. "He doesn't hate you. Your husband, on the other hand," I started to say as her mouth twisted into a snarl.

"Ex-husband," she clarified. "And I feel like I owe you an apology," she said, and I swallowed hard.

"Me? Why would you owe me an apology?" I asked, wondering where she was heading.

"Because I stayed with Richard for so long. I feel like I

allowed all of this to happen to Mac. I know you've picked up the pieces. I'm sorry I let him break for so long."

My eyes instantly welled up. "Oh jeez. We can't both start crying during the game. Mac will be mortified." I tried to laugh. "That wasn't necessary, but thank you."

After the game ended, the three of us went out to dinner together and took our time, eating and hanging out. It was so much nicer than I'd anticipated; I was always a little unsure of how Mac felt when it came to his parents.

True to her word, his mom didn't drink. And when we dropped her off at the hotel that night, Mac walked her into the lobby and talked with her for a few minutes before giving her a hug. She waved at me before she disappeared.

Mac opened the car door and hopped in, his eyes red.

"What happened? Is everything okay?"

"Yeah," he breathed out. "She apologized for everything. And wishes she could take it all back and do it different but knows that she can't."

"That was nice of her to say," I said as we pulled out of the parking lot.

"Yeah. I mean, now that she's not drinking, she said she sees it a little too clearly. And she's having a hard time not hating herself for it all."

I imagined what that must have felt like. To have numbed your pain with something for so long, only to have it all come crashing back in high-definition once the haze lifted.

"What'd you say?"

"I told her that I didn't hate her. That I wasn't angry with her anymore and that if I could forgive her, then she needed to forgive herself too," he stumbled on the last words, and I knew that he was getting choked up.

I reached across the seat for his hand and squeezed. "That was very mature of you."

"I thought so too." He smirked as he brought our linked hands to his lips and pressed a kiss there.

"Oh, I keep forgetting to tell you!" I practically shouted. "Rocky texted. She said to tell you she's watching your games online, so don't screw up." I laughed. "And that she misses us. Mostly my cookies."

"Man, that girl." He shook his head. "She's something else. Is she getting better?"

"She said she was going to therapy and it seems to be helping."

"That's good. I was worried about her for a minute there," he admitted. We both had been.

"I know. But she's tough."

"She's fucking inspiring," he added. "Anytime I want to give up, I channel my inner Rocky," he said, sounding all badass and tough. "Don't tell her I said that though. She'd never let me live it down."

MAC HAD FINALLY taken Coach Carter up on his offer and called his brother, Dean, the sports agent. Dean Carter was patient and answered all of Mac's questions, but in the end, he said the whole draft process was a fluid beast that moved quickly and adjustments were often made on the fly and at the last minute. Basically, he said that nothing was guaranteed, and the call hadn't done anything to help ease Mac's state of mind for the upcoming draft. We still felt completely in the dark.

And as the season started wrapping up, I learned that hitting only one home run wasn't necessarily what the scouts and the Major League teams were looking for. They wanted 'power hitters,' even if that meant that they struck out more than they didn't. Because when they did get hits, they made them count and scored a bunch of runs. I thought that was some stupid, illogical crap, but what the heck did I know?

Apparently, having some of the best stats at Fullton State didn't always mean anything more than you might get your name on a plaque and break some school records.

Baseball was weird.

And I was starting to resent it.

The day the draft started, Mac and I sat alone on the couch of my apartment with the television on and his cell phone at his side. I'd never seen him more uneasy than he was during this time. He didn't want anyone else to share this moment, too on edge to have witnesses to whatever his future ended up being. We both had no idea what would happen, and neither did anyone else, it seemed.

A bunch of Mac's teammates were at the baseball house, but he couldn't stomach the thought of being around them if his name wasn't called.

"I wouldn't be able to take the looks on their faces. The

way they'd feel sorry for me but thankful that it wasn't them at the same time." He pushed up from the couch and wrapped an arm around his stomach.

I knew how sick this was making him.

The not knowing.

The waiting.

The silence.

It was all out of his hands now, and that was both terrifying and a relief. He'd given baseball his all this past season, and I knew he couldn't have played any better. He knew it too. But for whatever reason, none of that seemed to matter now.

When the tenth round started up, his phone beeped out a text message indication, and he grabbed it so fast that I thought he might crush it. I watched his expression morph into something unreadable as he put his phone on the coffee table in front of us and leaned back into the couch, staying quiet, like he'd been since the whole thing began. I looked at him and waited for him to share what he'd just read.

He finally turned to me and blinked before looking away from my eyes. "They think Dayton will go soon." His tone was undecipherable.

"Who's they?"

He shrugged. "I don't know. That's just what the text said. He must be talking to an agent or something."

I didn't know what to say. I honestly had no idea how to deal with all of this. I couldn't be my usual positive and happy self. Draft days weren't technically about keeping a positive attitude. We were beyond all that now. We were in business mode. So, I wasn't sure if we should be happy for Dayton or be mad at him for it.

The announcer said Dayton's name, and I saw a small smile creep across Mac's face, followed quickly by a deep breath as his chest shook lightly. He grabbed his phone and typed out a text—I assumed he was congratulating Dayton.

"I knew he'd go," Mac said while staring straight ahead at the TV.

"Yeah?" I asked, still at a loss for the right thing to contribute.

"He's a pitcher. He had a great season. It wouldn't have made any sense if he didn't get the call," he added, and I wondered if he was explaining it more for my benefit or his. I only understood half of what he was saying anyway, but I got the gist.

That night he barely slept, tossing and turning the entire time, and when I woke up on day two of the draft, he was already out of bed, and his side was freezing cold, like he hadn't been there for hours.

Mac refused to eat. I baked cookies he didn't touch. Ordered pizza that he ignored. I had to remind him to drink water, or he would dehydrate himself without even thinking. He barely talked out loud, staying in his head, and I tried to understand how he must be feeling, watching his dream slip by with each hour that passed.

Each time a new round started up, I swore he held his breath in anticipation.

Or maybe it was dread.

And as they continued to dwindle, I watched the light drain from his eyes after each one completed without saying his name.

"It's not going to happen," he mumbled under his breath at one point.

I knew he wasn't talking to me, but I stupidly answered him anyway, "It's not over yet. You don't know. There's still hope."

He shot me a look that would have broken other females. But I fought with my inner little girl, reminding her that this wasn't about us and to not take it personally.

But hope wasn't enough. The last round came and went, and Mac Davies's name was never called. My heart split in two inside my chest. I felt the ache of it.

The sheer devastation on Mac's face only lasted a moment before he pulled himself together and stood up. "Can you take me home, please?"

"Are you sure?" I asked because I wanted to be the one who took care of him, but I also understood him needing to be alone.

"Sunny, I want to go home."

"What if your teammates are there?" I asked, figuring that he wanted to avoid them if possible.

"I'll just walk." He ignored my question and started to grab his things, so I reached for his arm, stopping him.

"I'll take you. Talk to me," I begged, and he looked right through me, neglecting my request.

We stayed quiet the entire drive back to the baseball house. I wanted him to say something to me, but I was scared to push him too hard. When I pulled up, there were a bunch of cars at the house, and I noticed Mac suck in a breath before opening the passenger door.

"I need some time."

"Away from me?" I asked with a shaky breath.

"Away from everyone," he replied. "I can't do this right now."

"Do what?" My eyes started to fill with water. "Are you breaking up with me?" I asked through my shock.

This stubborn, pigheaded boy was not freaking dumping me now, after all we'd been through.

"It's better this way. Please, Sunny, just go. I don't want you here," he said before shutting the door and disappearing without giving me a second glance.

My heart split inside my chest. It pulled at me, ached with each beat, as I replayed his harsh words.

"*I. Don't. Want. You. Here.*"

I convinced myself that Mac just needed some space, and I respected him enough to let him work through the fact that he hadn't gotten the one thing he'd always wanted more than anything. Baseball had been his dream, his goal, and now, it was gone.

It had to hurt like hell. But having him walk away from me, from us, hurt like hell too. I felt like we'd taken a thousand steps backward and we were back in the place we had been last year all over again.

I pulled at my necklace; it usually calmed me, but now, it represented a lie. If Mac didn't want to be with me, then I couldn't wear it anymore. I started taking it off when my phone pinged. I reached for it, hoping it was Mac telling me he was an idiot and was sorry, but I noticed Chance's name instead.

CHANCE: HOW'S HE DOING?

ME: LITTLE JERK BROKE UP WITH ME.

My phone rang instantly.

"Hey," I said as I tried to hold myself together.

"It doesn't surprise me," Chance said, and that wasn't very freaking reassuring.

"Gee, thanks."

"No, Sunny. I just meant that he is probably going out of his mind right now. He just lost everything he's ever wanted," Chance explained, but I had known that already. I knew how badly he wanted to play professional baseball.

"I know that."

"But you don't. I mean, you understand, but you don't know how that feels. He's not himself. He probably won't be for a while. This is something that takes time to work through and accept. It won't be easy."

I sniffed into the phone. I didn't mean to start crying, but I couldn't help it. "I never thought he'd break up with me because of it. Stupid, right?"

"Not stupid," Chance breathed out. "It won't last. You know that. I know that. But right now, he can't see straight. Hell, he can't see at all. Cut him some slack, Sun. I'll talk to him."

"You might make it worse," I said because Chance had everything that Mac wanted. There was a good possibility that Chance talking to Mac might exacerbate his feelings on the situation.

"You're right. I'll give him some space too." Chance started mumbling to someone in the background, and then he was back. "Hold on. Danika wants to talk to you."

Danika got on the phone and started yapping a mile a minute. At first, she apologized about Mac, but reassured me that this split was only temporary. She told me not to worry about it before launching into some diatribe about her clients needing more than only she could provide.

She explained that she needed help with the division she'd started at her dad's company, which she'd told me a hundred times before, only she was truly serious now. She offered me an official job. One with a salary and benefits and everything.

I practically screamed, "YES," into the phone.

Even though my personal life was falling apart before my eyes, I had no reason to turn down Danika's offer. I had fallen in love with New York, and while her high-end real estate clientele seemed super intimidating, it also sounded exciting. And nothing job-wise had even remotely excited me, so I took it as a sign and accepted.

What the hell else was I going to do with my life?

THREE DAYS HAD passed, and there was still no word from Mac. I texted him. He never responded. I called him. He refused to answer. It was like I'd never existed. How he could go about his days without talking to me when all I did was think about him twenty-four/seven boggled my mind and twisted me up inside. I was coming apart without him, and he was what ... *fine*?

Three days turned into a week, and my sadness turned to anger. *Screw him for letting me go. Why did I always have to do all the fighting in our relationship? Why was it up to me to keep us together and make us okay all the time?* Mac Davies was going to feel one hell of a shock to his system when he finally woke up from his daze and tried to find me ... 'cause I wouldn't be here!

Ha!

Good luck locating me in New York. Jerk.

On day nine, I began packing. My lease was ending at the apartment, and I wanted to spend a few days back home with my parents before I headed across the country to start my new job and life. Without the one person I'd thought would always be there. I heard my sliding glass door open, and my body instantly tensed. *I forgot to lock it?*

Of course, this was how I was going to die—right after being brave enough to move away.

The sound of shoes heading toward my bedroom made me go rigid. I stared at my bedroom door and waited.

It was Mac. He looked awful. Worse than when he had shown up at my house on Christmas night. His eyes were swollen, and there were big black bags underneath them. He hadn't been sleeping—that much was obvious.

"What are you doing?" he asked as he walked right into my bedroom, uninvited.

"What's it look like?" I threw back in a *screw you* tone as I folded more clothes and set them inside one of my open suitcases.

"Where are you going?"

I pondered whether or not I should tell him even though I assumed he already knew the answer. Asking me was merely a formality. I was sure Chance had filled him in.

"New York," I answered without meeting his gaze.

"What a coincidence."

I stopped folding and glared at him. "What is?"

"I'm going there too."

"Why would you go to New York?"

"Because you'll be there," he answered so simply, so matter-of-factly, like he hadn't broken up with me and tried to discard me in the midst of his grief while I was grieving too.

Baseball hadn't just broken his heart; it'd broken mine too. But Mac didn't care about my feelings. He only cared about himself.

"I didn't invite you." I tried to sound tough, but us being apart was stupid. We belonged together. But I wanted him to grovel a little at least.

"Well, my girl's going to start her career there, and I'm going to support her. It's the same thing she'd have done for me if I'd gotten drafted."

"Your girl, huh?"

"Yep," he said, popping the P.

"Thought you didn't want me," I threw his words back in his face as I started to get worked up and emotional.

The past nine days had been hell without him. I hoped it

was just a phase that really had nothing to do with me, but it still hurt that he'd tossed me away like it was easy for him to do it. After everything we'd gone through, I figured we were stronger than anything. And all he had done was prove me wrong when he disappeared.

"I can't live without you. I'm just sad, babe. I'm so fucking sad right now, and I didn't want you to see me that way." Tears started falling from his eyes, and he didn't even stop them or try to wipe them away.

"But I'm supposed to be your partner in all of this. We're supposed to be a team. I'm the one who gets to see you at your weakest because it's my job to lift you back up. That's what a good couple does. That's what I thought we were," I argued.

"I couldn't get out of bed for three full days," he admitted, and I hadn't known that. I hadn't known that at all. "I didn't leave my room for seven. Colin brought me food. Left it outside of my door. This is my first time leaving the house."

I didn't know what to say.

"I know I fucked up. I'm so sorry. I didn't know how to deal with losing baseball. Hell, I still don't. I'm devastated, babe. But I can't lose you too. I'll figure out how to get through this whole baseball thing, but there's no getting through losing you," he said. "Please let me come to New York."

I stayed quiet for a breath. And then another.

I could make him suffer more, push him for more apologies or more groveling, but that would be my pride talking and not my heart. I didn't want to hurt Mac more, only to make myself feel better. And that was all that would be. I loved him. I'd always loved him. And moving to New York without him would be a terrible option even though I would have done it.

"I guess you'd better start packing. We leave in three days."

LIFE AFTER BALL

Mac

I WAS DEPRESSED. No. Depressed was an understatement.
I was fucking lost.

A shell of a person with no idea who I was anymore or who I was supposed to be.

When your identity was wrapped up in one thing for so long, who were you when you didn't have that thing anymore?

Every single notion I'd ever believed about myself came into question.

My dream of becoming a professional baseball player was gone. Just like that. It had disappeared as soon as they called the last name in the last round of the draft, and it wasn't mine.

The worst part was, no one had prepared us for this part. We spent our entire lives practicing, conditioning, and working to be a better baseball player. If we made an error in the field, we made up for it by taking five hundred ground balls the next day. If we struck out swinging, we practiced our stance at the plate and focused on our ability to read the ball as it came out of the pitcher's hand. If we were too slow on the run from home plate to first base, we did drills. We worked on speed techniques, so we could get faster. To improve our time. To beat out that throw to first.

We were never taught how to quit.

We didn't believe in giving up.

Our whole lives revolved around chasing this dream. From what we ate to how much sleep we got and who we let into our personal lives. Every single aspect of our mindset was on how to be a better baseball player and how to get to that next level. We were always climbing to reach that next goal. We were conditioned to never give up on that dream. No matter what. We were told that it was never out of reach.

Until it was.

Because no one had ever taught you what to do when the dream gave up on you.

No one had talked about how lost you'd feel when the one thing you'd been chasing your entire life evaporated into thin air.

Everyone walked away and expected you to pick yourself up off the floor and simply ... move. The. Fuck. On. Like that was even possible when your whole world had just been shattered into a million unrecognizable pieces.

Who were you anymore if you weren't a baseball player chasing a dream? What the hell were you supposed to do with your life when you'd only planned for one outcome? And even more simply, what were you supposed to do with your day when it'd always been planned out for you?

No one had told us what it would feel like when this day came. They all told us how we'd feel when we got the draft call, as if every single guy who'd ever stepped on that field was lucky enough to get one. Even though, logically, we knew it didn't happen that way, we always assumed that if it didn't happen, it was to someone else. Lots of guys didn't get drafted. But I wouldn't be one of them. Right?

You see, no one had mentioned that. They all just moved on, left us behind, without realizing that we were stuck in a sea of despair, feeling like we were going to drown at any moment. Because no one had fucking prepared us for this part. Not a single damn person had told us what *THIS* would feel like. How utterly painful and depressing it would be to lose baseball when you were not ready for it to be over.

No one had told you that you'd fall into a hole of sadness so deep that you didn't think you'd ever get out of it. And they sure as shit hadn't told you what to do after you did climb up from it.

"I'm here to tell you that it gets better. That there is a light at the end of the tunnel. And that you will be okay. But first, it's really going to fucking hurt. But that's why I'm here today. To help you through it and figure out your next steps.

"Your professional baseball dreams might be over. But your new life is just beginning."

The crowd stood on their feet, roaring and clapping as I tried to smile from the center of the auditorium stage as all the lights turned on at once. I'd just finished giving a speech to local athletes from all levels of play. Some were as young as high school kids, and others were seniors in college, about to play their last season.

Telling my story had only started getting easier more recently. There were times when it still hurt like hell, and I found myself getting emotional as I tried to speak, but knowing what I'd created for these guys helped ease the pain somehow.

When I hadn't gotten drafted, I'd thought my life was over. Even after moving to New York with Sunny. She had her new career, and I was still depressed and feeling sorry for myself. I had no idea what I was going to do or who I even was anymore. Nothing interested me. My entire identity had been wrapped up in being a ballplayer, and once that was gone, where did that leave me? DD's words echoed in my mind, followed closely behind by Hayley's. Both of them reminding me that I wasn't good enough to play professional baseball, that it was all a pipe dream. I'd wondered for a while there what they had always seen that I hadn't.

I'd spilled my guts to Chance one day over the phone in a tantrum of epic fucking proportions. To this day, I had no idea how he hadn't hung up on me.

I screamed.

I yelled.

I cursed everyone's existence for not helping when my world had crashed around me.

We ended the call and when Sunny walked through our front door after work, I did it all over again.

Her face lit up with a smug smirk in the midst of my absolute misery as she said, "That's it, babe."

"What is? What's it?" I smacked my hand on the table, hating myself, hating baseball, hating everything on this fucking planet, except her.

"You said that there's no one to help you guys navigate

what comes next, right? For those of you who don't get drafted."

"Yeah. So? What's your point?" I was being a fucking asshole, and I watched as she fingered the necklace that I'd given her for Christmas.

I'd started to realize that she did that whenever she was trying to stay calm and collected. She had been doing it a lot lately while I tested her patience.

"I think you should start a company that helps them," she suggested as she threw a pile of folders on top of the counter. "You've been sitting here, all sad and depressed, but I think it's because you've just been left in the wind to figure it all out on your own," she added.

The wheels started spinning in my mind immediately, like they had always been turning and were just waiting for me to activate them.

"I could start a nonprofit. One that deals with life after baseball, specifically when you don't get drafted. How to process that grief, that loss, and then figure out your next steps. Maybe I could have some sort of job opportunity board for all of the open coaching positions at various schools and travel baseball teams," I started talking, and my wheels would stop spinning. "You're a genius, babe. A fucking genius," I said before grabbing my girl and kissing her senseless.

"I think you'd be great at it." She gave me her trademark megawatt smile.

"I'd need funding," I continued brainstorming out loud. "Since this isn't something I'd want to charge the guys for. I want to provide a service. To really help."

"What about Chance's dad? I bet he would invest. He probably has retired baseball friends who would invest too," Sunny added with a know-it-all grin, and the two of us sat down for the rest of the night, plotting and dreaming and making a plan.

I called Coach Carter the next day, explaining to him what I wanted to do even though I hadn't researched every detail thoroughly yet. I wasn't even halfway through my planned speech when he told me to shut up before texting me a picture of him signing a check.

"Look, Mac, we always need write-offs, but this is something I can really get behind," he said through the phone. *"And I know at least twenty guys who will feel the same way. Just say the word. How big do you want this to be?"*

Shit. *I wasn't sure. "What do you think?"*

"I think this could be as big or as small as you want. You could have physical locations in every state or make it mostly online. It's up to you, but you'll need a staff. You can't be the only one who talks to all these guys. There will be too many," he said before sucking in a breath and blowing it into the phone. *"Unless you do big online meetings with multiple people at once."*

For whatever reason, my initial thought had been to be more one-on-one, but maybe that wasn't the best move. Maybe me talking to a group of guys at the same time and then putting those guys in touch with each other, so they had an actual support system would be the better option.

"I was thinking that I'd start small and grow as necessary," I said out loud, and he agreed immediately.

"I think this is going to take off though. So, make sure you have all the right people in place when you start," he said. "I'll get this check in the mail today, and I'll reach out to a few friends who are still in the city, so you can meet with them too."

Like the man hadn't done enough for me already, here he was, funding my business and sending me more contacts for it. "Thank you, Coach. This means the world to me."

"Mac, it's a genius idea. I don't know how no one's done it before now."

"Me neither," I admitted honestly.

Because if this had been available to me after the draft, I would have utilized it. If for no other reason than to have not felt so alone. I needed to hear that what I was feeling was normal but also that it would pass. Then, I was certain that I would have wanted to work there.

"Any idea what you're going to call it?" he asked, and I realized that in figuring out all the particulars, I hadn't even thought about a name.

"Not yet," I admitted.

"You'll think of something," he said, and I knew he was right.

This was a good thing, and I couldn't wait to get started.

EPILOGUE

THE OFF-SEASON

Mac

"**H**ONEY, I'M HOME." My silver-haired goddess waltzed through the front door of the Sutton Place condo we shared with Danika and Chance whenever they were in town. She had a giant grin on her beautiful face.

We were so thankful and lucky that Jack and Cassie Carter had let us move into this place, insisting that it was just "sitting empty, so someone should enjoy it."

But still, this place was gorgeous, and we never could have afforded to live in such splendor without their generosity. It had been a bit of an emotional adjustment for me at first, being around Chance. His life still revolved around baseball, and mine didn't. Hearing about it hurt. But the more I started to feel good about what I was doing for other guys, the easier it was to let go of the pain. This was important work, and I'd found purpose in doing something good that helped other guys like me.

And to be honest, Chance fucking Carter had more talent

in his pinkie finger than most of us had in our entire bodies. He deserved to be playing professional baseball. Even if I no longer was.

And I was okay with that.

"How was work, babe?" I asked, pressing a kiss to her lips.

"Awesome! I freaking love this city. And I love my job," she said, her whole face lighting up like the sun itself.

Once she'd started working for Danika and learned the ropes, Sunny had realized how good she was at finding beautiful places for clients to consider. She was excited and honest—two qualities that they seemed to adore in her. I completely understood their admiration.

Sunny and Danika made one hell of a team, and they were constantly slammed with work. Their division had grown so quickly via word of mouth that they both had assistants already. My sweet girl, who had had no idea what she wanted to do with her life, now had her own assistant. She was such a badass.

"Where's Danika? She left the office before I did." Sunny looked around the apartment for her best friend, seemingly confused by her absence.

"Chance took her out the second she got home," I said, knowing that tonight was the night Chance was going to propose.

He'd had the ring for a fucking year already, but he kept holding on to it instead of using it. He said he was waiting for the right time, but he'd confessed to me one night that he wanted Danika's division to be fully up and running before he distracted her with wedding planning. And now that our girls were a huge hit within the business, there was no time like the present. But his consideration for her success was just one of the reasons why I respected him so much.

I pulled out a bottle of wine and tossed a bottle of champagne in the freezer.

"What are you doing? Are we celebrating?" Sunny asked, her eyes wide.

"Yes, but not until later." I pulled her against me and kissed her nose. "You know how proud I am of you, right?"

She blushed and looked away from my eyes. "You tell me all the time."

"Well, I don't want you to forget."

"I'm proud of you too. Look what you built!" She pulled away from me and pointed at the framed baseball magazine on the wall that had my face on the cover.

It was a full-length feature spread, talking all about my business, Life After Baseball, and what I provided for players whose careers were coming to an end.

It was a really well-written piece that had made the business explode. Various coaches across the country singing my praises was one thing, but the nationwide exposure had taken the business to a whole new level.

I now had staff and locations in ten states aside from the main headquarters here in New York. Every person who worked for me was an ex–baseball player who had been through the emotional wringer when his time came to an end. I had study courses designed and set up that each staff member had to take and familiarize themselves with. I wanted our players dealt with from the same main angle and perspective.

Of course, every player was different, but the purpose of our program was to help guide them out of the dark and back into the real world. We showed them that there was more to their life than just being a baseball player. And we focused on all the things that had molded us, like being part of a team, and how we could apply that to other areas in our lives.

For example, every athlete had learned teamwork at an early age; how to take direction from higher-ups—coaches; how to deal with difficult personalities—other players; how to fight against adversity—people thinking you weren't good enough or beating someone out for a position; and how to be a leader. All of these were helpful tools that could be utilized, going forward, no matter what type of career they moved into.

"Chance is proposing tonight," I blurted out, and Sunny's mouth dropped wide open. "Wait! I mean, act surprised. Don't tell her you knew. He might not do it," I kept running off at the mouth.

Sunny started doing a little dance in the kitchen.

"How long have you known this?" She swatted my shoulder, and I growled. My girl was still always hitting me.

"I knew he was going to ask her soon. But I didn't know about tonight until today," I admitted. "But, babe, you can't tell her you knew!" I warned, and she pretended to zip her lips and throw away the key.

"I'm so excited for her." She pressed a kiss to my lips before hopping into my arms and wrapping her legs around my waist. "We're next, right?" she asked, and I pretended to choke before she said she was just joking.

I'd had the ring for about a month now. A beautiful square-shaped diamond, encrusted with yellow stones that matched her necklace. It was hiding in my old baseball bag in the closet, but I wasn't telling her that. Her dad had already given me his blessing. I'd asked him for it the last time they flew out.

Sunny's parents had visited us twice already, and if I didn't know any better, I'd think her mom was trying to convince her dad to retire out here. It was never going to happen, but I thought Sunny's mom enjoyed tormenting her dad.

Speaking of parents, my mom had bought her own townhouse and was officially divorced from DD. When she'd heard rumors that the old bookstore on Main was set to close their doors for good, she'd put in an offer, resuming her old title as event planner as well as owner. I'd never seen her happier. And the old store was thriving again with book signings and events happening weekly, all because of her.

I felt like I finally understood where my entrepreneurial spirit had come from, and it wasn't from Dick Davies. DD's blood was filled with dollar signs. He and I weren't the same. He'd tried to screw my mom out of substantial sums of money during the divorce by hiding it in things like Bitcoin and overseas accounts, but he had gotten caught and had to give her half of everything anyway. Apparently, he was pretty pissed off about all that. I didn't know because we still didn't talk. And as sad as that might be, I felt more relieved than anything.

The truth was, I didn't miss him, and I rarely thought about him. The guy simply didn't cross my mind. I was happier without his drama and negativity in my life. Sunny refused to let me feel bad about that, so I didn't.

I didn't have much to feel bad about these days. Things

had fallen into place when I thought they never would. See, if someone had told me back then that I'd never see the sun the same way again, I would have believed them. I would have agreed that it didn't have quite the same shine anymore. It was duller somehow.

But I would have been wrong.

Because life after baseball was shaping up to be more beautiful than I could have ever hoped for.

I looked at my silver-haired goddess and knew she felt the exact same way. I couldn't wait for the next steps in our life, and it suddenly took everything in me not to run into the closet, pull out the ring, and drop to one knee right here in the kitchen.

Chance would kill me if I took away his proposal thunder. And probably kick me out of the house. I could always do it tomorrow instead. That way, the girls could plan their weddings together at the same time.

A double wedding? I could think of worse things.

THE END

Damn. I'm not sure how you're feeling right now, but that story was such a hard one for me to write, but it was also SO IMPORTANT for me to tell. I wanted to talk about it. The part that no one tells you. How not every single guy gets drafted, but how badly they all want it. Some more than others. When they lose that part of them, it's devastating—to them and those around them. Most players keep it buried deep inside because it hurts so damn bad to think about, let alone talk about.

There is always a light at the end of the tunnel, but you have to get through the tunnel first. And sometimes that's a very isolating and lonely journey.

To everyone who wanted it, and didn't quite get it, you're still worthy and worth it. I hope you find a new dream and crush it. Baseball doesn't know what it's missing.

DO YOU WANT SUNNY'S FAMOUS COOKIE RECIPE?

https://tinyurl.com/SunnysCookies

OTHER BOOKS BY J. STERLING

Bitter Rivals—an enemies to lovers romance
Dear Heart, I Hate You
10 Years Later—A Second Chance Romance
In Dreams—a new adult college romance
Chance Encounters—a coming of age story

The Game Series:
The Perfect Game—Book One
The Game Changer—Book Two
The Sweetest Game—Book Three
The Other Game (Dean Carter)—Book Four

The Playboy Serial:
Avoiding the Playboy—Episode #1
Resisting the Playboy—Episode #2
Wanting the Playboy—Episode #3

The Celebrity Series:
Seeing Stars—Madison & Walker
Breaking Stars—Paige & Tatum
Losing Stars—Quinn & Ryson

The Fisher Brothers Series:
No Bad Days—a New Adult, Second Chance Romance
Guy Hater—an Emotional Love Story
Adios Pantalones—a Single Mom Romance
Happy Ending

THE BOYS OF BASEBALL
(THE NEXT GENERATION OF
FULLTON STATE BASEBALL PLAYERS):
The Ninth Inning—Cole Anders
Behind the Plate—Chance Carter
Safe at First—Mac Davies

ABOUT THE AUTHOR

Jenn Sterling is a Southern California native who loves writing stories from the heart. Every story she tells has pieces of her truth in it, as well as her life experience. She has her bachelor's degree in Radio/TV/Film and has worked in the entertainment industry the majority of her life.

Jenn loves hearing from her readers and can be found online at:

Blog & Website:
www.j-sterling.com

Twitter:
twitter.com/AuthorJSterling

Facebook:
facebook.com/AuthorJSterling

Instagram:
instagram.com/AuthorJSterling

If you enjoyed this book, please consider writing a spoiler-free review on the site from which you purchased it. And thank you so much for helping me spread the word about my books, and for allowing me to continue telling the stories I love to tell. I appreciate you so much. :)

Thank you for purchasing this book.

Come join my Private reader group on Facebook for giveaways:

PRIVATE READER GROUP

facebook.com/groups/ThePerfectGameChangerGroup

Join My Newsletter:

shorturl.at/duTYZ